GOING HOME

Volume Two

Hannah Duff

Jim Burnside was born in Belfast; grew up in Glasgow, Peterborough and Leeds and studied at Middlesex Polytechnic and Cardiff University. He worked as a teacher of English in Wales, London and Bradford before specialising in developing the communication skills of disabled and autistic students.

Visit his website at:
www.jimburnside.com or www.jimburnside.co.uk
Website design: Chris Marshall
Website: www.marshallmade.co.uk
E-mail: chris@marshallmade.co.uk

Editing with thanks to Jessica Macdonald.
Proof reading with thanks to Karamjeet Nahal-Macdonald:
www.FinalDraft.co.uk

NB. The author accepts responsibility to the intentional 'mis-spelling' of the word expertese (expertise).

All titles in the series GOING HOME by Jim Burnside will be available for order worldwide online in ebook or paperback and through all major chain and Indie bookstores, printed and distributed by Ingram's Lightning Source International or from Jim Burnside's website:

www.jimburnside.com

sales@jimburnside.com

FEVER THERAPY in print and ebook

GOLDEN DAWN, due September 2014

TALLY LONG'S PIE, due December 2014

Other forthcoming titles in this six book series:

LOOKING BACK

BISMARCK ON THE MANTELPIECE

With thanks to Karamjeet, Jess, Joe, Maria, Libby, Hugh, Peter and Violet who variously offered positive criticism, moral support, large glasses of wine, or helpful recollections.

For Duff.

'It will all be the same in a hundred years!'

Contents

Part Four

Hannah Duff, Part One

Chapter One *News from Nowhere*

Little Hannah was only four years old but her two elder sisters soon had her fully indoctrinated in all the necessary orthogenic reformations arising from their mother's death. The fact of the matter was that she had been closer to their mother and was devastated by an enormous sense of loss. Perfectly natural grieving was deep and long as weeks passed into winter and poor weather kept them all inside. Everyone was feeling blue and there was little incentive for conformity for the girls as the holiday had not yet risen above the horizon.

Harper's youngest, most intuitive child had begun to make her own inferences about the world. Hannah Drummond Wilson Harper the 2nd already knew how to question if not entirely see through the motives of others. Having quietly reflected upon the imprecations of unhappy adults she announced her own conclusions.

"A'm no' gonna be good," she stated quite innocently. This immediately got her the attention of both Elsie and Elizabeth, playing with her in the bedroom.

"Oh, dye hear it Elsie?" warned Elizabeth who had just started school and had committed to being *very good* at every opportunity.

"Mammy was good and she died."

They were stunned at the pure logic of Hannah's statement and for once Elizabeth was unsure how to retort. Little Han had made an insightful point requiring thoughtful evaluation.

"Good people don't always die," came back Elizabeth after a moment, with characteristic worldliness.

"Great Gran said the hen's goodness was the death o' it!" came the nostalgic explanation. Elsie blurted out her response to this perceived irony with a heartless laugh. As often with young children, Elsie could not always put her thoughts precisely into words. Instead she cried out loudly, "Great Gran only meant it tasted good, you numpty neep!"

"Yeah, but I heard Granny Jessie say to Harper that the good die young," put in Elizabeth a little more considerately.

"Well, I want to die too, so I can be with mammy," said Little Han without equivocation.

"You're a fool and no doubt, to say that!" Elsie snapped angrily. Pondering for a moment she added, "Harper and Margaret would be crushed if you died! They have enough with grieving for Mammy as it is!"

"Margaret hardly knew our Mammy," ventured Elizabeth, "She thinks Harper doesn't like her," she added with cold insight, cutting right through all the dormant issues.

"Well, Hannah thinks we don't like her either!" snapped Elsie, "Mammy couldn't cope with her when she was poorly . . . and I had to move into the box room and . . . she's gonna break all your porcelain ladies!" she blustered, having decided to let it all out.

"Yes, and Harper can't say her name," Elizabeth added, pointing straight at Hannah, calmly reposing upon her own official dogma. Little Han's lips curled in distress.

"That's because he just thinks o' mammy an' cries all the time," concluded Elsie, shrugging and parting her hands like a street trader.

"We'll just ha tay think of another name for you hen, don't worry!" Elizabeth indorsed thoughtfully, cocking her head to one side. She slid off the chair at the homework bureau to hug her four year old sister for her unaffected simplicity. The logic was clear – there could be no more 'Hannah' – that would serve to remind him there really was no other.

"Duff, we'll call her Duff!" Elsie decreed.

"Yes, we all went there with mammy remember! When Dr Coley made her better! Little Han loved playing on the sands at Macduff! You loved the sand remember? You kept saying it was 'Duff' and afterwards kept asking Harper to take us back! But after that Mummy got her cough."

"Aye an' remember going out to sea on the boat!" put in Elsie eagerly, with all the expansive love of that remembered day still in her voice.

Little Hannah looked from one to the other as she saw again spangled light on the water and felt the thrill of Harper carrying her on his shoulders. She smelt again salty breeze off the littoral and the musty harbour with its ceaseless industry – cranes and trains and shouting men. There were gulls screaming and windblown tide slapping the gunwale of a blue painted pleasure boat. Hannah remembered what then had seemed overwhelming beauty and was amazed by Elsie's suggestion.

"You cried cos you didnae want to come off the boat!" Elizabeth concluded, with the understated poise of a master of ceremonies.

The three Harper girls laughed long and merrily, lacing recollections with a sudden rediscovered passion – wishing with their retelling for golden days when their mammy was still with them. They spoke loud and bravely of the light of summer - so that sorrowful shadows in the corners of their room might retreat.

"But Duff was Mammy's name too," Hannah told them, with an innocent glow in her heart for such a happy solution. The decision was made with alacrity – a problem solved for the unthinking Harper.

Little Hannah learned at a very young age about life and death, bonding and separation. In her innocence she was just as eager to absorb the hard logic of her elder sisters, as she had been to learn from Great Gran or her ma about kindness and forbearance. A new mascot had been selected and a chimera driven away. Forevermore Little Hannah was to be known as 'Duff' except to those who would know her and come to love her as an adult. These of course would be people who had never met her mother or grandmother and who knew nothing of the painful 'namesake problem' as Elizabeth referred to it.

When old enough to reflect upon the past and make her own decisions, Hannah would allow the nickname she gloried in as a child to lapse - but for now it stuck. As the years wore on the handle would develop into more than a nickname. Holding the unique and inexpressible love she bore for her mother close to her heart, the association developed into a kind of happy alter ego. With the longest retrospective, the name Duff might have connotations of ill health and a decrepit body – as well as being a sharp reminder of her painfully joyous youth. Macbeth's witches never concluded the business of prophetic divination so circumspectly.

Harper was terrified of the future. It was a Friday night in December '96 when he realised that he had lost the will to live. Sitting for over an hour at Hannah's dressing table half naked and chilled, staring beyond the moonlit rooftops to the trees up the hill in Holyrood Park, he felt utterly drained, mentally and physically. Every instant, however outwardly pleasant or business like, continued what he had felt for the last six months to have been an ordeal. In his bereavement Harper sought imaginary rest and space of a type and quality eluding him and defying definition.

Thinking about routine commitments was oppressive to the point of physical sickness. No longer able to conduct affairs in an ordered way, he felt there was simply never enough time and never enough money earned. Although financially secure, his savings were ebbing as surely as family expectations grew. There were always outstanding jobs, endless chores, family and social commitments from which he wanted to run. Any nostrum Harper lived by held no deep meaning for him, whatever purpose it might be said to have served. He was living merely to survive and could see no end – imagine no relief.

In desperation he wrote to his only true friend Zachariah Williams, "My head is so full of trivial matters that abstraction itself begins to feel like an extremity bordering upon madness. In my heart's core I am defeated. In mental anguish, loneliness stupefies me Zach. I do not have enough energy to engage emotionally with my three charming daughters. In workaday life I am tethered and restrained. The passing of time has become torture."

He told others – family, friends and colleagues alike, "I'm as lucky as silver sixpence doon the back o' the sofa, wi' three pretty gilpies to keep me goin'! There's so much o' work and family - I'm always on the move, challenged by demand's o' the job an' interest in ma studies!" He lied.

They laughed because Harper told them what they wanted to hear. Yet he came to realise that in truth life was completely hollow and no longer reward in itself. Harper reached a point where it was becoming impossible to function. Worry and guilt worked together in a downward spiral, compounding depression.

It's just me! If I'd never met Hannah Wilson Drummond, I would have felt hollow in any case.

Wrestling with his demons Harper tried to think of some progressive event in recent months of operose routine. At length a smile condensed on his reflected image, in recollecting how sharpness met with the approval of peers at night school.

Re-running the scenario in his mind, he tried to recall details of a series of conversations about the American stock market leading to good fortune for all, "There is an international scarcity of precious metal for bullion," Professor Reid informed the group of insurance company and banking trainees, "The fervid debate between Democrats and Republicans about bi-metallism – I have explained bi-metallism – do we all understand this term, gentlemen?"

Guthrie on the third row, leaning against the radiator raised a hand and began to explain, "If you will allow, Sir . . . There is a fixed ratio – fifteen to one, between the commodity price for gold and silver, in the countries which accept both for coinage."

"Yes, yes Mr Guthrie. I don't need you to go over it all again for us, just indicate if there is a question . . . Entailing the starkest references to the crucifixion upon a gold cross of the workers he represents," continued the professor seamlessly, "by Congressman William Jennings Bryan, has led to a schism in American society. It is not a question so much of who is right and who is wrong – that may take economic historians another fifty years to resolve – with the comfort of hindsight," laughter echoed around the room but Reid was in his flow and did not pause, "It is all a matter of Confidence – most crucially that of investors. In an election year, this damagingly fierce debate is driving the US Commodity Market ever lower – influencing money supply as well as international trade."

Harper immediately bought low, putting half his savings into gold only, although many of his compatriots bought silver, because the ratio was fixed and the debate merely hypothetical. He sold high after McKinley's victory when the market bounced back - profiting as much again as an average bank clerk or insurance salesman would earn in a year, just from this short-term investment. Harper bought Reid a silver tankard with a glass bottom, 'So you will always be able to see what's coming, sir!' Ostensibly the present was from the entire group but none of the others had benefitted to the degree Harper had and he was glad to pay extra for engraving.

Other than occasional chats with Jim Reid, the teacher of Fiscal Law, Harper's only distraction from work or study related to career was in reading for pleasure for fifteen minutes each night before his eyes began to swim in his head. Realising that books, newspapers and periodicals were piling up around the bedroom - on the dressing table and on the floor - he had to admit to avoiding every form of distraction.

Habitually retreating with a warm drink immediately after a late supper he would light an additional lamp to fend off eye strain, adopting the qualities of a mediaeval ascetic in a cell. Rehearsed dialogues constructed in preparation for night school took place increasingly in his imagination only. Barely having time for the *Scotsman,* Harper still took weekly copies of *The Economist* which also piled up unread.

Determined to make the most of his studies, he wasn't ideological as much as sceptical of conventional wisdom. Desperate to find meaning in existence, Harper took turbulent voyages in search of the sterile islands of outmoded ideas. Cut off from a secure sense of belonging in the World, only warning voices of men stranded in the past came, filtered at times through the erudition of his mentor Reid. Unsurprisingly he began mumbling to himself in solitude, like a mad scientist rifling through obscure discoveries of the past, searching for the Philosopher's Stone.

In broken sentiment, Harper recalled demanding Jim Reid offer an explanation of the burned out church in the woods near Rothiemay. From learning a little of local Edinburgh history of which there was so much, Harper guessed its destruction related to the stand of local hero Thomas Chalmers and his Evangelical Free Church. Sympathetic resonance with Chalmer's views had been Morayshire's equivalent of the Jacobite rising. Reid told him the Disruption of 1843 arose from a blatant attempt at the extension of State control through the courts, "Chalmers came to represent freedom of speech and the principle of

Democracy, John. On the other hand, most ordinary churchgoers just wanted something to believe in," Reid explained.

For Harper, that tendency to be led was in itself the most corrupting weakness of all. He answered thoughtfully as they stood in the autumn chill outside the Old College under an insipid gas lamp, "I believe Darwin and Lamarck were right, sir. They established the scientific truth behind Hume's insight into Natural Law. It is evident to any rational man that we are living in a human jungle, where the greatest dangers are elaborately contrived deceits and illusions – especially those cooked up to embody the ambitions and vested interests of greedy employers."

Reid smiled indulgently at the statement of a suspicion voiced repeatedly, year on year by his smartest students, "I believe you are right, Mr Harper. Democracy is not a naturally existing form. It was nothing more than banal for Edinburgh Churchmen prior to Chalmers, to suggest that the comfort of the masses depended primarily on their 'right moral condition.' It might be controversial to say so but their contemporary Karl Marx came closer to the truth."

"And if he wasn't sir, he certainly has more popular appeal over half a century later. Either way we are back to a kind of dictatorship then?" Harper asked, looking up at the taller man stood smiling at the turn of the steps, as moisture filled his itchy eyes.

"Hmm, you refer to 'The dictatorship of the proletariat,' Harper. That is conceivable under direst economic circumstances. I believe you are right - unless we find equable ways of extending representative government, there will be upheaval at home and abroad."

Reid was Harper's only foil, indulging naiveté and pointing him to inspirational works by idealistic authors such as Edward Bellamy. But the Professor's judicious neutrality couldn't help the brilliant young man with his loneliness. As they parted company, Harper heading to his bus stop along South Bridge, Reid knew well that his mature student would return home to study into the small hours of the morning.

Remembering family commitments for Saturday morning Harper set aside his book - *News from Nowhere* by William Morris - to rub tired eyes and stretch out fully clothed on his bed - hours after the city had gone to sleep.

Scholarly investigation into Socialism reflected a fundamental division in society between owners and aspirants. Those with wealth and endowment played power games, buying and selling whatever they wanted, including of course people. They dabbled in politics and warfare - entertaining themselves with arbitrary, sometimes professional ambitions.

Reaching under his bed to slide out the bound hardback ledger used for a diary of his studies, Harper had begun writing irritably in order to pacify resentment,

"Friday, November 21st 1896.

The Good and Great contribute enormously but asymmetrically to our society - only indirectly to the quality of living for the majority of individuals serving them. They help their fellow men *incidentally*, on the back of self-aggrandising actions, aimed at extending personal wealth and power."

Harper reached for a three day old newspaper to de-tune his overstretched mind, before considering what more to write. He noticed an advertising feature article with a photo of his employer's store.

Ha! Jenner's caryatids . . .

Shaking his head Harper folded the inside pages of the Scotsman, still unable to see the point of such ostentation.

The wealthy engage other people to work for them. Or if they feel the need, they can crush good people they see as rivals – as challenging, irritating or unimportant.

In his depressive torment Harper thought of the heroic failure of William Coley, incoherent rage swelling in his chest as random impressions played through his mind. Picking up his pen again he focussed on the diary entry.

"Truly imaginative men are sometimes cheated out of recognition by less worthy rivals. Darwin, pre-eminent scientist of the Century was howled down by religious fanatics. Marx, the most clear sighted and rigorous philosopher of the modern era, lacking the possibility of reverence from a retrospectively safe distance in time like Aristotle, passed away in obscurity, with a sad little coterie of mourners at his funeral."

Harper laughed sardonically as he imagined Leon Wernerke's ideological forgers preparing for revolution. He envisioned class struggle driving armies of such determined socialists across the world. Again he picked up the fountain pen, to vent indignation burning in his heart.

'In respect to *News from Nowhere:* I don't imagine a great deal will change in the next hundred years. If I fell asleep and went back in time an equivalent amount I would be at a loss to offer inspiration, except perhaps to warn them that there will be a terrible hardening of attitude in our present era. In the words of Karl Marx: 'The proletarians have nothing to lose but their chains . . . they have a world to win.'

But looking forward as Morris invites us to - for a brief moment utopian socialists may seize ascendancy . . . like so many unswerving campaigners of the past. Failed republicans like Cromwell and egotistical Napoleon – who hardened his heart against Polish nationalists as he took on the rest of the world. Another striking figure within the last century, Robespierre, incorruptible opponent of the death penalty. Ha! How well his revolutionary principles endured!

In future Socialist ideals may be subverted by warfare, corruption or greed. By imperialism or brutal exercise of authority in the name of enlightenment, as with non-conformist values in the past. No doubt the Marxian vision will be lost in the heady lust for control following success. Power will one day slip through their fingers too because the exercise and control of power is ultimately about self-interest and greed - not justice. Class struggle, bubbling up in every grubby city I visit, will ultimately be subverted with lies. What would Hume predict? What are the lessons of natural philosophy?

The biggest lion sleeps while the pride risk life and limb making the kill. Then he gorges himself before others are allowed to pick over the bones. All he does is reinforce authority - his raison d'etre. That is the natural order of things. Improved education may be the only unbreakable mechanism of lasting change. Education for all but especially for politicians.'

Harper paced the room, looking out through the drapes at a murky night, musing on his lion metaphor for the Sovereign State before finishing his notes. Finally he wrote, 'I consider myself to know the British Lion well. This metaphor for the Civil State is reminiscent of Hobbes' *Leviathan*. It continues to be incredulous, repressive and essentially at war with itself. Exploitation and strife are eternal dance partners.'

Harper slept without dreaming. He couldn't envisage the future at all.

In the months following the loss of Hannah it was heart breaking for Margaret to see John Harper slide into the black hole of hurt and depression. At twenty one, finding love seemed easy and she accepted with alacrity that it might come and go. But Margaret was never so humble that she wouldn't want Harper to consider her someday as a replacement for all he had lost in the death of Hannah.

She let her sister Muriel in on the secret after a rare Saturday evening spent dancing. Oliver Thompson, the wide-eyed veterinarian who had doted on Margaret for years, accompanied Muriel's regular boyfriend Keith. But Muriel had a seasonal virus that came on suddenly after a couple of hours of energetic reels and she reluctantly cried off early. Keith agreed to drop Olly off in the borrowed rig, before returning it to Muriel's dad.

As they sat alone in their parent's home waiting for Anthony and Teresa to return from their pub, the suddenly recovered Muriel teased out Margaret's burning secret, "Come on, spill the beans . . . what's so important we had to dump Olly? And why are you so down in the doldrums?"

"I cannae stop thinking about poor John and his predicament."

"Oh fukubukuro! Didn't we see that coming!"

"I beg your pardon?"

"Oh, it's one of Keith's sayings. It's a Japanese word for lucky bag."

"Are you saying I'm chasing after party leftovers?"

"No, sorry! He's lovely, even if he does take himself too seriously. We dinnae want you doing that too."

"You said 'we' . . . I take it you mean Teresa?"

"Oh, it's obvious. She's been banging on for months about you looking sick as a parrot!"

Margaret's smile faded and she began to doubt whether Muriel would take her seriously. Her younger sister saw love as joyous benediction – associated as she was with a Diplomatic Service graduate trainee, who took foreign travel for granted. She'd been engaged to Keith for barely six months but behaved like they'd been married for a decade. Muriel leant towards Margaret to look into her solemn eyes.

Margaret puckered the left side of her mouth like she was swallowing a lemon. Tears of intimidation rose to just below the surface as she dropped all pretence, "I don't want this to sound as clichéd as poetry soup but . . . every minute of the day and most of my dreams are filled with his face. I swear Muriel, if he ever kisses me on the mouth I'll put a black silk court plaster over it and never speak again, I love him that much."

"Well, I fer one wouldnae want that. Who would we ha'e tae complain about the price o' fish?"

"Clearly he needs me more than ever . . . but if his thoughts turn in another direction Mu, I gonny be high and dry."

"Well, let him know your feelings, silly!"

"I cannae. It's too soon! I'm desperate but," Margaret looked at her hands, still embarrassed by thoughtlessly stringing poor Oliver along. "But what? Is John already seeing another woman?"

"I dinnae ken, but he has a shine for what's her name in Accounts you mentioned?"

"Marlene?"

"Yes, Marlene. I could tell by his tone of voice when he mentioned her one Sunday evening doing his expenses. But what if I make a play for him and he gets angry and I'm off doon the road?"

"Oh, that'd be dreadful," agreed Muriel, warming to the romantic theme, "Or worse still if some old Jezebel from Kennington's moves in after you've worked years for his family!"

"In the name of heaven, don't even say it!"

"So, what will ye do?"

"Nothing I can do. The girls are key for now. I'll manage their routines as best I can, short of moving in."

Margaret lowered her head again, pondering the next personal revelation. Muriel waited, able to read her sister's reserve like a magazine cover.

"I even spend my own money on them. You know, money he pays me."

Muriel laughed excitedly, "Oh, that's *crazy* woman! You *have* got it bad."

"Well I dinnae care what you say. It's my way of telling him I love him. He's learning Accountancy. If I avoid asking for more, he's bound to notice. That way he'll get the message. Elsie and Elizabeth are sure to tell because they notice everything, and they're starved of his attention. But look, there's something I wanted to ask you."

Muriel's kind eyes shone with delight, already committed as she was to playing matchmaker, "Ask and you shall receive! You want me to dance with Oliver, or tell him he smells like a horse's arse?"

Margaret didn't answer directly. Where Oliver and others of their small fraternity of devotees were concerned, much could be taken for granted and the subject of his acquiescent feelings was best avoided.

"Hannah used to make her own clothes and clothes for the girls. John taught her the skill, I know."

"Why are you looking at me like that?"

"I want to learn."

"So learn!"

"You operate a jacquard loom and an industrial sewing machine. You teach me. You can get patterns from work."

"Oh sugar and spice Margaret! When?"

"Next Saturday night. We can pretend we're going dancing to make him jealous. He'll have to stay in, if you're with me. We can even get dolled up and come back early, like we did tonight . . . you can teach me then on your sewing machine!"

Muriel sat back on the sofa, disappointed to have to make a commitment to forego leisure time in the context of such hard work at weekends. But Margaret smiled pleadingly and Muriel's soft eyes lit up with the mischief.

"You scheming hussy! It's him you should get to teach you on a Saturday night, instead o' reading all they bloomin' library books. What aboot the boys that adore us? They'll think we've become women o' the night, aff tae turn tricks."

"They can take it or lea'e it. Tell them the fairy Godmother is working tae rule – she willnae do midnight pick-ups since the last bitch complained!" Margaret Kemp laughed freely for the first time in months. Relieved to have cleared her conscience to Muriel, she had a bright plan for a future dedicated to the Harpers.

Due to time pressures Harper had taken to ordering directly from suppliers he represented at discount trade rates. Often at the end of taking an order he'd simply say to friendly retailers, 'Oh, will you keep three of those dresses to one side for me, until the next time I call?' More often than not offer of payment would be waved away with a knowing smile - followed by the meaningful handshake.

Seventeen year old Muriel, employed as a machine minder at Jenner's factory, was familiar with state of the art manufacturing specifications of the most elaborate ladies' and children's fashion. There was always demand for template patterns for the same items from families on a limited budget. The store and everything it sold gradually inspired and converted ordinary people in the capital and throughout the country.

Jenners and Kenningtons were created by and had come to symbolise tradition. Now fashion and poverty worked magically in conjunction, to recreate the symbol into a marketing reality. Relatively few people had skills to make their own clothes to such a high standard, so Margaret's plan could not have been designed to greater effect. It involved high skill, time and dedication but when the time came to offer finished articles to the girls, she knew John would be delighted. Margaret took up much of Muriels' spare time in learning basic techniques familiar to an industrial seamstress.

Elsie and Elizabeth had always been the best turned out children at their school. Seen together, the three Harper girls might be assumed to have ventured up from the smarter end of Inverleith, whenever they were seen in the park or on city streets. Determined to sustain that impression at all costs Margaret flushed with pride when occasionally mistaken as their mother.

Once there came a back handed compliment from two old busy bodies walking through the town side of the park, "Look how well that wee woman keeps her youthful figure wi' three bairns!"

"Oh aye, she's a bonny lass." Approval fell into Margaret's pretty, receptive auricle where it resounded all day - basso profundo. The most prurient fantasy followed when she was alone that evening. In a blissful state she prayed that John Harper, the true object of her self-seduction, might in wretchedness turn to see the light of love in her eyes and hear her heart beating in tune only with his.

Muriel was roped-in frequently to cover for Margaret as she walked the fine line between wider social commitments with old friends and increasingly becoming a surrogate for the deceased Hannah Harper. Subtle manoeuvring, involving rotation of the least maudlin or most enthusiastic escort also served her purpose, when Olly became too amorous.

If it was a working day when he was out of town, Harper felt under obligation for Muriel's efforts to underwrite his obvious need for a full time nanny. Margaret's social engagements were always planned well in advance and his homecoming seemed all the more enchanting for reaffirmation of a comforting pact. By the same token, in asking Muriel to oblige when she took time out with her friends, it could not be implied Margaret was obsessed with John, although instinctively he knew she was.

Chapter Two   *Smoke Brothers*

It was Thursday the 24th December, beginning of the winter festival –
with Christmas, as well as Hogmanay now seeing-in 1897 by popular
demand. Harper had taken his friend Jeremy to the Spotted Red Bull, a
favourite watering hole where he hoped on the off chance to see the
familiar face of Ali Macdonald.

Outside on the pavement a Salvation Army band were playing
Christmas Carols. A blazing coal fire radiated across the lounge,
warming half a dozen early arrivals while the majority standing at the
bar shivered in raw cold floating in from a door wedged open in
welcome. It was the rush hour prior to an optional holiday and the SRB,
as regulars liked to call it, was filling up rapidly.

'Just nipping down to the *SRB* hen,' as a mid-evening diversion after
washing pots and reading the form, or in response to the demand,
'Where the hell have you been? Your supper's cold!'

'Oh . . . just called in at the *SRB* on the way home, dear.' *SRB*
sounded like an altruistic charitable affiliation, possibly a worthwhile
sporting involvement that sat well with hard living patrons.

Pinder had insisted on buying the first round, so Harper went to
grab a table near the fire. The tall, robust man returned with two pints
at speed to the table where Harper was sitting, as though haste was
essential if they were going to drink their fill.

"Tell me the SP, John."

"The starting price, or the State of Play?"

"You know me John, I never bet unless it's a sure thing."

"Yeah, I know . . . and it's never a sure thing," Jez laughed his brisk,
affable laugh and Harper felt obliged to speak easily to his boss in
return.

"I've been looking forward more than ever to spending time with my
family, Jez."

"Oh yes, I agree like bells man. It's been quite a run-up to this
holiday!"

"You mean it's not always this busy?"

21

"No, no . . . I don't think it has been in past years, do you? Traditionally conservative Scotland is being influenced, in a positive way mind, by tidal forces of a much larger English economy." Harper nodded pensively and both men sucked deep draughts of their beer.

"Europeans, particularly Germans and of course our wealthy American cousins, started the trend of spending on gifts at Christmas. I think the English and their numerous colonial associates are merely following suit."

"Right, Jez. But it occurs to me that whenever there's money to be made our employers take any trend and promptly turn it into a fashion."

"Oh yes, John that's precisely what we aim to do. But don't knock it. Jenner's and the other large department stores in town have reacted to the consumer trend more than the populace we serve. It's called market creation old son. Edinburgh's citizenry, nestling around their northerly volcanic stump miles from civilization, have begun to feel emblematic of Empire. If not arguably at the very heart of Empire."

"Hmm, but we still feel like a colony."

"I dunno. There has always been a feeling of pride, a general conviviality around our great city which demands recognition." Both men smiled as they stoked up their pipes. On the cusp of his thirties, Jez was handsome and confident. Opening his overcoat and kicking back in his chair he folded long legs and began to pronounce an economic analysis. Harper imagined Pinder a younger version of Conan Doyle's scholarly investigator, Sherlock Holmes.

"Unlike London, Edinburgh always tries to have a feeling of setting the pace, rather than following it. You've been there haven't you?"

"Oh yes, several times – but never to Lambeth." Jez was completely unaware of the allusion to Polish counterfeiters so Harper laughed aloud at his disarming response.

"Oh, well you missed out on the best whores then. No, John, I think London is too big to care. But when the world wants to celebrate, Edinburgh throws a party."

"Well I know there's a lot of poverty in London, Jez and we are certainly better off for housing, health and education than Glasgow or

Manchester . . . but I dinnae see much evidence of investment from central government."

"Who cares if the English neglect us when it comes to investment? forget them, they only ever looked after themselves. Scotland still gets the orders. And not just for textiles John, also for ships and steam engines." Such was the popular invective around Kenningtons, at least among the travelling reps taking orders for manufactured goods. Times were good and employment secure. There was a new corporate identity extending from the top down, which encouraged loyalty and hard work.

When he thought about that conversation with Jez following the Christmas weekend, a couple of typical manifestations of this tenuous economic reality struck Harper. Firstly, he was on holiday with his kids, following a month of the most manic rush imaginable to take orders and get goods into shops throughout major urban locations of the United Kingdom. This was in fact a holiday Harper was obliged to take because there would immediately follow an almost complete suspension in business in the clothing industry. There were local exceptions – but Edinburgh had long ceased to rely upon a locally generated market economy. The development of rail and ever larger iron ships had seen to that. Despite cold weather, business would not pick up again properly until early March – everyone knew that. And then fashion magazines would see to it that business went crazy again.

Secondly, he was going on a works outing. Although Harper couldn't think of any valid reason why, at that precise moment - seven forty on Tuesday morning, 29th December - he was sitting naked in front of his dresser near the bedroom window, except for the kilt he had avoided trying on since the same time last year.

Staring indifferently at sky above the treetops lining Holyrood Park opposite, he felt a gentle brushing of the cat's tail against his left leg.

"Go on ye daft quadruped. I'm no feedin' ye at this time o' the morning! Ye eat more than I do fer Chrissake." Instead he reached down to stroke Molly, who jumped up onto the polished elm dresser where she rolled in front of him, purring in anticipation of affection. Molly took every opportunity to get Harper's attention in this elaborate manner. The tame 'Scottish Tiger' knew him for an easy mark – who often sat alone with her to talk nonsense when he was in his cups.

Now he tickled Molly's belly and the beautiful cat stretched out, pushing her paws against the mirror stand. Harper made a play of counting a double row of black spots on her underside, talking to her like a baby as he prodded them. When he got to ten, near her taut furry abdomen, Molly grabbed his hand with both paws and made a playful feint to bite his thumb. But she was gentler than any cat he'd ever seen and as ever her needle sharp claws were withdrawn.

"Oh well, I'm definitely not feedin' ye now!" Molly continued purring as she rubbed facial scent glands against the frame of the mirror.

In his underwear drawer were the plates. On an impulse Harper took them out to examine closely for the first time since he'd found them in the suitcase six months ago. Knowing perspiration was enough to soften dried ink, he avoided touching the stamp-facings with his fingertips. The built-up layer would be awkward to remove yet metal beneath was not worn.

Their condition speaks of tens, or hundreds of thousands - not millions of imprints. Wouldn't the Treasury love to know. Ha! Sod them.

Harper considered burying the counterfeit Bank of Scotland plates in a Hessian sack in the back garden, or winging them into the tide off the deep water harbour at Newhaven but for some inexplicable reason couldn't bring himself to do either.

I can never hand them in of course – that certainly would spoil things for everyone. I could never explain it all without damaging my reputation, as well as that of the man who investigated and cleared me.

Harper knew Somers would never come back, even though the status of the tentative investigation into alleged missing items was 'open and unsolved.' Harper had seen the search warrant destroyed. On the back of such action came silent agreement that Harper was exonerated. If the plates turned up now it would make Somers seem incompetent. Harper also knew from recent discussions with Ali Macdonald over a pint at the SRB that there was an active special unit still working on the case in a basement room on Bank Street. It gave him pause to think how a good record with the force might have saved him from damaging scrutiny although it had not felt so at the time. In the final analysis the team from the Treasury had taken a leap of faith - seeing him as one of their own.

Harper had not thought much about it until now – perhaps because it had all been too embarrassing. With over six months behind him since the devastating loss of Hannah and the trauma of detention, he could think about it all for the first time without wishing the ground would open up to swallow him.

The Treasury men had appeared at the Forbes late on the evening of the funeral. Between them they paid for several rounds of drinks although a few eyebrows were raised and conversation fell relatively silent for half an hour or so. But Harper read it instantly for what it was.

This is political. Someone high up told them to make amends, to contain any possible blow-back. They need me to keep my mouth firmly shut about this blunder and that's exactly what I will do.

Somers worked quiet charm on local notables, family and friends alike. He spoke freely about shared interests, revealing a little of opinions and personal background but nothing about his work. The Inspector made a firm friend in Dr Payton and his stunning wife with whom he sat for over an hour, talking mainly about symphonic orchestras he'd heard playing in London and his favourite composer, Beethoven. He was gracious but did not outstay his welcome.

When Harper's immediate family began to leave just before midnight, Somers made his excuses shortly after them. With a telling look across the room to John he conveyed the thought: 'You my friend are a special case. We're letting you back in the water but the hook is still in your mouth.'

25

Harper rose to accompany Somers down the street but the Treasury man made a point of publicly shaking his hand.

"Mr Harper . . . once again let me express my deepest sympathy for your loss. Thanks for clearing up the matter we needed to talk to you about. If there is anything else you can remember please get in touch with me personally."

Harper walked outside with the Inspector to his borrowed motor vehicle, a neat little Farnell truck hired from the Station Hotel in Elgin. Keith Somers gave Harper an enthusiastic demonstration of how it worked, as if all the controversy between them was forgotten. Cranking the starter handle vigorously he climbed behind the wheel as the engine of the little three wheeler hissed into life. Harper stood with his mouth slightly open as he waited for D I Somer's parting shot, smiling benignly when it came.

"If you find them, dispose of them properly now won't you? Good luck for the future!" Shocked, intimidated and relieved all at the same time, Harper made no attempt to reply. He was still the host and this was shaping up to be a long night.

"For fuck's sake! Enough of bad luck" he murmured as the aptly named Orange Box faded into the velvet night. Wandering down to the river John needed to smoke and enjoy his own company for a while. He knew if he walked to clear his mind the wake would still be in full swing when he returned. After all the bustle, he'd seen local Bobby Bill Stevenson was hemmed into a corner by a table covered in untouched drinks purchased by everyone who loved him. Standing in shadow beneath trees on the far side of the bridge, Harper looked back up the street at noise heard from afar. It was Wilson's raucous, piggy laughter, underlain by Donald's humorous, warm growl - rarely in evidence unless he was thoroughly crocked.

McIntyre had found a true blood-brother and could be heard by the entire village opening his shop to dig out a particular bottle of aged malt he'd hidden there. It would serve to educate the Englishman 'in finer subtleties of the water of life - the best possible way of tying one on, son,' he explained. In Wilson, McIntyre had at last encountered a man as fearlessly balanced on the edge as he was - someone not afraid to open his mouth and speak his mind. Donald was not about to let Ted escape.

Harper smiled to himself at the fleeting recollection of Wilson and McIntyre, enthusiastically playing darts against the outside of the butcher's preparation shed in the small hours of the morning – a fixture he'd chosen to keep well away from. When the pipe was finished and he was strolling back to the lock-in at the Forbes, a compelling aroma of frying fillet steak was drifting along the street from accommodation at the back of the butcher's shop.

Detective Sergeant Garner turned out to be gradually more lucid and friendly as he became drunk that evening. The gigantic fellow stood at the bar all night, buying drinks for anyone who would accept his dubious company. At first there were no takers at all. Then a few. Then by three or four a.m. there was a garrulous forum of old familiars, laughing and shouting across the bar room at one another.

Jack Garner dipped into his pocket two or three times but then found that glasses were filled and paid for before he could take his wallet out to pay. Bill Hendry knew what they all wanted and that they were not about to stop. The hotelier had an understanding with Harper that formed part of an easy tradition. Whenever a man requested a round be bought, all still able to stand up at the bar were included in it, even if their glasses were half full.

When Garner had eventually drunk his fill he'd lost count of what might have been spent, yet was clear headed enough to realise he'd come out well on top. His wallet was still fat, and Rona refused to let him pay. Confounded earlier in the day by his professional status, she now plied him with drinks as if he was a favourite uncle.

Garner wanted to bare his soul to Harper as a former Bobby. "D'ya know, me old tulip, I'm glad for once me quarry has turned out to be innocent. I've never known such a thing in all my years of service."

"I'm glad too Jack . . . and I'm sorry for takin' the wind oot o' yer sails!" Harper held out his hand for Garner.

"Ah, no hard feelings John. Ted an' me, we were taking the piss. At least ye di'nt scuttle me nob." Harper offered a thin smile in response, guiltily thinking of Blum, whose nob he had most definitely scuttled.

Garner made several attempts to find the words for something he found extremely difficult to say and in the end he came to it.

"Y' know John . . . what I regret most – I long for my own lost innocence as a white haired boy. D'ye know, out . . . out on the fens, shooting ducks wi' a punt gun."

On the verge of stupor Garner had been poetic in his good humour. Despite the sadness of the occasion this had been a traditional Highland wake and the gigantic stranger had fit in well. His maudlin tone gave cue for recitation and more arcane forms of jocularity. No-one was sober enough to sing but Henderson took up the violin and played a couple of sweet laments. Although it was the hour before dawn and blackbirds could be heard rehearsing in the mist humped forest across the river, Rona came round the bar room proffering an ashet piled high with bacon sandwiches.

Above all else, Harper recalled with satisfaction how Somer's team had taken trouble to redress the question of Stevenson's involvement in Harper's detention earlier that day. If anything, Bill's reputation was enhanced in the end. To cap it all no-one had a fight - not even Jim Lorimer, or Andy Murdoch. Hannah would have laughed and *that* was the entire point of the tradition. All in all it had turned out to be a good way of saying farewell to friends and home for John Harper. At least it had left them all with something to gossip about in Milltown of Rothiemay. And that, he told himself, is what makes the world go round.

As is the case with all the most monumental hangovers, Harper's recollection of the night of Hannah's wake filtered back very slowly. Like all who had ever emerged intact from such a whipping of the cat, Harper hoped there was nothing of potentially greater embarrassment still lurking in the recesses of his mind.

That was it!

The one thing Harper found impossible to envision in reflecting upon the past was the question of what was yet to come. As he held the counterfeit Bank of Scotland plates in his hand, he could hear again

Hannah's exalted laughter. Soft indigo light seemed to appear in the room beside him, as he imagined her thoughtful presence and gentle touch. Harper sighed with bittersweet wisdom, knowing it was time to begin thinking again about the future.

The plates in his hands symbolised Hannah's ribbing sense of irony. Her temporary reversal of fortune with the fever therapy. Even her knowledge that everything in this world is scam, or sham – except the virtue of hope itself. A souvenir of a wild but ultimately happy time, they belonged to no-one now but him.

Harper decided he would clean the plates with methyl alcohol and hide them from the children at the back of his sock drawer. Each time he looked at them from now on he knew all these wonderful, bittersweet memories would come flooding back. At last he felt ready to forgive himself.

As he opened the drawer to replace the plates, Molly stamped her front paws into the pile of underpants and socks, tipping one pair onto the floor which she immediately dived after. Harper laughed aloud as he stood up to look with dismay at a hairy paunch, bulging over the adjuster strap of his Buchanan dress tartan.

Muriel had persuaded Harper to order the kilt one night when he was slightly the worse for wear, blatantly trying to impress the girl. The sett was maroon check on buff ground with black stripes running through it, though not as bright as expected from looking in the kilt makers sample book.

What reason have I to be proud of some imagined tradition? It's not Lennox or Hamilton, Campbell or Macdonald, romantically linked to some historic act of valour or treachery. Who cares about the past anyway?

Harper felt no affiliation whatsoever to any mediaeval clan or extended family, much less any minor baronet or laird for whom his ancestors might reluctantly have raised arms in rebellion. But dress tartan was something everyone talked about locally. It figured large at this winter season of celebration, as in the summer when there were games and festivals.

Ali Macdonald had summed up the revived tradition aptly one evening in the SRB – a favourite haunt for off duty policemen, "It's a tradition which differentiates us from the fuckin' English, Harper," This assertion had not required further explanation. All present reached as one in silence as if to say, 'I'll drink to that.'

There was still shelter in routine and for a time Harper could avoid what was preordained. Margaret Kemp was too valuable to him as a component in family life and routines to dismiss without the disapprobation of her family and a significant number of mutual friends. There was no good reason to do such a thing, apart from the subliminal issue of her trying to insinuate herself into the widower's life and his bed.

At first, indifference to her was protection in itself. She was young and uncommitted. Harper had his family to think about and was de facto her employer. But she had been taken over four years ago in Hannah's absence and was effectively now a surrogate mother to his children. The burning question was to what extent Harper might allow Margaret to become a surrogate wife.

She had one or two male friends and suitors whom she clearly kept, quite literally, at arms-length although whenever Harper met them, the lads patiently pursuing her seemed creditable and keen. By her own confession, Margaret had for a time been genuinely worried about Harper but as the months rolled into years she came to see him as invulnerable.

It was clear to him that the smart young woman was privately committed to grabbing him if she could and had dug in to wait her chance with solemn dignity. Some months ago Margaret had stopped mooning over him – so the boys who called when Muriel stood in added to the tantalizing sexual allure. Apparently determined to express no direct interest until he was good and ready, Margaret Kemp burned with the honest anticipation of an urbanised Jane Eyre.

Evenings when he studied were the hardest for Margaret. She sat in his home waiting for the man she loved to return from night-school, hoping he would ask her to linger and sleep with him. But he always made for the dining room with his brief case, like a monk retreating to his cell after compline. When he turned up the gas lamp and gave her an austere look it meant, 'thank you and goodbye.' Insurance industry examinations were a convenient barrier but the sad and purposeful look in his eyes said, 'this is not a mutual feeling Margaret. I'm not ready to forge another bond, however keen you think you are.'

For Margaret, innate mechanisms of sexuality were understood and accepted, "His memory of Hannah clouds interest in other women," she told her mother, in the kitchen of their home off Willowbrae Road.

"Yes dear, you're far too sage to doubt it. And it's only right that John studies to elevate his status. Hard work disnae always amount tae happiness. No if ye work every hour o' the day just tae break even, like your faither an' me!" "

"Hmm, but he disnae need to keep the world at bay as he studies."

"Oh nonsense. You know where he is, if you have him in your sights," Teresa looked up thoughtfully from the dough she was kneading for onion bread, "Although I think you should find an unmarried man and start a family of your own!"

Margaret did have him in her sights. She teased him proficiently like a kitten playing with a mouse – even though it drove her to distraction wondering about women he might meet and fall in love with on his constant travels. Secretly it charmed her to think Harper was still faithful to the memory of his passed wife. It might take a couple of years before that hurt even began to fade.

Teresa reminded her that, 'In posh society, folk in mourning keep themselves aloof frae mixed company for a year at least.' Margaret laughed as she glanced unintentionally at the calendar on the kitchen wall.

Like a chump, Harper wrongly imagined another effective barrier between himself and Margaret's unsolicited attention was his overtly enthusiastic interest in Muriel. Margaret took it for what it truly was – the foolishness of a lonely, older man, testing his ability to attract the opposite sex. The fact that Muriel was her younger sister and engaged to be married, simply reassured Margaret of Harper's subliminal interest in her.

Muriel Kemp was not only thoroughly delightful in character but also quite exquisite to behold. Her beauty burst out in every sense, like over-ripe fruit - and all the vigorous boys who knew her ached to taste it. She smiled so much she had developed laughter wrinkles as a child. Creases appearing suddenly around dark eyes that accompanied frequent expressions of delight, would take Muriel from attractive youth to gloriously beautiful woman in a breath-taking instant. Those endearing lines on her face were set in the most fulsome, smooth complexion anywhere to be seen. Jet-black hair tumbled in waves around high cheek-bones and her strongly humorous, fair face. Delightful enthusiasm for everything in life shone through amethysts for eyes no King could purchase for a Queen. Most tellingly, a closer look was always necessary, even when a man had seen Muriel before. Usually the greetings of others were met with an instant, welcoming smile. The amethysts were set against magnificent lashes, a bonny nose and strong classical brow. Muriel was not so pretty she might snap like porcelain though, nor so matronly she might ever put on bulk, stepping heavily on rounded heels. And her voice was laughter itself. It was clear to everyone who knew her that Muriel's sparkling, timeless beauty would always remain.

Unfortunately for the eligible male population of Edinburgh, Muriel had a steady boyfriend, Keith Morrison, who was tall and equally handsome. Morrison was a genial soul who played rugby union for Herriot's whenever he could and was training to be a Secretary in the Diplomatic Service. He wasn't around that much but for any of Muriel's old school chums it would be taking a big risk to chance their arm. She took all their salacious flattery in her stride but when asked about plans for the future would quietly accede that they involved, 'a move to London, then who knows where? Maybe somewhere in the Caribbean if we get to choose.'

She joked about looking beyond Keith's career to their retirement but no-one mocked. Enthusiasm would no doubt carry them forward. It was all a matter of knowing what to volunteer for. Muriel tended to express her worries like her delights – with a sweet smile and shrug of exceptionally contoured shoulders. Then her favourite tight black cardigan would fill reassuringly with the slightest lift of a gloriously proportioned bosom.

Muriel and Margaret played an exceptional and impenetrable double act. Together they were often raucous in confidence. Muriel, less discreet than Margaret, could be flagrant. Although they usually remained behind the invisible lines of propriety, it was only concern for the feelings of individual people that could stop them in full flow. Where Margaret was dauntless, Muriel was outrageous. Individually they were introvert and extravert but together both became equally charming and hilarious.

Mistakenly trying to use his easy familiarity with Muriel, Harper sought to deflect Margaret from entertaining amorous notions about him. The simple fact was that he could not imagine Margaret's sister as ever having been a child. Muriel had imperturbable balance – she was a gem. Harper realised that she reminded him of Hannah – at least how he might have idealised his deceased wife, unburdened by responsibility in her late teens.

When Margaret teased him about his obvious shine for Muriel, Harper expressed the view that easy friendship with her sister was 'purely platonic, as they say.' Yet he pretended it could be much more. Tuned to one another the sisters saw through his show immediately, agreeing it was no more than, 'typical, red-blooded male behaviour.' Speculating privately, 'If he might take us both on at the same time,' Muriel and Margaret roared with laughter at Harper's lame strategy. They had no secrets at all – and both women laughed till they cried. Harper had no idea. If he had known how Margaret schemed, or what was in store for him, he might have run a mile – or jumped in sooner perhaps.

The occasion for the wearing of traditional dress was more than just Hogmanay. Working her charms on him one afternoon in late November, Muriel Kemp prevailed on Harper to make a commitment he otherwise never would have entertained. He turned up for a meeting at work with Jez Pinder from Accounts, feeling a little self-conscious. Jez agreed to meet Harper in the staff canteen at one thirty, to give feedback after an end of year briefing with Mr Nichol, the Operations Manager. It was not the end of the fiscal year so Harper was keeping fingers crossed Jez would overlook unevenness in his annualised performance, especially the dry time spent in Northern Scotland last spring. Harper was also feeling guilty because his commitment to the job had tailed off significantly in recent months.

There can be no team briefing for field reps at this busy time of year. In any case meetings with Jez are always held on the run. This will either be bad news, or no news.

Straight and direct but with a practical joker's reputation, Pinder was generally thought to be a good sort. Jez was late for the informal meeting and Harper was grabbed by a bevy of machinists on their break. Whatever the women were talking about there was a general buzz of excitement in the atmosphere. Marlene from Accounts was there, sitting opposite Muriel Kemp and two or three other familiar faces.

The Accounts Supervisor asked his advice: "John, you know all the best hotels in Scotland don't you?"

"If I didn't know you better Marlene, I'd say that sounds like a proposition." There was giggling and Marlene conceded her slip with a knowing smile.

"Go on Marlene, please! What's the occasion, someone getting married?"

"No, staff outing!" interjected Muriel over her shoulder. She was turning at one hundred and eighty degrees to talk to a woman on an adjacent table, her voice drowned by two simultaneous conversations.

"Lomond Castle Hotel, and yes as a matter of fact my son was thinking of having his wedding there," answered Marlene.

"Lomond Castle, oh yes, I know it. Very much geared to the tourists but the room rates are no' bad off-season. I visit the local kilt makers. Wool from that area is amongst the softest anywhere, they get so much warm rain."

Muriel turned to join the conversation, "What's the hotel like Harper, tell us?"

"Oh, very grand I'd say, Muriel. Quite traditional. They treat their guests like royalty. The entire place, the hotel and its shoreline setting, has an atmosphere of tranquillity and grandeur that might easily go to your head. They organise ceildiths and boat trips for residents. There are woodland margins with wildlife for miles along the loch side. It's incomparably beautiful there, especially when the sun shines. Of course the whole area is steeped in history - much of it extremely unpleasant," Harper added with a smirk.

"Oh, so there are a few ghosts walking the muir?"

"I'd say there are a few ghosts walking the corridors." The women all laughed, then looking at one another stretched their mouths, pulled doubtful faces or tilted heads in consideration. There followed a cacophony of discussion in which all seemed to finally reach agreement.

"Book it then Marlene!" they all chorused. Glassy eyed with the eagerness of alleviating mundane routines on a subsidised weekend trip, the women turned now to the handsome interlocutor, who'd unwittingly convinced them all to throw in their merk and venture forth together.

"Thanks, John!"

"That'll do nicely then!"

"Well done – we knew we could rely on you!" each of the women called out in turn.

"What do you say John – you're gonny come?" came an enthusiastic suggestion from the irresistible Muriel. There was pause as the request registered with Harper. Then a chorus of, "Aw come on, come with us!"

"You'll love it!"

"We can hae a pic-nic at Rest and be Thankful an' visit Helensborough in the afternoon, if it's no' a wash oot," put in the lovely Marlene, thoughtful as ever.

"Have some fun, while there's fun to be had!" croaked slightly over the hill Janet Dixon, Muriel's Machine Room Supervisor. A wicked smile played across her eyes that said, "There's no man in my life."

"Oh, go on John, you could get Great Gran to come down from Rothiemay to look after your kids for the weekend! They'd love to see her!" This last suggestion came so fast from Muriel that Harper failed to register fully that it missed an important logical step.

What did register was that Muriel knew his situation intimately. Her idea was a good one, for all sorts of reasons that were nothing to do with a weekend staff outing in the run up to Hogmanay. It flashed through Harper's mind that if Margaret was not invited to come on the weekend trip too, it would cause awkwardness between them. It really would look like he was making a play for her younger sister. Muriel was way ahead of him and she was right. Deciding to prevaricate until he knew more he said, "Oh well, I'll have to see."

"What's that then old son?" Sitting down on a chair that he had reversed, Pinder spread long legs at an angle seemingly impossible for comfort. Sharp creases of his trousers hinted at another juncture in time when serious business might need to be discussed in professional detail. Harper looked down at them in dismay, wondering not for the first time if he had overdone the trips to Rothiemay.

"Oh . . ," Harper began, but Muriel Kemp cut in on him - her face and voice resonant with the prospect of a great holiday adventure, "We're all going to Loch Lomond for the Hogmanay trip. Are you coming too Mr Pinder? Spouses and friends are allowed but its adults only."

"Wild horses wouldn't stop me darlin' and I plan to sit next to you at dinner!" There were hoots of ribald laughter, followed by affirmations from all.

"This will be fun!" said Muriel, quickly mentioning to Marlene, "I'm gonny need a chaperone!"

"Don't look at me!" protested Janet her overseer and there were more peals of laughter.

"Only, I need to know now chaps. Jez, could I take a deposit from you? It's all heavily subsidised you know," reasoned Marlene.

"Yes, Mr Nichol says you have to arrange insurance cover," stated Jez in a matter of fact tone, "Give me details Marlene and I'll make the phone call for you. And I will be the first to pay." There was a congratulatory ripple of approval from the machinists as he took out his wallet.

"There now!" Marlene looked across at John in final imprecation.

What could be better - why look a gift horse in the mouth?

He laughed before he spoke to lighten the tone, "I'm tired of hotels and travelling you know Marlene . . . luxury for me is sitting at home reading a newspaper or going for a walk with my bairns." They all jeered him smilingly.

"Will ye listen to it?"

"Oh, he's spoilt by the expense account!"

Taking Harper's forearm comfortably between her two hands Janet said, "Oh, poor John, you just come home and spend the weekend with me then!" There was outrageous laughter, undermining the last vestige of his reserve.

He held up a hand to stop the barracking, "But I will *reluctantly* agree to this. Since the venue in question is probably the closest I'll ever get to an earthly heaven," again they all chuckled, "On the proviso that I can persuade my children's grandmother to come down from Rothiemay and that Muriel's lovely sister Margaret travels to Loch Lomond with us as her chaperone, as much to protect Muriel from Mr Pinder d'ye ken, as from myself?"

There was sudden movement of the group back to the looms when Mr Nichol unexpectedly stuck his head round the door. Despite the formality for off-site insurance still to be arranged, Marlene accepted Harper's deposit for two and he stood to leave with Jez, nodding goodbye to all the ladies in the group. Muriel Kemp returned his glance with a smile like the blessing of Athena.

"Oh Jesus!" whispered Harper softly to himself as he headed after Jez in the direction of the Sales Office, "What have I just done?"

Came the day, Saturday 2nd January 1897, Harper dreaded what he couldn't avoid. He had heard all the stories of similar events from previous years with a gentle warning from one of the buyers, Arran Hogg to, 'be careful not to come back with more than you left with.' Whenever he met his 'oppo' Hoggy, Harper always replied to the last

37

comment from their previous encounter. Aquiline and fair, dependable and outwardly innocuous in many ways, Hogg was nonetheless too fast and witty for Harper. Perhaps he had little else on his mind than making others laugh, since he always seemed to change the subject before Harper had time to think of a suitably droll response. The next time they'd met in the lift Harper asked, "Did ye mean that stag's head in reception Arran, or some of the stamped silverware?"

Hogg just smiled knowingly. As ever he came back with a lame joke to illustrate his word of caution, "Did ye hear about the Haymarket Hector wi' clap, who decided to throw his sel' oot o' a tenth storey window?" Harper smiled and shook his head, "His last words were, "I'm a gonner 'ere!""

Harper wondered if Hogg had first-hand knowledge of such disorders but he didn't ask that. Instead he said, "Hoggy, your jokes would make any fellow jump out of a tenth storey window!"

Harper had to pack briskly to make the pre-booked train journey, meeting Muriel and Margaret at Waverley station. The plan was to catch the early express to Glasgow, where they would have a light morning meal before assembling for the coach out to the hotel. He was slated to share a bedroom with three other gentlemen, whom he had identified as Bobby McGregor the eternal bachelor from Retail Sales Men's Wear with a reputation for being a womaniser, Accounts Manager Jez Pinder, and the inimitable Arran Hogg. There would be safety in numbers, even if he might have to endure lascivious anecdotes and Hogg's intermittent farting. Hogg always seemed to leave one in the lift whenever they were going up to Accounts together. The critical issue was whether Muriel would keep Margaret occupied. Harper wanted to treat her - for her to have a wonderful time, without any implication being built upon his best intentions.

From the first moment of the friendly meeting at Waverley there was a light hearted, convivial atmosphere to the entire adventure. Harper felt only a hint of the designs of Auld Clootie as Kennington's clan gathered. Finely dressed scrubbed up work-colleagues shook hands, engaging in casual chat. Some with nothing to say to those only vaguely familiar in their daily work routines nodded politely. Harper decided with a silent prayer and a thought for Hannah to remain sober at all costs – to be nothing more than an observer – Odysseus washed ashore on the tide.

Shaking his head Harper declined a bottle of Dryborough Ale. Hoggy opened his own which he pinioned between his knees before handing one to each of their two room-mates. It was twenty past nine in the morning.

"I'm gonny begin as I mean to go on," Hoggy informed Harper, clicking bottles with McGregor and Pinder.

"Breakfast!" alleged McGregor with an eager smile.

"Breakfast!" agreed Pinder.

"Breakfast!" Hoggy concurred, taking a swig of the popular brew, "The most important meal o' the day!"

Harper was hoping to make it through to the beginning of the next working week without being implicated in some outrage that might result in him losing his job. But ribaldry even amongst salaried and management staff present was such that by mid-morning any illusion of sustaining an element of propriety throughout the weekend had been shattered.

There were two coaches carrying the full contingent of a hundred revellers. Their drivers managed to pace each other steadily, climbing the gentle slope towards Dumbarton. There the road forked left to roll along the Argyll coastline. One coach was a monster from a past era with an internal capacity for thirty with room for another twenty two sitting atop. Originally designed for the run from London to Birmingham she carried enough coal to run all day and night without stopping but was slow and precariously cumbersome. The other was nimble and fast though extremely noisy in comparison with the old steamer. She had the new internal combustion motor, popularised by the designer Daimler. It had been built so Harper noticed, by an English franchise.

The relative rate of progress of the two coaches and novelty of their design and performance on switchback roads became focus for great levity among the trippers. If there was a notional speed limit of fourteen miles per hour in urban areas, the drivers ignored it out in the sticks-certainly at least heading downhill when new records might be easily attained. Any well-founded concern for country people who might never have seen any kind of motorised vehicle travelling these roads at such speed turned into vaudeville, complete with singing and impromptu comedy. Traditional folk songs and music hall numbers alike were spontaneously adapted to extract the last ounce of foolish banter.

The call and response tune *When the Chariot Comes*, adapted recently by American railroad workers into, *'She'll be coming round the mountain,'* became *'We'll be falling down the mountain.'*

Lyrics from Rabbie Burns' *Coming through the Rye*, *'If a lassie meets a laddie,'* was conjured into, *'If a drover meets a coacher, coming round the bend,'* and so forth.

When it transpired the driver was a taciturn old cud, apparent to some from the moment of first encounter in Glasgow, they baited the man mercilessly to get a rise out of him. A chorus of: *'We'll be cold mash and mutton by and by,'* began to rattle along the enamelled steel tube within seconds of him meeting an unexpected motorised wagon, coming at speed from the opposite direction on a tight bend.

It was a new phenomenon of the Highlands that in appreciation of Wade, Telford and McAdam who'd built the roads and bridges, those plying for hire or reward, lucky enough to be equipped with new internal combustion machines were going to get the most out of it. Time was money in the most technically innovative country in the world. Yes, distances between major cities and sea ports were great and connecting roads tortuous but it was clear from the outset of fast road transport, regardless of potential hazards, that the Scots were never going to hang around.

Soon enough the coaches stopped at Helensborough. It was a brisk but lovely day, with flat-calm sea and clear blue sky. Whilst some wanted to stretch their legs along the shore others remained on the buses, anticipating an alternative jaunt out to woodlands at Rhu, for those leaning toward temperance.

A dedicated hard-core formed up briskly as 'The Crooked Arm Brigade' to head on-the-double across the road to the Sinclair Arms

Hotel, with Harper in tow for ballast, 'After all,' they concurred, 'tomorrow will be a Sunday.'

Several swift swizzles later a slightly raddled Hoggy decided in the clear afternoon air that if Muriel Kemp would not reciprocate his endless, burning desire he would pick her up off the west shore and carry her into the brine.

"If ye'll no marry me I'm gonny droon us both!" he declared. Too late for intervention Muriel's screams of protest could be heard from afar, "I never said that! I never impugned yer manhood!" Quieter, more quarrelsome imprecations followed as she emerged from the tide sopped through, thumping him gamely on his shoulder. Luckily Muriel was wearing casuals and had a change of clothing for the evening.

"John – do something about this!" ordered Margaret. The She Wolf never roused Caesar's Ironclad Sixth so quickly to skirmish. Hoggy's broad smile turned honest when Harper swept him up in his arms and carried him out to deeper water. The two men wrestled as the coach party applauded, cheering them on. Harper was surprised at Hoggy's strength for a man of average build, how quickly he managed to wriggle free and get purchase on him.

Up in the Cairngorms that evening, so the weather map in the Scotsman had predicted, clear skies were to bring another night of the coldest temperatures on record – minus 41 degrees was expected. Harper remembered seeing this in a flash as he felt the numbing bite of the Irish Sea on the inside of his thighs. Resolving not to take the ardent fool any deeper, Harper tried to pitch him from where he stood. For his part, the sharply dressed buyer decided to take Harper down with him at all costs.

As the quick minded Hoggy flew in his beige morning suit into the lapping waves, he pulled firmly on the lapel of Harper's jacket. Harper went headlong after Hoggy, taking the salty slap open mouthed with the jacket yanked over his head. Despite embarrassment he came up sharpish with a triumphant grin on his face. From the shore Harper's attentive quartern of bliss clapped her hands, jumping up and down with her younger sister.

"Good Christ, let's get out o' here afore we freeze tae fuckin' deeth!" Hoggy advised, sitting in the water with waves lapping around his chin.

"Fuck me gently!" exclaimed Harper, now gasping for air, "I think Nimrod the Great Hunter has been bitten aff an' carried away by a dogfish!"

"Aye, or mebee it froze solid and broke aff, same as mine!" Hoggy's lower jaw shuddered as he spoke, lurching around in circles to get his bearings, as salt water clouded his eyes. Harper let out an irrepressible laugh as a streamer of sandy water ran down from his friend's hair. They trawled side by side towards the beach like shipwrecked sailors, laughing as they stumbled through the shallow waves.

"Who the blue blazes would want a life at sea?" demanded Harper, still breathless from the Arctic shock of the cold water, "What the hell happened to the Gulf-stream back wash?"

"That's just a summer advertising gimmick to get the English tourists in!" replied Hoggy.

Their coach arrived back from the woodlands at Rhu just in time to save the two men from foundering. Everyone else in the shore party ran to climb aboard in front of them, hooting with derision – to ensure they had a dry seat but mainly to avoid being dripped upon.

"Is this part of the entertainment Jez?" asked Bobby McGregor, tears of laughter floating still in his dark eyes.

"Oh yes . . . and I plan to pay them, Bobby. We'll hae a whip round later tae cover my outlay," Jez replied, creases of amusement puckering his cheeks and lining his high forehead.

Harper and Hoggy were obliged to wait, shivering at the back of the queue as Muriel and Margaret explained their situation, working their charms on the taciturn driver. When everyone else was seated he allowed them to climb up. For the first time that day the frown on the surly fellow's rigid, square face began to melt as he caught sight of the pair standing marinated like Admirals of the Narrow Sea. Clearly he'd seen much worse on a Saturday night in Glasgow, "Oh well, at least yis are no covered in vomit!" he observed with a guffaw, "Come ahead boys!" It struck Harper that the driver was that rare sort of man who actually delighted only in confrontation.

Hoggy and Harper climbed onto the front platform of the vehicle, where they stood beside the driver smirking back at them. He had to turn away to hide his glee at seeing two toffs in suits drenched to the skin. Glancing across the road at stragglers running back from the hotel he stuck out his thumb, directing Hogg and Harper, "Move down the aisle gentlemen. You might want tae hold ontae grab handles on the seats as you drip dry."

"Damn. My socks are wet Hoggy! I hate having damp socks!" complained Harper. Again there was hilarity and jeering from their audience but Margaret and Muriel shone with delight for their hero.

"Smoke!" demanded Hoggy, "I must have a smoke tae calm ma shaking bones. I thought the bastard was trying tae droon me!"

"What about me, you silly arse-worm?" scolded Muriel, "My new boots are ruined!"

"And her skirt," Margaret added fiercely through baby-blue eye liner, "What about her skirt?"

"Sorry," Hoggy intoned lamely to the floor.

"What was that?" demanded Margaret.

"Sorry!" Hoggy said a little louder, "I on'y did it cause I love you." There was rumbustious laughter along the coach at this beseeching plea for absolution.

"Well, I suppose I forgive you. But you have to polish my boots and pay for my cleaning," Muriel blustered with coquettish dander.

"Now that you've repented, you're absolved of your sins!" Harper invoked above the drone of the motor. Looking around to engage the audience he circled Hoggy with his arms, "So brethren, let us conclude this immersion ceremony. I baptize you, Arran Columbus Hogg - In the name of the Father and of the Son and the Holy Ghost," he incanted, making the sign of the cross over Hoggy. There was more hilarity and now even the taciturn driver began to guffaw, his pot belly rising and falling under the rudimentary steering wheel of his prototype 'frost of ninety-six' motor coach, as it cruised along the loch side road. Harper attempted to conclude Hoggy's confirmation with a Pontifical slap and they wrestled again in the aisle.

The two men made great play of emptying sea water and sand from their pipes, Harper knocking his out gently on top of the younger man's head. With a smile of gratification Jez took briars from each in turn, to

43

fill with dry tobacco. He dutifully provided a dry Lucifer, which he struck and held for them to avoid drips – as if this was the sort of thing Jez was used to seeing every day, up in his carpeted office on the fourth floor.

Surrounded in white tobacco smoke, Hoggy turned to Harper, holding out a hand for him to shake, "Sorry pal – for spoiling yer quiff, ih?"

Harper popped the pipe in his mouth as he reached across to take Hoggy's hand. He respected Hogg and held no animosity at all, "Me too Arran, me too! Unrequited love's a desperate thing, son . . . sorry for gi'in' ye the full sheep wash. At least now we're smoke brothers," said Harper lightly, to take any churlishness out of the matter.

The two men gave up trying to speak in competition with the roaring motor climbing towards Rest and Be Thankful, where the plan was to stop and stretch legs for half an hour while taking in the awesome view. There was a hired photographer on the other coach, intending to use the location as backdrop for recording some of the days' events. Hoggy and Harper moved as little as possible to avoid squelching in their own puddles, or dripping onto people in adjacent seats. When they stopped the two saturated colleagues stood on the corner of the landing next to the driver, allowing other passengers to get off the coach quickly. Without comment the two men went eagerly to search their overnight bags. Crouching behind the rearmost seats where there was some coachwork to hide behind, they fumbled for dry clothing. Harper found himself smiling unexpectedly as he pulled on a new pair of beige Oxford slacks.

The photographer had his work cut out, shepherding the contingent into rank. He had to persuade one of the drivers to manoeuvre his coach for him to stand on the steps with the tripod adjusted for declination, so he could take in the magnificent backdrop. His frame was a glorious midday with the sun at its zenith above frosted slopes and softly breathing forest. Golden light smiled through virgin blue sky, giving a little comforting warmth to heads and shoulders. Rabbits emerged to investigate unfrozen patches of grass near the woodland fringe. Rising eddies of moisture hinted at all the seasons to be seen in a day, as shadows ran from the sun. But to Harper's dismay, none of the urbanites would wait to ponder the most stunning natural beauty he'd ever seen in all of magnificent Scotland. Dry cold quickly rose into feet and there were not enough benches for the full contingent to sit down, so the revellers gradually drifted back to consume their picnic inside the buses. This resonant elevation of earthly nature, trumpeting glory of heavenly tides beyond the chasm below, invited contemplation. But Caillech, the blue faced hag, had to await another perfect time beyond Beltane for these her youngest children to see themselves as part of her picture.

Margaret noticed Harper still shivering and without a word took off her fisherman's roll neck sweater, tossing it to him as he climbed back onto the coach. The garment was knitted from fine, black Arran wool and would give him the appearance of a field preacher from a past era, but he wore it gladly.

As Jenners' weekend tourists came through Reception at Lomond Castle Hotel, laughter rose and fell amid the chatter. For just a few minutes after they had all passed by, levity seemed to have dispersed along the carpeted corridors of the fine hotel and there followed a little respite.

Slanting sunlight fell through leaded windows, reflecting off Meissen pottery and suits of armour, as the party stowed bags and rested a while in their rooms. But night fell quickly and muted sounds of waiters setting tables, surrounded by the aroma of roasting fowl, told the visitors it would soon be time to dress for dinner.

Bright laughter visited again with a knock on a door and quiet solicitation from a remote corridor, "Hello, is that the Metropolitan Male Quartet?" chimed Muriel.

"Oh no!" answered Bobby, who had opened the door.

"Oh yes, I'm afraid so!" cried Jez the joker from within. There was another chorus of, "Oh no!" from Hoggy and Harper, as the heavy door swung shut and the sisters flounced into their bedroom, ostensibly as Muriel explained, "to advise you boys on your kilt fittings."

The feeling of unwelcome intrusion quickly moderated into one of mild annoyance, instantly accepted by the girls but met with their teasing provocation, "I hope you're all suitably attired, as this will be a grand occasion and we want you all to dance!" demanded Muriel. Harper turned away smiling to himself.

"Oh yeah!" replied Jez, suppressing a snigger as he checked a close shave in the mirror, running fingers through lank black hair, "I'm suitably attired!"

"I've never been quite sure what's de rigueur for the upper classes?" asked Bobby McGregor disingenuously, ever the tavern fox. "Me neither," granted Hoggy with a straight face, optimistically looking to Muriel with whom he was clearly smitten.

"Is it tackle in, or tackle out John?" queried Jez, coming to the point with the tone normally reserved for asking directions from old ladies in an unfamiliar town. No one laughed - which was in itself a perilous measure of the controlled hilarity building within the little group. All five looked at Harper who remained deadpan, though a curling line of lips and softening of his voice gave a hint of flippancy to the response which was quintessential Morayshire, "Dinnae ask me guys, I'm no' the traditionalist."

"Oh, but you go to night school, so you're definitely the one closest to being upper class. An' you're a fully apprenticed tailor!" came back the delighted McGregor, roguishly warming to his own line of reasoning.

"What's that got to do with it?" demanded Harper.

"Well surely it was part of your training to discreetly discover the lie of the land? You know, ask a gentleman which way the pendulum swung and all that?" Harper studied McGregor's expression, trying to think of a level riposte to his baiting humour. Everyone in the room waited.

"Either way Bob, I'm no' showing my dick to anyone, especially not these two poor girls, who may have had too much to drink at lunchtime!"

The dam burst in a tide of warm hilarity, sweeping ornate coving and rattling carefully painted windows. Their vigorous ribaldry might have been overheard outside on lawned gardens and along the adjacent frame of the stone building, though any listener would simply have smiled at

46

their pleasure. There was a pause in the chorus of merriment, then another measured voice, "Oh!" cried Margaret, feigning offence, "I never touched a drop! Muriel . . . how about you?"

"Me neither! I cannae believe he just said that about us . . . that we might want to look up his kilt!"

"It's no you two I'm concerned aboot," testified Harper, again flatly affecting the guileless Northerner, "It's Bobby McGregor."

They all looked at Harper aghast as he paused on the brink of allegation and scandal, "I'm embarrassed tae say it but I think he might be a secret meat flasher. He telt me he just wants tae get us aw pished, then scandalise the women folk at dinner!" The girls squealed with delight as McGregor's bewildered face puckered with the outrage of undignified ridicule.

"Dye mean in the middle of aw the speeches and toasts?" cried Muriel.

"Precisely! That's when he plans to do it! When the MD, Mr Kennedy is raising a glass to the vision of Kennington-Jenner's, or even toasting her Majesty the Queen," said Harper, in a tone of dry innocence and bogus concern.

"Harper is going to great lengths to deflect us from a genuine line of enquiry here – if you'll pardon the expression," declared Jez, looking down at Muriel and Margaret, "I believe he knows the answer and simply will not tell us."

"Yeah Harper, tell us!" chorused Muriel and Margaret, echoed by Hoggy and Bob.

"I think we just grab him and sneak a peek," suggested Hoggy, the manic shine in his eyes seen on the beach at Helensborough returning in an instant.

"Oh no!" stated Harper with his Morayshire drawl.

"Oh yes!" contended Pinder, "We need to conclude this matter now for the benefit of all, or we'll be late for dinner!" Once again the girls squealed with delight. Harper backed into a corner, though it was Margaret and Muriel who led the advance, marshalled by Jez.

Thus it was that the cornered rebel, John Harper, came to entrench himself atop a massive mahogany wardrobe of neo-colonial design while the frustrated but determined Kemp sisters, whose direct assault he managed to beat off, attempted in dénouement to dislodge him by tipping the heavy closet away from the wall.

Certain events in a man's life are unrepeatable and should never be mentioned lightly, even if everyone he knows occasionally speaks of it with a wry smile. Such was the event with the wardrobe. Later Harper was in denial. Eventually he came to sublimate entirely the point in time when, sitting cross-legged on top of the wardrobe, he said to Muriel Kemp in order to stop her tilting it, "Okay! Okay . . . I'll show you what's under my kilt, if you show me what's under your bodice."

This bravura was spoken as much for the lads as for the lasses but if at some deeper level that was in fact what Harper had wanted – well that was precisely what he got. An 'eye-full' so to speak.

Both Margaret and Muriel folded arms down to their waist and in one movement lifted outer garments and trusses up to chin level. Harper's eyes nearly jumped out of his face, as once again the laughter hit the rafters.

As senior man Pinder read his cue, slipping out of the bedroom with an endearing smile and casual salute to Harper, squatting just below the high ceiling. Jez was followed by the hooting McGregor and mildly scandalised Hoggy, who affirmed later he would gladly have swopped places with Harper. In retrospect Hoggy told his friend, "I am deeply grateful to you Harper, wishing only that my gaze dwelt longer on the astounding wealth of fleshy delight revealed to entice you down from that wardrobe. In fact I'll probably go to my grave thinking about it!"

As they scooted along the corridor there was a yell of finality from within the bedroom followed by an almighty crash, as Harper leaped towards the nearest bed and the wardrobe went flying to the floor. The three men accelerated their pace guiltily towards the staircase, laughing uncontrollably all the way down into the bar. But there it was – a choice moment in life that no-one could have imagined or scripted.

They were decent girls for sure. The event simply showed how men tend to underestimate women, also the lengths they will go to if directly challenged. There was also an important caveat in Margaret and Muriel's view, that Harper really did need a 'boost' so to speak, "Or a 'boob' maybe?" Jez quietly insisted, when Muriel tried to justify her actions to him later that evening in the bar.

Determined to avoid further scandal, Harper was relieved that the table settings had been arranged by Marlene to mix up cliques. He found himself sitting opposite Eugene and Morag Chomkho, who were surrounded by other lesser lights. Harper knew Yevgheny, 'Gene' to his friends, to be a huge, garrulous Ukrainian, secure in the upper echelons of marketing. The vigilant Eugene represented a new breed of ideas men but was overly career conscious for Harper to warm to. Harper had met his wife previously but others at the table had not had the privilege.

As the meal progressed slowly between served courses, the volume of conversation became gradually raised. Politically reactionary Gene was unremittingly outspoken in his views, yet the man could also be humorous and inquisitive, so Harper made some effort to tolerate him while they made conversation.

To the left and right were a store man and a shop fitter, Jock Laing and Kenneth Whittle, with respective wives Alison and Janet. Harper realised that he had been selected as a foil for people who were either unselfconsciously dull or excessively loquacious. He wondered momentarily where in Marlene's imagination he seemed to fit on that scale.

Eugene's pallid but pretty wife hailed from Glasgow but seemed reclining and cautious, in contrast to her man. Morag's bright blue eyes played approvingly on Harper from a safe distance as her husband sat forward, leaning gigantic elbows on the table. Harper could not help imagining her repressed and ill matched sexually to the Visigoth sitting next to her. Harper rebuffed a flashing image of the seventeen stone bulk of her eager husband, working himself to a climax over Morag's anaemic frame.

Eugene conducted the conversation as though it was just another early morning team briefing. The seasonal five course meal passed quickly and lightly enough, once their leader was satisfied that he'd secured salient facts about all his acolytes and started to hold forth. Chomkho seemed to store each item of personal information offered, as if they were ledger balance entries that might connote into a rolling total, informing month end bottom line profit or loss. Throughout his inquisition the giant kept smiling, as though intentionally conveying the message that, 'Good business is fun and should be engaged in by all.'

Eugene was a proud, egotistical racist, repeatedly alluding to, *naïve* Poles, *pitiful* Russians, *calculating* Jews and other minority groups for whom he declared his distaste. Not meeting explicit challenge, he felt free to begin telling racist jokes.

"Sure you're not a Jew, Harper? You look like you could be – especially with having been trained as a tailor an' all." Chomkho narrowed his eyes, wheezing coarse laughter at his own disarming provocation.

"Gene, you look like a Police Chief who might relish his newly received orders to direct the latest pogrom," Harper alleged coldly. Opening his mouth to reveal half chewed food, Chomkho roared like a lion at the clever response, "I'll take that as a compliment," Eugene decided with his boorish equivalent of subtlety, when he finally finished bouncing up and down with laughter at Harper's measured affront. Clearly tyranny was a topic close to the Sales Executive's heart. Harper merely fuelled his imagination, allowing Chomkho to wax lyrical for the edification of all.

"There are millions of Jews in Poland, Lithuania, Russia. They take over all the businesses in the towns. They own all the property. Now they've started all this revolutionary crap to divide people. They won't be satisfied until there's a war. They want all the monarchies of Europe beheaded and nobility thrown in jail."

"You must be from a noble family then Mr Chomkho, eh?" suggested Harper.

"Ha ha ha ha ha ha ha Ha!" thundered the giant, enunciating each "Ha!" through a succulent mouthful of potatoes and gravy. The last 'Ha!' was particularly strong in case anyone thought he was just vacillating.

Availing the booming volume of an enormous physique, Eugene's insidious prattle resounded across the table, to intimidate his audience. Laughing continuously at his own thoughts, imaginings and verbose constructions, Chomkho alone delighted in his own company. He laughed at his own jokes so much that from a distance it could be construed that others in his presence indulged him by laughing as well. The complex fellow was so quick, he filled in the spaces for the dullards around him. Gene was playwright, lead and support in his own comic opera.

"I find that if people are treated badly, they respond badly. Unlike you, Jews have no country to return to, even if they wanted."

"Why should Jews have a country? Catholics don't!"

"Well, they had the Papal States, at least until '71 and there's always Poland."

"Come again?"

"Oh, just ignore me Gene, I tend to become obnoxious when drunk!"

"Well ease up a bit, Harper!" Gene ordered brusquely. Sawing briskly enough at his turkey to scrape the bone china beneath, he glanced disdainfully at Harper's half empty wine glass.

As the evening wore painfully on, Harper began to healthily despise his superior. Intellectually astute, this brushed and suited bully, though educated, seemed to the misanthropic widower much less genuine in his sentiments than other tough men he had known. Davy Lennox or Ted Wilson, even the intolerant Donald McIntyre, were less dangerously bigoted. Harper found himself wondering silently about experiences that might twist people like Chomkho out of shape.

What social mechanism is at play here? Why does education and obvious intelligence fail to generalise itself in salutary effects upon the character of an individual? How does an antagonistic fool like this get through the selection process to make a career in management? Is this what employers want?

When waiters came with the third course, Harper had not finished eating his roast turkey dinner. Unavoidably engaged with listening and responding to the alarming buffoon across the table, he'd not eaten his fill. As a social gathering this event was largely pointless and unpredictable. Nonetheless, that was what made it interesting and valuable for Harper. Life had whatever meaning he wished to imbue it with. Without realising it, the reactionary Chomkho was helping to liberate John from dejection.

Like a dedicated anthropologist in the wild, Harper continued to listen and learn about racial prejudice. Transfixed and bemused, he heard with incredulity the expressed sentiments of a talking Gorilla, while at the same time questioning the generosity of his own soul.

Who knows what is real for another man? How can we evaluate individual expressions of animosity? What I do know is, it demeans the gentility of our simian ancestors to compare them with this goon.

When the plates had been cleared, more wine was served with coffee and dessert. Harper decided at that moment he was glad to use the repellent Chomkho as cover for his imminent escape. Glancing across the room to exchange waves and broad smiles, Harper established that Margaret and her sister were evidently having a wonderful evening. They were sitting together close to Mr Bryant, one of the company's dedicated textile mill managers. Next to them were some of his engineers and their wives. This was select company indeed - a compliment for Muriel and her sister.

Although he would never ask, Harper knew that this too had been arranged by the talented Marlene and he smiled to himself, remarking another curious instance of the minute, internalised workings of society in play.

Hmm – 'Chance and natural selection' gets you onto the top table. Or more simply, 'Bright eyes and big tits.' Well at least I've seen them naked. Mr Bryant never will.

Chomkho laughed at Harper through a heavy smoker's cough, as he studied him like a boxing opponent between rounds. Having caught the warm exchange of glances with Muriel, Eugene considered it moot to comment upon this, as with everything in his Grand Vizier's purview, "I think you're going to have to join the queue for a crack at that one sunshine."

Harper stared at the Sales Manager with open hostility, inimical scrutiny cutting through noisy conversation around them, but otherwise Harper ignored Chomkho's spicy observation about Muriel. Instead he rose to politely dismiss himself from each of his dinnertime neighbours in turn, including the little kept woman from Glasgow. Chomkho had seen fit to refer to her indirectly several times, as an adjunct of himself without formally introducing her. Harper did not look again at Chomkho as he withdrew. The conceited windbag was beneath contempt.

Smoking as he strolled along frosted margins of Loch Lomond, Harper intended not to 'practice to deceive - to skip and cavort like a romanticised Jacobite,' even one popularised with the acuity of a smart lawyer and endorsed by a corpulent King. When it came down to his soul, no matter how many deft days Harper enjoyed in his prime, he planned at that moment to remain a slightly embarrassed widower. What he did fancy was to lose himself along the glorious tree lined water margin, to let his soul heal under the sheen of a billion flashing stars, for as long as he could endure the coldest night in living memory.

Looking back at his own footprints Harper could see huge icicles growing on the waxy trees. Kicking a small branch from the bank, he watched it skid across the frozen surface of the glorious loch but it did not reach moving water. Unencumbered by doubt or responsibility, at last Harper felt happy and free.

By morning Lomond would be locked in a moment of crystal hoarfrost, to be immortalised in paintings and greetings cards. This relentlessly cruel world was a puzzle, clearly not meant to be solved in its stark beauty. Musical whoops and scratching from behind convinced him that, in desperation to come to terms with it, the whole of humanity was quite irredeemably insane.

Sorrow was waiting behind every hill and bend – so why not breathe in the fresh air while he might? There was a clear difference between self-inflicted solitariness and the alternative of becoming a social pariah. With a smile Harper realised Marlene had chosen him as a foil for

Chomkho because she knew that he was balanced – forthright and rooted in self-confidence.

She had also judiciously kept him away from the girls who would tease him mercilessly, until they got a reaction from him despite his broken heart. Marlene was a kindred spirit, maybe too like Hannah for him to consider as a partner. With a tearful impulse of recognition Harper realised he had grown to love Marlene as a friend.

Pondering his oppressive situation, he turned towards the massive Baronial house with its overspill of yellow candlelight illuminating wild Celtic prancing within. In that moment Harper finally came to terms with conditions of a lonely life, accepting that he was truly inspired by the warmth of some of the fine people he'd come to know – and by one affectionate soul in particular.

Stepping through a revolving glass door into the warm lobby Harper met Margaret coming the other way, accompanied as ever by Muriel. They were followed by a casual troop of admirers, mainly machinists and shop girls, with mooning bachelors roughly aggregated around their rooming arrangements. Margaret walked slowly as she gazed at Harper through blue eye liner, swinging hands and hips as gracefully as a water carrier. A silver lame evening gown cast warming light, reflected from a hundred sources onto Margaret's diamante earrings. Anyone in any doubt beforehand could see at a glance that she looked every curved inch like a lady. In that precise moment though, Margaret was preparing to take a step beyond appearances.

Catching her eye, Harper opened his mouth in greeting but before he could speak she gripped the lapels of his jacket, kissing him with an open mouth in a forceful embrace that was blatantly sexual. Standing on her toes she pressed her breasts into him, as he leant against the frame of the beautiful etched glass door. Holding a portable camera above the level of Margaret's shoulder, Jez said 'Smile!' before Harper could release her from the unexpected clasp.

There was a pop and flash of powder and simultaneously needles from the Christmas tree fell onto Harper's left shoulder. A large crimson bauble painted with white snowflakes brushed his ear as Bobby placed a twig of mistletoe on top of his head. Harper groaned a smiling protest through Margaret's open mouth so she released him, having staked a claim in the simplest, most direct way imaginable. The stunned Harper was momentarily speechless in voluptuous embarrassment.

"Believe in your own salvation!" prompted Hoggy in a moment of drunken lucidity, leaning close to Harper to resume banter from earlier. Instantly a broad grin broke across Harper's face - for perhaps the first time in his twenty seven years. The impenetrable dryness of Moray fell from his face, before the boundless drollery of the waggish Buyer. For a few moments Harper actually allowed himself to laugh freely. No-one apart from Hannah had ever got through his armour so easily. Slapping Hoggy on the shoulder he thought of replying, "Dominus vobiscum!" but for once the smile enveloping Harper's face and glint in his eye spoke for him. The midnight ramblers moved off to sober up a little in the grounds without further discourse.

"Now she knows what he's got under his kilt," McGregor murmured to Hoggy, as they retreated through the lobby into the iron grip of the night.

"Harper!" called Jez, as he approached the revolving glass door. Harper turned to look – still ruffled with embarrassment from the encounter with Margaret, "Happy New Year Matey!" he called with a wink and a sly grin.

Chapter Three   *Light Angels*

Prepossessed by the physical aspects of sensual minutiae, Margaret and Harper developed their love affair with slow mutual consideration. As the months went by each became engrossed in the company of the other, to an extent that outward observers might have felt aptly Victorian. Every time he smiled the sun came out. Every time her voice thrilled with enthusiasm as it so often did, Margaret's presence in his life seemed more congenial. Harper knew he could wait until the wounds healed, if they were ever going to and through it all Margaret's appeal kept him upright.

Continually looking forward to encountering one another, their eyes met over increasingly remarkable distances. Margaret raised her hand to wave, acknowledging his look from a hundred yards down the hill at Parson's Green, or from within a meandering crowd of Sunday walkers half way along the rural road. They connected without imposition, smiling to touch for re-assurance without lingering.

As they sat together on the sofa discussing hum drum problems at work, she placed her hand affectionately on the top of his thigh. Harper's mind reeled in amazement, without need for comment. When other people were around he would reach out his hand to briefly touch her fingers, withdrawing immediately. Wary of condemnation, they adopted a public school greeting meant to uphold secrecy. Both knew it meant more than 'Hello' but were constrained by convention and circumstance. When she arrived late one morning with a heavy cold she groaned, "Oh, I just feel like getting back into bed!"

Harper was bursting to say, "I'll come with you!" but refused to sell himself short. Something in his mind told Harper love always has conditions and it teased him to the point of delight to consider Margaret's. She was in control and cool in her ardour. She might even find someone else. Love shone like spring sunshine but remained a subject beyond discussion.

Always, there were her eyes. Harper saw Margaret's confident gaze in his dreams. Whenever his mind wandered or he was bored they were there, watching him with veneration. As winter turned to spring, he found himself searching her eyes for measure of her mood. She in turn searched his, for reassurance that he was still interested. Their trust in one another, neither explicit nor sexual, was assured by Margaret's commonplace gumption. The harder she worked, the more he voiced appreciation.

"You know," he said one evening in March, shaking his head slightly as he handed Margaret her coat, "I have to say, you are very special. And I would have been lost without you Margaret!"

For both, their quiet affaire de coeur became deeply sensual in anticipation. Harper thought about Margaret constantly when his mind was not given over to business. Recollection of his beloved Hannah actually made his love for Margaret all the more poignant. First he had to admit Hannah had been right . . . he *could* love another woman.

Returning from Newcastle on an early afternoon train on his last working day prior to the Easter weekend, Harper's viewing through the window was flooded with afternoon light from a reviving landscape. Stretching legs in the empty carriage, he allowed himself to think of the myriad ways Margaret had tried to entice him.

A flush of visceral desire burst in an instant from either side of Harper's stretching spine. Passionate release bypassed trapped genitalia, rising upwards through his stomach. In a moment instinctual craving for Margaret exploded into his brain, moving sharply downwards from his head to his heart. In the most tangible sense Harper was engulfed with untamed desire. Thinking again about Margaret's New Year kiss, he came as close to the intensity of orgasm as he might had he taken her to bed. In that moment of prurient longing, he also knew what must be. Harper realised that he needed to reorganise all his priorities to accommodate this lovely young woman, if she would commit to having him.

What made that fateful moment extremely sweet was Harper's awareness that Margaret could not have made her wishes more clearly explicit. In cool, temperate style she'd won him over - influencing his impartiality with sage earnestness through endless, whispering days.

The lenitive chemical catalyst of soft voice and blue eyes had distilled kind amity into his heart. Daily offering the inclination of smiling face, proud little chin and uplifted breasts, Margaret Kemp had utterly seduced him. Or perhaps in meditation so far from home, the cold logic of his situation tricked Harper into seducing himself.

As he came through the front door, Harper handed Duff some flowers, "Run ahead and take these to Margaret," he whispered.

The look on her face as she stood in the kitchen with a chopping knife in her hand was consummation itself. Margaret hugged Duff then feigned surprise, "But surely you've got the date wrong, its no' my birthday until next month!"

With a smile he gave her a box gift-wrapped at Jenners – containing an expensive silk scarf, "See if you have a dress that might match this," he suggested softly. Margaret's genteel smile said it all. She knew her dream had come true.

Later that evening John Harper called on Muriel, "I need you to spend tomorrow afternoon and evening with the girls, if you will?" Muriel laughed her sensational, raucous laugh showing teeth amid intuitive glee, "Nothing would give me greater pleasure John . . . sorry! Mum's the word!" she added, putting her deft hand on his arm as he stood at the back door.

Then Harper asked Margaret to, "Accompany me on a secret mission of great importance which I can discuss with no-one but you."

"Oh, well I think I'd better just play along with that," came the tentative reply, "though I'm not sure whether to bring dancing shoes or my muddy boots."

When the girls pressed him on the nature of that mission they got a bluff and misleading response, "Don't tell anyone, especially not Margaret but we'll be surveying higher ground where I can look over fences . . . to check the distribution of large women hanging out red bloomers. Mr Kennedy the Managing Director of Jenners asked for *me personally*. But I need a female accomplice, or I might get arrested." Elizabeth squawked with glee.

"Naw, he's fibbing!" said Elsie shaking her head.

"Can I come with you? You're going to climb up Arthur's Seat aren't you?" asked Duff, "That's why you gave Margaret a scarf!"

Elizabeth was scandalised that such a fun adventure, whether it involved red bloomers or not, might be conducted without her. Standing in the doorway with hands on hips her mouth was wide open, as she hesitated to say what she wanted to say. Finally, after half a minute of incredulous scrutiny, she spun off and away without saying goodbye, as Margaret and Harper prepared to leave. The front door closed and happy voices were heard heading off up the hill.

Elizabeth came back a minute later, storming down the stairs to confer with Muriel and the other two associate members of her committee.

"What do we want to do this evening?" asked Muriel, politely deflecting the anticipated bluster, "Shop for Harper's messages first then later a story . . . if we can pick out a good one that none of us have read, yeah?"

"Muriel will you listen? He's gonny ask her tae marry him!" declared the scandalised Elizabeth, "They've just gone walking through the rye!" She paused for a moment as the bombshell struck the other two.

Muriel half laughed, half cried out in amazement at Elizabeth's precociousness, needing to put a hand over her mouth to stifle an uncontrolled reaction to the correct reading of such a tremendously romantic moment. Duff and Elsie parroted Muriel's stifled cry of amazement - because they too were at a loss for words. Muriel's feigned confusion did seem to fit the overwhelming scandal of the moment for the Harper girls.

At length Elsie spoke, in her slow, considered manner, dark eyes soft with sorrow, "Oh, no, what would mammy have to say?"

"Oh yes! I'm afraid it's true . . . he gave her *flowers and a scarf*," Elizabeth recapped, quicksilver eyes and schoolmarm voice all severity.

"But people do that to say 'Thank you,'" pleaded Muriel in exasperation, careful not to play her hand too strongly, lest Elizabeth read disingenuity as sharply as she read Harper's intentions.

Duff sped out of the room with tears running down both cheeks, cut in half by the thought of her mummy's memory causing Elizabeth's trenchant condemnation of Harper and Margaret. Letting out a strangled wail, she ran blindly through the hallway out of the front door. It was as much an instinct to avoid the surgical cruelty of Elizabeth's jealous logic as the need to follow and congratulate Harper that incited Duff to run after them.

At a framed rotunda gate to the park wall, the child stopped with hands covering her face. Margaret glanced back at a turn in the pathway and noticed her, "Look, there's Duff," she told Harper.

"They're obviously playing hide and seek. Come on, Muriel will watch her . . . let's go."

"No, no. Something's wrong . . . she's crying, see how she's breathing." Looking at one another for just a moment both simultaneously voiced the same conjecture, "Elizabeth!"

As no-one had followed they walked back in the direction of the house, speaking softly to console Duff, who would not utter a word. Intuitively, Muriel was waiting for a while before following, expecting Duff to return. Margaret met her sister at the doorstep. Consoling the child at a pragmatic distance, Harper caught the gist of their brief exchange.

"He didnae consult the Oracle."

"What?"

"Mother Shipton has declared against it!"

"Eliz . . . Oh, I'm going Muriel, I dinnae want tae hear it! We'll take the bairn."

In a second Margaret turned, moving quickly away from the house and any further controversy that might emerge from it. She was not about to derail Harper's anticipated move in her direction.

"Mammy said I was no' tae ever say bad things that might hurt Margaret's feelings!" stated Duff, wishing for a simple solution. Margaret's mercurial features flashed with fond appreciation.

Promptly lifting the child in his arms to avoid further embarrassment, Harper walked ahead of Margaret back towards the park gate. Outwardly cheery at the prospect of taking Duff along with them, Margaret resolved not to entertain awkwardness. She knew instinctively the moment she had lived for had come at last.

It's Harper's initiative, so I will let him deal with the child too. This intrusion could dampen his resolve to say whatever he needs to say.

Margaret smiled blissfully as Harper headed towards the city, with Duff sitting on his shoulders. Everywhere she looked springtime colours, emerald, white, yellow and purple were bursting through dank earth of woodland margins. Weak sun kissed their faces as they walked. Rankled by the effect Elizabeth clearly had on Duff, Harper mused on the controversy his proposal might trigger. Glancing at Margaret, he suddenly found himself bemused by crystal eyes and sharply cut features under a modish bonnet.

Oh my Lord, just look at this appealing twenty-one year old mademoiselle! She may well turn me down. What if Margaret sees me as I see Marlene? A bright star, out of reach for all practical reasons.

Stopping at a bench below Duke's Walk Harper squatted to sit in yellow afternoon light. Turning to Duff who sat watching him with sorrow in her innocent eyes, he took both of his daughter's hands in his.

"There's something I need to ask you, Duff," he began.

"What is it, Harper?" replied Duff with the gentlest respect. Margaret waited politely, charmed to smile as ever with a devotee's smouldering stoicism.

He's about to ask permission of his five year old daughter to remarry. Then no doubt he's going to turn to me, to ask me the same. This man will draw humour from every situation.

Constrained not to laugh, Margaret found the scene played out before her so teasingly comical, she almost burst with ecstasy. This was Harper's way of defusing the bombshell while asking her by proxy. Her genial face beaming with delight, Margaret Kemp imagined she was experiencing as much elation as it was possible to encompass at once without heart failure, or the overwhelmed mind being staggered into unconsciousness. She fought back laughter - concerned by the effect it might have on the child.

Harper spoke with complete alacrity, beginning his explanation in simple good humour, "Duff, you know I loved your mother with all my heart." Listening devotedly, the child inclined her head forward to study her father's face.

"I love you too Duff. And Elsie and Elizabeth."

"Thank you Daddy!" Duff replied, waiting patiently for the right opportunity to hug him.

"Now I have come to love Margaret too," he affirmed, "And I need *you* to help me explain this to Elsie and Elizabeth."

"No bother, Harper. I'll tell them what mammy said!" promised the innocent. Harper cleared his throat dramatically, like a circuit judge about to pass sentence. Looking over his shoulder he caught Margaret's eye, holding it with his Morayshire bluff, "If Margaret might feel the same way, I wish to marry her," added Harper, glancing back at his daughter. Seeing tears of joy filling Margaret's eyes, Duff immediately jumped off the bench to embrace her. Standing on tiptoes she kissed Margaret on the mouth.

"Well . . . What is you answer, Duff?"

"Oh, you know Daddy! Margaret loves you! I won't let Elizabeth stand in your way!" Finally joy burst out with the sunshine glimmering on St Margaret's Loch. All three laughed aloud, Margaret leaning forward with a smile on her face to indulge the child, returning her kiss. Resisting the urge to wipe away wetness deposited on her lips, Margaret stood up to hug Harper too. A single tear of joyful release rolled down her lovely face, articulating a deft, shining plait of the Weaver's Answer, "Thank you so much, Duff!" declared Margaret by way of consent, as she stroked the child's hair at the back of her head.

They strolled through the park, then along the Royal Mile to visit Camera Obscura on Castle Hill. Duff struggled with the stairs, so they found themselves in the midst of a Church of Scotland Women's Guild party from North Deeside. When they reached the viewing room, both took great pains to point out familiar landmarks for Duff who had trouble distinguishing the area near home, due to Calton Hill being in the line of sight.

"Take me there after you marry, Margaret please Harper," she entreated, pointing at the folly, "And you can get married at the nice church with the basket on top!"

"Which one? Oh, St Giles,' as long as there are no baskets inside," answered the Episcopalian turned agnostic.

"Actually, we might have to start attending Church more regularly," suggested Margaret with a smile, punching him with a straight fist into his ribs as he flinched.

"What was that for?"

"You know fine . . . Presbyterianism has a special place at the heart of this city. And don't use language like that in front of the child," she hissed.

"I thought you were brought up a Catholic!"

"I was brought up a *Christian* and taught to respect all religions."

"Oh well, we'd better call in at St Patrick's on the way home then," Harper conceded with disarming alacrity.

But the smile faded from John Harper's eyes as he breathed deeply, gazing at the gloriously feisty Margaret Kemp. She was no longer someone to compare with another. Margaret was a discretely gracious individual in her own right. Mumbling something inexplicable, seeming to come from an incoherent Caliban, woken from slumber in his elevated cave commanding the coast below, Harper stood up at last, straight and tall.

"A good punch in the ribs was all I needed to bring me to my senses," he muttered reflectively, "Maybe you should have done that before!"

"Come again?"

Clearing his throat, this time Harper spoke with resolve more becoming a man than a cave dweller, "Pardon me, what I meant to say is that I love you, Margaret Kemp. Will you marry me?"

"Oh, so you are not getting the child to do your talking for you this time?"

A small group of new initiates to Edinburgh's breathtakingly romantic panorama turned on fashionable heels to pause and smile knowingly.

"Yes, of course John Harper, I *will* marry you. What girl in her right mind would decline you, given the chance?" she added, with a glorious smile.

Echoing murmurs of approval came from around the little darkened observatory, as John Harper laughed brightly once again with the glad voice of a boy.

"Oh and I love you too, as if you didn't always know it," cautioned the gentle Margaret. With a tone he knew to be the closest she might ever come to scolding, she added, "Just don't ever take it for granted."

To a ripple of applause for principled affirmation, with smiles from the little group of observers and with little Hannah clapping loudest in their midst, Margaret kissed John eagerly and he folded her warmly in his arms.

A small coterie of politely garrulous women flocked and fled like grass parrots around the bright mural, pretending not to be pre-occupied by what every eye was in fact drawn to. There were speculative glances in the direction of Hannah, then toward Margaret's gaunt face and flat abdomen, yet none of the women in the coach party ventured an alternative opinion.

One stately diviner in particular, as sumptuously attired as any Lady of the Guild from Cults or Bieldside - tall, fair and sinewy under crisply cut hangings - levelly assessed Harper, as a divorcee and philandering rogue. Had he dared return her Ladyships' sensational inspection, he might have fleetingly considered declining Margaret to elevate his status, so bold was her scrutiny.

But that might have involved a golfing weekend, to slip arsenic into the snifter of one of his watery-eyed Lodge associates. The sophisticated, forty something enchantress pondered Harper's face until a friend linked her arm to draw the woman away. Out of politeness the satisfied little group turned as one to clamber downstairs, just as more of their associates formed at a discreet stalking distance behind.

Margaret took Harper's hand for the first time ever, thrilling to the longed for touch. Duff took his other hand, satisfied to have witnessed what seemed such an artless development.

Words of wisdom echoed up the stairway from below, "An ideal place to propose to your ain true love, don't you think Euphemia?" said the modest lady to her judgemental friend. "Oh, Veronica, please!" said the other, "The next you know there will be weddings and funerals in here too! Besides," she said after a pause, "what kind of rite could they have? There isn't room to swing a bloomin' cat by its tail!"

"Well no there isn't, but I don't know what you're implying!"

The curious sound of politely insouciant laughter came back to the new couple as the flock of old birds gathered again, spilling out ahead of them to the cobbles and unbroken April sunshine. Their laughter was restrained rather than fervent, yet heedless of the couples' feelings nonetheless.

Harper showed no concern for joyous ribaldry started among the merrymaking cluster of women tourists by his public declaration and proposal. Much less was he interested in whom among them might have risen to gladly partner him across a dance floor. He wanted only Margaret. Her love had already saved him from mistrust.

Margaret had waited over four years for this exquisite moment. Despite the new reality that Harper had declared his love for her, in a sense she could continue to wait. To Harper she seemed exactly what she was, despite her intensity - young, inexperienced and preciously vulnerable. Her family, with whom she and Muriel still resided, were not wealthy. Their rooms in the house off Willowbrae Road were not large enough to command much in the way of rental, so their parents encouraged the girls to stay and contribute to board and lodging.

Anthony and Teresa Kemp had humbly agreed conventional moral standards and expectations of conduct. From their father, Margaret and Muriel learned of the world, and by their mother were taught caution. These were two complimentary assays – the touchstone and the hallmark, one couched as theory and the other invariably practical. Expectation would apparently deliver the world to the feet of stunningly attractive Muriel, whereas probability instilled balance in Margaret's sharp mind. She planned to carry forward professional discipline, in work as in her new relationship.

Although Harper was tendering her promise of a change of status, it still felt to Margaret like a transaction and she was determined not to sell herself cheap. Now they could talk openly about it. At last the flow of dialogue Harper missed greatly following the passing of his remarkable wife began to return.

"That painted old vamp would have smuggled you onto the bus if you'd offered to carry the lunch hamper."

"Ha, ha . . . I'm not old enough, or innocent enough!"

"Oh, she wasnae innocent. None of them were!"

"Well, they would'ha dropped me off at the bottom of the hill once they'd turned over ma wallet."

"Why, have ye run oot o' cash?"

"No, but when they saw pictures of my family . . ."

"It sounds to me that deep down you dinnae believe you're an eligible widower?"

"Well, I could sum that question up in five minutes, even if I ran on."

"Harper, no-one said it would be easy, but if you ran anywhere, I'd follow you." Margaret placed herself in front of him as if he was about to bolt, still holding his hand.

At that moment the sun came out in the sky and Harper's beaming smile reflected glory he saw in his heart. A small dream he'd had after months of the darkest night, was turning into a beautiful story. They were heroes walking through the Athens of the North, benevolently tuned to every consideration within their compass.

"Well, this is your reward for being so patient," he told her with warm love light in his eyes, "And I have to admit I wanted you so badly!"

"Ha, ha! You getting all this?" asked Margaret, looking down thoughtfully at Duff.

"Oh, yes Margaret, I knew this was going to happen *ages* ago. Mammy wants you to *always* be kind to one other!" The child wrapped

66

her arms around them as they crouched down to her on the esplanade at the end of Castle Hill, laughing at her stunning revelation.

Although Duff's precocious insight astounded Margaret, this glad understanding endowed her with power. Power in turn lent added allure. Taking on Hannah Harper's family was a consensual choice she was proud to make on her own terms and her own family would be heavily involved, as would Harper's. The discretion of a long engagement would be mutually workable, considering the difference in their ages and status, not to mention resistance already encountered.

Ideally, she needed time to identify features of the panorama they were walking into. Harper's studies would eventually generate increased salary from finding a job in banking or life assurance, so he told her with confidence. Margaret's nominal status as nurse or midwife could provide additional income when Hannah started at school, she mentioned in return.

Standing at the edge of the water, Harper leaped into the air with feet tucked under and arms raised joyously in the air, "I'm not suggesting this ken? It's a neutral statement but we *can* live together." He stopped in the middle of the busy thoroughfare to search Margaret's face for her response, "I will tell your parents, if you can't. They'll understand if I explain that we plan to wait for a couple of years. Who really cares what people think?"

"I care, Harper. I care very much. I want them to think well of me." Gently spoken concerns elicited the protective response she most wanted to hear.

"Oh, but what you decide is up to you Margaret. This is Edinburgh after all, the open forum of new ideas,' Harper looked around with a benign smile, as if he might see a legendary figure step right out of the stonework to advance up the cobbles and shake their hands, "At different times our city has been the breeding ground of radicalism, romanticism, the elevation of paupers and women but it's also the home of freethinking individuality - of emancipation itself!"

"Ha, ha! The Edinburgh I know, is the place where folk are sure to offer their opinions without being asked!"

"Oh, I think we're both ready for that."

"*We* might be. I just hope the girls are too."

"Well, that settles it then . . . we'll bring the wedding forward. Get your diary oot an' pick a date hen."

Margaret's gleeful smile was the only endorsement needed. They gazed into one another's eyes for a lingering moment, until Duff broke their attention, "We shouldnae go in the Castle, daddy. It's noisy and dusty with workmen. Get a slider instead and save the money," she said, pointing with her middle finger to the ice cream stall.

"Oh pity, I wanted to show you both Richard Ansdell's painting, *The Fight for the Standard at Waterloo*. His works are brilliant. They show dramatic moments with wonderful colours and light. He created moving subjects, which I imagine most artists would avoid."

"Well, another time maybe! I've lived here all my life and you tell me something new about my home town every day!"

Margaret smiled diffidently at Duff, who surprised her even more than Harper, but she took the child's hand as they turned to walk down into the town.

All that each had gratefully forecast essentially fell into place, within gentle minutes of chat. Zig-zagging down grassy slopes, they ambled towards a bursting haze of unseasonal warmth bisecting the valley along Queen's Street. Pleasant radiation reflecting off bald cobbles and recently rolled tar, mingled with uprising moisture drifting from awakening trees and manicured lawn. Holding hands round every turn and flight of steps, they followed undulating pathways towards the crouching stonework of the town.

Duff sat on Harper's shoulders, singing her way through a popular children's repertoire, taking requests for the 'Skye Boat Song' and 'My Love is Like a Red, Red Rose.' She caressed them both as a much younger child might have, while they strolled along. The child yearned to embrace family again, for hurtful separation had blighted every moment of her life so far. As she listened to healing love revealed in every earnest step they took, her skipping heart lifted in joy at last.

By accepting Duff's presence, Margaret and Harper were including her in the reformation of their family, knowing they could never have had such conversations in front of either of her elder sisters. Elsie and

Elizabeth would both have questioned too much – although from entirely opposite motives. What Elsie would have been magnanimous in accepting, Elizabeth would have examined rigorously for authentication.

As they approached the corner of Bank Street, Harper set Duff down and the child ran with Margaret to buy pastries from a street vendor. Gorging on mille fuilles - enormous Napoleons filled with custard and topped with icing, embedded with almonds and chocolate – they drew attention from pigeons and seagulls.

Harper flicked morsels of puff pastry and nuts high into the air for the birds to swoop after. Over-faced Duff dropped half of hers onto the bench. Her dad demonstrated how to feed it to the gulls.

"Watch they dinnae poop on yer heed," cautioned Margaret observing from a safe distance.

"Oh, they're far too canny for that!"

Duff laughed at Margaret's exaggerated common dialect, calling back in mock refinement, "No Dear, I wouldnae want dung in my hair! Len' me yer pretty bunnet while I feed the birds!" Flabbergasted at her cheek, Margaret gaped in amazement.

"Have you met my youngest daughter?" Harper asked playfully.

"No, I'm not sure I have. Who does she get it from?" queried Margaret, a little abashed.

"I have no idea," claimed Harper with a defensive laugh, "It could never be me!"

Duff laughed at them with her whole face, head and chest. As she curled shoulders forward slightly, hilarity bent her tiny back and knees. So happy was she in that special moment of adult recognition that her body kinked. After all, how significant was a generational age gap of seventeen years in the undying clockwork of eternity? Duff's merriment was bright, resonant sound, deeper and fuller than her quiet speaking voice. Charmed by that amiable tone, Margaret and Harper were astonished to admit they'd never heard the child laugh so freely before.

For the bride-to-be, astonishment was compounded by realisation that Duff's manner conveyed more than an impression of her mother's captivating geniality. In that instant Margaret felt she could come to terms with all the skeletons in Harper's cupboard - but knew she would never be able to ignore this living presence.

After climbing the Scott Monument and walking round the town window-shopping, Harper insisted on buying afternoon tea at the Balmoral Hotel. Despite his earlier 'neutral statement' regarding a long engagement, Margaret caught the glint of an ulterior motive in his eye. She noticed him checking room rates when they walked through reception, then as they waited for the waiter he excused himself to disappear for two minutes. Something told her he wasn't planning a discounted party rate for wedding guests from Morayshire.

When she questioned him, he just smiled guiltily, mumbling about arranging the evening's entertainment. "Woman is fickle!" is all he would commit to. When she pressed further he appeared self-conscious, looking at his fob watch as if there was pressing urgency.

Margaret's sparkling eyes reflected the unreleased tension that had been growing between them for months. With understated intention, Harper hurried Duff to finish her battered plaice. Margaret offered the child a neat linen 'kerchief to wipe sticky fingers.

He whisked them along Princes Street to Hamilton and Inches jewellers, before the shop closed at six, for Margaret to choose rings. In his jacket pocket were two tickets for a performance of Verdi's Rigoletto, booked discreetly along with a double room, by cash down payment to the clerk at the hotel. Begging Margaret's indulgence would be the difficult part, even if he never touched her in public again until they were safely married.

Having committed himself to loving her, Harper could not wait to possess her. If need be he had to express that precise thought to Margaret this very day. Reconciled to the notion that presumption might backfire, if necessary he was prepared to get down on one knee to ask forgiveness.

But once inside the jeweller's shop, he could see Margaret was in her element and not about to rush this moment. If it meant another two or more consultations with the enthusiastic Mr Inches, still she would innocently pander to every word of advice.

"It's not unusual for a couple to shop together," he assured them. "We can indulge your fancy, Sir, Madam, with the range on offer, or make your own custom made designs to order. Have you an idea what kind of engagement ring you prefer? Platinum or yellow gold? Perhaps a gem stone arrangement?"

Harper could see it was Margaret's time to shine but couldn't help seeing the contrast with Hannah's experience. They'd scrimped and saved for everything. With a glad heart he could spend money, now no longer an issue for him, on this vivid, loyal soul.

Margaret studied the rings without wishing to try them on, as though intuition was focussed instead on the token of his love. If it came out of a Christmas cracker she would wear it with delight. Each ring presented for appraisal required a glance to Harper from her. He could sense her body trembling with excitement from her tone of voice. It mattered a great deal to Margaret how their bond would be consecrated.

"They're all lovely Mr Inches but none of them are practical for a woman doing daily chores."

"Now, there's the voice of wisdom. At this point I invariably take the opportunity to counsel the younger generation on matters of practicality. Budgetary considerations follow betrothal, as surely the weather follows the sun."

"Oh . . . look!" breathed Margaret huskily, "May I?"

"Of course Madam, one at a time is the only house rule."

"I would say that applies to the lads as well as the lassies – no, Mr Inches?" chimed in Harper. Inches barely ghosted a smile. He'd heard all the laddish banter before and was planning a life in politics, so preferred not to be quoted out of context.

Reaching her hand to the tray on the counter before her, Margaret removed a white gold ring with an aquamarine stone, which she slipped onto her finger. Smiling provocatively she posed with hand stretched against the matching background of the blue silk scarf Harper had given her.

"What has Andrew Carnegie got to say about this?"

"I'm not sure, he'd probably run it past JP Morgan for stock valuation before committing himself."

"Oh, Margaret that's beautiful," chimed Duff, "It matches your eyes perfectly!"

"It's a blue diamond, just over one and a half carats. I will leave you good people to discuss your choice," offered Inches, aware that the price tag was several times the benchmark three month's salary.

Harper put his arm around Margaret to reassure her, smelling soapy freshness with a hint of moderately priced scent. It would wipe out proceeds from the speculative investment prior to the US election but the positive flow of Margaret's good intentions felt like treasure already stored up in heaven.

"No, John! I was joking, I didn't mean . . ." but John was not listening or, if he was he intended to act swiftly to avoid embarrassment, "I will pay for it now, Mr Inches and return it to you for adjustment when Madame has had time to show her mother and sister."

"And Anthony! Elsie and Elizabeth!" urged Duff, "And Molly . . . she'll love how it sparkles. She can chase light angels when the sun shines, like when you wash the bottles!" Margaret laughed indulgently but Inches said nothing. Close inspection of Harper's fine business suit told the gentleman he had just made a thirty five guinea sale.

Hiring a cab so they would have more time to dress for the evening, they set off to return Duff to the care of her elder sisters and Muriel. Margaret's heart sang in her breast. To sit next to Harper, confirming textures and immaculate odours she had only ever mused upon from a distance, gave her an inconspicuous quiver of excitement. Watching every movement and gesture with glad light in her eyes, brighter than the fine gem pushed back on magical, nameless Anamika, Margaret felt that regardless of sorrow burdening his brave heart, John was truly in love with her.

I will save him from himself. He'll lead me in the dance until he falters, then I'll show him how strong I can be.

"When you go back for the ring fitting get something for Elsie and Elizabeth," Duff instructed Harper.

"You are clever, what a grand idea!" agreed Margaret. Harper opened his mouth to protest, like a frog catching flies on a river bank.

"What would you suggest?" asked Margaret, before he could voice an objection.

"Oh, every girl wants a wristwatch," purred Duff with self-assurance, "but they on'y make them for ladies, so I think it"ll hae tae be bracelets or beads."

"Oh yes . . . beads . . . I think beads would be preferable to bracelets, or ladies wristwatches," Harper stated mordantly, nodding with fake interest, "Especially as I've just spent the holiday money for our next trip to Ramsburn."

"Did you? That's okay, Harper. You invited them all to come down here," Duff reminded him with bland enthusiasm.

"So, I did. Isn't it amazing that you remember what I said over a year ago?"

"They'll all want tae come to your wedding," she added quietly, "I'll write to Great Gran Han and tell her the date, so she can ask Mr Grant tae step in."

"See what happens when a child spends too long with adults," observed Harper, as Duff ran along the path to be first with the restorative news. There was no question in the child's mind that what she found easy would be awkward for Harper and impossible for Margaret. A wry smile played around her lips as Elizabeth greeted her, suggesting disingenuously that they had been worried about her. Duff had been entrusted with the momentous task of briefing Elsie and Elizabeth about the day's events, and informing them that Harper and Margaret had 'tickets for the opera.'

When this euphemism was conveyed to Muriel she smirked knowingly across at Harper, standing in the hallway. There was something intensely erotic about Muriel his mind would not connect with given all the circumstances, so he just smiled back at her lamely.

After half an hour of excited questioning and reassurances, followed by another half hour of Margaret trying on dresses hastily collected from home, the new couple were ready to step out together. The girls and

Muriel embraced Margaret, telling her how happy they were for her and Harper.

"Well, have fun! We won't wait up, will we girls?" she promised, looking down at her three charges, craning their necks for a glimpse of the polished prize Margaret wore on her finger. As she stepped into the living room where they waited for the cab to arrive they could all see radiant serenity on her face. Harper's thrall had transported Margaret into a daydream. Even Elizabeth was at a loss for an objection.

Curling her shoulders unintentionally as she carried her overnight bag down the path, Margaret could not help smiling with unnatural guilt. But as Muriel and the girls called good wishes from the doorway, she lifted her head to wave over her shoulder. Wheeling after Harper in a sky blue satin evening gown and small organza hat, she looked as proprietorial as the cover girl on Sears Roebuck's mail order catalogue.

It had been so long that he'd not known where to start. She seized the initiative, throwing off her clothes briskly, to slide between perfect sheets. Pressing her generous bosom lightly against Harper's naked back Margaret clasped him warmly. Intuition told him to wait and not to speak, that passion and humour follow like butterflies rolling in flight, vigilant for one another along a summer lane. He wanted to say, "You are mothering me like a little boy!" but was afraid that teasing her might break the soulful charm of gentleness, plumbing fathoms of his resounding soul.

At last turning to kiss and caress her, Harper searched Margaret's eyes for assent - but she seemed distant and unsure. Measured curiosity took them through estivate fields, where both were rapt with fragrance, contour, texture and taste of skin, hair and wrinkles.

"You're bum is cold!" he grumbled against her flat belly, hesitating between caresses and the passion anticipated.

"My bum is always cold. You'll have to warm it up." Turning over she backed into him, suggesting rest rather than activity. He floundered without a cue, kissing her back tentatively for want of a lead.

Postponement led to an interval of fire burning underground, which Harper knew would eventually lead to spontaneous combustion.

"I think I've been struck by lightning!" he whispered at last, reaching for her breasts beneath the sheets. Laughing confidently as wildfire surfaced she turned to offer the sensual cascade of her neat little body. Silky hair and warm breath; fulsome breasts and supple belly, moved onto him - with the gentle assumption of heavenly shape over exploding space.

Images larger than life flooded Harper's neglected senses, as love transported him above the treeline. He glimpsed again in three dimensions many faces from his beloved home – some deprived but none derelict. He saw and heard the family rooms at West Port, the garrulous crew at the Station, then again the prettiest woman in the entire city moving passionately in his arms, as his ordeal resolved in compassion.

He laughed so loud, at first Margaret thought she had maimed him with her energetic movement.

"What? What is it John? What was so amusing?"

"Nothing . . . nothing. I daren't say."

"I'll be offended if you don't! I want to get off on the right foot in our marriage. No secrets we agreed!" She rested on top of him with her hair draped over his chest.

"You and Muriel, that afternoon at Lomond Castle. If I live to be a hundred I don't expect I'll ever see anything so daringly funny. That's when you got me going. That moment of boldness . . . coupled with seeing your pretty lips every morning!" He placed his lips ardently over hers before she could move away.

"Why did you never tell me? You could have said!" she tried to say, as he pressed home the kiss with what seemed exaggerated ardour, now that the act of love making was complete. Showing tenderness to Margaret, restrained for so many months, bordered on compulsion.

"I waited so long to give myself away but it was worth every minute! Let's do it again," she whispered. There was laughter and relief following such bewildering pleasure, their joy all the more intense for how well they knew one other and the confidence each had in the other's good graces.

"Good Lord woman d'ye think I'm an automaton! And people will talk aboot us if we're late for the show!"

And so the opera was sandwiched between tender spells in their room at the Balmoral, making the Duke of Mantua's dalliances seem inconsequential, curse or no curse. Harper on the other hand really was bewitched. Re-running details of what they'd seen and felt earlier in the evening as they watched Rigolletto, both smiled at the promise of embracing again soon, without imprecation or sacrifice.

As Margaret bathed, Harper stood naked - looking down through lace curtains at the Scott Monument and Edinburgh Castle, on bustling brass plate traders privileged to live where they worked merging casually with an endless stream of transient visitors. This was Harper's fine city now, as well as Margaret's. It was their proud country; their time in the sun. Everything imagined to be worthwhile and all they might need, was here in reach. Their situation could not have been re-arranged to have felt more right.

Tinged a little by regret and non-conformity their hearts were lifted the more so in fulfilment, overflowing in true romance because they had been tested and had endured. When they had nothing, they had found one another. More than this, each affirmed a permeating sense of belonging, in a place where the emblem of common currency was nothing more sophisticated than the decency and kindness of ordinary folk.

Returning from the bathroom rubbing her hair with a towel, Margaret asked frivolously if there was 'minor royalty, or nobility in residence?'

"Where, in the Castle? Oh no, they'd never come here! Not since George the Fourth in 1822," pronounced Harper, "If they were in town they'd prefer to stay here in the hotel."

"So why are they rebuilding the old hospital in the Castle?"

"Hmm, to restore it as a National Monument I imagine. They've been talking about it for a generation."

Margaret pretended to wave politely across illuminated parkland just in case. She drew up a chair to ponder the splendid view from their fourth floor window in silence. Harper pulled up the sash to smoke hispipe. Through circling blue smoke and the ping of a dead pine match in the glass ashtray came soft flat sounds of a warm, early evening.

Harper caught the sharp measured raking of iron horse shoes on cobbles, as two mounted policemen rode slowly along Princess Street from the direction of North Bridge. Reminded of a time when incoherent anxiety gripped his heart and he needed a confidante, Harper could not resist a peek over the ledge. A broad smile of recognition instantly spread across his face. Standing naked at the window he resisted the urge to call down to Macdonald and Lennox, as he watched them on their late evening circuit. They might have to come up and arrest him for gross indecency.

He decided instead that his former colleagues would be amongst the first he'd call upon in his new career as Life Assurance agent. Harper imagined how he could iron the hard bumps of his own life into a cautionary tale of woe for them. They didn't know it yet but their best intentions were already as safe as a deposit in the Penny Bank.

"You're gonna be working for me soon boys!" Harper muttered to himself. Turning from the window he caught a pleasing glimpse of Margaret slipping back into her nearly new satin evening gown before heading to the ballroom. She went back to wipe moisture from the mirror in the bathroom and apply a dab of rouge.

From somewhere down on street level came the bright, optimistic sound of an accomplished musician energetically rehearsing his score from Chopin's Second Piano Concerto. The one face he could never have seen when he made love to Margaret came to him now, suddenly filling his mind's eye. Harper let out a long, audible sigh for the gun stone of eternal loss that heaved once again through his gut. Briskly tapping out ash from the pipe, he wiped tears away with the back of his hand before Margaret noticed.

I don't want her to think I'm the court jester, even if my back is hunched with care.

Chapter Four   *Christ in the Curtains*

Duff wept silently up in her bedroom, alone while her sisters conspired to overturn Harper's suggestion that she share a room with Elizabeth. Margaret had moved in almost a year before and proved to be a tough arbiter. They had needed the table to do homework and since their teacher insisted they ought to share loaned out text books to prepare for attainment tests in Mathematics and English, there seemed a certain prevailing logic to it. This trivial nonsense naturally tended towards the exclusion of Duff.

"She's not at that level but Elsie and I are," went Elizabeth's Pythagorean logic, "So she should move into the smaller room."

Margaret gave her assent without comment or concern. The day following Duff's bedroom move, a telegram came with bad news from Rothiemay concerning Great Gran, which Duff could not accept as true. Seeking refuge in her room from useless talk, she lay on her bed pondering what appeared to be a crucifix in the overlapping curtains. Duff imagined feeling the guilt of Original Sin, although she was unsure of the basis of the idea. The shadow of the crossbar window frame cast by streetlight on the drape, was reminder of the ultimate sacrifice. It spoke of atonement and salvation, but in her sorrow Duff could not tear her eyes away from it. Whenever a momentous event occurred, she tended to notice the awful pattern in the curtains. Imagining it to be moving, Duff could easily personify the eternal dynamic of the Crucifixion re-enacted in her own room, with shouts and groaning while recalling echoing admonitions from the Minister. The message was simple enough for any child to grasp.

Elsie says Adam shouldnae have had sex with Eve. Original Sin brought all these problems. Temptation and evil make everything bad happen - even when we think we're doing fine. That's why we suffer and need to be saved.

Duff just wanted her pain to just stop for one minute – she didn't want to explore inescapable conviction any longer. Great Gran was gone forever – that was all she knew. The awful grief of that separation felt all-consuming. She'd loved Great Gran Han more easily than anyone, even Harper, or in a sense her own precious mother who had been too ill to spend time with her. She might have been eighty years old but she was Duff's very best friend, ever. Great Gran Han had been there for her when she felt desperately lonely. She had only ever told her off once, the time when Sally got in with the hens.

Duff bawled with grief, turning her eyes away from the shadow of universal brutality in her curtains. Pulling the pillow down hard over her head she gave herself up to impenetrable sorrow.

School! I have to go to school. He can't afford to take us all to the funeral – after all the times Great Gran Han looked after us!

The hurricane of doubt in Duff's distressed heart lost intensity as it drifted over the land of thought. Swinging out of bed the next morning she sighed deeply as she caught a glimpse of herself in the mirror. Dragging back the tangerine embroidered curtains with angry contempt, she glowered out of the window at the street below. Determination began to rise in her simple soul.

For weeks winter had gripped the land in a mailed fist of weeping iron. Freezing fog clung to desperate trees, licking around opaque skylights and cracking brittle tiles. A vain orange sun called to Duff, through a morning pall that would break a brave girl's heart.

Half term was three weeks ahead and as a consequence Harper was planning to go to the funeral on his own. Grief welled up again as Duff thought of the pervading injustice written into every line and page of her childhood experience so far. She was only six but dread filled her heart at the prospect of demands Almighty God could make, even upon his only begotten son.

No wonder he never appears any more, after what happened to Jesus. Maybe we've all been sent to Coventry worse than peeping Tom.

Duff tried again to persuade Harper to take her to the funeral that evening. But Margaret put her foot down, declaring that she would not allow it. When Duff asked why in a simple way, fire flashed behind her fierce eyes, "Because your father cannot afford a week's wages for rail fares!" The other two didn't seem to care that much, so there was just glum silence at the dinner table.

Duff felt about to choke on food she couldn't swallow. Burning in the heat of isolated embarrassment, incoherent rage flared under her brow. Margaret was becoming her rival and oppressor, as surely as Great Gran had been mentor and friend. Her incoherent feeling was about the unique quality of love that can never be assumed. Duff had learned young to introspect disappointment, so she forced her meal down and said nothing.

Why does Margaret not know how much Great Gran loved us? It can't end like this!

On the morning of Wednesday 31st of January, the day prior to Great Gran's interment, Duff was woken from dreams of induration by conspiratorially whispering Harper crouching at her bedside, "Don't make a sound or we'll both be in trouble!"

Instantly rolling out of bed Duff smiled thankfully at him. Harper could see signs of tension in his daughter's pallid face. There were impression lines of hair she'd slept on pressed into her cheek and red blotches under her eyes. Harper's appreciation competed with a feeling of sympathy as he reached out to place a hand on her shoulder.

A change of scene will do her good.

Without delay Duff brushed her teeth and washed her face. She combed wavy auburn hair and donned weekend clothes. Tiptoeing downstairs with her Daddy, she lifted a winter coat from the hall stand without so much as a cat's padded creak on a loose floorboard. They were gone from the house and down the hill at the bus stop at Parson's Green before either spoke of their collusion, "Why just me Daddy?" asked Duff.

"Because you and Great Gran Han were so close, sweetheart. I didn't want to argue with the others at dinner last night. But you were right. I couldn't sleep for thinking about it."

"Thank you Harper! I love you so much," attested the prodigy. Harper hugged his youngest daughter with a smile the size of San Francisco Bay.

They caught the early train to Elgin where they met up with Zachariah and Annie Williams for a late lunch. Harper's conversation with his oldest friends went some way to salving a guilty conscience, "Margaret is young and impetuous," he told them, speaking plainly in front of Duff whom he knew to be trustworthy, "She disnae understand the complex history I have here, Zach. And I canny expect her to blithely accept it all."

Zach held his counsel but watched Harper receptively as they ate. Annie used her woman's prerogative to speak for the betrothed in her absence, "I think most of us had a little growing up to do at the age of twenty-three. She hasn't met your wider family John. How could she evaluate relationships which you no doubt avoided discussion of, because they involved mention of Hannah?"

"I will admit they've not been foremost in my mind. I've been studying so much, I barely get time to write home."

"Well, if you assume anything dear boy, assume Margaret will want to call the tune from now on."

"If you assume, you make an ass out of u and me!" chimed Duff, between mouthfuls of pasta. Annie laughed at the child's attempt to break the tension with a stab at humour.

"Suitably rebuked, Duff," agreed Zach, "We should let Margaret speak for herself."

"But I think the bairn has helped you set a precedent. I expect we'll see a lot more of you in years to come. Once you're married you can bring Margaret. She'll love it here," ventured Annie.

"Yes, in fact you are officially invited to come and stay with us. We have plenty of room. Annie can show Margaret the tourist attractions, while briefing her on how to deal with your fierce temper and dark moods."

Harper opened his mouth to protest but all three of them were looking at him for assent.

In the early evening Zach took them to the station in his rig, where they caught the six o'clock train to Rothiemay. Harper knew he could not have faced that heart breaking journey without his dear little side kick Duff, to help close the circle. Going home was not just about his feelings for Great Gran. It brought back all the sorrow of losing the sweet companion lying alone in the churchyard.

He had left a cursory note for Margaret, asking her not to worry about money. Although feeling guilty, there really was nothing more for Harper to say that might have made Margaret feel better. His 'neutral statement' had indeed led to many shared mealtimes, followed by intimate evenings together, that naturally led in turn to Margaret staying over. She had a key to her parent's house, so was never grilled about hours she kept. Anthony and Teresa couldn't disapprove of what they didn't wish to ask. In the event Harper had his cake and ate it too.

If Margaret changed her mind and broke off their engagement that would be too bad. In any event Harper decided, he would not argue or try to force any issues. Nevertheless, allowing Duff to come with him to Great Gran's funeral might take the gloss of things. When it came down to family issues, Duff's gentle impressions would carry equal claim on him - for now at least.

Harper had no idea there were so many old people in Milltown of Rothiemay and the surrounding district. Hannah was amazed and for once in her sweet short life never got a word in edgeways. No matter, she learned more of social graces and kindness in the watery eyes of Great Gran's kindred spirits then in a year of RE lessons at school.

The Kirk was packed and latecomers stood around in the vestibule, craning their pious necks like Glasgow Catholics at eleven o'clock Mass. Mr Duff, the Laird, was the first of five locals to stand up to offer his perspective on the life of a scion of the 'Community of Change' that in his nouveau riche view, 'carried forward the stamp of tradition.' Others had more claim to have the final word but the young man spoke directly of 'privilege' as if it was a personal trait of character, not a matter of wealth.

If Mr Duff got them smiling; Jeannie; Frank and Jessie got them thinking of all the little remembrances that characterised sentiment and then Payton's eulogy reduced them to tears.

"In all my years as a GP, privileged to have served this broad and flourishing community of crofters; millers and brewers," he pronounced, "I have never met a more beneficent, or humbler soul than Great Gran Han. Hannah Drummond lived close to the land and the seasons but closer still to the whispered Word of Our Lord. She knew tragedy and how to face it down, seeing wistful, golden days beyond the time of a beloved husband, an only son and a charming granddaughter. Never flinching from sorrow, she unfailingly offered succour to those in pain, or in need. She knew love and loss in equally great measure but through it all her smiling, humorous mother's heart carried an example of magnanimity to us all. She rose every morning at dawn in summer and had worked half a day before the sky lightened in winter but still found time for the Women's Guild and visiting the sick or disfavoured, with consolation, and to furnish what help she could. Her life was a lesson in wisdom, tempered with humility. As a widow, she carried on traditions of excellence inspired by her late husband John, creating conditions to rear the finest lambs in the region – loving the creatures that brought her good fortune, the dogs and the sheep, as much as the land that is mother to us all. I can't help but say, that if any of you were to rise early tomorrow morning, to walk the pastures of Deveron, nearby Ramsburn, you might still catch a sense of her kind spirit walking there. Great Gran Han's life was appreciation and blessing to all who knew her. As the blessed, we thank the Almighty for the example of that pure, harmonious life."

Margaret spent the first summer of a new century working, saving and planning for a bright suburban wedding. She and Harper made excuses to the girls then shipped them off to Jessie at Milltown of Rothiemay for the summer. The formidable trio travelled together on the train to Keith, where they were met by Uncle Alex with the rig. Margaret intentionally delayed close scrutiny from Harper's wider family, by fixing a date with reverend Gibson for late September at the Abbey Kirk. There would be plenty of opportunities to visit Morayshire after the wedding. Of course they were all invited, if they could tear themselves away from harvesting routines.

On his Stag Night - a modest affair at the SRB involving a lock-in with half of the local Constabulary, Kennington's Sales team and the contingent from Reid's night school class – Harper told Zach, "I have been lucky twice and I believe that luck will continue. In fact I have been lucky in love and lucky with money . . . I'm the exception to the rule."

"Yeah, I can see that lad. Sometimes Fortune is perverse. In your case it has involved the harshest trials. Take my advice. Don't think too much. Just accept whatever comes. You have a kind heart John – that's all that matters!"

If Zachariah knew something more about that perversity he was keeping it to himself, at least until the effects of strong drink wore off.

A number of friends and relatives came for the shindig. Jessie made it and so did John senior with Isobel. Bonnie came too but Hugh made work related excuses, sending Douglas in his stead. The Paytons arranged cover, as did the Stevensons. Donald closed his shop and let the customers go hang for the weekend.

Anthony laid on a refurbished coach and four for the arrival of the girls with the bride and her mother, which he drove himself in top hat and tails. Everything was picture perfect; the rings; the dresses; the hymns; the speeches and the behaviour of all the guests, right down to the totally reformed Harper and his battalion of smiling cronies.

It was an affair restrained in the round, yet characterised by the three most amiable, blue silk attired bridesmaids and the most voluptuous maid of honour of the season. Margaret's matching smile was as delightful as it was beguiling, however. No-one was going to upstage her in this fairy tale moment of loyalty fulfilled, not even Muriel the enchantress.

Harper married his children's nurse, as much through her ambition as his lack of preference. No-one could ever measure up to Hannah in his esteem, yet no-one would have wanted to take over her role except Margaret. He married her because she loved him enough to make that sacrifice.

After the wedding Zachariah William's handed Harper another envelope, with another cheque for five hundred guineas.

"Oh, I can't accept this!"

Harper held the cheque signed by Zachariah out to the old tailor as they stood on the pavement on the corner of Marionville Road.

"Why does he never visit?"

Zachariah slowly shook his head, "There are too many complications, which it is not my place to discuss. But this money is for the girls. He knows how you've suffered. He wanted me to say that 'this is the least he can do.' Please accept it, for my sake if not for him."

"Complications?" asked Harper contemptuously, "That are more important than a son getting married? What could that be Zach, other than a partnership with his wife's family?"

"That's not what should matter to you," Zach told him, folding his hand over John's forearm and turning the envelope back toward him, "The point is, he would spend this at a National Hunt meeting without blinking. And that doesn't include his veterinary bills, or overheads. So put it away and thank God for Providence and a bright future."

"You're going to tell me everything Zach. Everything!" hissed Harper, as Margaret approached with the photographer.

"I will John. I promise, I will. Now put it away!" Anthony was standing nearby at his rig, waiting to whisk them up to Waverley, from whence the newlyweds would travel by rail to stay at Rusacks' Hotel in St Andrews. Harper turned to meet Margaret and the camera, with the light of love in his eyes. He had begun to understand better than most what money could buy but knew that it didn't include love.

In contrast to the girls' deceased mother who had been perennially funny, understated yet unambiguous in all expressions, as well as slow to anger, Margaret seemed at first a little immature and brash.

Observing the rapid development of a clinging physical relationship between their understudy mother and their overstretched father, the girls came successively to envy, then conspiratorially censure. They were naturally jealous. Tense dynamics of five sets of individual relationships become competitive and strained.

Margaret recalled how Elizabeth the virago had set the scene on the day of their first assignation almost eighteen months before the marriage. Although weddings and their paraphernalia always have a magic all their own, she had patching up work to do when the gilt very quickly wore off the gingerbread.

Harper tended to run for cover when issues of control and authority surfaced and naturally enough Margaret tried to dominate proceedings in his absence. Following a precedent she had set from the outset when he was around, Margaret attempted to buy off Elsie and Elizabeth overtly, with treats or distractions. But her new role, in all its maternal demands, had changed imperceptibly. There had always been a professional, caring relationship - but no real emotional bond. Margaret knew this deficit to be a function of her characteristic reserve and she found it hard to change.

As they re-evaluated their relationships with one another, a kind of mutism by default descended upon the Harper family. It seemed each member of the household was afraid to utter a sound. Evening mealtimes and weekends became strained. Margaret waited for, even came to hope for petty disputes that might allow her to express herself and exercise benign control. She felt it necessary to use daily concerns to demonstrate prowess as an arbitrator – to corroborate her role as aspiring matriarch.

"Pick that up!"

"Bring down your laundry!"

"Put that plate in the sink!"

"Wash up for me, now please!"

"You'll be late for . . . oh they've gone!"

Nothing met with an objection, much less a voluntary response. The girls were wary but she had them too well drilled for rebellion to ever be likely.

Thirteen year old Elsie never challenged her step-mother, except with the worldly sadness in her eyes, or the gentle imprecation of a nervousness voice.

Elizabeth the Oracle waited for leaves to be scattered and incense burned. She knew her moment would come. But for now her pretty freckled face locked up, eyes focussed upon nothing. Elizabeth brooded, computing every petty offence, while keeping opinions to herself.

Unfortunately Duff seemed too young to matter for Margaret's practical purposes. Somehow she could not rise to the challenge of bonding with her. Duff was Harper's soul mate re-embodied and a constant reminder of her own inadequacy. Nurturing that relationship was in truth the only way in, if she wished to make a triumph of managing Harper's family - had she been blessed with the magnanimity to know it in her heart. Duff was potentially a conduit back to Elizabeth and Elsie, who had been Margaret's allies in the early days of their mother's absence. Lonely and starved of affection they became bitter too. But Margaret never quite saw it.

Instead she resolved to be her own woman. Children's rivalries and squabbles, the daily grind of modelling motivation and routines, rose before poor Margaret like a stone wall. She wrongly presumed the impassive Duff had little or no influence upon her father. Worst of all Margaret failed to learn the lesson of Great Gran Han's funeral. In reality there was a mutual, intuitive compact between them which Margaret couldn't see. Psychic recognition persisted between eldest and youngest which in essence intimated an understanding of all the lost love.

Harper became as sensitive to Duff's moods as a dedicated zookeeper with a favourite tiger cub. The logic was simple: every time Harper looked at Duff he too saw her mother. Each time Duff met Harper's eyes, the child registered vulnerability borne of an enduring tension between love and loss. There would always be a new context but there was always a developing history. Whenever Harper gave time to Duff, the child accommodated her torn family as a whole. She reminded him at every opportunity of Granny Jessie and the aunties and uncles. For Duff, holidays were not holidays unless they could be spent in Milltown.

As school vacation approached in the spring of 1901, inevitable conflict arose around planning ahead.

What Margaret found astonishing was how Harper could read Duff, detecting subtle changes of mood and teasing out small ways in which his beloved had tried to curtail the child. Margaret began to think of her as precocious and manipulative, whereas for Harper, Duff's company was evidently as refreshing as sunshine on a rainy day.

Margaret's first, most singular challenge was to fit in with Duff's explicit demand that family holidays be spent as always in rural Morayshire. Margaret was out voted - not that there was much democracy involved. Elsie and Elizabeth lit up at the prospect too. But it was Duff who cut the ground from under her when she dared to propose alternatives, with the same bell-like, clear voice which had charmed her with its innocence just a couple of years before.

"You have to realise my mummy's family are *our* family, Margaret. Dinnae fret though, they'll love you just as much as they love Harper - and Elsie and Lizzie and me. And *you* are gonny *love* the farm . . . and the dogs and hens and coos."

"You're too young to know the meaning of the word love."

"I know adults forget what it's like being young," replied Duff pensively. The comment stung Margaret because it was true.

She withdrew to the kitchen and her chores where she gripped the edge of the Belfast sink, breathing deeply to contain resentment of the child. Teresa would have slapped Margaret down for such cheek at Duff's age but somehow her wisdom was beyond reproach. What fazed Margaret most was the disturbing insight in the child's words.

Margaret felt herself to have grown up too fast, almost obsessed by involvement with the Harper family from the age of seventeen but now she realised that much of the past eight years of tribulation had been experienced in parallel. There was so much she didn't know about the Harpers . . . because it had been too painful to discuss.

They're planning to spend Easter and summer holidays with Hannah's family, not Harper's . . . but why? That family connection is stronger than Harper's own parents', so it seems!

88

Margaret was confused. All her instincts told her she had made a huge mistake and when he came home from college that night they argued.

"What's wrong with you? Why are you objecting to a free holiday in a beautiful location?"

"Because I've married a bigamist!" she snapped at him, for want of an insult more appropriate to the complex circumstances. Although he realised this was an improper choice of word, Harper was mortified at his young wife's outspokenness. She sulked off to grumble to Teresa while he tackled a mountain of dirty dishes. Harper was speechless too. He fell asleep on the sofa awaiting Margaret's return, wishing only to wrap his arms around her without further argument.

One glimmer of hope for Margaret was the benevolent disposition of Elsie towards her. On the morning of 12th May, Margaret came downstairs at 8.40 am needing a cup of tea before the early service at the Abbey Kirk, to discover Elsie at the door to the kitchen.

"No! Go back . . . you're not allowed in here."

"What?"

"It's your day off. *Mother's Day* and you're not allowed in the kitchen. In fact I want you to go back to bed."

"Whatever for Elsie?"

"It's a surprise. Tell daddy before he gets up. I've made you breakfast in bed."

"But I've just brushed my teeth," Margaret teased, glancing over the top of Elsie's head, which came up to her chin, "Oh my word . . . what have you made?"

Margaret glimpsed a bizarre arrangement of toasted bread covered in a thick layer of whipped cream, topped with a carefully arranged circle of sliced peaches and interspersed with hothouse strawberries. From the tell-tale white line along the fine black hair of Elsie's unnaturally red upper lip, Margaret could see that she had sampled her preparation.

"Don't look please! It's a surprise," she said gently, ushering her step-mother away from the kitchen area. Margaret turned on her heel as she made for the bottom of the stairs.

"You've done all this on your own, without Elizabeth or Hannah to offer assistance?"

"No, they're sleepy heads Margaret. *This* was my idea. But *they* have planned dinner!" Elsie added circumspectly, "And gave me some of their piggy bank money for a present. I'm not giving it to you unless you get back into bed!"

Margaret came back along the hall to wrap her arms around Elsie amazed to find a lump rising in her throat, as tears of joy welled in her eyes, "Okay, I'll go back to bed, on one condition," said Margaret, lifting the Sunday paper off the door mat.

"Okay, whatever you say."

"As soon as you've finished making breakfast, get Lizzie and Duff out of bed. Tell them to put on old clothes. We're going to the stables at Spylaw."

"You're taking us to see the horses?"

"I'm taking you riding."

"Ooh, how wonderful! Can Muriel come? And Gran and Grandpa?"

"Okay we'll see. I'll ask them."

Margaret was back in control. All she had needed was tuning-in to the love of the universe which happened to run through every unaffected moment of Elsie's beating heart.

Harper was delighted with the plan. Ten minutes later as he perused the front page of the Observer, Elizabeth backed into their bedroom. She was holding a tray presenting their syrupy breakfast, bedecked with a single orange rose in a vase, with an envelope containing a card propped against it.

"Surprise, surprise!" cried Duff, running into the bedroom with a bunch of the remaining roses, their uncut stems still wrapped in paper.

They took apples for Anthony's true cab horses on their only day off. There were a dozen ponies which Margaret's father ran or rented to other cabbies, though not all of them were stabled or pastured, even on a Sunday. Muriel helped Margaret find two old saddles, neglected for years from when they were teenagers. Harper smiled benignly as the women bridled two of the smaller ponies, Bruce and Domhnal. Moving briskly they tried to impress their father with their competence.

Harper noticed the ponies were wary of strong scent and quick movement but seemed well used to meeting many types of patron. Bruce and Domhnal were well-groomed animals, strong and fit by even the highest standards and Anthony was clearly proud of them.

When Harper commented favourably as he lit up a pipe, his father-in-law engaged with him, throwing out his chest.

"The toffs around Inverleith and up in town don't like to see a worn out pit pony pulling their Hansom. It might be a dying trade John, what with the cars and omnibuses but I still earn my crust. It's wicked though, what some of the licensed cabbie's do to their beasts."

Anthony stood at the entrance to the whitewashed, stone built stables, narrowing his eyes at the former policeman, hoping he was not indifferent to the plight of horses generally.

"Hmm, so I've noticed. That cruelty helps the competition, no?"

"Quite so John, that's exactly what it does," agreed the proud little Englishman, "But I keep my end up, in anticipation of a revival of fortune."

Anthony wore a dark brown stable hand's overall and Wellington boots, although there was no ordure on the lane. A strong pony, Magnus, was saddled ready for him to guide the pupils.

The yard smelled of honeysuckle blossom, drifting from a nearby woodland margin. A dozen butterflies danced above them to the murmuring tune of a hundred meticulous bees. Harper noticed with pleasure that the busy stalls presented less of the hot stink of ordure than the King's Stables near West Port Police Station, where falling standards easily met with a reprimand.

"I'll hazard you take what you read in the newspapers very seriously Anthony?" Harper narrowed his eyes, tilting his head slightly in confidence.

"Oh, the War in Africa? Well they *are* making a meal of it lad. Half a million mounts they want. But soldiers they give them to are not trained to look after them. General French's cavalry rode five hundred poor creatures to death in one day." Anthony was spirited in his anger. A vehement sense of injustice penetrated the white tobacco smoke, as well as the holiday atmosphere.

Muriel and Margaret smiled at the men as they led Elsie and Elizabeth, mounted on the two small ponies, out of the stables. Duff stood at their feet, looking up and listening as they talked of the Great Game.

"Oh yes, the relief of Mafeking . . . Our Cameronian riflemen used to be able to march sixty miles a day under a blazing sun – now they ride half that distance at ease on a foundering mule."

"It's not just the poor horses that suffer, Harper. War is wrong. All war. It's despicable. Who does it serve if not The Devil?"

"Well the Germans don't want war, if their Chancellor Bulow is to be believed."

"Three plus one? That'll never fly, son. They are all furtively advocating conflict between Japan and Russia. Meanwhile the hero of the hour, young Winston Churchill, is currying favour with the Yanks."

With a roguish glint in her eyes Teresa came to interpose her vivacious persona, before the men became sombre. Smiling at Duff she took her by the hand, "Come on, you two great equestrians! Lead the girls up onto the field and give them a riding lesson. And no more politics on the Lord's Day. You shouldnae talk of such matters in front of the bairn."

"Oh, that's alright Granny Tere, they've no been swearin', an' I like to listen."

"Oh, but men are boring dear, especially when they talk about politics. You'll learn soon enough!"

Harper smiled and found a murmuring laugh running over his vocal chords, even if he disapproved of the sentiment. Teresa was appealing in her feistiness. He could see Muriel's charisma in her mother, Anthony's thoughtful morality in his own charming wife. As he watched Margaret making final adjustments to Elsie's saddle strap before she entered the field, Harper felt blessed a thousand fold - for every day she had turned out to rescue him from dejection over the past eight years.

Anthony Kemp was a new type of Edinburgh Saxon, more attuned to urban living than many of the locals, 'The last time I was down in Norwich,' he'd told Harper at their first meeting in their pub, the Broadfield Arms, 'some uncouth sod told me to fuck off back to

Scotland.' Clearly proud of his adoptive home he reminded Harper, in appearance only because appearance was all he had ever seen, of his own father. For a moment Harper wondered if memory tricked him about this image – but recalling what Zach told him referencing the National Hunt, all of the scant information fell into place satisfactorily.

From out of nowhere came an oblique resolution to continue close ties with Hannah's family. They *would* go to Rothiemay in the summer.

"It's always wise to make the best of a bad situation," Harper advised Anthony reflectively, apropos of nothing.

"Indeed John, for we never know what tomorrow brings," he replied, as though reading the young man's thoughts. Tapping out his pipe low on the wall Anthony swung up into the saddle of the waiting pony.

The girls were excited and though they each had a trot around the paddock, closely following Anthony on Magnus, it was Elsie who seemed most reluctant to go home when time for the feast drew near. Her eyes were alive with the fire of enthusiasm for the first time in years. Teresa and Muriel encouraged her with riding tips and banter but as she confidently trotted the bay appaloosa, Domhnal around the field one last time, Elsie didn't need instruction. She was a natural rider, pressing down a little on her stirrups, firmly guiding the pony away from grazing in long grass at margins of the paddock near thorn bushes, with a tight rein. A connection had been made between Elsie and Domhnal.

"Please Margaret, let me take him home! He can crop the lawns for us," she pleaded from a distance, looking like she might spur her pony like Annie Oakley, take the fence and never be seen again, "He'll fit in the shed and I can trot him round Queen's Park!"

"And who would clean him out?" asked Harper.

"Elizabeth can do that! She likes the smell o' horse muck." Elsie joked at someone else's expense for the first and only time ever in her life.

"Eeeeugh! I do not. I hate the stink of horse muck!" shouted Elizabeth, sunk in Bruce's saddle like an inept aristocrat.

Duff's raucous laughter floated across the paddock from the fence, where she balanced between the women on the top bar. The ponies seemed to smile as warm sunlight cut through a curtain of sea harr, turning grey sky to blue. An eddy of fragrance and buzz of insects presaged the turning of a glorious day. Just as surely as her heart going out to the Leopard Spot pony, another connection had worked between Elsie and Margaret.

As Anthony took them home in his Hackney coach the young woman put her arms lovingly around her step-mother, nestling into her neck as Margaret chatted with Tere and Muriel. Harper delighted to see her surprising display of affection even though it was downplayed so casually.

"It's been a picture day in the book of life," he suggested with a smile.

"Yes, Daddy, the world is talking to me, though sometimes it plays unexpected tricks," replied Elsie, with a warm smile of her own through narrowing eylids.

"What is it saying?"

"Everything is in *perfect* harmony. *None* of what worries us is real," she mumbled with a relinquishing yawn. The combination of an early start with the fresh spring air had apparently done for her. In the flowering of adolescence Elsie was suddenly exhausted.

Margaret's fast wit and sharp tongue could never resist giving testimony. The nursing job at the Royal Hospital for Sick Children that Margaret had taken when Duff went to school had become her life. It was her custom to always say what she felt, perhaps in the unspoken fear she might become surly and change for the worse if she didn't. This was the quintessential Margaret, although she didn't necessarily like herself for being forthright, "I'm married to my job," she told people.

Word got around quickly within her wider family and social set that the lady saw herself as a factotum, reluctantly doing what was necessary to bolster family income, instead of doing what came naturally to a young couple. Had she been employed at the Royal from seventeen, might a career in hospital management have beckoned? Annoyingly there were several nursing sisters and a matron with seniority who were younger. Margaret felt them to be less competent and was candid in telling everyone who needed to hear it.

When she came home on the afternoon of the board interview it was plain at a glance to Elizabeth that her step-mother had not been selected for promotion. Elsie was pre-occupied with homework and Duff was reading quietly in her room when raised voices snatched at their comfort from below.

Coincidentally Margaret's framed wedding photo with glass front lay smashed against the cast iron frame of the fire. She presumed Elizabeth to have played a part, when reaching for fruit from a bowl on the display cabinet for her packed lunch. Elizabeth denied the assumption vehemently and as she did so, cold censure descended over her brow, solidifying into a Gorgon stare.

"Why would you do that, you poisonous little witch?" Margaret shrieked.

"Do what?" protested Elizabeth, with surprise in her voice.

"You smashed it! You're the jealous one!" Margaret continued with the same abrasive squawk, "You've always been jealous, for every one of your twelve damned years! No-one can breathe without *your* displeasure."

"What are you talking about? I haven't done anything."

"Well who did it then?" demanded Margaret, "There was only you in the house, I saw your sisters leave! There was only one apple left for you."

Elizabeth answered with the clipped poise of an offended Headmistress, "Then you can assume it was Molly on routine patrol who brushed it with her tail."

"Molly never breaks anything."

"No? Apart from the doors and carpets she rips to shreds!"

"She steps around vases and tea cups!"

It wasn't so much that Elizabeth was disrespectful in her response to the accusation that gave offence. Yellow roses and starry-eyed smiles face down in the tiled hearth did not mean that much - after all the frame could be fixed and glass replaced. Yet Margaret felt an overwhelming sense of bitter irony. In that moment of frustration she felt all her efforts of the previous nine years, all the good intentions – not forgetting the love of her life, that best ever dream come true – had also been smashed and soiled. When the dam broke Margaret gave vent to all her quietly contained indignation. In the past she had always felt subordinate – now it was time to take charge. She trembled with rage as Elizabeth defied her.

"Oh, so that's certain then . . . I am a vandal *and* a liar . . . because I hate you and I'm jealous of your influence over Harper?" Margaret seized Elizabeth by the top of her right shoulder before slapping hard across her face.

Unflinching defiance and cold resolution stared back at Margaret, from twelve year old grey eyes that held the wisdom of time without end. She was about to strike again when the straight lines of the child's brows and lips began to re-shape - perhaps into momentary contrition. Margaret paused – her right hand still raised.

"I told you Margaret," Elizabeth informed her slowly, without raising her voice, "It was the bloody cat that knocked your wedding photo off the mantelpiece." Fingers of both Elizabeth's hands were stretched wide apart, elbows crooked in emphasis. She rose slightly forward onto her toes, speaking again with white hot rancour, "Why don't you get Harper to put up a bloody picture rail!" In terms of intellectual vigour there was a role reversal – essentially Elizabeth the adult, speaking to a child.

Utterly intimidated by the day's failures, Margaret burst into tears. Without speaking she hugged Elizabeth – pulling her tightly into the crook of her arm and chest. She wept freely and deeply, clinging on to the young woman as she released all her distress. Margaret gulped for air as she tried to speak, "You are *so* beautiful . . . and wise . . . I had no right to speak to you like that."

"Well, Margaret don't run yourself down, it happens to be true," With perfect comic timing she added after a pause, "I did chuck it in the fire." Margaret released her hug to look questioningly at Elizabeth.

"No, no! I'm joking of course. God forbid anyone would ever dream of doing such a wicked thing."

"Oh and like a fool that's what I accused you of," confessed Margaret embracing her again.

Molly and Elsie appeared on cue, respectively to investigate and repair the damage. Duff was keeping out of the way. As quickly as rage turned to remorse, remorse turned to laughter.

Margaret found herself at Elizabeth's mercy however. Her spirit and temperament was so like her father's. Margaret's hair fell over Elizabeth's face and she found herself unable to look at the child again until she let anxiety out, "I am desperately sorry – please forgive me for that. It's just been so hard for me to do this. I loved your mother too, you know," she sobbed through her laughter, infected by Elizabeth's drollery, "And you . . . you girls are wonderful. I understand all that you've been through but I'm really doing the best I can, Elizabeth. You have to help me."

"This is *our* family Margaret, not yours," she stressed, "*You* have to join us. If you make the effort Jessie will love you. And the Wilsons, Robertsons and Harpers too."

Elizabeth patted Margaret softly on her back as she clung to her with a pounding heart. It had been so long since anyone had hugged Elizabeth that it felt painfully intrusive for her to experience so much fondness in one moment. Elizabeth noticed something again that she knew but had taken for granted.

Margaret smelled different from her mother. Perfume she wore was young and oily, more like freesias than roses. Breathing in the scent deeply to savour its novelty, Elizabeth decided that she liked it - but her face still burned long from the slap. It was another trivial reminder of the nature of injustice.

On a warm Sunday night in the last week of May, Duff persuaded her sisters to camp out in the garden. It was a bank holiday with no work in the morning, so Margaret and Harper agreed to it. Elsie helped bring chairs and old blankets which they draped over the washing line to make a rudimentary encampment. Elizabeth made lemonade and iced buns for their midnight feast and Harper showed them how to bake potatoes in a garden fire. Once Molly had joined them they set up an improvised mosquito net over the entrance and lit candles on a small table so they could read.

For the first time Elsie asked about the confrontation between Margaret and her sister. Pallid eyes watched impassively for signs of movement from the back door of the house but their parents were in bed. Elsie's concern was persuasive enough to warrant explanation. Elizabeth looked at her elder sister indulgently, as Duff propped herself smilingly on a large embroidered cushion.

"Margaret is a dear individual in her own right and Harper clearly needs her, even though in children's folklore Elsie, he should never truly love another. Adults are strange it seems to me – they trade themselves in transactions, like they would when purchasing a new suit of clothes."

"She was angry with you because she thinks you're jealous? That you broke the picture deliberately?"

"Frankly Elsie I'm scandalised by that thought! I *am* allowed to be myself and *she* can think whatever she likes but the evil was in Margaret's mind."

"Does that mean you don't accept her as our mother?"

"No, I think she's marvellous and we're all lucky to have her."

"What then? Explain the problem to me."

"I would just never lower myself in that way."

"What, marry a man with three bairns?" asked Duff.

"Yes, exactly. I mean, clearly Margaret sees herself as having made a huge compromise." The two elder sisters gazed at one another for half a minute, before Elsie finally spoke.

"You think of it as a kind of prostitution?"

"I imagine Margaret sees it as amounting to the same thing at times, otherwise she'd not have been so angry at me."

"You two witches! I'm no' listening to this gossip anymore! I'm away tae ma bed," hissed Duff. She was gone in an instant, with Molly running after her.

Elsie had to cover her mouth, she laughed so much. Elizabeth hugged her, laughing hysterically too. Elsie went inside to persuade Duff and Molly to come back to the tent, with a promise not to gossip any more.

But in Elizabeth's rapidly crystallising, axiomatic mind, Margaret's frustration arose from an unhappy compromise and that did amount to dishonour. She would accept Margaret because evidently the woman worshipped Harper – but the high-minded Elizabeth would never completely trust her stepmother again. All three sisters agreed that Margaret had made a fundamental mistake in trying to avoid their mother's extended family at Rothiemay prior to the wedding.

For her part, poor Margaret was neutered by Elizabeth's inflexible thinking. As with many parents and one or two of her school teachers, Elizabeth saw that an outward appearance of harmony gave the lie.

From May 1901 until she left home four years later, Elizabeth was in control of the dialogue in every conceivable way – how it was conducted and when it was closed. It was her home. Her indulgent pa. Her employee nanny. Streets ahead of her sisters in expressive reasoning, she didn't need to justify herself in their terms, whatever their objections. Elizabeth Harper realised that the world would conform to her own strict interpretation of it, just as long as she believed her own invective.

Elizabeth could apply intellect with energetic purpose, occasionally unbridled fury to any given situation. She was switched on all the time, showing few areas of weakness. As they settled in their room at night she lectured Elsie, her only confidante.

"On the whole people are mindless conformists, slowly shuffling through life Elsie - like traffic at either end of Leith Walk. They rush around madly when they aren't waiting in line. Most of them don't challenge the mindless presumptions of order. The pushiest bitches get the best jobs but only if they're wealthy, or well connected. And by the way the best jobs don't include teaching, unless you're prepared to leave the profession if you marry."

"Well, I'd like to be married and have three children, like mammy. *And* I want to be a teacher. I can think of nothing finer."

"Well you'd better join the Suffragists and the Labour movement too, or find a wealthy husband."

Surprisingly Elizabeth was only drawn to people who were nice. If they turned out not to be as nice as they first appeared to be she went to war with them. Having mugged them for the wherewithal, she burned them to the ground and moved on, like an accomplished dragoon in Napoleon's Grand Armee. Elizabeth's deprivations drove her to search for status and refinement in others. That endowment alone would help her move forward.

Volunteering for everything possible outside of home life to get away from Margaret, Elizabeth succeeded at everything she attempted with relative ease. Coming top in annual school tests and examinations year on year was taken for granted and there was always a library book by her beside.

Having mastered basic techniques of the violin at nine, she practised unconditionally each evening for three years, to improve sufficiently to be noticed. With tremulously dramatic poise and uncompromisingly elevated elbows, Elizabeth projected sweet fluidity through her playing. A hint of determination in her manner got her noticed early, even within the ensemble section at school. Within three months of taking up the instrument she had been recruited into youth orchestra performances where her tutor encouraged her to learn solo pieces.

Superior talent drew Elizabeth to an elite at school – or more precisely they were drawn to her. Her diary was full of rehearsals, concerts and birthday parties – seemingly always at the smarter houses bordering the park, or down the hill towards Inverleith. Every imaginable accommodation was made by Harper and Margaret through Anthony to take and bring her home safely.

Elizabeth's sweet young life became a microcosm of the kaleidoscopic social connectedness of twentieth century Edinburgh – she began to speak like a blue-blooded socialite. With each passing day her refinements became more seamlessly patrician, her eyes seeming to turn greener, her nose more fashionably retroussé. It was more than coincidence – Elizabeth was evidently 'to the manor born.'

Chapter Five   *Going Home*

In contrast to her sister's flourishing, Elsie waned silently. Large like her mother, perhaps blighted by circumstance, she intentionally disguised the slow atrophy of her fevered body with the deep breathing of a carp rising in an artificial lake. Always trying to merge with the background, occasionally surfacing with laconic humour, she inspired delight in others as well as affection. But in recent months Elsie had rarely moved out of the safe shadows – and it was a long time since she'd caught any flies.

Elizabeth had been alerted by Elsie's silence more than by her coughing. She stood at her bedside staring in horror at blood on her lips. By instinct she felt a welling panic and without hesitation went to seek the moral authority of Duff.

"Come quickly and see. Don't be upset, just tell me what to do. Maybe she has a nose bleed, or bit her lip."

Duff stroked Elsie's cheek, smiling gloriously at her as she opened her eyes.

"You are poorly Elsie. Why didn't you tell us?"

"No . . . I'm fine . . ."

"Elsie stop it! You have to tell us, so we can tell Margaret. She's a nurse remember?"

"I feel sick and achy, Duff. Blood came in my toilet, not just from coughing. I'll be alright though when we go to Ramsburn next month. Jessie will look after me! The country air will help to clear it."

"Oh God, its TB! Bloody silly fool! That's why you didn't say anything," Elizabeth scolded. Turning to look at her, Duff put a finger up to her lips, "Elizabeth, you go find Margaret before she heads off to the Royal. Tell her we're going to stay off school with Elsie while the doctor comes."

"No, you'll get it!" protested Elsie with a renewed flourish of coughing, as Elizabeth lent over her bed to hug her, before darting off down the stairs.

Both her sisters saw the vulnerability in Elsie's soft, round form and timid eyes. By the time Margaret made the inescapable connection and

Tuberculosis had been confirmed after a visit from the doctor, it was touch and go whether they could save her. From that moment onwards Elizabeth and Hannah loved their elder sister like a baby. They visited her each day in hospital, thinking and talking about nothing else.

Elsie Harper's name was on everyone's lips, school chums, family and friends, even people who knew her only through association, enquired after her comfort and state of mind. Elsie came to represent the benign optimism of every beating heart in her neighbourhood. Simple good nature and confident humour was what best characterised her. Somehow that alacrity exemplified the family who prayerfully held her at its centre. Moreover, Elsie's illness brought celebrated recollection of the generous woman who had borne her.

Deep concern for Elsie's wellbeing struck home when it was mooted by Dr Foxworthy with precise scientific rationalism that, "These things take their course." Harper had heard it before. He knew that particular caution to be the closest the little man would come to preparing loved ones for the worst. But that same evening all in the Edinburgh branch of the family stoically agreed with Anthony's assertion, "Elsie will surprise us all yet."

Elsie did surprise them all but not in the way Anthony desired. After brief remission in early July the teenager gladly unhanded disquiet for a burdensome future, on a working day just forty-eight hours before the beginning of summer holidays that she had been so looking forward to.

Jessie Wilson smoothed things over with the Reverend Blair regarding, 'Issue born out of wedlock' and a plot was dug out next to her mother's. With reflection, Elsie's short story was testimony to the sad affairs of Hannah and Harper, for anyone who had really known them as a couple. Their sweetest daughter became an afterthought carved onto a family headstone in rural Morayshire, which few would have time or opportunity to commemorate.

The mourners left Harper alone in the front pew of the little church, where eleven years before Reverend Blair had conducted their vibrant marriage. Whereas memories of Elsie burned in her sister's fond hearts,

Harper was dumbstruck with grief. Margaret stood at length, to leave him for a few minutes with his perplexing sorrow.

He recalled that two years prior to the wedding Blair had flown in the face of a whispering congregation to baptise illegitimate Elsie, whom they had just now buried. Harper smelled stale air, suggestive of mildewed prayer books and slowly oxidising timber, earthy riverine breeze from under shrunken doors and a hint of rich soil from the shoes of doughty farmers.

It all came back. Elsie had been their love child. She represented something stronger than conventionality – a connection borne of passion, that creed and conviction would normally not permit.

What was it Zachariah had told him when his life was boiling over, when he sought advice about Hannah's pregnancy? 'Seventeen can't marry twenty four. Her family have to take responsibility and yours will need to help you. So make your plans like a man.' He heard himself murmuring the reply he'd made that day, 'Don't worry Uncle Zach, I won't let you down.'

'It not me you should be concerned about, John. Make sure you don't let that lovely girl down.' Zach's assurance that day had made him laugh but Harper remembered the shameful deceit of his adoptive family – how none of them had taken responsibility for telling him the truth. Even now Harper's heart was swamped in angry fire as again he felt blows delivered by John and Hugh, whenever he'd dared to challenge their authority or their word.

They were not to blame. There is no real order to society, much less to struggling families. There is just the mindless organic thriving of humanity. Families constantly make and break themselves, while civilization remains in turmoil. Mine was a momentary reaching out for a hand to hold, as Hannah and I were swept along on the tide.

Harper wept silently and painfully as he saw again brave Elsie's optimistic face, her strong little chin, lifted in a characteristic smile.

What did her life amount to? Did we offer some security? Some vision of hope she might hold onto? School and work routines swallowed up any true engagement. What did she say to me?

Harper struggled to remember Elsie's words and their significance. She had been left with only him to love, at a time of innocence when Hannah had died. Yet Elsie had actually been more expressive in recognising her own needs than he had. She had frequently demonstrated love for him, with appreciative hugs and words of approval. It floored him now to think how little he had reciprocated – how little he ever really had to offer Elsie, or anyone else for that matter. In the silence of the Kirk, Harper imagined hearing his daughter's words of consolation within.

I'm with Mammy now Harper, so you are not to worry. Who you are is all that matters. Mammy says, 'Play your game with dignity. Run with the ball at your feet and keep your head up!'

Through his tears Harper saw their first baby again scowling at the light, cradled in her mother's arms. They walked through woodlands back to Ramsburn after Blair had baptised her. That night he heard Elsie crying and went to lift her from her cot. She responded immediately to his touch but wouldn't go back down without protest, so he walked the floor for an hour whispering sweet nothings.

Harper longed to feel again her tiny movements. He tried to imagine once more her fulsome baby smell. An indeterminate blend of talcum and mild soap, mixed with Elsie's natural odours, had made his mind reel with pleasure. They had been blessed with a tiny love child and joy was complete. The future didn't matter. The future had been in his arms. It lay quiescent in his warm bed. But now it was gone.

In his mind's eye Harper watched for as long as he could, an image of Hannah running after Elsie through the farmyard. He smiled to recall how the toddler had wandered off on her own to feed the chicks, a nappy trailing around her knees. Their love had inspired him. He worked from dawn till dusk without complaint and the only reward he looked for was the narcotic of those effusive sensations, of warmth and caring.

There is no man as proud as a young father an' I was the proudest young bugger in the county. But it made me unselfish.

When Harper's anguish subsided at last below concerns for the rest of his family, he rose from the front pew with stiff knees and a new mission. Smudging away tears with the back of his fist, he breathed in deeply for the first time in an hour, perhaps for the first time in years. Making the sign of the cross like a Spanish Catholic, he headed off to find Reverend Blair in his cottage.

Blair greeted Harper warmly, inviting him inside. Shaking the old cropper's soft arthritic hand, Harper declined tea, explaining that his wife had left him to his grief.

"Invite her in John, *she'll* take tea perhaps?"

"No, no you don't understand. I told her this morning I wanted to talk to you privately, Jim. I expect she will have gone back with Jessie and the bairns. There are things I cannae say to anyone but you Reverend. That's why I wanted to see you alone."

Blair gestured with his right hand, ushering Harper to make himself at home. Scent from pale golden roses mixing with dusty odour of threadbare furniture offered a sense of courageous familiarity. Both men sat forward on their armchairs as Harper began his disclosure.

"There so much I want to impart to you, sir. I feel very guilty that it has been five years since we visited."

"No, surely not. You and the child were here for Great Gran's memorial service."

"Aye, sure," Harper accepted the correction, levelling at Blair, "But that does nothing for my conscience."

"Go on John, take your time. A wee dram perhaps?" the Minister offered conspiratorially, beckoning to the drinks cabinet beside him. "Oh, well why not? I think the sun is well past the yardarm."

Blair poured two large glasses of the finest local malt and both men sipped slowly at the pale yellow spirit, observing custom by warming and rolling it appreciatively. As Blair relaxed with the assurance of the eager moderationist, Harper put his glass to one side and sat forward in his armchair.

"Elsie's passing has crystallised something deep in my skull, Jim. Sorry, I cannae find the right words tae express this," he added, shaking his head. Blair could see that Harper's eyes were red from sleeplessness and distress but he waited indulgently.

"I have come at last to accept my own salvation. Life has been desperate for years – all I ever had was hope." Harper scrutinised Blair's face for a reaction. It struck him suddenly that from his expression, the Minister appeared guilty about his role in some of that difficult history, as though this statement amounted to an accusation.

"I need to tell you, as a man of God who will understand, that I hear words spoken in my ear. Sounds from another room." Blair removed half framed glasses perched on his nose, placed them on the sermon he was scribbling for Sunday and crossed his legs, "Go on, John."

"For years I have felt Hannah's continued presence. My daughter Duff, I mean little Hannah, says this too. It's like a man still feeling his leg after it has been amputated. I believe Elsie has gone there too."

"Speak freely."

"Well, I couldn't remember her voice . . . then it came back in floods when I cleared my mind of other thoughts. Like giving your full attention when someone is talking to you." Harper paused in his explanation as if to underscore how important this was. Blair studied his face but did not interrupt.

"It felt like she was there in the kirk right next to me man, no' interred in the ground." Blair searched Harper's grief stricken eyes, stunned by the quiet simplicity of his words.

"John, I know many people of faith. I'm glad to say I've often been reassured by those for whom *I* was expected to provide comfort in *their* hour of grief. They often speak of crisis ghosts and visitations from those suddenly taken from the world. But yours is a true affirmation among a sea of sorrows, spoken without fever or confusion."

"Aye - and from the man who caused greatest controversy among your parishioners over the past fifteen years," Harper added with a wry smile.

He searched Blair's eyes waiting for an affirmation - but none came. At length Harper remarked dryly on the Minister's palpable doubt, "Judging from your response Jim, perhaps you're losing your own faith as the years roll on?"

"Yes son, you are right. I don't know when but maybe I've been thinking more of my own inevitable demise. It isn't matters of the afterlife or salvation which cause misgiving, so much as the combined experience of every broken hearted loss – my own and those of others. I've seen too much suffering. It's the seeming arbitrariness of their passing which hurts me most. Sometimes lives have no apparent meaning, unless it lies in the elements of tribulation - whether a body responds to suffering altruistically, or with self-regard. Too many never make it through Seven Ages, to exit stage left."

"I can associate my ain queries wi' that notion. Elsie may have crept like a snail, unwilling to school on occasion - but I never believed her a less sympathetic figure in the sight of God."

Blair watched Harper's expression as he sipped his pick-me-up, eager to gain some insight without inviting the devil to the door. Harper drank some of his bracer too. The excellent whisky seemed to breathe its sizzling ether up into the trunk of his brain, enlivening sense and loosening his tongue.

"I went through years of scepticism, especially with my philosophical studies. Yet nature is an astounding phenomenon, which we are here at the heart of and able to question. I am reconciled to the thought that this universe is a design. I suspect it's in the fundamental geometry of that design that there will always be something else we cannae understand."

"The Mystery of Faith."

"The Mystery of Scientific Rationalism. It's one and the same to me Reverend."

"Hmm, Wise saws and modern instances. Let me ask you . . . and I can see how sincere you are, so do not imagine I am debunking you . . . what led you to this conclusion?"

"It's in the nature of prophetic vision. Death is the temporal reality but somehow time must be an illusion. Ignore the pantheon of deities, strip away arcane ritual, and theology is essentially trying to express that notion – whether churchmen agree or not. I believe Hannah is still alive in spirit, I *have* to believe - for my own broken heart."

Blair looked uncomfortable, sighing like a split log in a diminishing fire. Harper held his breath, afraid that Blair was about to reduce his naïve assertion to ungodliness. But that was not it at all.

"Hannah meant a lot to me too, John . . . In fact I privately came to question if life had any fundamental purpose or meaning, after her untimely death." The two men stared at one another as realisation dawned for the first time in Harper's mind. Long before he'd gone to work at Ramsburn there had been a rival for Hannah's affection.

"So it's true? The rumours were true? You *were* in love with her?"

"I'm only human, John. There are as many kinds of love as there are lovers."

"But we're no talking aboot the Bride of Christ here, Jim."

"No John, we are not." Harper waited indulgently as Blair examined his recollections of Hannah.

"The truth is I would have asked her to marry me if you had not fallen in love," Blair shook his head slowly, "I don't think she ever fully realised it."

"Aw Jim, women have a way of knowing these things! For what it's worth, she thought the world of you, old son. If I hadn't snatched her from under your nose, I feel sure she would have said yes to your proposal."

"Well, she will live forever in my heart, as I know she does in yours."

"Okay Reverend, I'll no' dare to intrude into your private thoughts. I cannae accept that one man's inspiration is another's impediment."

Blair smiled warmly, gusting an awkward reply, "No, no - quite the contrary John. Your kind words have stirred my heart. I will pray for you and your family – all of them. In Prayer we refine and dedicate our best intentions you know, so try to make that a habit."

The two men embraced warmly, parting under a rose tree shading the threshold of the Minister's cottage. Blair watched Harper in awe as the earnest fellow strode off across granite chippings, toward his pretty young wife.

Margaret was waiting alone under a gently waving Yew tree. Evidently Elizabeth and Duff had gone ahead with their aunties and Jessie back to Ramsburn. Margaret looked arrestingly beautiful, wrapped in her black dress and veil. Grief endowed her look with the gaunt prescience of a mediaeval Madonna. She was Giulia Farnese in mourning, though Harper remarked from a distance that she had taken up a fashionably masculine habit. White smoke swirled around her head.

"Good Lord, Margaret! They don't approve of women smoking in public round here."

"Oh, well would you prefer if I did it in the lavvy? Or maybe when I'm hanging out the washing?"

"Do whatever you want, woman. You have my full backing. Just don't feed them to elephants in the zoo."

"I love you, Harper. You have *my* full backing." Margaret lifted her veil. Placing her hands behind his head she kissed him firmly on the mouth. He could taste the sharp flavour of a Scotch mint, competing with the stale odour of tobacco. She was tense, clearly worried about the impression she might make on the Wilsons and Harpers having met them only briefly at her wedding. They smiled warmly at each other, as he stated his intentions for the week ahead.

"If I had the time I'd visit every single person I know in the town and wider area, especially my own adoptive family but also the Barbers, Lorimers, Murdochs. I should also pay my respects to the Stevensons . . . the Paytons . . . and the Laird's family, the Duffs . . . an' then there's Donald McIntyre. If I don't spend an evening with him and his drinking cronies, the old bastard will bear a grudge."

"Oh my, the terrible things a man has to do to earn respect in the community! Harper if you want to move back here just say the word.

I've spent all my life in one place, at school and work. I dinnae have that number of people who give a care about me. I don't even *know* that many people."

"I plan to spend tomorrow visiting Marnoch and Auchterless, then Zach and Annie Williams up in Elgin."

"That's fine with me but shouldn't you spend more time with Jessie?"

"Oh Lord, I'm dreading that!"

"Whatever for – I thought she regarded you as her adoptive son?"

"I'm dreading the reproach that they had not seen Elsie since the wedding."

"Huh! Well what could you have done about that? John, no-one could have predicted this. They know consumption takes one out of every two unfortunate enough to catch it. When Jessie was a girl it probably killed one in four of all the people who died."

"Yes you're right and that's all the more reason to show her respect, the fact that she's sixty one years old. Margaret, I plan to beg her forgiveness for neglecting her over recent years. I will remind her that she is the real head of the family, the model of true compassion and Christian sentiment."

Harper stopped in the flow of his vaunted speech. Margaret knew there was something more he wanted to say, that would have come naturally if Hannah had still been his consort. She decided not to laugh and hold her tongue even though his manner of speaking had been self-mocking.

"Jessie practises Margaret, but she disnae preach."

"Oh well that's me told. Thank you!"

"I'm also gonny give her money for all her kindness over so many years. I need tae tell her that I love her, just to be sure she knows it."

"Fine, how could she ever doubt it?"

"By reading *me* Margaret. I've been full o' doubt."

"Well, the Lord fears for him who fears to doubt," Margaret stated, without a hint of piety.

"I will offer myself thereby to the totality of God's grace, as I have experienced its measure so far in this world."

"Oh well I don't think you need to be saved twice!" said Margret through a teasing smile, taking his hand.

"Ha! You're debunking my need for forgiveness. What kind of Catholic are you?"

Margaret smiled warmly at her dear man, pondering an apt reply. If this was the closest they would ever come to a major rift, it would be a bargain. Margaret knew in that instant, having hitched her wagon to Harper's star, she would never feel insecure.

"I'm the kind who measures repentance like salt in a cake recipe, John. It should make the other flavours stand out but never be tasted itself." Harper laughed disarmingly at his beguiling companion.

"When I have reaffirmed my relations with the Wilsons, I will take you, my scheming temptress, for a circuitous walk through the woodlands surrounding tortuous, secret Deveron."

"Oh, is that a promise?"

"Yes, you're on a promise but only after I've explained all the ambiguities of hypocrisy, compassion and living faith - in this rural community."

"And gossip? Will you tell me some gossip? It goes well with smoking at the washing line and I'm new to both these pleasures."

"Nae bother hen. I can show ye how tae light a Lucifer in a force nine gale *and* I will maliciously repeat all the gossip I can remember. If we're still talking at the end of the day, I'll offer you my humble conclusions - derived from years of worry mind - without once mentioning Hannah Wilson's influence over me in the living years." Margaret narrowed her eyes sceptically, titling her head to one side but said nothing.

Holding hands affectionately they walked up through the woodlands to Ramsburn. Though he tried hard to make conversation, telling Margaret the ancient history of the area, Harper actually found it impossible not to think of Hannah. Jessie and her family immediately solved that problem for him. As soon as they arrived at the farm Jessie fussed over Margaret, asking her all about her family and work at the Royal.

111

Harper's bride was the guest of honour and felt easier in the company of twenty–one year old Frank who was bowled over by her, and his five sisters, than she had been lately with Harper. Conversation went on into the small hours, fuelled by strong drink and delightful humour, to be remembered another time in gladness. Routines of the farm were left in abeyance, with Jeannie and Betsy telling Margaret all their private affairs and ambitions long past bedtime.

As an inevitable part of the ritual Duff and Elizabeth kept vigil with a midnight feast on the stairs, accompanied by their young aunties Fiona and Elsie.

Kate Robertson sulked because at sixteen she had issues about parentage and felt she was being excluded from the adult forum. Jessie intimated to Harper that her adopted daughter only wanted an excuse to slip off to meet his brother Ewan.

"Should I go over and speak to him ma?"

"Oh, I imagine being a Harper he'll know what to do." Margaret laughed openly, at Jessie's biting satire.

"I don't doubt it but I *meant* to offer him advice."

"Oh, I imagine being a Harper he'll not welcome advice," Jessie's indigo eyes flashed with flinty humour. Her prodigal son in law put down his glass and reached across the sofa to embrace her.

The summer night was sultry and blankets too heavy on their bed. Waking in a sweat next to Margaret, in the room where Hannah had spent so much time with him, placed a silent proscription upon desire.

Sounds of the farmyard drifting through the open sash worked better than an Ingersoll pocket watch to indicate the hour. Harper knew within an instant of opening his eyes that hands on the dial were approaching nine and the working day was half over.

Rolling naked out of bed he went without a word to dress and shave. Within ten minutes he had hitched Jessie's pony and trap. Immediately after a hearty breakfast provided by Jeannie, Harper headed out on his social calls with Margaret smiling at his side. This day he hoped to make an easy and permanent accommodation with his beloved. He prayed she might try to understand his complex set of relationships, perhaps continuing to respect him despite his paradoxical views. In any event he intended to make his position clear regarding the bond with Hannah's mother and the young aunties and uncles. As he turned right out of the end of the lane and trotted the pony and rig up the gentle slope he spoke quietly, looking up at the same undulating horizon he'd felt to be a trap, less than a dozen years before.

"This connection will never be cut, Margaret. The Wilsons are more than family tae me. They're my true friends. Their closeness is the touchstone for any worthwhile relationships I may seek from now on. And I have tae think o' Duff and Elizabeth."

Margaret was no cipher to be cancelled in an equation. She went straight onto the offensive, "Well I think it's a scandal that you let her be called that." Folding her arms she looked away across fields to the west.

"Because?"

"You know why. Because you don't want to be constantly reminded of her mother."

Harper opened his mouth to speak but then clamped it firmly shut. He had been about to tell Margaret the first piece of gossip regarding his conversation with Reverend Blair. Margaret realised she had just put her foot in her mouth and Harper decided not to compound the folly. She was right of course but neither of them ever spoke of it again. One way or another, little Hannah's nickname 'Duff' was to stick with her for the rest of her days.

As the warm thundery summer wore on, excitement mounted for Harper working notice for Kenningtons. He thought respectfully of Dewhirst whom he planned to meet up with in Otley while breaking in Cameron Young, his replacement.

Sitting around an open fire quaffing Timothy Taylor's exceptionally smooth ale, the old man seemed spare and distracted. He looked more like an Alpine woodsman in his green Bavarian felt hat and open neck shirt, than the sharp dresser Cameron had been told to expect. Long hair had turned white, hiding his ears. Roger expressed worry about his wife's poor health and their general lack of funds, "My grand villa on Pool Bank is up for sale," he told them.

"But you saved so hard to get that man! It was your dream."

"The tree-lined gorge it sits by was my dream Harper, not the rotting wall plates I am too decrepit to replace."

"I sometimes think we spend all out time mastering life, only to give up on it!"

"Isn't that the truth! But I'm happy to compromise. At least I have my woodland walks. To be candid I'm more interested in them than supping ale I can no longer afford . . . My liver you know," he added by way of explanation, tapping his vast abdomen. Nonetheless Roger did sup too much ale and became taciturn as the evening wore on. Harper remained clear headed and indulged the man good-humouredly. On the late evening train to York Harper remarked to Young how economic circumstances and ill health often oppress an otherwise exceptional man, leaving him empty handed and with nothing to say.

Prior to fond farewells and a drinking bout at the Spotted Red Bull, Harper took judicious care in seeking out and saying goodbye to each and every individual known to him by name. Contact details were duly logged in his address book on the back of a promise, "I'll visit you soon on behalf of the Widows Fund." He shook hands with every single one of them, nodding and smiling moderately before walking away.

On the weekend of the twenty third of August, 1901 he returned with Margaret to fetch their two daughters from Ramsburn. In the spinney behind the house Blackbirds sang their hearts out, as a fine summer evening descended like a two handed blessing from boundless deep blue sky. The story of travail in Jessie's leaky eyes as she emerged from the farmhouse to greet them carried intimation that Apollo must give way to Dionysus. She chattered brightly, wiping wizened hands on her apron. Her solicitous tone betrayed the want of company, of opportunity for affection.

"I wasnae sure when tae expect ye but the timing's perfect, dinner'll be an hour. Jeannie and Frank are still at the milking. The young ones are practicing with their sett for the ceilidh tomorrow."

Harper jumped down from the rig, paid the cabbie then wrapped his arms around the sprightly little widow. Jessie Wilson gasped and made herself rigid, pulling away from the smacker he left on her cheek. Margaret smiled in embarrassment, as Harper fawned over the older woman.

"My God woman ye're a sight fer sore eyes! It's me ye should hae marriet all they years ago Jessie, if on'y I'd chanced ma arm!" Jessie looked at him askance through a puckered smile, as though he had lost his mind.

"Oh my word . . . now the true confession, Margaret," she intoned, winking at her, "As if hitching a woman thirty years his senior would not constitute the biggest scandal since Gordon Cumming cheated the Prince o' Wales at cards!"

"Oh, I'm sure you'd charm that one eyed old cud more than his American heiress, Jessie if on'y he knew you!"

"Aye mebbe but d'ye think he'd he give up his monkey fer me?"

"I think he'd give up the monkey but the eighty thousand dollars a year might be a bit of a wrench," put in Margaret. They laughed generously at her caustic irony.

Jessie Wilson hugged Margaret warmly as she stepped away from the turning rig and Harper waited politely for her to usher them inside. Setting aside banter, he read her like a book. Surrounded by activity and the strains of responsibility, Jessie was benevolently alive but lonely. Attractive and scrupulous in all her dealings the feisty matriarch carried a debit for the affairs of the one man she had ever loved. Even eighteen years on she still clearly missed Frank.

After a fine super and a few drinks Harper spoke about mysteries of faith with alacrity and obvious sincerity, "I was sceptical," he declared, "Now I believe." With imperturbable sincerity he spoke warmly about the importance of friends and family but also of, "The true family of Greater Humanity."

Margaret and the Frank bantered with him mockingly but the girls were quietly influenced by such plain speaking in a man of the world.

"Well, I think we should attend service on Sunday. Jim will be delighted tae see us all," declared Jessie.

"Here now, I took you for the humanist-atheist ma!"

"I've more cause than most tae be a non-believer son but I'm wise enough tae hedge ma bets. Especially now that I've put in ma three score years and running fast intae the ten."

"Hmm, sounds tae me like double cropping. Fine if ye read the daily weather forecast."

"John, I never miss the weather forecast. No matter how much I celebrate life, I'm always up wi' the lark. And I make the best o' every situation, no' just what I take to market."

Indeed there was much to celebrate in Jessie's household. All six of her young family had stories to tell and all were obliged to eat with the Harpers. Frank held sway with his cutting wit and anecdotes from the working day. He knew everyone locally and they all respected him. He talked seamlessly and entertainingly about each significant event, from haggling with drunken contractors buying his lumber to the graphic details of delivering a calf straight after breakfast. Easy laughter flowed with the food and drink.

Margaret's gentle questioning of each of the girls in turn brought a running commentary from Frank. He evaluated their boyfriends, or prospects at work or school, with humorous brinkmanship. Occasionally his twin sister Jeannie rose to the challenge, putting him back in his place before he went too far. But they all seemed happy, including Kate who had invited Ewan Harper on the pretext of him spending time with his adoptive brother. Her fierce eyes showed a simple appreciation for John Harper, amounting to unquestioning affinity.

"Well, blessed are those who mourn, for they shall be comforted," said Harper quietly. They all looked to him in silence, "And here's tae Jessie and the glory days she has created for us aw!" he added with sincerity, raising his full glass.

"Slaintje!" said Frank setting off a chorus, "Good cheer!" added Jessie, looking across the vast table contentedly at John Harper, the flatterer. She was reconciled in the outworking of destiny, to have lost an unfaithful husband but reformed a prodigal son.

In the warm gloaming John Harper sat in the garden with Ewan and Frank, discussing their plans for a finished timber stock yard. For an instant he felt dazed by the perception that this was where he belonged – where his wife and daughter had been laid to rest and his legal relatives ground out a living each day.

The last slanting rays of a red sun, reluctant to set, glimmered through the fox wood. Thirty yards from where he sat, Hannah had greeted him with news of her remission from cancer. His heart was here, along with remembered sorrow and unspeakable joy. Although he said nothing Harper had half a mind to visit Mr Ross, the Laird's Factor over at the castle in the morning. He could put his name down to take the next croft that came up for rent.

Frank lit pieces of wood in a garden brazier and Ewan turned the conversation to the desperate plight of Afrikaaners and the brutality of Kitchener's scorched earth policy.

"I cannae believe what they bastards are doing in the name o' King and country, in the Boer republics," he began, settling into a garden chair with his drink, "It makes me ashamed tae be British."

"You're no British Ewan," taunted Frank, "You're an undercover Jocobite, waiting fer the next uprising."

The moment was gone. An impulse to suggest a business partnership with the two young men had eluded Harper but his feeling of unjust displacement remained.

In his new career as Life Assurance agent Harper met a great many people. From the outset it was essential to his career that whenever he stepped out over the threshold, he was happily prepared to engage with any one of them. Doing the rounds like the milkman or the postie, the man in the suit was accepted just as readily by one and all. He was acknowledged a true gentleman, honoured and respected by all his clients, in so much as they regularly handed him their hard earned copper and silver.

In order to increase his scope for doing business Harper had a telephone installed at home. Following listings taken from the directory provided, he approached subscribers politely and systematically according to which area they lived. Bills were enormous but legwork that followed from a flood of contacts more than compensated.

As long as he avoided the office and distractions abounding there, Harper instinctively knew it was only a matter of time till he became top dog on the Sales force. Experience as a travelling representative for Kenningtons and Jenners had taught him how to manage time for maximum effect. Being punctual. Wearing an immaculate suit. Talking to everyone he met with unfailing respect. These were the simple ingredients. Conducting business successfully had been a way of life for Harper at Kenningtons. It was a comfortable affair to apply such standards to the community at large, as it had been to the bourgeoisie he was used to trading with. It was obvious to Harper where to start – on the high street. Above all, he knew that avoiding uninitiated work colleagues was a matter of necessity.

Other direct selling agents on his team felt the need to be gregarious. They shared notions and anecdotes about business; set up team-work arrangements with more experienced colleagues to secure agreement with difficult business clients; chatted up the receptionist who took their messages. They used their charms on the office girls to speed up newly signed schedules, occasionally waited for the boss to get a decision on a suicide. Then there were frequent compliance briefings and training refreshers – all very high minded but completely pointless if you knew what you were doing and didn't need to hear it all again.

Inevitably there were doubtful observations from the stragglers. They all had weary legs and leaking soles. One or two despised and mimicked grubby clients with their wide-eyed bairns. Everyone knew the legend of some old hen still chipping in weekly for her man who had died a decade before. Others liked to retell the easy selling of indemnity to window cleaners, steeplejacks and fishermen.

These men went to the pub early and finished their rounds late. For them every day got a little harder, whereas for Harper the job was joy itself. With a quarter of a million clients available in Edinburgh alone he found himself picking ripe apples in an autumn orchard. And he didn't need a ladder. Harper was already on top of it looking down. As an approach to selling policies, he simply used the weight of logic of his own experience to cut to the chase.

Spotting the McClenaghan bairns from a distance he took a short cut across The Links, stepping unannounced into their game. Dribbling the football away from them, in the direction of the pavement opposite their house, he ignored protests and raucous insults amid the laughter, "Gi'e us wir ball back ye old bam pot!" and in a lame attempt to distract him, "Look mister . . . ye've got dugs keech on yer Oxfords!"

Balancing a brief case with one hand above his head, he stopped dead several times, easily evading tackles from left and right with deft flicks of either foot. As the youngest child advanced with a laughing growl from between two piles of coats, Harper finally back-heeled the ball for the other two to turn and race after.

Waiting patiently in the living room of a proud terraced house on East Hermitage Place, he knew the conclusion of business would be a matter of forced logic and determination to put a case against another man's willingness to cast his fate to the wind. At the time Harper had no idea how strongly this discourse would come to characterise all the other instances where good fellows would, 'need more time to think about it.'

To occupy himself, as Charlie, the Master of *Ben Lomond* finished his supper, Harper re-read the article he'd cut from the newspaper back in June about the collision between *Banffshire* and *Ben Mohr* in the

Thames estuary. He decided to let that costly misfortune do the talking for him.

Charlie McLenaghan was a fine Hibernian in all respects. He and his wife were originally from Stranraer where they had felt a little conspicuous, even among the itinerant Irish. Joining the Merchant Navy at seventeen, Charlie followed work from there to Glasgow and then on to Leith and the finest merchant fleet to grace the High Seas. Now he travelled to all points of the compass with his eyes on the horizon, when they weren't plotting the stars. Bearded and broad with handsome, slightly sagging features giving testimony to all he'd seen traversing a million miles of ocean, this Captain commanded deepest respect from first sight.

A ten buttoned and braided long coat hanging in the hallway told Harper of his recent return from duty. Charlie would want to relax and share stories with his devoted Sandra. Evident from the number of bairns running in and out the house with bats and balls to the Links was the impression that whenever Charlie did return from sea the McLenaghans paid scant attention to the phases of the moon. After months apart, withdrawal would seem immaterial to the mood of an upstanding Catholic.

The good man settled across from the suited landlubber, sleeves rolled and a second cup of tea balanced in the steady palm of his left hand. Charlie smelled of Old Spice and Carbolic but underneath the competing fragrances was the stench of bilges and rust that would take another long soak in the tub to leach out.

It occurred to Harper this persuasion of the Widows Fund might be stretched thinner than Tasmanian Merino, washed too many times in brine – mistaken perhaps as an expensive luxury, rather than absolute necessity. Equally he realised it was his given task to evoke as much warranted pride in Charlie's bairns as in his Ben Line uniform. Knowing there would be no sale without an open discussion, he planned to cut straight to the objections. Tapping a Parker fountain pen impatiently on his notepad, Harper stuck nervously to small talk about the loading of general cargoes of beer and wool and glass.

At last Sandra sat down beside her husband and Harper waited smilingly for her to give him full attention.

"Life and work are tough enough . . . but what would your circumstances be if there was no breadwinner in the family, Mrs McLenaghan?" Harper asked the key question then kept his mouth shut until the couple engaged with one another.

Sandra looked guiltily at Charlie, "Er, well . . ."

Charlie indulged Sandra, tentatively allowing her a voice. Harper stood up, slowly approaching Charlie as Sandra began to express predictable reservations, "I really don't know. I'd have to sell the house I suppose."

Harper handed Captain McLenaghan the newspaper cutting, to distract him and prevent interruptions as his wife responded. He returned to the sofa, watching Sandra benignly all the time as she expressed her fears.

"Women always worry more about these things I know, although the man is the breadwinner. I'd try to find work but . . ." She looked at Charlie, who glanced once at the article and then disconcertedly back at her.

Significantly Charlie did not put the article to one side, even though he knew every line of its content. He placed the extract from the Herald on his lap, clearly intent on reading it again. Sandra searched Charlie's eyes, unselfconsciously showing all that love had offered and still promised, until the old salt cracked a smile. Placing the fine china cup back on the saucer he reached out a huge weathered hand, to gently clasp Sandra's work dressed knee.

Here it comes, at least he will acknowledge her concerns.

"Well, I don't know. Who *can* predict the future? The Lord giveth and the Lord taketh away. I'm forty-three but I have struggled to save all my working life Mr Harper. It seems the only thing that changes each time I return home is the cost of living."

"But you wouldn't leave port without insuring a cargo, Sir – or if you were the consignor, at least checking to see that the vessel was registered with Lloyds. Am I right?"

McClenaghan levelled with Harper, taking the measure of the man for the first time, as he would a newly arrived Deck Officer. There was surety and understanding in that gaze that did not require formal agreement, although Charlie was inclined to say, "Damned sure, you're right. I'd lose my job and never work again if it wasn't."

Harper changed tack and tone while keeping the same business minded rigour. He had adopted Jim Reid's courtroom manner, "If you don't mind me asking, do you get much chance to read, Sir . . . I mean weather permitting?" asked Harper as he unclipped his brief case.

"Oh God, yes. It's the only thing that keeps an Officer of The Watch sane at times. Why, what have ye got for me lad?"

"Typhoon, by Joseph Conrad, Sir, a Mercantile Master like yourself. I'll be keen to get your impressions on your return, if we don't have time to conclude business while Ben Lomond is loading. Would you look at your diary and suggest a date for us?"

McClenaghan laughed generously, showing the true nature of his incisive mind, "Fine, fine. I'll sell one o' the bairns tae a travelling circus," he agreed, turning respectfully to his wife, "But I'll tell ye now lad, I'm a slow reader and I spend my working life in a den o' thieves – ye'll probably ne'r see this again."

"I think Jamie's your best candidate for a life in the circus – he was doing cartwheels in the park when I was walking down from the bus."

"Oh, no! He's my bonny lad!" protested Sandra, "He's just at that age when the world is still interesting to him." All three of them laughed lightly, as Harper wrote the appointment date in his diary.

Harper habitually rehearsed all their names, including the bairns, personalising the closing of every deal as carefully as if it had been Old Man Shelton signing off the purchase of five hundred yards of prestigious jacquard textile for drapes. He never wasted time speaking to men unless he could confirm straight away they were in fact married and the wife was at home. Each working day consisted in delivering and polishing a well-rehearsed script.

Crucially he never spoke to their fears or guilt – only to the fact that, "You work hard every day Mr . . . , out of a strong sense of duty and pride. Look at it this way - the big city is reaching down to give families security in the future. It's nothing new; we have the first Emperor Napoleon to thank. When a fellow went off to fight there was a distinct possibility he'd need more than nursing care if things went badly for him." He would wait patiently until the point had been acknowledged, since there was no need to sell it to himself. Only when a word of agreement came did Harper break silence and steadfast scrutiny.

With his pen placed on the table between them he sat silently, or smiled genially at the smallest child in the room. More often than not the wife would go without a word for her purse, or her man's wallet. The first instalment mattered in principle but the rest of the revenue flow could be entirely flexible. At all costs it was essential that the policies never lapsed.

"I'll call again . . . let's see - next month, on the seventeenth Mrs McClenaghan." When objections came he would reply with ease, "Oh just put the money in a jar in the kitchen, most of my clients do. This is life assurance hen, no' the butcher's bill. Ye can always raid it at Yuletide an' I'll call another day," he catechised with an easy smile and a laugh, a jolly friar dispensing absolution on his rounds.

The flow of new business fluctuated with the vicissitudes of transport and weather, paperwork and unpredictable people. But it settled down within limits of feasibility, at around five or six contracts a day. Typically this level of activity translated into a three figure number, invariably heading the sales chart in the boss's office at month end.

Arthur Burns invited Harper to talk to his sales team, the best of whom could not seemingly aspire to half that level of consolidated enterprise. On a Monday morning in early January 1902, they filtered into the conference room at the office on David Street, displaying a mixture of admiration and dread. Burns was concerned that some of them might give up too easily, rather than try to emulate the trailblazer.

When he began speaking Harper radicalised them all, including his experienced manager. He sat on the edge of Arthur's desk, never raising his voice above conversational level. As an individual with no time to spare, he went straight to the point, "It strikes me that this is a uniquely difficult industry to operate in, lads. There will always be pressure to work more efficiently, against a backdrop of legal and bureaucratic constraints that tend to militate against that. If you can think of ways to speed up the processing of business, share them if you will. But I wonder if you can. I am at a loss to do so and frankly disappointed at how little I've achieved in my first quarter."

Dumbfounded, they all looked for a cue to Burns, who stared in turn open mouthed at Harper, waiting for something more, "This is an important, almost missionary venture, yet extremely inefficient in the manner it is conducted. All I can add is that at some point you want clients coming to you. You will thrive, or decline, according to the number of referrals you receive. Please ask for referrals *every* time you do business. It will strengthen what people believe about you personally. You represent the company – the foremost of its type, so credibility is not an issue. Efficiency *is* however. Encourage clients to talk on your behalf."

A dozen men sat in silence, cowed by Harper's mystique. Burns wondered how he had achieved his spectacular success but was afraid to ask in case the bubble burst. At last a hand went up at the back of the room. Tim Blackman, a Southerner from Berwick with large, genial specs and impressive sideburns waited politely for acknowledgement before making his observation, "How do you do it John? Give us a breakdown. We all want to know."

"Well, I'm not going to patronise you with sales training patter. Let's assume all present know how to prospect a client and close the business. But look - always leave with a laugh and a joke. Always tip yer hat to the man sat sullen at the table. Thank them with your eyes and leave them with dignity after the sale. That's the beginning - always open up with personal information on following visits but never re-sell what is assumed – that's why they call it Assurance! And again, ask for referrals," They waited respectfully for the coup de grace, "The rest is a question of time management."

Former City Police colleagues signed up for Harper en-masse at two meetings arranged at the end of a Tuesday shift, a week apart. At the first session he kept it short, insisting he was not there to complete business. Harper wanted the word out though and commitment at the follow-up if anyone came, "Just ask yerselves what the Widows Fund can do . . . not for you personally mind, because it cannae add a minute tae yer lives gents . . . but for those ye'd leave behind if a horse kicked ye in the mush, or God forbid if ye had tae break up a football dispute in a local park."

There was sardonic laughter at Harper's reference to the cruel murder of a Glasgow Bobby but the point was made.

"What if ye've nae bairns and yer no marriet?" asked Jim Connolly, a rookie with a reputation to make.

"Then dinnae spend yer money on laced mutton or a Copper's nark," cautioned Harper, staring in disbelief and shaking his head slowly. Jim coloured self-consciously, suddenly thinking about his girlfriend.

A dozen men at the first meeting brought thirty more. Harper was glad he had invited Blackman in support. Tim chatted casually with the off duty policemen, as Harper breezed across town in a cab to find Arthur and get him to open up the office. Within an hour they'd collected another box of application forms. What wasn't filled-in that night they left with clear instructions for Sergeant Chambers to have signed by others Bobbies out working their shift. Tim promised to collect them the following Tuesday but Harper called on Friday evening, before the weekend went mental, with a bottle of Rosebank.

Chambers was delighted to see him and they promptly began chatting politics and literature.

"The Heart of Darkness?"

"No, I saw the review but no I havnae read it yet," Harper told him.

"Don't buy it, I'll sell you my copy when Lennox gives it back."

"Oh, so you lend tae your friends but sell tae the general public eh?"

"That's right, efter aw, you tend tae lose things pal, eh? Like evidence central tae the biggest bust in the history 'o plodding . . . ye daft we bugger," Chambers reminded him, with a stern look over the top of his glasses.

Harper tried hard to remain deadpan but his eyes betrayed scintillating humour, "Well ye can see I'm still working tae put food on the table Sarge, so I've no' gone intae production."

"Not yet! As soon as ye do I'll be calling on ye for my cut."

"What aboot that old scunner, Mark Twain?" ventured Harper, in an attempt to change the subject back to Chamber's comfort zone.

"What?" The big man straightened up from where he'd been leaning on the counter, snapping his fingers to assist recollection. In one deft movement demonstrating the economy of command, Chambers resolved that it was time for a fortified cuppa which Harper would join him in. He lifted the counter flap, waving his friend through into the sanctum sanctorum without need for explanation.

Anyone distracting him at this peaceful hour of the turning week had better have a bloody good reason. Sergeant Chambers was renowned for thinking on his feet but now was a time for thinking sat on a padded office chair.

The two men moved out of sight of the reception area into a space where they could observe Brodie's lustrously polished shoes descending the second flight of stairs, where they returned from the Royal Crest casting coloured light onto the carpet.

"Double Barrelled Detective Story? I thought it was very clever," said Chambers, probing into a bag of sugar with a teaspoon.

"But wasn't that what Friedrich Nietzche was trying to say aboot academia? If we analyse things too deeply, we miss the point?"

"Well exactly, but it was Twain saying that aboot Conan Doyle."

"Nah man . . . Conan Doyle's hero. Why can we no' accept Holmes fer what he is Dennis? The man's a genius!"

"Because every story is a projection of the author. Twain goes oot o' his way tae make that point."

"Bollocks, they're no supposed tae mention that. Sarah Bernhardt never looks directly intae the camera!"

"Hmm, Diderot's Fourth Wall."

"Eh? I dinnae ken whit yer bletherin' aboot man but I'd still rather read The Hoon o' the Baskervilles," said Harper, reaching for the mug of tea proffered by Chambers.

"That's because you're an ignorant wee bastard. Ye never went tae school in Edinburgh, whur ye'd a had a proper education. Possibly the finest in the world, so the legend goes . . . An' dinnae mention Nietzche again, the low brow Neanderthal. According tae the papers when he deed last year he was a degenerate racist, wi' a dose o' the clap. I hae enough trouble wi' 'The Will Tae friggin' Power' son, keepin' bastards in line when they come in here drunk on a Saturday night."

"D'ye mean the criminal fraternity Dennis, or the boys on late shift?"

"You ken fine who ah mean, Harper. I covered fer you a number o' times when ye stepped o'er the line. We Polis Sergeant's hae a lot o' responsibility."

"Sorry Dennis, I'm sure yer right but ye shoulnae speak ill o' the deed," said Harper, with poker faced drollery.

"Shut up an' pass me yer mug," said Chambers, whipping the top off the bottle of malt his friend had bought him.

"No Sarge! That's sacrilege! Just gi'es a spot o' your Whyte an' Mackays," Harper cautioned quietly, knowing Brodie would censure Chambers for drinking whisky neat, if he caught them on the hop.

"There are things to be said in favour of the exception Harper, provided that it ne'er wants to become the rule," said Chambers, pouring two generous measures of the malt.

When Millar and Dyce arrived with the first arrest of the evening an hour after the pubs had opened, Harper promptly rose to his feet, shook Dennis firmly by the hand and headed out through the raised counter flap. Chambers lowered it, snapping home the locking bar on the inside. He went under the counter and Harper assumed he was looking for a charge sheet, so turned to go. But Chambers whistled sharply through his teeth, "Oh, now you're doing it again, man. See this fiddlestick?" he said glancing at his colleagues, "He'd forget tae get oot o' bed fer Kirk on a Sunday."

Harper reached for the evidence satchel Chambers was proffering. It was full of signed documents.

"By the way Brodie and the Management are put out that you didnae invite them. Ye ken whit nit-picking old farts they are. Think they micht miss a trick."

"Tell him I'll phone."

"Not good enough, see him on Tuesday at the Lodge," called Chambers, "There's a quiz night comin' up. He wants you on our team. And Maureen says you're to come over next Sunday at two." Harper saluted crisply then headed for the door, smiling with his eyes.

There was laughter in the footslogging daily routine – always. Familial, heartfelt, self-deprecating, unforced, howling, infectious, common, loving, hopeless, ironic rather than mordant – but taken together irresistible. Harper didn't generate amusement intentionally – rather he discovered it about himself, like a crazy pocket miner in a Western adventure story.

This was how he responded under the natural tension of interacting with hundreds of different people, each with a unique story and the need to relate. He simply smiled and said whatever came into his head, hoping never to give offence. But he could have asked any one of them if it was all right if he moved in for a few days. The vast majority would have gone straight off to change bed sheets and fetch another plate of mince and tats. Within a year of joining Arthur's team, Harper was firmly established as Scottish Widows' top salesman.

Everyone involved seemed to celebrate that success. The bosses spoke of him smilingly behind closed doors, like some thoroughbred Arthur had discovered with a low handicap. His peers tried hard to draw the man into conversation – to pick his brains in hope they might capture the essence of Harper's balanced approach to the job.

Margaret, who had been cold towards him for months since starting such a demeaning job, suddenly began to show renewed affection. Characteristic self-possession which had always drawn him to her shone through her pale blue eyes again, like the light from an unflawed diamond. Thankfully Margaret also began to hold her head up again, showing renewed pride in herself for the first time since their wedding. Her tone in speaking to everyone, including Elizabeth and Duff, became cool and understated again. But there was renewed laughter and hope in her sweet voice too. She naively announced to Harper, "I'm actively planning for the future."

"Oh, well I just hope that fully involves me," was all he could think to reply. Evidently the thought of *planning* whatever it was, allowed her to smile like a Yellow Tara – empty of ambition yet blessed with prosperity, flowing through open hands. For a couple of weeks Margaret became as serene as Jetsun Dolma, the Mother of Liberation. Then suddenly the Buddha smile faded and she didn't speak to anyone for several days. Harper was too pre-occupied to ask what had happened and her plan was shelved.

Part Two

Chapter Seven   *Nor'easter*

Within two years Harper was in a salaried position as Team Leader. In less than five, Sales Manager at Head Office, dealing exclusively with corporate and business clients – offering company pension schemes and underwriting the value of key personnel.

Wednesday afternoons were spent at the golf course, at a select time less busy than the weekends where distinguished members of his clientele regularly saluted from a distance. Harper quartered and scrutinised their leisure time as voraciously as a hawk on the breeze hunting the Royal parkland beyond.

"How's it hanging, Don?" he intoned softly, entering the Club Professional's shop. Resident pro Donald Glennie had long been in Harper's confidence and effectively in his pay as secret agent. Don advocated team pairings to provide him access to big hitters in the world of investment, as well as the world of golf.

"Tucked away nicely under my combos John, Elaine says there's a cold front backing from Southern Europe. Can ye believe that?"

I'll believe anything you tell me, son. Just don't expect me tae repeat in court."

Laughing gently, Don craned his neck to ensure the high handicap pair who had just stepped out were no longer within earshot, "I need some more of your business cards. Every established member has had word from me at some point. Walter Bradshaw er, East Lothian Construction isn't it? Wants tae insure his boys fer code of practice. He's been griping for months John, since one of his roofers slipped an' broke both legs," Don shook his head, as if every missed opportunity for a backhander was nothing short of a scandal.

"Oh aye. You dinnae need tae say a thing Donald. Just tell me how tae work my handicap up an' doon the ladder old son," said Harper, practising his swing with an imaginary putter, "I'll dae the rest."

"Well that's easy pal. Just ha'e a skinful the night before an' ye wont have room on the card for yer score. It happens tae me aw the time."

Harper laughed but he knew it wasn't as easy as that. Don could play a tournament *with* a skinful and still beat everyone.

Glennie, himself a former travelling salesman, spent so much time with his accomplice that some of their august associates assumed Harper was another professional and came to him for advice on stroke play.

Harper was such a natural athlete that he would gladly help them win while discreetly losing himself. In doing so he never chatted idly nor mentioned business, unless they shared confidence with him over a pint later.

"Well thanks man, you know how much I appreciate all your help!" Harper declared graciously, handing Don another ten business cards taken from a silver holder in his bulging wallet.

"I'm glad to oblige, John," Donald told him, "As far as I'm concerned I'm helping oil the machinery o' big business. Every enterprise needs insurance," stated Donald with unequivocal humour.

With the intention of being discreet and gentlemanly in all his dealings Harper openly took the hint regarding the latest referral, Bradshaw. In turn it seemed only fair that Harper, the comptroller, thoroughly evaluate the need of Glennie's paramour Elaine for indemnity, in recognition of services rendered. But Donald intimated the impressively low premiums might still be a stretch. "I never realised they got relatively lower with age?" he told Harper, smiling and shaking his head.

"The bairns ha'e moved on Don, so you're less likely to work yersel' tae deeth, or jump in the tide."

"Your right, I never think of doing that any more. Clever bastards!"

"Exactly."

Harper waived his commission fees on the policies, chipping in the first annual instalment for each by cash. It was clear to both men that if Donald got struck by lightning out on the thirteenth green, his beloved Elaine would never need to work again.

As the girls sprouted and blossomed through the golden years, no-one in the wider family was more vociferously delighted with Harper's success than sixteen year old Elizabeth. Recognition and achievement translated indirectly into deepening association with other families of well to do students, within a growing circle of friends.

It was too early to 'go for a walk in the park' where they would encounter the boys, so Sophie, Olivia, Isla, Jessica and Emma crammed intimately into the terminus of Elizabeth's bedroom, swopping competing stories of adolescent outrage and autonomous identity. Duff was a silent observer, whom they were careful not to shun.

Least mature and most indulged by her parents, robust redhead Olivia tried to instigate 'syllable salad,' a playground game that had produced merriment for them years before, "Itshay, iveway okenbrayed imayway ailnay."

"Upidstyay owcay!" came back smouldering Jessica, the most incisive of the group.

Genial Olivia laughed at the spoonerisms, as well as the fierce put down. An accomplished linguist, she was the one most receptive to playful neologisms.

Elizabeth looked across the room to where blonde, 'Superior Sophie' was brushing Duff's hair for her. Duff caught her eye in the mirror and smiled. Elizabeth knew her sister could always be trusted not to say anything. Duff was the least challenging person in the world but she saw everything. Elizabeth smiled back and Duff waved at her reflection.

"Iwayayvotgaywayimayeriodpayway," murmured Olivia, hoping for a sympathy vote.

"Oh well at least you won't get pregnant tonight," ventured Isla. Isla was the least cultured but in many ways the most attractive and funniest of the clique. Clearly concerns about unwanted pregnancy were high on her personal agenda. Olivia laughed her fulsome, disarming laugh and even straight-laced Elizabeth cracked a smile.

"Ewayanwecayetgaywayumsayidersay?" she continued, eager to win approval somehow.

"Iskayaywayormayikeitlayway!"

"I believe vodka is the least likely to smell on your breath," asserted Superior Sophie, a hair clip perched in the corner of her mouth.

"My ma would absolutely mill me if she caught me or my sister drinking spirits," cautioned Emma blandly. Snapping chipped fingernails self-consciously she added, "My brothers are always drinking. They waste their money an' get in fights."

"Well that's no reason to wrap yourself in cotton wool," objected Jessica, the bas bleu, "If I wanny drink, I'll bloody well drink!"

"Yeah, an' if ye wanny get pished . . ."

"Right, I'll get pished."

"An' if you wanny fight?"

"Damned right Emma, I'll have a ruddy fight!"

"Not with me though?"

"No, not with you!" said Jessica, hugging Emma amid a round of coarse laughter.

"If anyone might have answers to the dilemmas of youth we do," Elizabeth told them all mildly, "A healthy self-image is vital, and hating parents does not always help."

"Oh, I hate my mum," protested Isla, "She makes me work like a black."

"Don't say that," cautioned Sophie.

"But it's true!"

"No, fool it's racial and unacceptable!" hissed Jessica. They all laughed mercilessly at Isla's naïveté, "Blacks; Coalminers; Bag Ladies – all exploited people, Isla."

"Well, what should I say then?"

"Say something you've thought about first," advised Elizabeth, reaching a gentle hand out to stroke her friend's hair.

"I think being a Suffragist is de rigeur, as long as no-one gets hurt," declared Olivia.

"Yes, no question about it, that's why I want to stay on and study History," agreed Emma, "The professions are the battleground."

"Yeah, there aren't too many peers or baronets queuing up to be fish wives or sack makers," Sophie added, to another pulse of raucous delight.

"Dressing up smart with a little make up to attract the boys is permissible though," ventured Olivia.

"Sure, you know what? That's the first sensible thing you've said all evening - attract them - but control the bastards," suggested Jessica,

"The fashion is smart Indian cheesecloth, long loose skirts with a tight jacket. Maybe a neat French beret is okay, as long as it's no' black."

"Ye wouldnae want tae look like an Onion Johnnie," cautioned Olivia.

"Yes . . . all in all that outfit will make you look attractive *and* slightly older," concluded Elizabeth, "But what colours though? Nothing a man would wear – jade green?" They spent the next ten minutes talking French berets.

When Elizabeth and her pals left for the park to seek out boys from school, Duff stayed in to do her homework. She wanted no part in Sophie's attempt to purchase alcohol.

Any accepted social contact however tenuous, fed into Elizabeth's inspired romance of becoming a fine lady. For his part John Harper was not averse to spending an evening at the Usher Hall listening to Tchaikovsky if it meant ultimately signing up a few more parents or the occasional guest conductor.

When it was rumoured on a discreet but unofficial grapevine that Lady Graham was seeking a governess for her son James, Elizabeth took a lot of trouble composing a letter to suggest she should look no further. Amongst other things she said of herself, 'I have the educational grounding, balanced refinements and exemplary character that might be adapted to the requirements of mentoring exceptional young children. I have a genuine interest in Physical and Natural Sciences, as well as Classical Literature and Humanities. If I may rely upon her Ladyship's discretion, can I mention the insight that my parents are actively promoting - the intelligence that I play lead violin in various Edinburgh youth orchestras and have passable ability to converse in four foreign languages? This is in marked contrast to my childhood tendencies for impromptu drama, midnight feasts and dressing up of Molly our cat, with the assistance of my sisters. I wish to plead that formal education has not entirely dulled my instinct for play.'

She added contact addresses for referees wheedled out of Harper, for which he made brief, light hearted phone calls to confirm. Elizabeth glibly stated in her letter that she would be delighted to hear again from her Ladyship. She'd neglected to mention her relatively young age of sixteen but once the letter was posted that seemed irrelevant. What did age matter in the light of such precocious talent?

At night Elizabeth lay awake for hours fully clothed on top of her bed, imagining she could hear the calls of a small child. There would be wet-nurses and nannies for that contingency so she would need to resist any natural, brooding urge.

What if they don't want me? Maybe my letter was too cheeky. I'll have to find some other opportunity of that ilk. But nothing could ever be as good.

She imagined bright stars above her head, filling the vista of unbounded sky beyond the roof. Praying and dreaming that the great gearwheel of the heavens might sweep her up with the Hamilton-Grahams - onto another wider, more gracious plane of traction, Elizabeth lay awake into the morning hours.

Life was fine, yet somehow experience had always limited her and she yearned with all her heart for connection with something sublime, glimpsed in early childhood but never fully recognised. She had been born for something very special but still couldn't see what it was. Intuition whispered of something elusive – singular, dedicated like her mother yet still freewheeling like enigmatic Harper, her exceptional, adored father.

In her meditations Elizabeth finally came to terms with the haunting desire for safekeeping that had always confounded her. For years she had been reworking the derelict stonework of ruined childhood into something grand. The unbending ridge timber was her impartial and total love for virtuous, unworldly Elsie - whose passing broke her heart. The re-dressed capstone was notional reverence for a darling mother she'd never truly known.

Elizabeth knew she could become the perfect mentor for the infant son of the Duke and Duchess of Montrose. Still fully clothed at a little after five, as blackbirds stirred in the woodland margins of Holyrood Park, Elizabeth fell asleep - alone in a world of her own imagining, surrounded by beckoning hands and entitled voices.

Several weeks passed and school dragged on towards the usual closed options for Elizabeth. Then at last a fine envelope with black copperplate handwriting landed on the mat, with the gas bill and a weekly letter from Jessie at Rothiemay.

Elizabeth's exultant shouts could be heard throughout the house and half way up the street. She ran upstairs to hug Margaret, standing in her dressing gown on the landing. Harper shook his head as he observed, "This is the least lady-like behaviour I've ever seen from you Elizabeth, and after all it's only an interview."

But she was undaunted, "Oh thank you! Thank you! Thank you Daddy! Lady Mary suggests a trial period where I see how I get on with her son James! I can't believe it. Thank you, Harper thank you," she kept saying, over and again.

It was clear to his tempered, astute slip of a girl what connections can do – what they can give and what they can take away. Harper absorbed her joy with satisfaction, remembering wealthy affiliates who had sponsored him indirectly at an early age. In recent years Elizabeth had developed understanding and natural appreciation – not always acknowledged by Margaret perhaps. In retrospect it appeared that she knew instinctively her dream was about to come true – that her future was resolved.

Five weeks following Elizabeth's departure a sepia postcard came, showing a photograph of the exterior of Brodick Castle. Elizabeth described details of her room adjacent the nursery, the location of which was proudly circled in pencil on the image.

"How cryptically delightful," stated Duff as she examined it, "To describe living in such a magnificent place, yet how cadaverously sad to never really belong there."

"What? There you go again, using your fancy words like they actually mean something . . . explain yourself!" demanded Margaret contemptuously.

"Maybe it's selfish – but I want attachment to a place that belongs to me. If I was in Elizabeth's shoes I'd save every penny to achieve just that! I wouldn't want to be the unknown ghost in someone else's library."

"Tosh! They wouldn't let you in their library, you'd study all the time and never do any work! And it sounds tae me you've got expensive notions." Margaret hammered a ladleful of burnt oatmeal into Duff's bowl to emphasise her point.

Duff sat at the table stirring porridge she could not bring herself to eat. Gazing at the postcard of wooded, grandiose Scotland she felt that by degrees she had become completely hollowed out. For Duff the image conveyed elitism wrapped in most hurtful romance. The hypocrisy of false idealism made her feel like weeping. There was some inexplicable folly in Elizabeth's actions and ambitions. Duff wanted to argue with Margaret, tell her that 'aspiration always has its price' but a lump rose in her throat.

In a way Elizabeth had bought into something intangible, without even seeing it as a compromise. By the same token she'd traded worldly ambition for refuge, without hesitation. Elizabeth would always be her wonderful, talented elder sister but her deference exemplified everything Hannah wished to avoid.

"Its moral cowardice," she griped but the words stuck in her throat.

"What?" demanded Margaret, "What did you say?"

"Nothing, nothing important."

Duff still missed her sister achingly. There was indisputable logic in her privileged choice of career but although Elizabeth was always supposed to be the front runner, Duff saw her now as a Judas Goat. As she re-read the postcard for some hint of love, tears welled into her eyes. This had been the only contact in over a month. There was no generous invitation to visit. No pleasantly indiscreet anecdote about the noble family Elizabeth associated with daily . . . just a postcard. The harder Duff tried not to be insulted the more it galled her.

When Hannah came home from school that day she reflected on the fact that they were all gone now except her and the house seemed empty. Margaret had a full time nursing job at the Royal Infirmary, not that they needed the money – she just couldn't find enough to do at home. She told everyone that she had gone there seeking informal advice from the Gynaecologist, then ended up applying for a job on the spur of the moment. She told Harper bitterly that she'd 'lost interest in other people's children.'

Madness! Why don't they have a baby if that's what they both want?

Duff brooded miserably upon the fact that even poor old Molly was on her last legs. Her teeth were gone and both thyroid glands had swollen massively. When Perez the vet removed one, Molly was obviously stressed. But he assured Duff she'd recover with a bowlful of whole milk each day and a spoonful of cod liver oil added to her food. On removal of the second gland ten days later, the poor old cat immediately became hyperactive and breathless as her overloaded metabolism spun out of control.

Two months after Elizabeth's auspicious departure, Harper persuaded Duff that the beautiful old mouser had to be put down. They sat together into the small hours of the morning, stroking and speaking gently to her but in the morning when Duff rose to take her to the vet she'd already had a heart attack. No other living being had displayed so much trust to Duff in her thirteen years.

"Oh Daddy look, she must have been panicking for help!" Duff said, pointing to where Molly lay on the dining room floor beside her tilted over basket.

"I'm sorry, Duff. I wish we'd stayed with her till the end."

Harper lifted the old girl in his arms and gently closed her eyelids. Duff righted the basket for him to lower Molly's chilled and rigid frame into her blanket.

"You bring it. I'll go fetch a spade," said Harper, lifting the wicker bed for Duff to carry.

When Harper finished burying Molly inside her basket in the back garden Duff bawled like a nor'easter driving sea spray onto an outcrop no sailor had lived to speak of. There was no-one to share her grief. No-one to properly celebrate childhood remembrances of the joy Molly left behind. Duff felt there was too much missing in life that could never be replaced. Her sense of aloneness felt like the end of an era. She cried indignantly for Hannah, Great Gran, Elsie and Molly - as well as all the people she loved who were no longer part of her daily life.

Margaret had spoken occasionally of wanting a child of her own. It was clear to Duff now that her step-mother waited only for her leaving home to begin life anew with Harper. Although Duff admired Margaret's endurance, she also had to accept the absence of genuine mutual interest between them. They lived in parallel – frequently nodding at one another like busy neighbours in a hurry.

By the age of thirty-eight Harper made Superintendent of Scottish Widows, with thirty five days annual leave and an executive expense account. They also provided him with a company car, ostensibly to help him supervise agents in the field and service a widespread, demanding clientele. The car proved more trouble than it was worth and its cost, if not its worth, was more than a small house.

Arbitrary corporate extravagance surrounding Harper's advancement gave cue for Margaret to think again about their future. On a Saturday in April '06 when the Beeston-Humber Landaulette had been delivered at the beginning of the new fiscal year, Harper drove them along the coast road to St Andrews with Duff brooding in the back.

Walking on the beach they both hugged her warmly, making bright conversation to cheer her up. Margaret probed for smiles of approval in her step-daughter's gentle eyes but Duff was reluctant as ever to speak about what seemed obvious.

"What's the matter, honey bee?"

"I can't help worrying about my future, Margaret. Wondering if I'll ever get the chance to show what I can do. "

"Ha! I remember being your age. It seems like yesterday. Now I'm thirty and I'm still terrified of the future."

"When I was your age I was making horse shoes for a living. I wisnae sure who my parents were, or if I'd stay another day. I think I hated everyone," Harper declared insensitively.

"And look at you now, sitting on top of the world," said Duff through a wan smile. Moisture filled her eyes but there was assurance in her voice.

"That's because I knew I had a role to play which I gladly accepted."

Harper the arbiter walked in the middle, linking arms with both of them. Later he bought them steak dinner at the golf club where he applied for membership.

Recalling the counselling of his mentor Zachariah, Harper spoke all the while to Duff like an equal. Amid shimmering light and sounds of porcelain and glass, the Buddha smile returned at last to the immaculate face of Margaret Harper. Listening indulgently to the conversation she mused silently upon an inner secret that could never be voiced. When they finished their meal Harper reached across the table to hold her hand.

"I could sit and look at you all night," he told her.

"Oh, you don't have to do that," she laughed easily, switching on her fascinating smile. Duff approved of the long love between Margaret and Harper and resisted the urge to say, 'Stop now, you're making me feel like a gooseberry.' Instead she too smiled gloriously, tilting long hair forward over her face in self-conscious embarrassment.

On the way back to Auld Reekie Margaret realised that amongst all freedom, the greatest joy would lie in starting her own family. There was only one obstacle causing division, one haunting spectre disturbing her brooding peace of mind. The enigma of unfulfilled happiness lay sleeping on the rear seat of the car.

From the earliest age Duff had been a realist. By mid-teens she could instantly see either alacrity or deceit in another's eyes. Often she saw both together in the same instant - looking beyond contradictions in many an individual whom others rejected. As a consequence Duff made many loyal allies and without overtly trying, attracting the widest circle of friends. Looking with honest clarity upon the hard world she was growing into, the teenager understood her own popularity and returned humour and warmth in all situations.

In school as in social settings she was usually the last to speak, but when she did others tended to listen. In all exchanges she sought resolution rather than conflict. Hannah Harper became disarmingly insightful, rarely expressing cynicism as much as compassion. People who knew her well expressed appreciation – close associates naturally but especially her teachers. In nature, Duff was Elizabeth's aristocrat without the landed wealth.

For her step-mother Margaret however, Duff was a banshee in the flesh, not simply an omen but haunting, tangible remembrance. In every waking moment and not a few of her dreams, Margaret saw Harper's deceased wife Hannah in *their* lovely girl.

Now she sat rigidly, framed by the light of a glorious June evening, nursing a cup of coffee that might protect her from the requirement to reciprocate Harper's anticipated touch.

"Where is Duff?" he enquired gently, aware of a pattern where his wife would spurn amorous attention.

"Gone to Isabella's house, to do her homework," she answered snippily.

"What's wrong woman? You look like you've been handed a life sentence for murder."

Margaret's eyes filled with distress as she balanced the cup on the arm of the sofa, "Why have I been cursed by guilt like this, Harper? I think of her all the time and it makes me feel like an auxiliary!"

"It's all in your mind," stated Harper, "Just accept her for who she is. You know how much she means to me. Don't be bloody jealous woman!"

"Yes, God damn it Harper . . . I *am* jealous," she shrieked, "But not of *Duff* you fool!"

"Then you're fixated," Harper snapped back angrily, "Why did this not matter years ago when I swept you affy yer feet?"

"Because each day Duff grows more like her mother," she pleaded, her mouth stretched in passion as the burden of inmost sorrow was voiced at last. Margaret wept inconsolably before Harper's insensitive bluster, buried under the tragic guilt of her own damnable confession.

As if the perception needed reinforcement, Margaret noticed how Jessie Wilson almost fainted with astonishment at the beginning of their summer holiday at Rothiemay when the living image of her beloved daughter turned up on the doorstep. No-one needed to say it and Duff herself was fully aware of the impression she made. Loving reverence in her grandmother's gasp spoke volumes to authenticate Margaret's envy.

Her aunties and uncles liked nothing better than to celebrate Duff's legendary mother by talking up the resemblance. Kate Robertson told them blandly she'd idealistically named her three year old daughter after their adored step sister – Hannah's mother.

"I wis a pushover at the time," explained Ewan, "We agreed that one afore she even got pregnant, didn't we hen? I think if I'd said no she'd ha' foun' another man! She loved yer ma that much." Ewan had also followed in the footsteps of his adoptive brother by not bending to convention by getting married.

"Well I hope the child has better fortune in her life than Hannah Harper," Margaret said coldly, "Some families crave a bairn and others treat them like dolls bought in a toy shop in the town."

Iron vehemence lay behind her fine pale complexion and tightly plaited tresses. This was the one and only time Margaret gave a hint that Hannah Wilson Drummond Harper had taken her into complete confidence from the outset. Harper the local hero was above the politics of ecstasy but Jessie, clearly gobsmacked had nothing to say at all. The whole family stared at Margaret across the vast dining table, not daring to question her statement - wondering at her hidden depths and if she was maybe just a little crazy for obviously hating Duff.

The cause of Margaret's rage, Duff's likeness to her mother, lay in the teenager's movements - swift graceful turns and the sweep of long skirts. It was in easy smiles energising her face with ribbing, conspiratorial humour. Above all reminiscence flowed from the glint of dark green eyes and a voice that even in speaking quietly, which Duff invariably did – still sounded like warm laughter. On occasions when Duff sat down to play the Bechstein with Fiona, who was taking lessons from Mrs Payton, Margaret almost swooned with inarticulate regret. She told Harper in private, "I never minded being a stand-in John. But now I feel I'll always be second best."

Shaken by the depth of her alacrity, Harper floundered for the appropriate response. All he could find to say was, "You're not a stand-in, Margaret. You're the woman I love and want to spend the rest of my days with."

Despite his reassurance, jealousy curled and jaundiced Margaret's pleasant features like leaves of a yellowing chestnut in a dry month. It put a hard edge on her voice and drove her to solitariness and dispute.

Aloof and long-suffering in the mode of the teenager he thought he'd left behind at the forge, Harper carried Margaret's unpredictable swings of temper dispassionately – not unlike his enormous golf bag.

As Duff's abilities strengthened with learning and experience she grew more confident in her own status. Her peers especially wanted to be approved by the gentle sage. Adult members of the wider family, Harper and Jessie included, respectfully prompted Duff's balanced thoughts and opinions.

Jeannie and Frank, Betsy, Elsie and Fiona, who had always adored her, began to treat her like a celebrity. Duff had nothing to prove. Her sweetness and intelligence won high appreciation from all the people who mattered to her - with the exception of Margaret, who simply couldn't compete. For Margaret, Duff was the monopole - the magnetic grounding of all her best intentions. Jeopardy lay in the fact that Margaret couldn't reject her without rejecting Harper. On the other hand, how could she embrace the girl without conceding her own compromised feelings? Unable to come to terms with her, Margaret increasingly kept Duff at arm's length – avoiding contact whenever possible. Worse was the fact that she consciously tried to divide Harper from Duff at every cut's turn. That wasn't as difficult as Margaret expected it to be as Duff advanced into teenage years, spending increasing amounts of time with friends. Both Harper and Duff were sensitive to the dynamics of Margaret's invidious attitude.

In the Easter holidays of 1907, as he prepared for the working day, Duff visited her father in the corner box room he used as a home office.

"If only she saw herself as others see her," Duff complained wearily, "She's gorgeous, Daddy! Much prettier than poor mammy was. She's foxy and funny and she adores you! Why does she feel that I'm her rival? She has a phobia we should pity. You need to help her."

"Humph . . . in the first place, you're too inexperienced to know what attracts a man. Pretty is temporal, beauty eternal. Your mother was the most attractive woman I've ever seen in my life, Duff," Harper declared. His expression carried a word of caution for his daughter, never to quote that opinion.

That evening he tried to lay down the law in a priestly manner but it served only to concretise the alignment of a triangular relationship, "This is not a problem of Duff's making," he told Margaret quietly, "You have to treat her fairly – as an individual in her own right. It's as simple as that. Your jealousy is detestable and unkind." Margaret stood wounded, still in her nurse's uniform, tears filling indignant eyes.

"I have never been unkind to Duff. What on earth are you talking about?

"You don't know what I'm talking about?" he repeated sceptically, "You drive her away with mealy mouthed resentment, then scold her every time she comes home late!"

"That's not true. She has her own friends! Duff *defies* me because you encourage her."

Harper let her defence hang in the air, determined to make his point.

"*She* defies you? You see *self-expression* as defiance. She told me you hate her, that you avoid her," he said with stripped sentiment.

"You know why! If she even frowns at me I feel guilty," Margaret yelled in response to his accusation by proxy.

"Then ask Dr Foxworthy to set up a meeting with Ford Robertson the Psychiatrist!" said Harper, knowing there would never be resolution to such perverse alienation, "In the meantime I'll buy you a bike, or you can try filling my pipe with Indian Hemp."

"Why not drag me up tae Muschat's Cairn and strangle me by the roadside. It's no' far from where ye asked fer my hand in marriage . . . or ha'e ye conveniently forgotten that?" Margaret was crushed. It was the only time in a dozen years that John Harper had deliberately hurt her feelings. He knew that in days to come she would turn her shoulder from him. But over the years he'd grown used to that.

Hannah Harper walked alone through Holyrood Park towards Portobello with no idea of where she was going or why. School was out of the question today. She wasn't upset but needed time alone to think. Talking wouldn't touch it and her diary was not the right foil for this occasion. Besides, Duff knew that Margaret occasionally went into her drawer to take a look at what she had written.

Spring sunshine sparkled on the sea, highlighting a kaleidoscope of a million lapping ripples. In the distance a dozen or more cargo vessels plied in and out of the wide Forth estuary, their speed and direction marked by the only clouds in the sky. Duff took off her shoes and socks at a bench on the corner of the promenade and made for the cool sand. She wanted to explore a notion that had come to her more than once in the night, prompting the need for solitude and firm rationalisation in the cold light of day.

First she allowed bad temper to leave her, with the breeze racing into her face off the sea. Sitting on a wooden groyne Duff removed her hat and shoved it into her school bag. Adjusting clips to stop zephyrs flicking hair into her eyes she focussed on internal thoughts, ignoring the possibility of interaction with any of the handful of strangers walking along the shore.

I am alone. Ultimately we are all alone. Every one of us. We reach out to touch. To be embraced. But it is only when we accept the solitary nature of being that we begin to have compassion. Love is borne of loneliness and loss.

Duff smiled and walked back along the beach, satisfied with a positive outcome beyond persistent nightmares of uneasiness and negativity. She stopped outside the Spiritualist Meeting Hall on Bath Street, wondering why there was an attraction here. Her mother was talking to her maybe. And Great Gran Han and poor Elsie.

The horses. We need to go see the horses at the weekend. I'll ask Margaret tonight. In fact I will tell her that she's coming with me. Grandpa will be delighted.

At a grocers on the corner of Portobello High Street, Duff broke into her bus money for the week to buy carrots and a bag of large cooking apples. Walking briskly to a florist further along, she bought pink and yellow scented freesias decadently heat treated and imported from South Africa. Their sensational fragrance would delight Margaret, who Duff knew to be a simple soul despite her animosity. The intention was to repay unkindness with consideration. Hopping on the Leith tram for three stops, she had only to walk round the corner of Inchview Terrace to catch a bus up the hill to school.

When her class teacher demanded to know where she'd been Duff politely explained, "I had an important appointment that I couldn't miss but it really is a private matter."

Mrs Mercer scrutinised her moderately before replying, "Don't let it happen again Hannah, or I *will* speak to your parents."

"It won't, but thank you Mrs Mercer." The strangest things happened to girls at times; who could predict? It was important to build trust before probing. Mercer made a note of the event in her diary for future reference.

In spite of discrimination against girls there had always been extra school work for Duff. With indirect prompting, Harper had asked Margaret to visit Belle Vue back in '05. She discreetly requested that the Dominie, Mr Bruce, assign homework through subject teachers delivering the academic syllabus for boys. Bruce knew Mrs Harper's request was politically loaded. Their daughter was keen if not exceptional. Regardless, it was only a matter of time until he would be called to account by his Board and no doubt also by the press. His staff were not in fact 'delighted to oblige' as he falsely gushed to Margaret but he made a point of directing them to offer the same homework they would for boys, even if she might not understand it.

An hour later, after the meeting, Bruce smiled peevishly as he made the rounds to give bland direction. He expected Hannah Harper to struggle without formal grounding not on offer, yet he brooked no pessimistic discussion with staff.

"I will check on her progress," he told each of them, male and female alike, in turn. They were on notice to ensure it was done, "Expect more," was all he added by way of explanation. In the event Duff was given not only homework but attainment tests for the long summer holidays.

This controversial theme arose as frequently as any political topic, usually followed by disputes or at least strong differences of opinion. Margaret demanded of Duff in the coarse vernacular she tended to slip into along with loaded invective, "Why on earth d'ye want tae do school work when others are oot in the sun? Wait till yer my age lassie, ye'll ha'e had enough o' working," this just before she set off with Grandpa to the station, as she headed north on her own this time. "Go tae the Ceilidhs," Margaret added. "Find a man like Kate Robertson did. Dinnae end up on the shelf like Jeannie and the others. If you tell those farm boys ye speak French, they'll think ye have airs an' graces."

"You're perfectly right, Margaret. I'll make sure to strike a balance!" was all Duff said in response. But Margaret could have saved the invective. Duff was smart enough to see her education going nowhere. After all, she was a girl.

"What are you going to do when you leave school?" Harper asked one late summer evening, over his newspaper and reading glasses.

"I want to work for a bank," retorted Hannah without conviction, "Maybe with your connections you can set something up for me? After all its twenty eight years since Sophia Jex-Blake and her contemporaries broke into the all-male medical profession," she added in playful provocation.

With all her heart Duff wanted some day to be a University graduate with a good enough degree to qualify to study for an MA. She might study Literature, Languages or Economics, since Natural and Physical Sciences were effectively barred to women. But that undisclosed desire lay too close to her heart to be trampled upon in discussion with Margaret. Without him realising it, Harper's question had put her on the offensive. The dam was leaking.

"The University refused to award their degrees!" trumpeted Margaret in her sermonising tone, "Most decent men would refuse to go to a woman GP," she added, leaning forward to thread a line into the eye of her sewing machine.

During this difficult period Elizabeth had been frequently cited by Margaret as an ideal of how opportunity might be grasped, with presentation of the right feminine demeanour in conjunction with modest intelligence. Now she seized the opportunity to reinforce Harper's query. The implication of Margaret's advice was clear – like her sister, Duff had intelligence but needed reminding, "Polite feminine conduct is important and even that might land a woman doctor in trouble if taken the wrong way."

"You mean I should smile and speak with a plumb in my mouth, so I can get a job working as a domestic servant for some noble family?" queried Hannah disarmingly.

"Well yes, something along those lines," Margaret agreed tentatively.

The crack in Duff's mild disposition was spreading as irritation built into wrath. She knew well that Margaret's ideal of Elizabeth's situation in working as a Governess, advocated so frequently in the abstract, incorporated the notion of her leaving home.

At every opportunity Margaret felt free to enthusiastically praise Elizabeth, who didn't look anything like her mother and didn't trigger neurotic alienation.

Of course the oft cited Duke and Duchess of Hamilton – who had long since acquired the beloved status of close relatives - came into the equation too. According to Margaret's reductionist thinking, intelligence was simply the application of learning, "And Lady Mary saw that in your sister."

"Well I suppose that must be how she got to be a Duchess. Or at least one of her Hamilton forebears back in the thirteenth century," Duff remarked dryly.

"Precisely, they just made the mistake of not having enough children," said Margaret, deliberately alluding to another contentious issue.

"You mean *male* children," stated Duff, now on the brink of bursting with rage. The conversation ended there, to be re-visited at a later date. Harper folded his legs and lifted the broadsheet; Margaret rattled off a hem and Duff withdrew to her bedroom. Natural habit throughout her life had been to seek solitary refuge in meditation.

She lay on her bed staring at a photo of her mother surrounded by three majestically attired daughters. Duff had been barely three years old but even then there had been a visible resemblance. She smiled with satisfaction to remember the feel of green silk trimmed with black embroidered lace against her skin. No scion of aristocratic stock had ever been dressed more fashionably than the Harper girls. Duff's smile transformed into a rapturous laugh.

She found herself praying on her knees like an Episcopalian as she had been taught as a child. Shutting her eyes and placing fingers together, the teenager whispered doubts for her mother's consideration as though she was there right next to her in the room. Duff believed with all her heart that her mother Hannah was alive in another, higher realm. At times in the past when she'd cleared her mind to listen, Duff imagined her speaking in reply. Elsie had known it. Harper knew it.

Margaret knew of it. But what Hannah took as solace, her step-mother regarded as sorcery.

Contemplating her mother's presence, Duff reflected on gender biased views about intelligence. Margaret had a view that Duff was instinctually opposed to, yet there was no-one else to discuss it with. Now with knees trembling, itchy eyes tight shut and her forehead resting against the candlewick bedspread, other impressions faded at last.

Childhood images of Rothiemay flashed in rapid sequence through a sleepless reverie into Duff's mind. Hens and sheep; barking dogs, singing blackbirds and softly stirring Highland light flicked across the silver screen of internal memory. At last a half remembered tone of voice came back on a stunning wave of excitement. There before Duff stood her mother. Emerging recovered from her sick bed she held out welcoming arms, a smile of recognition on her face.

It goes deeper Duff – intelligence is not simply animal shrewdness. Life and learning may be one and the same struggle but the best use of your mind, dear child, is to enrich thinking itself.

Duff imagined Hannah advancing towards her to place a hand on her head then passing on instantly with the speed of light, leaving only thoughtful illumination behind. She was fully alert in an instant with eyes open.

What convinced her of the reality of her mother's spiritual attendance was a dreadful sense of loss, starkly contrasting an aura manifest in the room just moments before. Forfeiture made her want to follow, cry aloud for the conduit to remain open. She rolled onto the floor exhausted, still trying to recapture the authoritative wisdom glimpsed from higher consciousness.

Duff resolved to learn for herself – to read everything she could get her hands on, to 'enrich her mind.' The following day she asked Mrs Mercer her English teacher if she could join the Literary Society at school. Mercer already thought the world of Duff and said she would be delighted to direct her reading. For years she had attempted to inculcate in Hannah's class a sense of the paramount importance of education and freedom of thought.

"They are opposite sides of the same coin," she told Duff again, "If you will allow me to stretch the metaphor, they lead to the only valid success in the world."

"Yes Miss, I know, but it helps if you already have the coin!" Duff observed with a wry smile.

"Indeed Miss Harper, wealth does tend to make doors open," agreed her mentor, "But if you have none there is always the library."

One true friend, Isabella Stuart, who normally sat beside her in class, lived nearby on Lilyhill Terrace. Isabella was the best possible foil for Duff's commitment and all she learned. They went to the library together, practiced conversational foreign languages, talked about family and gossiped about boys. Mature for her years, Isabella was discreet but at times outrageously funny. Above all she was ambitious and capable.

Duff started to read newspapers Harper had delivered to the house, at first removing them from the waste bin to sneak up to her bedroom after he'd finished with them. Predictably, Margaret noticed and interfered, making sure The Scotsman was promptly used to light fires or wrap potato peelings.

Despite the gift of freesias and subsequent trip to see the ponies at Spylaw, it was evident that a siege mentality had developed at some point without Hannah being aware when or why war had been declared. All she knew was that it began around the time of the arrival of the brass-eyed monster that conveyed Harper to work on rainy days.

Duff's intermittent access to the national daily helped her form nascent political views. It became clear that the latter part of the first decade of the 20th Century was a time of fervid social change, demanding huge investment on the back of political reform. In relative naiveté and isolation, Duff's internal dialogue was the best foil for resolving these perceptions but she and Isabella also saw the evidence with their own eyes. Walking through crowds of vagrants around Canongate and on a trip out to the Hansom Cab asylum at Craiglockhart for a recruitment taster day, they caught glimpses of both derelict and destitute souls there and at the nearby workhouse. In parallel to the massive industry of the burgeoning city and worldwide markets it catered for, there was an enormous burden of abysmal health care and the most desperate poverty.

Following a brief chat with the senior matron, they had set off with a nursing sister to view the geriatric wards but got no further than a connecting corridor where some poor soul had defecated copiously in the middle of the floor. The nurse had left them to take a fifty yard detour through another entrance off the courtyard and gone off to find a cleaner.

As they waited on a bench in the hospital grounds for three other girls more interested in leaving school early to finish chatting with overworked medical staff, Isabella queried what Duff had gleaned since starting to read the daily papers.

"Hmm, *bloody* good question. I'm not at all sure. The thing is Is, *ideas* seem more dangerous than the very worst excesses of human behaviour." Duff paused to let the message sink in.

"Okay, I like it, but give examples please."

"The strength of populist movements –Suffrage and Labour for a start - depends more on press coverage than who actually makes the most sense."

"So, examples?"

"So, they quote outraged idiots with a stick up their arse who want to deny us the vote. Judges and local councillors. Politicians who don't want things to move too fast, even for people suffering desperate neglect like we've seen today. "

"Oh, yeah. God help those poor old bastards. And these people here are the *well to do!*"

"Quite so, Is – imagine life in Craig House Asylum, even with poultry and pigs for some of the patients to manage. The ratio of medical staff to inmates is impossible and conditions are squalid. The fact is we live in a brutally heartless society."

"How does that relate to what you're saying about news?" Is stretched long legs out in front of her on the bench, as she threw pieces of a lunchtime corned beef sandwich to a squirrel hiding behind a Beech tree.

"Well the clearest example is the reality that strident anti-feminism gets more press coverage than any women's political movement."

"Ho, you do have the extended code. What the hell is strident ant-feminism?"

"Dinnae be dense, ya glaikit hallion. An' stop feeding meat to a fickin' herbivore. What you have to understand is that our time is characterised by aggressive, reactionary politics - of men shouting loudly, rather than listening."

Is offered Duff a bite of her sandwich, which she accepted gratefully.

"Hasn't it always been this way?"

"No, I'm not sure. Things change imperceptibly. The whole point of being well informed is that it lulls you into riding the crest of the wave. But what I believe is that things are critical right now. Ordinary people have had enough."

"Why now? You heard what the matron said about Darian House Hospital?"

"No, I wasn't listening. It sounded like patter – you mean *Bedlam*, and the death of the poet Robert Ferguson?"

"Exactly, this is your point though, she said things have changed immensely for the good since then, Duff."

"Oh Is, don't be taken in so easily. Why d'ye think they invited us here today? No medical doctor worth their salt wants to work in a place like this . . . and anyway, this disgusting shite hole is just one example of what I mean. The same problem extends to everything in the public realm. They throw money at a problem rather than sit down and plan how to really solve it."

"Well, at least *they* throw the money in the first place."

"Yes, because the proceeds of a budget always find their way back to the people in control. Besides, the elite don't throw *their* money Is, they throw *tax payer's* money."

"Wow, that's dead dodgy – you mean all the politicians have their noses in the trough?"

"I mean noses, trunks, beaks, bills . . ."

"Balls, arses and feet?" Duff's invective was shattered by a release of hilarious laughter, with both her and Is laughing so much they almost cried.

At last deceivingly pleasant voices came from behind, as their three school friends emerged from the office area of Craig House, each carrying a buff envelope containing an application form. Duff and Is rose as one to greet the others. Neither gave any hint of the deeply troublesome impressions they had just been discussing.

In response to Margaret's default use of the Scotsman, Duff developed a purposive routine in which she rose early to take Harper a cup of tea and the morning newspaper. Later when he'd cast it aside or agreed that there was no time to read it in the office, Duff would hide it in her school bag to read later. Soon a sense of critical irony began to develop in her conversation, which Harper noticed with pleasure. He started to smilingly encourage her, occasionally discussing main articles in the news.

The Scotsman, Edinburgh's creditable national newspaper was always punchy, declamatory, and thorough in investigative style.

"Like a successful illusionist with a discreet private life, it appears more left field than its naturally conservative readership," he explained to Duff thoughtfully, much to Margaret's chagrin.

"What accounts for its perennial success, is their ability to predict a mood of blustering resignation. People read it, talk about its fulminating articles then let off steam themselves. It's always safe to radicalise readership when there's no need for any of them to take decisions or assume responsibility for outcomes."

"So Daddy, The Scotsman is a safety valve for a nation boiling with resentment and frustration?" ventured Duff. Harper smiled affectionately at her, shaking his head as Margaret bit back on her anger, "You're too damned clever for your own good, child," he teased.

"You can say that again," Margaret added in a grumbling tone.

Duff noticed that Margaret coloured with embarrassment, almost choking on a mouthful of food. The playful instinct to reach out and pat her back faded with disappointment, as it struck Duff that her step-mother always sat on the opposite side of the table. Unlike many adolescents, Duff acknowledged that her own deep craving for affection tended to make her feel morose.

Through exposure to constructive discussion initiated by Harper at mealtimes, Duff began to develop a sense of hopeful idealism overlying her own intuitive insight. In her teenager's way she thought she saw through the entire square, greedy system.

"Genuine issues of Scottish Nationalism, as well as questions of individual rights and freedoms are not being addressed by the Westminster Government," she told Harper blandly at their next evening mealtime, as if he didn't know it. Harper smiled as he challenged his daughter to say what she would do about it.

"Well it's essential to have a voice. Working people need political affiliation beyond the main political parties, otherwise they tend to codify opinion into their own dogmatic canon and ignore the public."

"Ha, ha, isn't that the truth. Political pressure groups in other words. And how would you advocate the conduct of the discussion outside of Parliament?"

"In the press of course. I don't know enough about History but I imagine there must have always been a middle way in politics, provided the debate on reform was honest and inclusive. Otherwise wouldn't we still be living in the Dark Ages?"

"Hmm, did you find one of your mother's books on Buddhism?"

Margaret blanched but said nothing. She was awaiting an opportunity for them to stop speaking in generalities. Margaret's confidence lay in simple, moralising tenets of hard work coupled with ritual observance. Eventually the conversation would turn her way.

"Yes, Daddy I did read them. And I do think progress is a matter of listening to opposing views and searching for compromise, a form of dialectic Buddhism if you like," she looked to Margaret for acceptance but saw only the glassy eyes of ignorance.

"And would your religious pacifism, or whatever it is you advocate, work against the repressive Russian Monarchy with their Okhrana? How would you respond if they took your money for union affiliation then threw you in jail because they've infiltrated the leadership? Or worse still, slaughter hundreds of innocent protestors like they did in St Petersburg a couple of years ago?"

"No, perhaps it won't work but life here isn't that bad. If you can't have what you want there are always alternatives. Edinburgh is a place of alternatives." Harper smiled warmly, reaching out to take Duff's hand. In her naïveté she had learned very little about vested interests.

To complement emerging political awareness, Duff also discovered a developing sense of History. Increasingly Harper looked forward to engaging with her after mealtimes as a way of encouraging that mutual interest. Kicking back one evening he filled his pipe with the curtain parted and a window open to the summer air. Margaret brought him a glass of Malt and he invited her to pour herself a drink and sit too. His appreciative eyes followed her exquisite form as she crossed the room. Harper encouraged Duff to settle with them and talk about anything that was on her mind.

"I don't entirely blame the English for Scotland's failure as a great nation," she informed him, "Rather, the fault lies in our deep social division."

With a smile Harper endorsed her opinion wholeheartedly, telling the story of The Clearances – something she knew had been glossed over in school History lessons.

"Go on," he prompted, thoughtfully sucking his briar pipe. Margaret listened indulgently, perhaps silently evaluating notions she had never thoroughly explored before.

"Division lay in the Highlander's association with the Irish, I think."

"Hah, there's a popular view!"

"I mean in respect to their tendency to pursue the lost causes of Old Religion. The smartest people are often the most naturally conservative don't you agree?"

"Oh, so you retain a high opinion of the Irish?"

"Hmm, this'll be due to that Journalist from Edinburgh," chimed Margaret, between sips of Sherry from a tiny crystal liqueur glass, "You remember, the Temperance Lady who campaigned for women's education."

"Ha, yes let me think!" said Harper, "I know who you mean Margaret, Isabella Tod, the Suffragist. Is Margaret right, Duff?"

"Yes, you're both right and Margaret Byers, the Liberal Educationalist," Duff agreed with enthusiasm.

"I remember, the one awarded the honorary Law degree a couple of years ago, from Belfast University?" Harper recalled with a smile.

"Dublin, Daddy."

"Oh . . . I could have sworn she lived in Belfast."

"It was Trinity College Dublin who awarded her the degree."

"Okay, I stand corrected."

"Ha, ha! You don't know everything," said Margaret gleefully. She stood up to refill her tipple, warming at least to the fortified wine, if not the conversation.

"Then there was Ann Jellicoe. We mustn't forget her. She opened up Alexandra College and the opportunity for women to get into Royal University," said Harper, having fallen straight into the trap. In a roundabout way Duff was presenting her case without having to open the debate.

Margaret looked at Harper and shook her head just once. Duff seamlessly turned the subject back to Irish History, before Margaret lured her into provocation, "Yes, despite their opportunism the fighting Irish never had stability at home, yet they were the traders and mercenaries of Europe. Mrs Mercer says if they weren't England's first colony, England would be Ireland's first colony."

This time Harper laughed aloud at Duff's incisiveness, "So you think there's an underlying affinity between the two countries?"

"Of course, dating back into the mists of time, probably before the Kingdom of the Two Cities."

"What do you mean, Belfast and Dublin?" queried Margaret, content to sit back with her second glass now, pretty legs folded under her backside on the sofa.

"No, Dublin and York I think she means, Lovecurls, a thousand year old Norse Kingdom that lasted over three hundred years," Harper observed lightly. He tasted his Macallan, trying to recall what little else he knew.

"I don't think I ever heard of that . . . were they the Goddodin?"

"Ah, now you're talking," said Harper, launching into an explanation of Scotland's oldest heroic poem and how it was written by a Welshman named Williams.

Glad for once to talk and loosely picking up the theme, Margaret went on to hazard whether Williams might have been a Jewish tailor like Zach. Following a complex time of tension, laughter and light entered their home again on the back of Duff's optimism. But there was still potential for dispute. In contrast to views held by Elizabeth and Margaret, Duff expressed distaste for all forms of monarchy and aristocracy, "The legal investment of Sovereignty in the hands of any one individual, symbolic or elected, is a Procrustean Bed."

Margaret laughed aloud, "What on earth does that mean? Are you talking about crusts of bread handed out to the poor, or just talking a foreign bloody language?"

"No, steady on my love, it's a Minoan Legend Duff is referring to, about forced conformity," Harper explained, tapping out his pipe in the ashtray, "One size never fits all."

Richly aromatic tobacco smoke filled the room. Duff rose to pin back the open window, letting in soft fragrant air from the woodland margin beyond the wall of the park.

"So it's not just Catholics you don't like? It sounds like you are a Republican?" Margaret demanded with a raised brow, looking like she might take personal offence.

"No, you're right as a matter of fact. Both Royalists and Unionists seem to betray their own cause. They even show a lack of historical awareness."

"How so? History's all that Orangemen ever talk about!" pronounced Margaret fiercely.

"No, that's not a sense of history. They celebrate events reminding people of wickedness and confusion in the past."

"So they're in danger of becoming another outmoded lost cause?" asked Harper with genuine interest.

"Just so . . . all that matters nowadays is equal opportunity and justice, not constant gloating over the outcome of a hopeless rebellion crushed more than a hundred and sixty years ago. These intolerant people reinforce division, teaching the young to hate, instead of seeking common ground."

"I thought you said the Irish were smart?" Margaret reminded her.

"I think they are, despite all the jokes about them. Many Irish families settled in parts of England – Newcastle, Yorkshire, Liverpool and London. They built all the canals, railways and roads. But Orangemen are not culturally Irish Margaret, they're Scottish." Margaret laughed in astonishment at Duff, who shrugged her shoulders disarmingly.

"But surely you don't want to depose poor old Bertie?"

"Maybe. Why should I be subject to a profligate drinker, gambler and womaniser? Besides he seems to think we're all Socialists now." Margaret's jaw dropped.

"Never! What a tangled web we all weave. The *King* is a Socialist? But what's the point in studying History then, if we all have equal rights?"

Duff had become the prodigy they all imagined her to be as a small child. She had a firm grasp on the building blocks of analytical thinking that any undergraduate would have set store by. Delighting in the harmony of engagement, she decided to allow Margaret the last word.

"Where are you going young lady?" snapped Margaret as soon as she rose, "Pour me a sherry and tell me this Minoan legend aboot the bed, Honey Bee. I want tae hear aw the steamy details."

Harper laughed freely, noting how Margaret loosened up with a drink in her.

What worried and oppressed Duff as a young observer were limitations she saw imposed upon ordinary folk everywhere. Poverty and ignorance, ill health, alcoholism and violence seemed ubiquitous. Following in Harper's footsteps she cast doubt on conventional thinking promoted in the press as an antidote to increasingly widespread social disruption. In many ways Harper was the typical conservative Scotsman reader, less vocal now he rubbed shoulders with the Great and the Good. It seemed to Hannah most of what she read amounted to sanctimonious moralising. What was clear was that the wealth of nations was built on the suffering of an endless army of poor and elderly.

Despite the shock of this discovery and perhaps due to an absence of external influences other than the redoubtable Harper, in her fifteenth year Duff was already a very smart, freethinking individual. Her sparkling eyes shone with humorous enthusiasm, especially since Margaret began to gradually moderate her egocentric rivalry. It seemed to friends that Duff's face was constantly ready to erupt in laughter. Several boys her age at Bellevue High School were already besotted by her irresistible charisma.

Chapter Nine   *Lamb's to the Slaughter*

Willie, Walter and Jim fought and gambled out of sight for the chance of carrying Duff's books. They took the blame for whispering about her in assembly services, causing an outburst of laughter that annoyed the Head teacher. Willie Proven, Walter Chalmers and Jim Dick could not have been christened by their doting, worthy parents with more naively inappropriate, nor perennially embarrassing names.

Willie, son of a Potato Merchant was tall and fair, athletically balanced, tough and handsome. He had a reputation for using fists in a flash against blatant unaccepted use, or any imagined play of words upon his proud name. His reaction might depend on borderline misuse of the middle phoneme in the word 'Moon' as opposed to the third phoneme in the word 'frog'. That is to say in context of the mistaken use of his name 'proven' as in a case presented in a court of law, as opposed to Proven rhyming with 'oven.' Daring brinkmanship on the part of certain classmates constantly led to trouble. In any event retributional violence could not protect him from deliberate misuse by masters.

Occasionally the Dominie, or Rector and in particular Dan Thompson the Physical Education Master, reversed Christian and surnames when conducting a roll call. Thompson deliberately milked the opportunity to raise a laugh, intentionally using the abbreviated first name as his gaze fell on the lad. He knew it would fire Proven up for a match of any kind as his natural, pugilistic captain. Willie boiled at the sardonic attention drawn from his peers. Throughout his school years Dan's calling of 'Proven Willie' with a straight face and no pause was cue for other boys to giggle and bait the lad. If they laughed too much and it led to a fight, they would be first under the cold showers after the game.

Willie wasn't so straight backed that he would go to the masters to insist upon always being called William. He advocated informality but sighed with relief when they used his full Christian name. Connotations for ridicule seemed interminable to Willie especially from older, bigger boys.

Then in teenage years as he grew tall and lank, innuendos started to come from girls. All of a sudden the Black Swan of crazy fortune was cast in a different light. Suddenly Willie had the antidote to inflammation filling his brain with vehemence, making his fists permanently curl. He could turn it around and use it.

Willie started to pronounce upon the conjunction of his name with a reputation for manly prowess, like a weather beaten Viking of a hundred raids. He became sage and raconteur, standing tall at the centre of the crowd - though Willie's fist might still flash out, into an unbridled mouth.

Jim Dick, son of an Abbeyhill motor mechanic had always been a harder nut to crack emotionally. The other kids saw it and left him alone. Smaller than Willie, Jim was nonetheless trim and athletic – a natural born fly-half with a reputation for riding tackles.

"I'm gonny be a Journalist when I get oot o' this place Wull, so I'll need a thick skin tae get alongside people, ken? Ah dinnae gi' a jig if they rip the pish oot o' ma name – it might he'p tae break the ice when I go after a story."

"You stick wi' me just the same pal. I need people around me who'll sympathise an' report back on bastards steppin' o'er the line."

'What a Charmer!' by comparison was still small and sallow at fourteen. Walter Chalmers was the Tailor's son. Open-faced, gentle and assiduous, he made the most loyal companion. The three friends complemented one another. Walter helped Willie with homework, Willie defended Walter from bullies and Jim kept his ear to the ground for calumnies and vilification behind their backs.

Well into his first major growth spurt by the summer of '07, Willie at fourteen began to make great play on aspersions cast by all and sundry about other unusual names - regularly triggering hilarity with some item gleaned from a history lesson, the daily paper, or a newly published telephone book.

In his naïveté Willie thought wrongly that the ability to make others laugh might impress Duff. Typically he would launch into laddish conversation as he waited for her in the street, with mention of names more preposterous than his own.

"Reginald Bastard," he stated coolly. Taken unawares Duff howled with outrageous laughter. Willie tried hard to keep a straight face.

"Never, I do *not* believe you! And that breaks the rules Willie, making it up. And in any case it's a bad word, so don't repeat it please!"

Willie whipped out the newspaper cutting taken from the obituary column of the Times. He watched her with an exculpatory smile as she read, saying over and again in his mind, 'Please love me Duff, as much as I love you. I'm funny and smart and look I even read the Times for you! Yes, yes!'

"Oh God, the poor man!" exclaimed Duff.

"What? He was eighty-four! He'd had a good innings."

"No – silly," She slapped him on the upper arm, "I mean imagine how the poor man felt being called Mr Bastard all his life, with idiots like you taking their end."

"How dye do?" parodied Willie with a posh accent, offering Duff his hand, "I'm Mr Bastard . . . But would you mind awfully just calling me Reggie?"

She laughed disarmingly, flicking long brown hair out of her eyes, shaking her head but beaming at the rogue. Willie loved her so much he felt himself colouring red with embarrassment. Duff took his hand as part of their play. So innocent was she that Willie could have jumped on her right there on London Road, with a dozen passers by watching.

As they neared Bellevue School a coterie of friends merged to read Willie's scandalous cutting, each of them in turn howling with disbelief.

"Here's another," signalled Walter, with characteristic composure. Walter waited till the girl's adulation for Willie subsided a little before taking out a business card from a locally based English architect. He explained ponderously about his dad planning a warehouse extension to cater for increased demand from the new housing estates over by Newhaven.

"Get tae the fickin' point Walter," counselled Archie Soutar, one of Willie's tough fellow travellers.

"Sorry pal, just tryin' tae improve ma comic timing."

"You were born nonsensical Walter. Ye couldnae be any funnier if ye tried," submitted Souter, himself an aspiring comedian.

Walter handed the card to Archie who stumbled over the reading and never quite made the obvious connotation, "Ih? . . . Richard . . . Richard Pry . . . Price is it, Walter?"

"Gimme that ya numpty," ordered Jim, snatching the card from the younger boy, "Sometimes I think I'm the on'y literate one in the entire bloomin' school."

Jim's freckled face clouded for a second as he read Walter's contribution. Oh I ger it! P-r-y-c – maybe he's called Prike but the letter y sounds like 'ih' - like in *wychelm*. The letter c is as in *camisole*," he explained, with a wink and leering glance at Duff.

Two or three of Willie's female admirers tittered at Jim's reference to underwear and moved in close to their hero.

"So, I infer from my well reported aptitude from working Latin conjugation - that people who don't know the man might think it says 'prick' – 'Dick Prick' in fact."

Willie whipped the card out of Jim's hand and turning to Walter smiled down at his best friend, "I like that, Walter. Norman English mebbes, or Welsh? Well done for finding a professional dignitary who might want tae ji'n our club man! I think that's outstanding by the way."

A ripple of approving laughter ran through Willie's gang - mostly girls a year or two younger, likely to burst into flames if he even smiled at them. Two or three other boys queued up to examine the business card and newspaper cutting, grinning as they peered over Walter's shoulder. Walter beamed in the light of Willie's approval.

"Aye, thanks Wull. I'll bet they builders workin' fer ma da gi'd the poor man a hard time."

"Nae doot aboot it man . . . 'Dick Prick' . . . Whit a fickin' handle ih? Beats the one Gavin Walker found in the paper last week – what wis it again, Jim? Hedley Cockshott? "

"Aye hilarious man! It conjures up visions o' accurately guided ejaculation."

A couple of younger camp followers made an instant vaudeville of pretending to do just that, until Willie threatened to skite them 'for being rude in front of the lassies.' Evidently use of the foulest language and worst behaviour, like all the other good things in life, was the preserve of those with pretentions to authority.

"Aye, an' that wee fella in the first year whassisname - Eric Boocock?" Walter prompted.

"Aye yousuns, dinnae keep rippin' the pish outay him, ken . . . aw that shite about him hiding 'ahint bushes in the park wi' 'is parsnip oot. Must be hurtful fer the poor boy."

"Aye, ah ken fine Wull," said Jim, "Ye wouldnae want the wee stalker tae get a complex aboot 'is name!"

Willie handed the card to Duff for perusal without looking at her. He felt that he could only look at her so much without falling on his knees to beg her to be his girl forever.

Once again Duff bubbled her regal laugh. All Willie's girlfriend admirers, by default Duff's aspirational ladies-in-waiting who planned to marry well by association – three or four of them who even at eight thirty a.m. trailed everywhere in Willie's wake - laughed with Duff on cue. There was general hilarity as the card was passed among other boys and girls, gravitating to the bunch near the school entrance.

"Which is worse Walter? Reginald Bastard, or Dick Prick?" asked Willie.

"Mine I think Wull – Dick Prick. It's more derogatory ken? At least if yer just a bastard ye retain some vestige o' egotistical pride, even if everyone who calls ye that evidently does hate ye."

"Aye thurs a few o' them aboot!"

"Exactly my point. Dick Prick on the other hand is a double insult of Chaucerian quality. There can be no mistake aboot the intended vulgarity o' it. It raises imagery not on'y o' insults hurled by a wronged woman in unthinking fury at a man but also the purulence of his overused appendage."

"Thanks a lot, Walter. How d'ye think that makes me feel?" said Jim.

"Sorry, I thought ye' didnae care aboot folk laughin' at yer name?"

"I was referring tae yer use of English ye wee mugger."

"That's true though Walter, ah couldnae ha' put it better mysel'. Full points tae Walter then Duff?" asked Willie as they walked away towards the boy's entrance.

"Full points to all of you for Chaucerian quality," she agreed, heading for the girl's line up at the other side of the yard.

"Last man . . . don't get caught wi' that card in assembly! Plausible deniability will no' save Walter frae the tawse if his name is mentioned," Willie called over his shoulder to the still quietly scandalised group of followers, all with cheesy grins on their faces.

"Yeah, yeah we ken fine big man . . . you'll find out who grassed and' there'll be consequences," Archie quoted from a well-known script.

"I like you Souter. You catch on fast," concluded Willie with a seditious wink.

Together with their beloved Duff and her pal Isabella, Walter, Willie and Jim were a caucus for every kind of confident social initiative. They exemplified an unlikely combination of interests, reflecting diverse backgrounds. Friendship for each was motivated as much by reciprocal interest brought to the circle as by what each individual saw in Duff. She was the unconscious catalyst because she was gregarious, kind and maternal. Children of unrecognised petite bourgeoisie growing into a world of polarised ideals, with stark extremes of poverty and plenty visible on every street, these friends agreed they were taken for granted as much as the hardcore in the roads.

They sat smoking and drinking among the yellow flowering summer whin above Queen's Drive, setting the world to rights. Is pointed out that the most demoralising element was the fact that parents were obliged to pay for education beyond Elementary level and in exchange expected humility and fear of failure, "My ma and da separated ten years ago. He teaches at a lycee in Paris and says it's all free if you can get in." She didn't mention the fact that her mother would struggle to pay her fees if she stayed on.

Trepidation was reinforced regularly with all kinds of moralising, often Biblical invective from parents and teachers that could never be qualified or argued. The friends had heard it all before but Jim especially loved to parody, perhaps dreading winter mornings with freezing fingers stuck to a grimy engine block,

"If you dinnae get oot o' bed in the mornin' ye'll end up in the City Poorhouse!" he shrieked, quoting his ma. Willie laughed like a drain but Walter's eyes fixed in fear, as though recalling some indescribable avatar.

"If ye were in the Poorhouse ye'd no complain aboot ha'ein mince an' tatties every day!" chimed Is, to general approval. Willie as ever missed the point, advocating different pie crusts rolled and baked over a deep plate.

"If ye were spiking recovered hemp in the Poorhouse, none of you would ever shrink frae hard work!" offered Duff with the hesitant metre of Weston, the school rector. They frequently mocked but on the whole subscribed passively to a system most had come to despise.

On the back of the hard invective, easy solutions were strongly advocated in terms of planning a career. Mr Brunton, the Careers Teacher, did not make a habit of indulging an open discussion leading to an evaluation of interests and talent. His guiding philosophy was, 'any job's a good job and it should never take more than five minutes to choose one.' Guidance consisted of, "Here's my list of suggestions. I think you should do this." Any reservations were silenced by the authoritative swirl of his scrupulously chalk-free master's gown.

There was the Army or the Polis for lads if they showed some respect and could follow orders. Girls, if they *really* wanted to work until they married, were steered towards opportunities in teaching or domestic service – if, as Margaret kept insisting, they were 'personable enough.' Failing entry into one of the professions or a vocational calling, there was always factory work - machine minding, blowing of bottles or casting of bricks. Brunton optimistically pointed to the recent trauma of the Boer War and a potential increase in hospital building with opportunities in nursing. A massive budgetary deficit and countless tragic cost to the nation was still lamented with stiff upper lip but soon there would be a trickle-down effect from all that colonial commerce and booty – mountains of gold and diamond. With sage, humanistic understanding of all things purposive in the world of economic transaction, Brunton also had expert advice to offer any lad who got a girl in trouble while waiting for Lady Luck to call, "The port of Leith is two miles down the hill son, and if that's too close for comfort, the Port of Glasgow is a short train ride away."

"Rumour has it that the man's got 'is ain commission network an' slush fund," ventured Jim.

"Oh God aye, just coont the num'er o' lads who've disappeart," Willie agreed knowingly, "He got my brother Errol intae Newtongrange as a shearer."

The friends stared at Willie as he sat on a log sucking his beer, wondering if Errol had been lost in the winding house fire back in '03.

Coincidentally it seemed, schools and education had become the subject of fierce political debate around the time of Hannah's projected leaving. Barely five years previously parents had demonstrated against James Gillespie's School continuing limited fee paying access for girls, although Hannah and Is both wanted to go there. They knew that Suffragettes had picked up the theme of equal rights, seeing fit to set fire to the new academy annexe. The general populace wanted free access for all to Further and Higher Education. Hopefully that would spell the end for elitist Academies. Nonetheless, as the school year drew to a close, Duff pleaded with Harper to let her attend St Margaret's or James Gillespie's, both of which he could easily afford. But when he told her, Margaret saw the request as a blatant challenge to her personally.

For her step-mother, Duff's disaffection with the normal path was maudlin and potentially dangerous. It also meant she would remain dependant for longer. Margaret was determined to see the back of Duff before getting pregnant with Harper's child. Somewhere along the line, her ideal had transmuted into obsession.

Hannah's acme report card lay on the table between them as the Harpers drank an afternoon cuppa, still in their respective uniforms – Harper a touch corpulent in white shirt and red braces; Margaret grubby and gaunt from a long shift at the Infirmary. After too much casual scrutiny of her attainments Duff had retreated to get a cup of tea for herself.

"She should accept her lot, come down to earth. She's just a plain Jane, so fancy education won't do her any good," Margaret declared with inimitably caustic style, as Hannah listened in.

Although she was no fool Margaret could never win an argument with either of them. Now the tables were turned. Duff's needs were vehemently cancelled out by Margaret in a no-prisoners declaration, "Two more years at a fee paying school? Are you bloody joking? You need to stop making demands on other people young lady and take responsibility for yourself! Just get on and find a job, like I had to at your age!"

Duff's smile faded but she withdrew with characteristic dignity. This chasm was predictable but still shocked deeply as it finally ruptured between them. Up in her cold bedroom Duff thought of her mother again, gazing at an empty fire grate.

Remembering a time long ago when loneliness mortified her in spite of vain hope, she wept silently for the love of Great Gran who had consoled her then. Duff could hear again the resounding melody of a sweetly played piano sweeping through the rooms of her memory. She didn't break though – instead she felt inspired. Suddenly she could see the face and hear the voice, which the act of simply trying to remember could never regenerate. Her mother was there in her mind's eye. Duff held her breath, sitting perfectly still for fear the impression might be interrupted or lost. The image became stronger, less dream-like and less fleetingly ephemeral.

Shutting her eyes she imagined them there – Hannah, Great Gran and Elsie as clear as day. The shock of that impression was tangible but Duff kept her eyes shut. These were her best teachers - her true advocates. She could hear them speaking, asking what she wanted, soliciting her to think sincerely - then do whatever felt right.

Duff found herself speaking aloud, "Thank you Mammy! Thank you Great Gran! Elsie!" With her eyes still firmly shut, she saw herself again as a child running to hug them. Belief in their watchfulness healed the greatest hurt in her young life – the knowledge that all faith in Margaret had been spurned, rolled into a ball and thrown back in her face. Duff might forgive Margaret - but would never truly respect her again.

The impression of a spiritual presence was so strong that Duff began to seek the same ethereal contact again each evening before she went to sleep. Interest was not borne so much of loneliness or isolation within her family as the strong impulse to experiment consciously in an area that fascinated her. Indifferent to Margaret's animosity, Duff was convinced that the spiritual contact was real.

After a week or so of the same strong impressions she discreetly arranged for Is to come up into her bedroom, to discuss the experience. Isabella Stuart was standing where Duff imagined Elsie to have been just half an hour before, "This is happening because I am open to it, Is. Mammy and Great Gran are active because I need them," she revealed.

"Jingbang jings Hannah Duff, that's truly scary!"

"It's anything but scary, Is. It's inspirational. I always talked to them daily when I prayed. Praying just gradually merged into a style of active psychic communication."

"Oh! You're serious. You think they still exist in some parallel dimension?" Isabella folded her lanky frame onto the corner of the bed, looking alarmed.

"Why shouldn't I? Our entire religious culture teaches eternal life. But you can walk all day and not find a single soul who actually believes in it."

"Oh, I think lots of people believe it but what about all the 'earthbound spirits' hoo ha Weston prattles on about?"

Hannah ignored the question because it seemed irrelevant to her situation. Instead she told Is what she really wanted to know: "I spend the time tuning into images or impressions from the past without specific thoughts or emotion, to prevent what might be my own superimposed direction. It's like listening to music without humming. I carry a question or doubt at the back of my mind which always draws an answer."

"So what do you plan to do with this amazing knowledge, Duff?"

"I intend to continue, Is. This may be the single most important thing I have learned in my entire life. I need to find out more."

Duff knew immediately what to do about the overstated opinions of 'the loud mouth,' as she came to think of Margaret. Paderewski the virtuoso pianist was coming to town and Duff planned to buy two tickets. She had money saved and knew Harper would not hesitate to say yes. The other ticket would go to Walter if he wanted to go. He could accompany her home after the performance. They could catch the motor bus from town or even walk. This was Duff's way of responding to Margaret's blatant opposition.

It inspired Duff to realise that she had come to know herself better as a young woman, due to not being sheltered or indulged. Relative liberty underwritten by Harper was well won. Underlying Duff's worry for the future was mild good humour and confidence that no-one could deflect. Most important of all, Harper told her with an almost passionate mania in his eyes, "Your mother would approve. In fact she would be delighted."

There were parks and gardens around town in which to squander long summer evenings with friends, when Duff found the atmosphere at home as uncomfortable as she did now. There was the magnet of Portobello, or Musselburgh, if any of them were so fed up they needed to mitch off school and didn't want to get spotted by someone they knew. On this occasion however, Hannah resisted the temptation, although everyone in her circle knew that her feelings were hurt. Willie kept pressing for a date in an attempt to 'console her' and although subliminal pressure due to the triangular relationships at home made Duff by her own admission 'more outgoing' she told him, 'it disnae make me *that* outgoing!'

When they had no pocket money the little group of friends would walk to the beach but this year they had all managed to find seasonal part time jobs from Easter onwards. Hannah's Saturday job, at the café on the pier, brought an element of financial independence as well as a reason to meet with friends at their favourite haunt.

Margaret's rigid transactional thinking about chores was water off a duck's back as Duff was always a step ahead with household routines, including school work. She didn't leave loose ends to be picked at; if she saw a job to be done she did it without being asked. In any case, following each wicked outburst Margaret usually preferred to avoid conflict, as she did now. Without a word but with typical ambivalence she pre-booked Anthony's hansom cab for the night of the Paderewski performance, as an obvious gesture of conciliation. Duff was afraid to mention the olive branch, knowing it empowered only Margaret.

To break the uneasy silence, Harper made a point of telling Duff that he was still annoyed with Margaret, "And by the way nothing could be further from the truth, you are anything but 'Plain Jane.' Also Hannah, you know I have always believed in the power of education to change people."

"But?"

"But Margaret is set against you going to Gillespies' Academy, it's just too expensive - although I will talk to her about the choices that face us. That I can promise you."

Walter and Willie were so different in nature and appearance that neither boy could see the other as a rival for Duff's affection. Jim was phlegmatic, in many ways similar to Duff. He knew that she hadn't found what she was looking for and there was no point eating his heart out, although he confessed to having a crush on her. But the other two were fixated.

Neither Walter nor Willie had any chance of winning her heart, though both went through life bemoaning the lost opportunity. There was never any plan beyond joyful innocence and friendship in a great town. Intellectually and emotively, Duff was the undisputed boss of their wide circle and Duff was easy. If it sounded like fun and hurt no-one they would do it.

Walking hurriedly along the pavement to school with them one morning Duff playfully cautioned, "I need to take care not to step on a line, or I'll end up marrying a fool." Undeterred both lads pleaded variations on, "Well if I was you I'd give up now, it's bound to happen. Just accept it!"

A moment later Willie nudged her gently in the back, looking down at edges of the stone slabs to see if his luck was in.

"Get off me! Get off," she cried as he pushed her again, hoping to see her take the double step that would land on a gap.

Duff jumped onto the asphalt roadway to run from Willie with her books under her arm. Long hair flapped indecorously over trim square shoulders. Willie and Walter ran after her like sheepdogs, trying to force her back onto the pavement where their chances would improve.

On another occasion days later, Willie and Walter lay in wait for Duff on a park bench on Hopetoun Crescent Gardens, far enough from school not to draw a crowd. They'd made a pact in their passionate dialogue to tell her officially, "We're both prepared tae *gladly* crawl o'er *broken glass,* if ye'll let us kiss yer hand. Ye'll feel the passion o' true love, like Prince Charming wi' Cinderella."

Laughing she declared, "Well I wouldn't want that! You might cut yourselves."

"Nae bother, Wull powdered the glass up small wi' a hammer," explained Walter, as if that would influence her desire.

"Well, think of a trial . . . any act of chivalry, or daring. We'll swim roon the end of Portobello pier when the tide's in?" suggested Willie.

"Lay down under a speeding railway locomotive?"

"Shut up Walter, I never agreed tae that!"

"You cannae both marry me! But it's gratifying to know this is still obviously a man's world," resolved Duff after a few moments, "So, like my mother Hannah . . . and indeed my charming step-mother Margaret, I'm inclined to bide my time. Ask me again in ten years."

"Okay then! But at least have a baby with one of us out of wedlock! Mind if it's Walter ye choose, at some point I might ha'e tae kill 'im."

"You potato head! How can you speak to her like that? And why would ye want tae kill yer best friend, even fer love?"

"Come on or we'll be late," Duff rose to walk on and Willie, who always travelled light, offered to carry her bag.

Duff's bright laughter resonated in Walter's head all day in school. Willie had shot Cupid's arrows and missed but Walter was thunderstruck. Hannah had secretly asked him out on a date.

Duff was reading in her room when she heard Harper's car pulling up on the street outside the house one mid-afternoon in early summer. He made himself a cup of tea and went into the front room with his paper where the light was better. Margaret was still at work but he knew Hannah was home from school. To her surprise he called her straight away. She left Angel Clare with his doting milkmaids to run down the stairs.

"Sit, I want to talk to you." Light rain was coming in from the west so he'd evidently thought better of mixing business with pleasure at the golf course.

"Yes, I'm fine thank you . . . how are you Daddy?"

Harper narrowed his eyes into a roguish smile, "God, you are so like your mother. Sorry, how are you Honey Bee?"

"Lonely, distressed, quite desperate about the future – my own included. No . . . just joking Harper, I'm fine, truly!"

"Well go and get yourself a cup of tea."

"No, I can wait. You came home early for a reason, so say what's on your mind."

"Okay, firstly: do not encourage that boy unless you intend to marry him." Hannah gasped, not expecting an inquisition on the broken glass conversation.

"Who said anything about marrying him? I'm far too young to think of such things, Harper. I asked him to accompany me to a concert. You never raised such objections with Elizabeth when she went to the orchestras with her friends."

"Don't argue Hannah. We don't need to argue."

"Does that mean I can't go?"

"Not at all – just be careful not to give Walter the wrong idea. His family are Jewish."

"And?"

"And nothing. But he has the status of a man in their community even though he is only fourteen. Look at the way he dresses. Which brings me to my next point."

174

"Oh God Harper you're too predictable. You were running a business at Walter's age . . . and within two years, running three businesses . . . and of course you'd already mastered the elements of working a fourth before you even took on the first. However did you learn to play golf? I'm surprised you could find the time!" Harper guffawed. Her tone was ribbing, but not sarcastic.

"You're right," he surrendered, holding up his hands. "But it was never easy to be so self-reliant. I was absolutely determined to better my place in the world, as much if not more so than you are."

"So, I have to leave school and find a job . . . is that what you're leading to?"

"No, most certainly not. I accept that education is paramount.

Your mother and Great Gran had taught you to read by the age of three. I encouraged you to develop the critical awareness you now so easily turn on poor Margaret . . . Look, I know she is single minded . . ." Harper gazed at Duff, looking for the right words to fairly characterise Margaret.

"Tell me Harper . . . she only wants what's best for me?"

"That happens to be true. But listen, what I mean to say is that going through a little bit of hell to get to where you want to be is never a bad thing. You have a way with words that she lacks. I know Margaret is brusque at times but she genuinely loves you."

"So I should just take the first job that comes along and one day I'll be Superintendent of a major financial institution. Is that what you're trying to say?"

"No but try to strike a balance. Stay on for the two years if you insist but forget James Gillespie's. Higher education matters, but it will work better for you in a vocational context. Unless you really do want to teach. Even then, believe me, there is a danger of institutional ennui that will probably stifle your imagination." Harper stared at Duff, probing for a thoughtful reaction.

"What? Harper? Tell me the truth; I'm old enough to be trusted. It won't break me."

"The Education Industry is an essential part of the free market economy. A revolving door that amounts to being a self-serving bureaucracy, like any other. Formal education is *not* about enlightenment and never will be . . . not in my lifetime and not in this country, as far as I can see. It's about bums on seats and 'how much can you afford to pay?'"

"Is that its only rationale?"

"Essentially, yes; Education is geared to conditioning citizenry to be good workers and consumers – even if what they consume is the notion that poverty is essential to create *their* personal wealth. It's not *specifically* intended to reinforce selfishness and discrimination but it does so more effectively than any right wing government policy. The further you go through the system, the more you will realise the hard truth of what I'm saying, even if you do attain to the expense account and pension fund."

"Oh, that *would* be a rare thing for a woman, but so-what?"

A paternal smile crept across Harper's mouth before he replied with a softer tone.

"So stay on for the additional two years at Bellevue but have no illusions about full time higher education. My advice is get a job and save your money. Educate yourself with commitment like I did. Real education is not so much a commodity, as an obligation to yourself."

As Duff went around the table to hug Harper, she could smell expensive whisky on his breath.

Hannah borrowed a cream lace bridesmaid's dress from Isabella, worn only once at her step-mother's wedding in Paris a year earlier. It had tiny yellow and red flowers embroidered into the trim and was perfect for the concert. She took the dress up a little at the waist to adjust it for length and dyed the matching summer pillbox hat a light peach colour, in reference to the pianist's mane of ruddy gold, wild hair.

Walter spent over an hour in the bathroom of his parent's home at Inverleith Place, bathing and washing his hair, shaving with the surreptitious use of his father's razor but also combing his thick brown hair for the best effect. It was the evening of the Paderewski concert and although he felt uneasy about the whole affair, somehow he had to try his best to cut a dash.

Duff had been absolutely clear in saying, 'this is not the beginning of any romance, Walter, whirlwind or the other kind. If you don't want to accompany me on that understanding, please say.' Walter had been more than a little disillusioned but if it got him next to her he would swallow his pride. Willie and Jim would hold him in higher esteem than ever when word got out and it would shut his ma up about 'finding a nice girl', which essentially hinted at the future prospect of an arranged marriage. In any event he would make up his own mind about things generally from now on, including his dratted mop. Forward combed was champion, as it seemed to make him less baby-faced, but his sister, Miriam, called him 'chubster' when he practiced his smile on her, so he went with vertical at the sides as well as back combed across the top, to give the illusion of an extra half inch of height.

Walter dressed slowly with a cultured eye and even borrowed his mother's iron, to press creases out of a new shirt. Standing in his clean underwear, vest and socks, he splashed after shave lotion onto his smooth face, now shorn of bum fluff. He shook the opaque bottle to confirm that there was plenty left and that his dad would not notice, before sousing armpits that were healthily sprouting adolescent growth. "What a charmer!" he muttered, smiling at himself in the mirror.

Then Walter made the fatal error all boys make only once, prior to their first date. The liberal dip of Old Spice on his unmentionables caused him to cry out in shock, and hop around the bathroom – first to grab a mercifully damp towel from the drying rail and then pronto over to the hand basin which he rapidly plugged and filled with cold water.

Having recovered from the astounding discomfort and resumed dressing with heightened awareness, Walter tried on his dad's monkey suit murmuring, "No, blast it. I'll look too Jewish. Why do Jews always dress like undertakers at the funeral of a Sicilian Seigneur?" Turning sideways he tutted at the fact that it made him look pudgy, "If only I was two or three inches taller I'd get away with it! Perhaps just as well. I don't want to end up looking like the Japanese Emperor!"

Walter picked out a magnificent town suit instead and shoving grey gloves into his coat pocket he rubbed patent leather shoes on the back of his trouser legs, stuck out his tongue and smiled one last time into the mirror. He picked out a grey homburg to match a thread of his dark pinstripe suit, with the intention of dressing down.

Anthony Kemp braked the landau and went to ring the bell. He was ordered by Walter's mother to bring Hannah inside. Scrutiny or not, it was her 'do' and she voiced her opinion freely, "Walter, you look as handsome as a prince!" she exclaimed, "Doesn't he Gramps?"

"Oh, absolutely Walter, a true gallant!" Walter beamed with the gentle courtesy that invariably bubbled just below the surface in any situation. He kissed his mother and smiled at his father the master tailor who had appeared momentarily at the door of the lounge to offer his seal of approval.

"Hannah, this is a great honour for Walter," he said, "Prod him in the ribs if he so much as stifles a yawn. And Walter don't forget, ask Paderewski to sign your programme! Speak Polish and speak up confidently. Don't throw away the ticket stub either. One day you will tell your children about this."

"Enough of children," hissed Mrs Chalmers, "*They* are still children!"

Anthony dropped them off outside the Assembly Rooms on George Street where they were caught instantly and fashionably in the flow of 'Paddymania,' spilling out onto the streets and pavements of old Edinburgh.

"The crowd seems to be mostly young women!" whispered Hannah. They mixed in casually behind a group of half a dozen smartly dressed friends wearing white hats. "Perhaps these are just the first to arrive?" answered Walter cautiously. They were still by far the youngest in the crowd, although suddenly much less self-conscious. Several men were dressed 'a la mode' in white tails and had grown their hair long or wore wigs to match the popular hero – stylised by the dilettante music press as, 'The Blacksmith.' They laughed effusively, already excited by what was in store, as Hannah and Walter listened to their banter.

"They say his compositions lack subtlety - but his playing is quite astounding!" said one aficionado, a man in his late twenties, "I think Beethoven begs that interpretation – and as for Chopin, he makes it sound like the master has risen from the grave to dance his own mazurkas!"

"His eyes are so intense," said a woman in the queue, "They would sweep you up to heaven!" There was laughter as the group looked admiringly at one another.

"And he smiles at everyone, like he's looking through you!" her friend replied.

"He doesn't just play the piano, he recreates the instrument into a projection of his own soul!"

"How wonderful! My mammy loved him," said Duff to her friend, "I can't wait." Walter walked tall that night. It was the germinal stage of a loving friendship that would define his life in symbiosis with Duff's.

Paderewski was awesome and the crowd were overwhelmed. He played Brahms, and they applauded an old familiar with so many cultured friends. He played Beethoven and they cheered the magnanimous soul of musical civilization. He played Chopin and they bawled recognition for love in chains to the gentle curves of the arched ceiling.

Walter was knocked for six by the musician, working what he knew favourable critics had described as, his 'transformational magick.' He was also quietly astounded to see the effect Thelema seemed to have on a number of women in the audience. Above all he was concerned for his vulnerable companion, who studiously absorbed every persuasive, ringing chord and every impassioned, floating harmony.

Walter watched Duff discreetly throughout the performance and saw her face was rapt in attention, but as the maestro moved through his familiar repertoire of mazurkas and ballades, she seemed to shrink in her chair, her face a tight line of sincere appreciation.

Walter had never seen Duff crying before and slightly envied the man who could do this. But he knew that her tears were not for adulation of the forge master of musical stone and metal working his aural filigree of finest gold. They were for the bright sounds of innocent youth, lost in the tidal song of the universe. Several mature women fainted as the performance reached a climax and the audience rose to rattle the chandeliers when Paderewski rested.

Predictably, the audience mobbed the virtuoso but Walter took Duff's hand and coolly walked away. Knowing that the maestro could not take a step without a running conversation all around him, Walter had asked the stage manager to request the autographing of their programmes before the performance began, and duly signed, they were waiting at the ticket booth. Not for the first time Walter showed the simple insight that made him uniquely reliable and endeared him to his friends

Walter was hooked, his head resonating with the dynamics of l'Heroique, played with verve and poise as a teasing encore. As they stood on the pavement waiting for Anthony, both wore beatific smiles that stayed with them for the rest of the weekend. Hannah had paid a very special tribute to her kind comrade that didn't need explanation. From now on the love of great music would be a central part of their mutual esteem.

Duff's extended schooling at Belle Vue consisted of fee-paid advanced classes in English; Maths; French; Commercial History or Commercial Geography; Domestic Economy; PE and Needlework - but no Sciences; no Philosophy and no Classics, all of which the boys had. Willie and his chums still went into school through a different entrance to the girls. For the most part, Bellevue boys were subjected to learning activities under the glassy eyes of Doctors and Masters, rather than lesser qualified, often temporary women teachers.

Willie and Walter came out at the end of each session with the same glassy eyes their teachers had. When quizzed by Duff, they were vague about whatever it was they were supposed to have learned.

"How can I keep pace with the syllabus if you two numpties cannae even take outline notes of the topics covered?"

"Outline notes? Should we be even doing this for Hannah, Walter? I dinnae ken girls are allowed to know the things we study, are they?"

Duff tutted and spun away at his effrontery. Walter came scuttling across the school yard after her to apologise on Willie's behalf, "You know it's on'y a question of masculine pride. He wants to be a bloomin' doctor!"

"You mean his ma and pa want him to be a doctor?"

"Okay, but what's the difference? They're the ones wi' the money. That's how any one of us ascends the ladder. Someone prods you up the backside, if there's no-one at the top tae pull you up."

"Willie needs more than a prod up the backside, Walter. He needs a fireman's lift. Frankly I'm not that strong, especially if you slackers don't bring me outline notes. It cuts both ways - you acquire the discipline to learn systematically and I get a copy of the broken down syllabus, with teacher direction. I'll even help with your homework."

"I don't need help with ma homework."

"No, because you want to be a Master Tailor but Wull does, even if he plans to join the Army as a Medic."

"Stop worrying Duff, you're a *seven percenter*."

"What do you mean by that, Walter?"

"Riley, the Maths teacher, says on'y seven percent stay on past fourteen. Straight away that means ninety three percent of the population are more glaikit than we are. Wull says we're a'ready the cream o' society!"

In contrast to what Walter described as 'the mind factory' Duff and her classmates spent endless hours under the burgeoning tutelage of ladies who barely met the approval of the School Board, given the new wider range of subjects requiring matriculation tests. Some of them had teaching certification, or more rarely degrees in the same limited and boring subjects presently offered as a syllabus for young ladies. According to Isabella, "Twenty minutes of History once a week plays perfectly to curriculum planning, because twenty minutes worth is all any of them know."

As long hours of late summer afternoons dragged on into the dampening chill of autumn, Duff longed only for escape into Carnegie's Central Library. There she devoured the works of Austen, Hardy and Dickens – anything to give a contemporary perspective to the overplayed romanticism of Stevenson, Scott and Burns.

Duff realised Harper had been right of course but discontentment served to inspire her, like a caged bird searching for an opening in the wire. She told Walter, "I feel like a turkey being overfed for Christmas -

but at least when I escape this reformatory each afternoon, I can forage for my own corn."

Because she was determined, some said driven, Duff's peers in upper school sometimes misunderstood her, perhaps seeing her as a rival. Despite being possessed with indulgent humour, some older girls decried a perceived hardness in Duff.

Lizzie McMurray and Norma Forbes-Drummond were the most respected prefects in school. They could do no wrong because they led vocal music classes and worked hard to put on plays and reviews.

"What more could a girl aspire to?" asked Isabella, when Hannah pointed out their road to success.

"Being rich or beautiful?" hazarded Duff, "Furthermore Is, they both have parents on the City Council and School Board. That's got to be worth another fifteen or twenty percent in a test."

The prefects supposed Duff to be blasé, or indifferent to the opinions of others. After all, she hung around with stupid boys! By reputation Hannah Harper was sphinx-like and enigmatic, unperturbed by criticism or scolding from stricter teachers whom Lizzie and Norma, like everyone else in school, had learned to tolerate and fear.

"You're seen as a maverick," said Lizzie, dutifully collecting plates at the end of lunchtime.

"What's a maverick?" asked Isabella.

"An unbranded range animal," explained Norma.

"A motherless calf," added McMurray, with more than a hint of aggression.

"Oh well, at least I'm clear what your intentions are towards me," Duff replied through welling tears of rejection, "I always thought it meant free-spirited."

But it was true that a handful of male staff allocated to teaching throughout the mixed school arrogantly gave credit to systematised, thoughtless bullying as a form of social learning. It came as no surprise for Duff and Is how well this paragon was learned by the most praiseworthy senior students, "Curiously," Duff told Is, "Their expertese in this area is not officially credited on Bellevue's published listing of *Subjects of Instruction and Staff.*"

Clearly rules were there to be broken, by inference because they were so numerous and arbitrary but not through any imagined initiative of rebellious pupils. Broken rules were a necessary concomitant of a schooling ethos bordering upon the military, in its crude assumptions about consumers. School rules were unimportant, intentionally petty in fact. What mattered was the visible and regular reinforcement of those rules - not conformity to them or their being breached, inadvertently or on purpose.

One evening at Isabella's house they took turns to brain-storm a transient short-list, before doing routine homework.

"You first Isabella!"

"Okay, No talking in line up."

"No talking in assembly."

"No talking in class."

"No running on the corridor."

"No lapses of uniform dress code."

"Good one, yet we have to pay for them. No eating outside the refectory."

"We have to pay for that too. No sleeping in class."

"No lapses of attention, or else!"

"No lateness, no absences without a line."

"That's two. No excuses for late homework, or poor quality handwriting. No spelling mistakes."

"Stop! That's three! No answering back."

"No tolerance."

"No blubbing, even when you've been beaten by someone who's socially impaired."

"So you agree with me?"

"Of course I agree with you. Those bitches are jealous because they are such tarts and you are so understated, yet the boys adore you! If ye could bottle it hen, ye could sell it."

"That hurt, about being a motherless calf."

Isabella came across the room to hug her friend, "You are an individual, no' a rebel . . . an' who could not love a motherless calf?"

It was difficult to stand back and take a view but the school regime amounted to crushing adversity for Duff, as for her contemporaries. Continuing hard times were accepted as the norm.

'Spud' Regan, Head of Senior School openly insisted that, "Every school day should be started with a hymn, a prayer and a bollocking." So oft quoted was his mantra that some staff at Bellevue High School arrived at the conviction Regan was the enlightened author of an infallible scholastic philosophy. This pedagogy of the oppressed did not aspire to being the equivalent of Evangelical politics popular in the middle part of the previous century but his approach was rudely honest, practical and certainly saved souls.

The mystery of Spud's wisdom was reflected tangibly in eager faces of rogues lined up each morning in front of him, as he rose to the lectern to deliver ruthless invective, following the hymn and the prayer. Staff arrayed behind him on chairs could relax, confident under their mortar boards and gowns that working life was sure, certain and purposive. They might have been a bunch of louse pricking pedants but no-one could ever accuse them of academic nudity. Grateful pupils who hung on Mr Regan's every word as a consequence would surely give their all in morning lessons.

Spud Regan, as his nickname suggested, actually looked like a sack of potatoes tied in the middle. His bald head was a massive raw, freshly peeled and washed King Edward. From a distance he looked like an Irish Heavyweight bare knuckle fighter. Regan's glance conveyed the hard glint of a less hirsute John L Sullivan, confident in his prime. All he lacked was the hair and moustache. Close up, so legend ran among older boys, it was best not to look at Spud at all unless you were ready to duck, or intended to kick him hard in the balls and leg it in an act of suicidal revenge. Every new arrival in school, as soon as they'd been initiated through various forms of ritualised bullying by older pupils, would be warned about him. Mr Regan taught by fear and rote. Coincidentally some of the children in his classes learned a little French, though the majority were merely conditioned to repeat words they did not understand, charged in the form of unthinking mandate. Those fated to hear the language spoken in clipped tones a little later in life were surely destined to experience the most terrible nightmares. Spud insisted that all conversational exchanges took place in French. This tokenistic intention merely ensured one-way receptive attention at the beginning of every lesson which he was happy to sustain indefinitely, even if most of them fell asleep. Conversational depth was in fact generally spare and meaningless.

One fine lad known as Nick Williams, only son of a widowed Belgian émigré who taught at St George's, spoke only to relieve boredom. Nicolas Willems was fearful that if he engaged with the Irish lourdin he might inadvertently expose himself to unwelcome discrimination. Established routine consisted of Spud singling out, ridiculing and berating each member of the group in turn during a ten minute drill before moving on to weekly dictation and grammar exercises. It was unwise to let attention lapse, despite the fact that this approach was boring and ineffectual.

Duff was actually interested in learning the language and had made reasonable progress over five years at Bellevue. Having a male teacher visit the senior girl's division room to teach them in their final year amounted to both novelty and affirmation. Unfortunately Spud noticed her looking out of a high window near the front of the class, searching the sky for signs of a change in the weather. Hannah was indolently wondering whether she could make it home without getting caught in the rain, when her turn came for the ritual abuse. With a diplomatic smile she rounded on the pugilist for his autocratic teaching style. He blocked and snapped at Duff's every turn like a sheep dog, as the others gaped at her tenacity and his mounting irritation. Determined not to be intimidated or break down and cry Duff responded in kind, raising her voice for emphasis, "Vous est un cochon impitoyable, monsieur Regan. Vous utilise ma ignorance intrinseque et jeunesse contre moi, mais vous et un pedant grossier. Un chien mechant!"

With a referees' outstretched arm Spud ordered her out of the room, speaking French with eloquent authority. For just a few moments the

185

semantics appeared impressively dynamic, rather than a rehearsed segment of uncouth burlesque. He sent Duff to stand outside his office, conveniently situated on the top corridor of the adjoining accommodation, where no boys would venture except for execution. Regan commanded the class to sit in silence as he followed her at a safe distance. Duff stood with hands behind her back staring at Regan as he barrelled towards her along the polished wooden corridor, his trailing gown wafting Old Spice in his turbulent wake. Despite breathing heavily through hairy nostrils, Spud wore a self-conscious smile on his piqued face and did not look at Duff as he entered the study.

Rummaging around noisily among storage tins in his tall equipment cupboard, he eventually found what he'd hidden from view. Assuming the old fool had mislaid his well-worn tawse, Duff tilted on her toes to confirm and was surprised to hear the sound of an unopened quarter of Navy Rum being snapped down upon the bureau table. Reaching to the gas boiler Regan poured a mug full of hot water onto concentrated Camp Coffee then stirred in three sugars before adding a liberal measure of Lamb's with just a splash of milk.

Spud marched off down the corridor in his worn, silent shoes heeling and toeing like a professional runner despite his eighteen stone bulk. Sticking his bull head around the door to the French group with the steaming aromatic mug hidden behind his back, he glowered at the class for two seconds before detouring to find Mrs Mercer. The following wave of laughter was actually more audible than the whispered conversation that preceded his visit, as he moved on apace.

Mrs Mercer left her English class with eyes down in composition, for a hushed conference with the formidable French teacher out on the corridor. She agreed with Regan's decision to leave Hannah Harper standing outside his office in the Boy's School until the end of the school day. It was a necessary example to any others with enough conversational French to have understood her tirade, although all she had done was throw back some of Spud's ritual abuse. Mrs Mercer agreed to telephone Gillespie's to request they take the girl on a School Board supported bursary as an outstanding pupil, if her father would agree to contribute at the existing level of termly fees.

Despite Spud's circumspection, everyone in school talked about what had happened. When Margaret probed to discover the reason for Mrs Mercer's intervention from Isabella Stuart's mother, the cat was waiting to jump out of the bag. Duff's classmate knew precisely what Regan had said and how Duff provoked him in response. Her dad had been born in Paris and Is had been there twice on holiday with her mum. Isabella's French comprehension was relatively developed, despite Regan's poor teaching. She couldn't wait to tell her mother about Duff's breathtaking put-down of the tyrant. Duff was clearly above it all looking down. In turn Isabella's mother couldn't wait to waylay Margaret in the Co-op.

Chapter Ten   *Hannah Duff*

They stood in the kitchen – Duff in her black and white uniform, Margaret in hers. Margaret brandished a butter knife and had made herself a cup of tea but didn't invite the recidivist to join her.

"Most remarkable are the lengths the school is prepared to go to - just to get rid of *you!*" Her sharp little voice flattened as its volume rose into a previously uncharted territory of annoyance. Margaret's face piqued with exasperation, brown freckles standing out against flushed cheeks as she railed against Duff.

She repeated what she knew of the most scandalous element of the mutinous story without inviting any perspective on the hearsay. When rage finally blew out Margaret demanded Duff's final word, as though sentence had already been passed and this was merely the observance of canonical judgement before execution.

Duff searched Margaret's face for any hint of compassion for a few moments before turning to walk out of the house in silence, "I'll talk to you when you're ready to listen," she called from the hallway without turning round.

Duff threw her arms back into her warm coat then dropping her brimmed hat onto her head, stepped through the front door with her school satchel. It felt very much like a rehearsal for the main event but there were still routines to consider.

Margaret bellowed after her, "There'll be nae mair money thrown at schooling. I'm adamant about that madam an' I intend to tell your faither. That includes new uniforms and buses oot tae Bruntsfield! If you know so much ye can argue in French wi' yer teacher then they've a'ready succeeded at Bellevue. And *dinnae* bother talking tae me at aw . . . Thur's nae mair to be said!"

It occurred to Hannah that the cultivated English airs and graces Margaret traditionally reserved for nights at the opera had lapsed along with her guardianship.

Duff called on Is and with brief explanation persuaded her to walk with her to a favourite spot on a small grassy plateau with elevation above Queen's Drive, a breathless five minute walk from home.

Unrolling a PE towel she kept in her bag, Duff invited Is to sit down on the lush grass. She turned the satchel strap side down and sat pensively beside her friend.

There were signs of activity on the horizon. Enormous cranes towered over a construction site to the north – no doubt another football stand, or just *maybe* a theatre. The town was pulsing with industrial self-appreciation, but in some respects it was all becoming too intense.

Is knew the issues and could see her pal was hurting. She waited for the lump in Duff's throat and tears just below the surface to subside. At last she let out her exasperation, "Why do issues of national importance have to be hammered out in my heart? Why are Suffragists so hated Isabella, forced to be militant? Nothing exemplifies this divided society so shamefully as discrimination against women."

Isabella leant towards Hannah, pulling her onto her shoulder with a long arm, "Talk to me if you can't talk to them."

Duff explained to Is that she longed with all her heart for her education to be extended, to attend Gillespie's and from there go on to university, "I imagine studying Literature or modern European languages. French, Spanish, Italian. I know I'll never be as good as you Is, but I would love to travel and teach abroad."

"Essentially we both want the same things. Maybe I could get mum to talk to your parents. She can tell them what a horrible man Regan is?"

"Nah! She's set against it. The arguement with Mr Regan is a side issue. He was actually very kind in the way he acted. I bet he's a brilliant chap, if only we knew him as an individual."

"Maybe that's your Achilles Heel, Duff, you want to think well of people who really are contemptible."

"This is not about anyone else, it's about me. All I can say is that I have never wanted anything as strongly in my entire life – except one other thing and that broke my heart many years ago."

"You're ma? You remember her well? Weren't you only three or four when she died?"

"Yes, I vaguely remember longing she would survive, thinking that for some reason a miracle had happened. The local doctor genuinely thought he'd cured her cancer. I feel that 'snatched away joy' now when I consider my own limited options. I could be going to Gillespies' at the start of next term. None of us can cheat our fate . . . but." Duff took out her handkerchief and dabbed her eyes, breathing deeply into her chest in order to avoid choking up.

"But what . . . you need to say it . . . get it out."

"If she was alive this doubt would have been resolved by now. Harper's indecision about paying to let me stay on would be condemned with ridicule. That bloomin' monster he drives cost more than a new house!"

"Yeah but that's not his."

"I know, it's essential to the business . . . his status as Superintendent and all that bilgewater. But my point is he earns a salary commensurate with the two tons of steel he drives around in. They're talking about buying another house near Duke's Walk, Isabella and he spends more on golf clubs than on my school fees. I know in my heart if my ma was still alive I would be attending St Margaret's. If I was a boy it would be a foregone conclusion."

"Oh Lord, that feels like the truth. It's not just a question of money then? I thought you said they wanted another child."

"Yes, the sad truth is Margaret has iron in her soul about that, Is. She's bloody loopy. She wants me gone before she has a baby."

"Oh, in the name o' the wee man . . . how selfish!"

"Yes, even Harper thinks she's batty. I've already thwarted her plans by staying on past fourteen. I heard her tell Auntie Muriel she wants a boy and plans to send him to Merchiston. Muriel's diplomat husband plans to send their son Joe to Heriots, so Margaret wants to go one better."

"Oh my, rags to riches! And her the daughter of a coachman. Sorry, no offence."

"None taken. The old cud has plenty of money, she just won't let him spend it on school fees for me. Their hypocrisy makes me want to retch."

As Duff hugged her knees, her view of burgeoning activity on the low horizon of South Leith misted over with tears.

The summer of '08 soon faded into somnolent hues of brown and surreptitiously autumn took with it Duff's childhood. Winter came with a bite, inspiring nothing so much as argument and militancy. Duff decided that to survive the choking indifference of her last year in a school system plainly biased against young women, out of necessity she had to be inured to discrimination.

She never took time off school - even when obviously unwell with flu. A classmate they knew well and liked, Eileen Cowan was one of several in the area who died following an outbreak of viral meningitis. Despite her spiritual awakening, the arbitrariness of living and dying was beyond Duff's understanding.

'What truly matters and what can ever really be decided?' she wrote in her diary, 'There are imagined alternative futures – but are any of them ultimately going to be meaningful for me, or for anyone else? I think the noblest thing any of us can do is alleviate the suffering of others. Everything else is just distraction. Why can't good people generalise this idea? Why does the world have to be so callous?'

Depression – had she known the word beforehand, or just then allowed it into her vocabulary? Either way depression was suddenly tangible. Duff knew it could never suppress her naturally buoyant energy and innocent romanticism but instead the darkness that surrounded her - the forbidding architecture of an urban landscape forming the bounds of her world - inspired rigorous scrutiny of every cogent idea and expressed notion. Duff avidly questioned everything. Yet everyone who spoke up in adversity was owed consideration in turn. Weathered stones of the old city streets she walked through with her friends demanded a toll of thoughtful commitment.

191

"There can never be any guarantee that the future will be better than the past," she told Isabella.

"Hmm, I think so too. The number of people suffering expands with the free market economy I guess," Isabella replied, with doctrinaire sarcasm, "And the growing population. I blame Adam and Eve."

"I was just gonny say – Adam and Eve, filthy shaggers!"

With the flash of a smile Duff's depression was gone, for the moment at least. It was a Saturday afternoon and they went to meet the boys at their secret place, between gorse bushes on the slope above the Rural Road.

Walter was blue with cold in the still dank air, despite his long coat, yet felt the need to suck on a bottle of Dryborough Ale like a vagabond. Jim and Willie were both smoking factory rolled cigarettes where they sat on a fallen tree. Isabella sat down beside them but Hannah stood, waiting for attention.

"By the way chaps and chapesses, I am no longer 'Duff,' so I've decided - not that names matter. From now on, call me Hannah. I'm gonny tell everyone."

"Well you know how much names matter tae us hen, so consider it done!" Walter told her.

"Why though and why now?" asked Jim

"*What* I am clearly figures more in this world than *who* I am, Jim. So I shall act accordingly."

"I dinnae ken whit ye mean hen, but we still love you for *who* ye are," vowed Walter, "You'll always be our Duff. Tell her Wull!" commanded Walter, with the unblinking loyalty of a Queen's equerry,

"Sure thing pardner," concurred Willie, pointing his hand like a Colt revolver at Walter. Willie had just discovered Western novels.

"But I don't want to be Duff. I want to be Hannah."

"Okay Li'l Sure Shot, Hannah Duff it is!" replied Willie. The little group fell into irrepressible laughter at his thick headedness.

"How are you ever gonny be a doctor?" complained Jim, "Ye'll mix up aw the fickin' prescriptions!"

Hannah frequently watched the world alone in silence from their secret place in the park. This evening a billion smiling stars looked fondly on Edinburgh, at its annual teasing personations. Reluctant to play along with Willie and the others, who were determined to cross dress in guising clothes and recite poetry for their neighbours, on the loneliest Halloween night Hannah had slipped out on her own to meditate.

A fire built by Jim and the others two hours before nightfall was still glowing in a ring of stones on the hillside but there was nothing to tell of who had built it, except a scattering of empty beer bottles. Hannah imagined herself a black alley cat sitting atop a high wall, gazing in wonderment past yellow gas lit windows, hunched spires and rooftops to an enormous flying moon. The self-sufficient feline saw the eternal wheel of dancing cosmos beyond and in the witnessing was awe struck by the phenomenon of her own fleeting existence and an absurd sense of self. A small lonely child on an all-embracing, wheeling carousel Hannah felt touched by dispassionate, gentle magic. That night she didn't want to ward off spirits that might walk abroad. Instead her heart opened to all that might converge to pacify her soul. For the moment she saw past the distracting fragmentation of her situation and striving; past the search for commitment and principles that might inform action, to faith in everything outside her reach that could not be controlled.

Since it was a Saturday and Guy Fawkes was not officially to be executed until Thursday which was a working day, many folk around the city had decided to light their Samhain bonfires early, in true Gaelic tradition. The sons of Thomas Hammond were evidently doing a roaring trade. Here and there rockets screamed into the sky, popping into bright orange flares. Every few seconds the crack of a squib detonating near or far gave depth to surrounding space that daylight would have hidden in plain sight.

Hannah felt she could reach down into a dozen nearby back yards to touch smiling bairns, scoffing apples and baked potatoes. Yellow faces glowed brightly from hundreds of yards away as clouds of burnt gunpowder drifted on the breeze. There was beauty in every creature with a beating heart, every meaningful paradigm of hopeful thinking. Hannah was still in her sixteenth year, naively confused and empty handed yet she was ready to submit to the challenges of humble existence. Terrified by the grandness and inscrutable subtlety of all creation, she was still poignantly in love with wild Life.

Remembering with a shock an early spring day when her mother had taken her to see a much grander light show, in the sky above forested Rothiemay, she realised the challenge lay in holding on to this clear vision. Despite all the hard knocks, Hannah remained determined to carry a dream of heaven glimpsed into uncertainty that lay ahead. She repeated a simple mantra,

Delusion is the real enemy, not depression.

Through weeks and months ahead there were many modest gatherings with lively juvenile excess and hilarious conversations. Any excuse would serve – this one going off to join the army, that one showing off an engagement ring with her parents' approval. Most of Hannah's friends had already left school and found jobs. Adolescence was short and sweet.

'Money gives you independence,' they all said, 'Yer ma won't even think aboot throwin' ye oot if you're puttin' food on the table.'

In amongst all the sudden changes were many private discussions with Isabella Stuart about the future. No matter how long they sat in the park together talking about it, neither of them could leave the subject alone. Nor could they decide with any certainty what it might entail. Isabella was more assured of the option of extended education, whereas Hannah considered Is to be annoyingly uncommitted to any of the courses available.

"What matters is the chance to go to university Isabella, to be respected as a woman with a brain."

"As opposed to just a woman, therefore having no brain?"

"Spot on. Even better would be options available only to men – Engineering, Banking, Medicine or Law. Please do it Is – do it for both of us!"

They talked anecdotally about their respective parents and families – how hard they worked and how their health and humour suffered as a consequence. They talked intimately and intensely, joking as girls often do about love and marriage. When they walked down through the park before Harper's evening curfew, Isabella and Hannah parted affectionately but with uncertain smiles, hiding diffidence and irresolution.

It was near the close of her final term at Bellevue School when many imaginative suggestions were made by staff to allow 'self-programming' latitude to prospective leavers – to keep them out of their hair near the end of an exhausting year. Project titles had been handed out to anyone unable to think up an excuse to disappear from under their teacher's gaze. For three days prior to Mrs Mercer's annual end of year art trip, Isabella and Hannah had been studying 'The Flora and Fauna of Holyrood Park' – unsupervised and dizzyingly confused by suddenly maturing sentiments of a handful of infatuated boys.

Jim had a job lined up at the Courier and in reaction to some overwhelmingly romantic, innate biological mechanism, he begged Isabella for an assignation. For her part Is had never seriously looked Jim's way in the five years they had known one another, yet found herself unable to resist his entreaties.

It felt strange to Hannah that when the group got bored sitting in the May sunshine and returned to the school library, to draw and make notes, that none of the teachers even remarked their casual studying of Darwin's Origin of the Species. From a table opposite, the girls were blatantly pursued by Willie and a couple of his tumescent pals.

Having resolved, 'Since I was named after a body part I ought to strive to become an anatomist,' Willie and his friends were studying the most popular page in Doctor Gray's Anatomy. Every few minutes there was an outburst of barely restrained laughter followed by a clamping of mouths, as a new initiate was shown the graphic content of that particular page. There would invariably be an exclamation of surprise as the freshman got his first glimpse of The Eye of Athena.

Duty Librarian Mr Harris, researching with a teaching group, shook his head as he looked away. Any attempt at discipline and good order had been abandoned this near the end of Summer Term.

A few girls who still had their combined Hymn Book and New Testament from their first year - a gift from the School Board for the edification of every student - discreetly circulated amongst friends, requesting signatures with farewell wishes penned onto the fly leaf. It was a time of strongly mixed feelings for all - with much barely restrained sadness for faces that soon would never be seen again.

Although at the time she had no idea, it would be on the day of Mrs Mercer's Art field trip, to sketch the recently revealed statue of Queen Victoria at Leith and draw impressions of vessels berthed at the Old Edinburgh docks, that Hannah's life was to roll forward, meshing beautifully into the unseen clockwork of fate. On the Thursday morning of her penultimate week at school, Hannah arrived with a heavy heart for all those she loved and would soon miss. There was so much that ought to be said and shared in life that could never be said or shared. Bellevue had been the social metier for people without status – de facto still children without the right to a voice until they started to pay tax. But there were several reasons why Hannah's heart was heavy beyond any possibility of discourse with her pals. Others around her seemed much less concerned about never coming back. Perhaps hers was the greater potential and therefore the greater loss.

With a two-inch brush and tubes of purple, white and green paint in her school satchel, Hannah planned to make a gesture of rebellion upon Victoria's voluminous behind. If the corners of the plinth proved too awkward to climb she meant to scrawl a Suffragist slogan on the flat stonework above the plac: 'John Brown's Spare Rib.'

There was literally no-one to share these thoughts with. Even Isabella had been given no hint of what was on her mind. It would be a calculated act – intended to draw attention to the hypocrisy of the world of men, of Sovereignty without social equality. Isabella's mother had gone to Margaret once before. This time she could not risk her finding out and pre-empting the gesture of defiance.

Brooding silently, Hannah hung back from the group as they headed for the bus stop. Smouldering with resentment she nervously wished her mood might elevate slightly, in case she inadvertently drew attention to herself. She was isolated and would act autonomously. They would expel her for sure – but that made no material difference, now that her educational future was a cul-de-sac. Being expelled was in fact part of the plan.

No-one else seemed to see Hannah's consternation, sitting at the rear of the upper deck as the group poured off the motorbus. All her classmates rushed off, twittering after the three old hens who led them from the front.

Perfect, the party are stretched out. Unsurprisingly there's no teacher to bring up the rear, to take responsibility for the total head count, or round up stragglers.

It seemed to Hannah that Mrs Mercer was more concerned about holding court alongside Miss Burley and Mrs Wainwright, attendant bright lights of the Senior Girl's School, than with worrying about unforeseen hazards. Leith traffic was usually slow and congested. Pedestrians could easily move in and out of queuing vehicles: draymen, deliverymen, collection men, cabbies and buses. It was incumbent upon drivers and animals alike to beware swirls of movement from every direction.

The bus had stopped in the middle of the road because a delivery van was blocking the fare stage near the corner opposite the statue. The driver smiled, doffing his cap to the excited party of schoolgirls as they flitted past him onto the pavement. Watching in his mirror, he saw the delivery man acknowledge him with a salute as he climbed back into his cab. Throwing his delivery manifest onto the crew bench, the trucker reversed and pulled away as quickly as he could.

Hannah and Isabella saw none of this but couldn't help noticing a filthy old man at close quarters in front of them as they rose to head down spiral steps from the top deck. They knew the major part of the man's history at a glance. Queuing patiently on the stairs as they waited for the full complement of passengers in front of them to step down into the street, they heard the old tramp murmuring something over and over, "Quick, get out of the house, get out of the house! Quick get out of the house . . ."

197

The vagrant was ragged and stale. Decaying floral fragrance percolated from every pore on his unwashed body and fumes of alcohol lay on his breath. Wearing a ragged grey raincoat over two jumpers he sported a long white beard. Despite apparent psychosis there was a look of annealed pride in the old man's placid blue eyes. He smiled apologetically at the girls as if to acknowledge his own repulsive appearance, which clearly announced his status as a homeless person. The old man looked and smelled like Jonah disgorged from the whale, disbelieving his own survival.

The conductress, an attractive middle aged woman with red hair pulled tight into a bun, offered him a knowing smile. She leant back against the stair pillar to watch indulgently as the last of her passengers for Leith descended. Although she'd not given the man a ticket, Hannah noticed he did tender coins in offer of payment. The inspector had already hopped on and off once that morning and besides the conductress knew how to work around the jobs worths.

"Jim, how long have ye known me, ye addled old Brandy shunter? Put yer copper away fer a rainy day man!" The grubby old man thanked her, saluting gratefully with a hand raised to tip a non-existent hat.

"Oh aye, you're so kind, so kind lassie!" Hannah saw his watery blue eyes burn with humorous recognition for the last time. Pre-occupied with shoving coins back into a trouser pocket he stepped off the landing without looking and rolled onto the bonnet of a speeding motorcar, which had nipped inside the stationary bus to make the turn out towards Newhaven.

Jim let out the faintest groan as his old bones tumbled along the splendidly polished frame of the hissing giant. But the loudest sound was the sickening crack of window glass against the vagrant's ruptured back. His body spun as it flew up into the air. All of the old man's weight fell upon one shoulder as he crumpled like a broken doll onto awkward cobbles.

The car screeched to a halt. Onlookers froze in dismay. Jim's left leg was twisted up behind his back at an angle only possible if it were completely shattered and limp. Hannah ignored the danger of oncoming traffic to run towards the injured man and kneel down in the road beside him. Reaching down to put a concerned hand on Hannah's shoulder, Isabella said she would run to phone for an ambulance then get Mrs Mercer. In a second she had spun away.

The old vagrant opened his mouth to warn Hannah away, like a dying dog who'd suffered enough pain. But she soothed him with kind words and friendly eyes, asking his name. Then for some unquestioned reason, borne out of the politesse of offered companionship, she volunteered hers.

"I'm pleased to meet you Jim Birnie, under any circumstances. Don't trouble too much but is there anyone I might inform of your indisposition – family, or a friend perhaps?"

"No dear, you're the only friend I need now. Thank you anyhow," he said with a wistful smile. Jim Birnie was unable to move. So badly twisted was he that even lifting him into an ambulance might finish him off. Failing that, the surgical team were going to need half a day on his spine and legs. Hannah briskly took off her uniform raincoat to fold it under his head.

With a grunt of dismay Jim muttered concern for the trouble he'd caused, "Uh . . . noo lassie . . . they'll all be waiting on the bus leavin'." Then he laid his head back onto the soft folds of her coat. Taking a deep breath he braced what muscles could still move into an enveloping field of pain. Awe-struck by the tortuous shape of his crumpled body, Hannah reached to take his hand. With a shock she realised it was calloused from years of daily toil. A lifetime of aspiration was conveyed in that gentle touch, staggering her imagination. Leaning forward she stroked Jim's forehead with her other hand.

A little knot of onlookers gathered around to offer advice and help. The bus driver squatted down next to her. Taking off his uniform blazer he put it over the old man. Hannah looked up to see tears welling in the bus driver's eyes. Somehow the man felt responsible for what had happened, more perhaps than he should. When she looked down again Hannah could hear the bell of an approaching ambulance, as life faded from Jim Birnie's eyes.

It's unbelievable . . . that they were so bright just moments before – and now they're glazed over, as if focussed again upon a distant horizon. One last unfamiliar road for the poor fellow to walk down.

There was a chatter of irrelevant observations among the crowd that gathered following his passing, which might rarely have accompanied such a man as he walked the streets – certainly never with approval or genuine concern. Two sage old dears engaged with the conductress Moira, who broke out a packet of cigarettes, offering them round as they waited for the next bus.

"Old Jim was frae Dundee," ventured the first, "Had a wife who died up there. Worked at the road mendin'."

"I heerd 'im say once he wis frae Orkney."

"Oh aye, true, he did."

"Aye, ken he left home at fourteen, so they say. Got used tae odd jobs an' a life on the road."

"Aye, there was nae work up there ye see," put in the second old hen, checking to see that her cigarette was lit.

"Aye, or mebbe worse, lookin at his age an' aw."

"Oh aye, ah ken whit ye mean sure enough . . . the bastirts prob'ly burnt 'ees fickin' hous' down roon' 'is ears."

"Chuck tough," concluded the first.

"Aye chuck tough," chorused her friend.

"So they say Annie."

"Anyways, Jessie - there but by the grace o' God."

"Anyways, Moira we shouldnae complain."

"Poor man."

"Aye, poor old soul," they all chorused in the queue.

"Horses woulnae ha' done that, mind," ventured Annie in conclusion.

"Oh, I think they would," contended Moira with an authoritative, gravelly voice, looking long at the critical passenger. She nipped out the cigarette she was holding at her side with a practised hand and spun away onto the deck of her bus to find the phone number for the depot.

As Hannah and the driver attended to Old Jim's last rites, Moira went to a nearby bank to call in the delay. This was a primary aspect of her training, so the inspector would come out with the next bus leaving the depot. Moira knew she would be tied up here for a while, making a statement for the police and it was wise to be cautious. She reached into her work pouch and took out a tiny spray aerosol of scent which she squirted liberally around her neck to mask the odour of tobacco smoke. Looking around as she returned, Moira could see two local Bobbies had arrived to direct operations. Trying to order the crowd to disperse or stand well back, met with bold impudence from people waiting in the lengthening bus queue. The driver was brusquely told to park his vehicle up against the kerb to avoid further accident.

"Come on sunshine, load up an' be on yer way, the punters are getting' restless. This Inspector of Pavements has breathed his last. Ye can visit him at the mortuary later if ye' like."

"Dinnae sunshine me pal, or you're the one'll be inspecting the pavement," the driver replied coldly, "And I think I'll load up in ma own sweet time, nae bother frae you *boy*. Ye can tak' a statement now, or no' at aw."

The Policeman opened his mouth to speak but something in the square cut and level gaze of the older man gave him pause. Turning away without further comment the Bobby went to assist the ambulance men turning their vehicle endways on to the dead body lying in the road.

Moira looked at her wrist watch, "Time seems tae be goin' very slowly this morning. It's still on'y twenty to ten an' we'll be on 'til four in the afternoon."

She locked her ticket machine and the take from the morning's fares into the storage bin in the cab, then went to give her statement as the driver waited with the vehicle, "Take yer time hen," he told her, "I'll sing them an Aria."

The ambulance men were loading the stretcher into their vehicle as the conductress approached. Moira rubbed manicured hands over her uniform where it wrinkled over hips and abdomen. Pulling the bobby pin from her head of magnificent red hair to make a good impression, she noticed the Police were taking their time with the driver who'd knocked the old man down, making detailed inspection of his motorcar to establish the manner in which it had been driven. Moira held back to do what she found natural in daily routines – she observed the world in its immediacy, absorbing wildness like a modern day Morgana.

The young man looks terrified. He'll no sleep the night.

The car owner was wearing loudly checked tweed, light coloured Oxfords and a rakishly matching golfing cap.

A man o' substance nae doot.

To Moira, the motorist giving his statement seemed very much out of place in this little hub of transactions, with its discreet locals and rough, swaggering itinerants.

He belongs in Burntisland, or St Andrews, where he'd been most likely heading - perhaps after a detour to a local bond warehouse to rescue a case o' Champagne, or some of his favourite Claret.

Having inadvertently despatched one of the locals, the young man's expression hinted at fear he might be buried up to the neck in sand by one of Buffallo Bill's Indians, left over from their recent visit. Leith after all was famous for its surprising cultural diversity. As a consequence toffs usually stayed up the hill in Inverleith, or travelled through briskly in pairs, unless Lord Roseberry was in town to reveal an effigy to twenty thousand cheering Royalists.

Only the Police and the trouble they dealt with so eagerly were consistent, in this place of eternal surprises. They were legendary - everyone knew what bastards they could be. Moira noticed with surprise when she turned around that her driver, William Macdonald, wasn't in the mood to entertain the regulars with his delightful floor show knowledge of Verdi. Instead her colleague was engaged in deep conversation with a school girl from Bellevue.

Mrs Mercer gave Hannah and Isabella leave to attend the funeral at Rosebank Cemetery the following Tuesday afternoon. Hannah knew this was the fine location in Pilrig on the edge of Leith, where all Edinburgh's down and out people had their final resting place. She had been thinking about the bus driver quietly ever since the sad event. The logic of her interest in him had not fully lined up behind the mixed emotions she felt, especially when to her embarrassment he'd lifted her coat up off the road and colour labelled paints fell with a brush to the cobbles.

Clearly he'd read her intentions like a Government Signpost prefaced with iron bars and a pair of Bobby's bracelets. The way he gazed at her before turning to look at the statue, then back at her – still politely holding out her coat – made her feel blameworthy, even though the plan had been thwarted.

She had not expected to see him again although he had asked her personal questions that very obviously went beyond the protocol of meeting over a roadside fatality – whatever that might usually entail. Hannah re-ran the conversation in her head many times.

"How old are you?" he'd inquired with sincerity.

"Sixteen . . . well, I will be later this month. In ten days actually."

"Whereabouts do you live, Hannah?"

"Why do you ask?" she demanded unequivocally. Rather than suffer embarrassment by explaining himself, William answered her question with one of his own.

"Do you imagine your parents would allow you to see me again – always given that you were willing to? I mean see me again?"

Hannah smiled knowingly as she wrote her address and telephone number on a slip torn from her art pad. In that instant she remembered the anxiety prior to her intended act of vandalism.

"It's funny you know but that poor man's death prevented me from being arrested for daubing a Suffragist emblem on Queen Victoria's bustle," she confessed, holding up her decorator's brush with the three tubes of paint.

"Wow! Aren't you the minx?" The handsome bus driver shook his head slowly with a conspiratorial smile.

"Well maybe it seems petty in view of what did happen here," she admitted, "But shouldn't it give you pause to think again before asking me to walk out with you, William?"

"No, not now that I have your telephone number!"

"In the name of goodness, William, never phone that number unless you want to buy a Life Assurance policy. I don't know why I gave you it. Nothing personal you understand but I'd never hear the end o' it!"

She had not discussed the brief romantic exchange with Isabella. More importantly Hannah was still determined to leave home as soon as possible, regardless of other contingencies – including interest from a chap built like a rugby player, with a face like stage actor Robert Bruce Mantell.

Hannah's sister had arranged a probationary job for her through a connection of Lady Graham's in Liverpool. Elizabeth had written to Hannah before Christmas, saying that she'd been asked if she might know of someone suitable.

'I unhesitatingly advocated my younger sister. It was all very simple. Effectively they will offer you the job because Lady Mary trusts me. All you need to do is swallow your pride, pack your suitcase and head for Monaghan, or Liverpool, or wherever they happen to be in residence.'

Hannah wrote back to her sister with a heavy heart, "I just can't take any more of Margaret's moral blackmail, or you can be sure I'd never even dream of this. It's no longer a question of my continuing education. In fact it never really was, although she was reluctant to allow me the two extra years at school.

I hear him sulking at night when she turns turtle and plays dead. He always has 'a little something for the weekend' on the bedside table. She makes him blow it up, like Casanova. I swear she has a magic amulet under her bodice too – either that or she walked in a circle where a she wolf peed. All this tension is down to me. It's her only way of turning him against me. And if she doesn't conceive soon she may never be able to. I can't take the blame for that Elizabeth.

If Lady Christina is such a perfect Bluestocking let your mentor, Lady Mary, read this letter and pass it on to her. She may change her mind and look again, if only on the basis of avoiding such a choked up reject."

Elizabeth had the good sense to make a tacit commitment on Hannah's behalf, conditional upon her finishing further education. Wishing to avoid contention she waited until a month before the end of the school year before writing again. Unwilling to involve her delightful employers she lay awake pensive in her room, wishing there was a vacancy at her home on the Northerly Isle of the Blessed.

Who knows how the story might have twisted in the interim? Harper's condom might have split. Hannah might have been awarded the bursary to the new Girl's Academy she applied for. Margaret could have changed her heart - before her shallow sea dries up.

Taking pen and paper from her writing bureau Elizabeth resumed the dialogue after a six month hiatus, with an apologetic but explicit tone.

'Hannah I really do not think Margaret is that fixated on your departure, besides, the last time a wolf was seen in Scotland was almost thirty years ago. In any event, I burned your extraordinary letter and told Lady Mary you were thrilled by the prospect of meeting Lady Christina in the near future. It is incumbent upon you to decline, if that is your intention.

Hannah, I cannot begin to describe how sweet life is here, although a close look at routines of everyone I know including the Duke and Duchess, would immediately give the lie to an Elysian notion that the good receive a life free from toil.'

Elizabeth rose early in the morning to walk down into Brodick. She sent the letter recorded delivery, for signature addressee only.

Hannah wrote back immediately, pleading with Elizabeth not to tell Harper or Margaret. She simply couldn't bear to discuss any of these

205

sensitive matters with her stepmother. Knowing that Elizabeth would ridicule her compromised principles, Hannah wrote simply, "Beggars can't be choosers."

Margaret was equally silent on matters of importance to her – not only the issue of Hannah's higher education, now thwarted. It was obvious to Hannah that at last Margaret had fallen pregnant, a source of great joy to all, Hannah hoped. What choked her was the knowledge that Margaret could not even bring herself to mention the fact – much less actually celebrate it openly. Hannah rejected the speeding misapprehension that Elizabeth had mentioned her plan to leave. Not sharing the news was simply typical of Margaret's instinct for concealment.

Doubtless Harper hadn't noticed, so pre-occupied was he with an endlessly rewarding career. In their parallel, compartmentalised lives Hannah felt her parents had become strangers to her and to one another. Resigned to fate she wrote accepting the job offer. All she awaited now was confirmation from the Leslie family in Liverpool. Hannah intended to intercept her mail, then pack and leave the following morning.

William Macdonald was a curious distraction from the anger welling in Hannah's heart. At twenty eight he was unmarried but too old to be of serious interest to her. The conductress he was paired with no doubt had some claim over the man, though she appeared to be almost twice his age. Moira had seemed overtly sexual in appearance and manner, yet there had been no wedding ring on her finger. Hannah shunned these thoughts about William - putting them down to fundamental laws of animal attraction – though she kept returning in her mind to the tears in his eyes for the old man. While waiting for the Police to finish with the driver of the car, William had divulged to Hannah that he had seen old Jim all over town.

"Moira would let him on for free in bad weather," he explained. "She'd leave a paper bag with a meat pie or a sandwich, on an upstairs seat for him to find. Old Jim always went to the upper deck," continued William, as though for some deeper reason it was necessary to give a full account to Hannah, "probably because it was a little warmer for him up there. Also none of the other passengers would have to brush past a dirty old tramp. But Jim was always grateful to the bus crews. If he had a cigarette, he'd offer it to them in return. He never chanced the arm to sleep on a bus when we headed back to the depot to park up for the night."

Clearly that honorific understanding with the old man seemed important to William. The sorrow of it also struck Hannah deep in her heart. He and his conductress Moira genuinely cared about someone that no-one else in the whole world seemed to bother about. Hannah was amazed. They were givers, not takers. The contrast with the callousness of Margaret, as with some of her school teachers, could not have been more profound.

Remarkably, Birnie's gentlemanly conduct and vulnerability elicited more genuine benevolence than her settled family bond. Regardless of what might be construed regarding William Macdonald in terms of his occupation, age or associations, he had spoken to Hannah like an equal. He'd made a judgement about her based upon his observation of unselfconscious actions. Looking past the school uniform and political activism, he saw an empathetic young woman, taking responsibility in the manner of an experienced nurse. That's what inspired him to show an interest.

In turn William had knelt over the dying man. He'd prayed for the repose of the soul of James Birnie with the stern assurance of a Baptist lay preacher. In the shocking severity of the moment Hannah had joined in his prayer, as piously as a pupil in the front row at a Spud Regan special assembly in the run up to Whitsuntide - when the Rector was relieved to see every set of lips moving.

Maybe the gates of heaven opened for more than Jim Birnie, Hannah thought. In that moment of recollection she felt touched by an angel. Hair on the back of her neck stood up in the cold of the familiar room she was soon to abandon.

A fearless psychic connection had materialised between them that could not fail to remind her of the relationship with her mother. Hannah and William had somehow been bonded in sorrow. Something spiritual about the instantaneous understanding between William and Hannah made it feel from the outset like more than attraction. As an inexplicable consequence of responding to the desolate suffering of another individual in his final moments, both were touched with the eternal light of compassion.

As Isabella and Hannah walked through the wrought iron gates of the fine cemetery on Broughton Road they caught sight of William at a distance. Immaculately turned out in a high buttoned frock coat, with waistcoat and rounded shirt collar, he gave the impression of being a man of circumstance. A black tie pin with an engraved square and compass gave a hint of activity beyond job and Kirk. Handsome, broad brush features reminded Hannah of her uncle Keith.

The set of the man told of an all-round athlete. Elevated chin and soft eyes suggested someone attuned to the vagaries of sky and weather. Huge musculature of arms, shoulders and neck confirmed the impression of a man born to the land. Hannah wondered for a moment if she should say something about him to Isabella. But her friend read the look, smiling demurely at Hannah as they approached the tiny chapel of rest. Was it that obvious? Hannah hated the way people jumped to conclusions – right or wrong.

But William's smile as she drew near obviated need for discussion, leaving no doubt in her mind. Neither of them had entirely expected to see the other at the funeral, so the pleasure of meeting again was all the more intense. Hannah saw benevolent light in the bus driver's eyes, going beyond glad recognition. She nervously introduced William to the amused Isabella but the smooth and affable way William spoke charmed them both. He offered his hand to each in turn, gently crooking fingers with the promise of Masonic assistance in any hour of need. Hannah recoiled slightly at this unpredictable stuffiness in a relatively young man. Even more bizarrely, Isabella curtseyed as if she might be newly arrived from the Court at Versailles. Indoctrination Hannah had resisted throughout her school career had evidently worked on her friend.

William Macdonald introduced the girls to a tall man standing beside him whom he styled as Pastor Bruce, "Here to give me moral

support, if I have the chance to say a few words on behalf of Old Jim."
Hannah shook her head dubiously but did not question William's concern. He certainly didn't strike her as a man needing moral support.

There were only a handful of mourners at the funeral service and cremation of James Birnie – though several times more than would have attended had he not been killed in such an unfortunate accident involving a bus crew as witnesses in such a busy location.

Moira the conductress was there at the far end of the pew, with a Chief Inspector from the bus company. A couple of Transport Sub-Committee City Councillors, responsible for the siting of stops and shelters, sat with determined politesse behind her on the second row.

A bevy of tearful Salvationists responsible for running the soup kitchen accompanied by two of James' itinerant fraternity, temporarily washed and brushed for the occasion, were more modest. The Catholic priest in attendance spotted them sitting at the back and directed an usher to invite them onto the front row.

To Hannah's surprise, the impatient motorist was there – no longer looking such a buffoon – attired instead in sombre suit with his head bared. On his left arm was a buxom, pleasant looking blonde, with a spoilt girl's wide eyes. The careless car driver sat self-consciously at the far end of the third pew from the front of the chapel, plainly squirming in the depths of his penance.

Before the service began there came an incongruous, almost unbelievable pop of a magnesium flare. A man in an inappropriately light coloured suit was taking photographs of the coffin, parked beside notaries sitting among the flowers.

"City Fathers Send-off Venerated Indigent," whispered William. Again Hannah shook her head again in confusion, "It's the politics of guilt – if you have to confess, make sure you do it to your own advantage. It's called, 'a photo-opportunity.' They're talking up the new electric tram system, with fixed stops and marked off lanes," whispered William to the two flabbergasted girls, "No doubt they'll all make plenty of money out o' it! And I'm gonny ask them for a transfer," Hannah smiled at him, deciding to forgive the Masonic handshake.

The letter came at last, elaborately phrased and reassuring as any missive from on high should be. It spoke not so much of Hannah and her promise as a Governess for the Leslie family, as discreet mechanisms of vetting and recruitment typically conducted by the elite of the Kingdom.

'You have been proposed as a suitable candidate for appointment by a personal friend of our family, on the advice of a close associate.' Close associate was a neatly ambiguous euphemism for 'your sister'. Hannah was warming to Lady Christina without even having met her. The spirit of the letter seemed to imply the Leslie's broad disavowal of the educational system and what it generally offered in terms of suitable candidates for employment, as well as a clear intention to develop alternatives of their own. It struck Hannah as interesting that, like the Grahams, Lady Christina sought an inexperienced girl with an excellent reputation but no formal higher qualification.

They look for Keepers. Bee Keepers, Book Keepers, Game Keepers – Kiddie Keepers. Docile retainers to maintain operation of the citadel.

In any event Hannah didn't care too much about the impression she might make on the Leslie family, whether they seconded Lady Graham's suggestion or not. She simply had to fly the coop, planning to look again at educational and work alternatives after arriving in Liverpool.

Hannah's last three days at school were excruciating. The more that Margaret and her Career's teacher rammed the suggestion of her taking up nursing, the more Hannah boiled inside at notorious injustices in the discriminatory treatment of women. Certain teachers who never usually gave her the time of day nodded in passing or congratulated her. For what, she had no idea. Prior to her last ever assembly, a first year messenger came with a note for Mrs Mercer, 'Take hymn books and Bibles girls!'

Spud Regan lauded Hannah in assembly as having, "displayed a paradigm of Christian Benevolence on behalf of her School and the wider Community." The dissembling old phoney read out the entirety of an Evening News press cutting, hailing 'Hannah Harper, A Good Samaritan,' attending to the comfort of a fatally injured victim of an unfortunate road accident, as bus driver cum-lay preacher, William Macdonald of Portobello, performed for James Birnie, a gentleman of no fixed abode, his last rites.

"One in the eye for the Catholics there too," joked Regan in 'leaver's assembly mode', which consisted of, 'A hymn, a prayer and a ten minute comedy routine.'

"Our lot would have insisted on sending for a priest," he intoned, "Just being flippant of course," he continued as the odd guffaw rose and fell among the rearward ranks of bleary eyed teenagers, "But as a point of information, it is of course permissible for Catholics, or indeed any Christian, to offer Baptismal, or Last Rites when there is absolutely no alternative. Consult Mr Weston in your scripture lessons upon this question, he added with a glance over at the Rector. Now, turn to Luke, Chapter ten, verse twenty five in your bibles."

"Oh Lord!" whispered Hannah to Isabella, "Not the Good Samaritan again."

Walter and Willie free-wheeled around the entire subject of life and death as Hannah sat beside them with Isabella in the library for the last time ever.

"Imagine . . . that that poor wee mannie was the end product of millions of years of unbroken evol-you-shun!" averred Willie, with the naked eye of the anthropologist. He looked to Walter for support.

"Oh aye!" Walter almost shouted with enthusiasm for Willie's insight, "It's absolutely astounding when ye think o' it, how we've aw come up frae the primordial slime."

Hannah and Isabella continued their sketches of Queen Victoria without comment.

"Aye that's the word fer it . . . astounding. Endless cycles of successful reproduction okay? - in which a living cell, part of the physiognomy of each parent . . ."

"Physiology!"

"Physiology, aye. That's whit ah said Walter, will ye no interrupt, this is an important insight here, rarely considered afore by scientists!" He shook his head, smiling benignly at Hannah before continuing, "Each parent . . . frae they we things that float in the ocean, right?"

"Plankton."

"Aye, ah ken fine! . . . Frae plankton; fish an frogs."

"Amphibians."

"Aye, amphibans. Then snakes."

"Reptiles."

"Will ya shut up Walter? Yer spoilin' ma train o' thought."

"Mammals. Sorry."

Now that Walter had fallen in line with a jaded look on his face, Willie the aspirational Anatomist tutored him by counting off a diorama of species on fingers of his right hand, "Sheep and coos, cats and dugs, aw that type o' thing. Fickin' quadrupeds ih?"

"Monkey and apes."

"Aye man, monkeys an' apes – in fact our nearest ancestors in the animal kingdom."

"Get to the point Willie," advised Isabella.

"Yes, Mr Harris is watching you," warned Hannah with a teasing smile.

"Well, all of that unbroken evolutionary history, comes tae an end when a person dies wi'oot offspring."

"And your inference is?" Isabella asked indulgently.

"A man should'nae take any risks wi' ees spermatozoa. He should start early. Each passing day is a threat to the survival o' the human species. I have a duty to generate as many descendants as humanly possible in ma sweet, short life. I think you two fine female specimens should he'p me in ma mission. We can start today if yis like."

The ferocious cry of outrage from the girls, with coarse laughter from Walter, immediately drew Mr Harris the head of Maths. He was supervising statisticians in a project report on pupils entering further and higher education, such as Willie and Walter. It was a nice end of term holding activity but if discipline lapsed, they would quickly get bored and he'd have to teach a lesson.

212

Harris came over to the girl's worktable, promptly expelling all four of them from the library.

"You two brazen hussies get back to your own division room in the girl's school! And you lads should know better as prospective sixth formers," he added, "You'd better not behave like this in my classes next year!"

Too late and with only superficial interest, her parents resumed the pressured discussion of Hannah's future that evening. Standing at the ironing board as Hannah and Harper finished their supper Margaret emphasised each point she made with a doughty welt of hot metal upon compliant cotton, or the occasional dismissive flap of Harper's shirts.

"Tell me if ye will," she began rhetorically, "What's so bad about nursing as a career? It put food on the table when your faither was building up his Widow's Fund round, going out in all weathers talking tae men who'd rather put money on a horse. Why won't you even talk aboot it?"

"Answer yer mother," snapped Harper, but Margaret was in a voluble mood and covered Harper's rhetorical assertion in case Hannah had a mind to object, "One way or another, I've been a nurse all my working life. It gave grounding to you and your sisters when you're own mammy couldnae cope with her chores."

Hannah had often wondered when that particular item might come up but it had been so long and was so unexpected, she almost choked on a mouthful of boiled potato and cabbage. Her eyes watered with shameful anger. Feeling cornered she put down her fork, trying to compose herself.

"She's got a good point, Duff," Harper stated quietly, "We all have to work for a living. If employment brings equality to women as you advocate, then work for a change within that context. There are women doctors now and that shows how the world is changing. Exceptionally talented women *are* coming through."

"Do you mean like Marie Curie? They refused to let her study at home in Poland, stole her research and gave her honours to a man!"

"I am talking about here, not Paris. Look how the Macmillan sisters are influencing Educational Boards up and down the country. There will be well qualified women in every type of occupation in the near future."

Hannah sat at the table with only a silent tear for reply. She felt like saying,

Yes, but that won't include me will it? Margaret has seen to that!"

Hannah already knew the line her father would take, about working and studying at the same time, as being the ideal way of tailoring professional interests to employment opportunities. Swept up in his intellectual purse seine Hannah knew there was no hope of wriggling past dense, existential logic.

It was what he knew of life's experience and it *was* perfectly valid but she just couldn't bear to hear him say for the hundredth time, 'This is the way it has always been - women can't be good employees *and* have children too.'

She knew that in Harper's view there was a Malthusian dynamic to the relationship between employers and women which gave them the lowly status of recipients of charity – rather like Dr Barnado's children.

Harper had seen that apocalyptic vision first hand and made the habit of reminding them, 'Overpopulated farms couldn't increase production because all the men left to find work elsewhere. It's no wonder Victorian cities filled up with the poor.'

Placing his hand on her arm, Harper spoke as gently as he could, "There's no need to fight for change Duff. It will happen naturally, as job markets create demand for women employees."

"Oh yes Daddy, they'll pay us half as much for doing the same job as the men. And who do you think might protect us from that kind of abuse? Kier Hardie, or Manny Shinwell? In the meantime, as women fight for justice, owners will recruit even cheaper labour from the Colonies – like the Indian dock workers down at Leith. And who speaks up for them? In the end it still amounts to exploitation and injustice."

"I fail to see what any of this has to do with nursing!" howled Margaret, forearms on the ironing board and curlers framing her tight little face, as her fierce blue eyes flashed with vehemence. She spoke with zealous confidence, inexplicably reminding Hannah of a snake charmer she'd once seen in Portobello. Hannah felt perplexed, wanting to look away.

"I don't *really* understand what you want Duff . . . But this time you're gonny listen to what I say," Margaret softened her tone marginally, for the benefit of her lord and master, "Mrs Mercer rang up again. What was it she said John?"

"She said you have natural ability as a nurse. Oh yes – and self-discipline, endurance and toughness. You are inured to the emotion of mourning, but have excellent humour and compassion for others, well beyond your years. She also said she'd written a reference for you, for some job in Liverpool."

Hannah needed to change the subject back to nursing almost as badly as she wished to vent her true feelings. Despite barely contained rage, she was suddenly burning with embarrassment. At last, after years of cracking under a ponderous weight, the dam of unvoiced feelings burst.

The clash of cutlery onto a plate of unfinished food seemed to snap back at Margaret's heavy handed ironing. Hannah raised her voice in anger for the first time in her entire life, "I do not want to be a ruddy nurse! Can you not come to terms with that simple fact Margaret? Why ever would I? Shall I elucidate? You may recall dear, I spent the formative years of my life completely traumatised by sickness and death. First my ma when I was three years old. Then Great Gran, whom I loved and knew better than anyone as a small child, when I was only seven. Then Elsie, barely two years after. To boot I've lived every day since witnessing my mother's passing under the rigid discipline of an aspirational matron! Let's face it, I just don't fit into your calculations Margaret. I need to think for myself, to act as an individual in my own right. In case you didnae ken, I'm a person with feelings, not a monad, nor a cipher."

Harper and Margaret looked at one another, trying to follow Hannah's line of thinking. Margaret puckered her face quizzically mouthing 'monad?'

Before either could speak she continued the tirade, but with a voice lowered back to its normal volume, "What I mean is, I am more than the product of other people's needs, individual or several. I refuse to fit the sum of *your* expectations for me, just because it's a convenient outcome of your efforts to support me for sixteen years that I become a nurse. I *will* experience choice in my life, even if it entails disappointment for you, or failure for me. Listen to me now, both of you!"

They stared at Hannah in silence, shocked by the intellectual tow of a long rehearsed argument, "Don't *ever* ask me again what I want from life, if you are not prepared to even consider the answers I give!"

With that Hannah stood up from her half-finished meal to sweep out of the room in silence. Neither Margaret not Harper thought to ask about Mrs Mercer's reference for the job in Liverpool.

The following day when Harper came down to read his newspaper and engage with Duff in her usual morning exchanges, he discovered with a sinking heart that she was gone. A scribbled note was folded on the dining table on top of the daily paper, next to the morning's post.

It read, 'Harper, I am so sorry for scolding you and Margaret. Still, I think my departure really is for the best. Please don't follow or try to prevent me from leaving! I have been offered a live-in job with a reputable family in England, as mentor for their two young children. I will write soon with the address and may telephone you at home if you feel we might actually be able to listen to one another. In the meantime try not worry about me. I am my father's daughter, so I will thrive. Thank you both for all you have done for me,

Love ever,

Hannah xx'

Harper read the letter twice while anxiously re-running the conversation of the previous evening in his mind. With a solemn face he turned to scan volumes arrayed above his head in the glass fronted bookcase that had become his office and study area many years before. He ran his finger over dusty antiquarian sale items including works by Hobbes, Locke, Hume, Kant, Hegel, Marx and others.

Despite open minded striving he had given up on most of them half way through and could never put any of it into a satisfactory moral framework – which was all that had really mattered to him during his time as a night school student.

In the midst of the Second Industrial Revolution, the present age of materialism, his golfing friends said that 'Science killed Philosophy, as surely as it put the last nail in the coffin of Religion.' That at least was the prevailing dark rumour amongst homespun intellectuals who would rather read a novel by Conan Doyle or Joseph Conrad, than speculate about where we all come from. After all, 'who might have a genuine perspective?' Harper asked himself. Some tenured genius at Glasgow University perhaps, though who would engage with such a person, other than a bar-room full of acned students?

What was once regarded as illuminating and precious is now a side issue. Possibly the historical dialectic can be best witnessed in church communities merging under one roof, who used to be at each other's throats - like at the Abbey Kirk where Margaret and I got spliced.

"Where the hell is it?" he said aloud. Harper knew precisely what a monad was but imagined Hannah's reference was to something with a deeper philosophical context, maybe from Pythagoras or Bey but couldn't remember precisely what. Finally his hand hovered over a work by the German Philosopher, Gottfried Leibniz. After a moment's hesitation he slid the book out and dropped it onto the table.

Having read around the subject of mathematical science as part of his study of Actuarial Accounting he knew a little of how probability interfaced with human psychology - but it had taken a prompt from his youngest daughter for Harper to reconsider some of what he had once studied as theory, in the light of personal experience.

Duff was entirely lovely, bright and sensitive – more insightful and constructive in her innocent expressions of doubt than her obviously brilliant sister Elizabeth. At least Hannah wanted to apply whatever she learned. Too late Harper realised that she was the one who deserved an opportunity to access Higher Education, leading on to university. Mortified, holding his head in his hands, he wept silently for all the small ways he had failed his delightful Duff.

Part Three

Chapter Eleven   *Daxy's Muff*

Hannah was searching titles on the low profile book rack in Clarissa's dormitory suite when Lady Christina appeared in the doorway. Strikingly beautiful in a burgundy evening gown made enticing by a voluptuous figure and yellow hair, she looked every inch a character from one of the volumes of Grimm's short stories.

"Oh, you're just about to read to her?"

"Yes, your Ladyship."

"No, no . . . you mustn't do that, not in front of the children. They're far too young to understand. You are going to be responsible for all aspects of their education."

"But . . ."

"No buts, I'm Christina, she's Clarissa and you're Hannah." Hannah laughed at her own folly, "Sorry, I thought you meant don't read to her." Christina laughed too and Clarissa joined in, shaking her head and pointing a middle finger, "Hannah, not Lady Hannah!"

"What have you selected?"

"Oh, that can wait. What would you like me to read?"

"Well, we did rather like Perrault, didn't we Clarissa? Or the brothers Grimm, or there's a new edition of Children's Favourites and Fairy Stories, that large red one."

"I want Mowgli!" said Clarissa, pointing at the book in Hannah's hand.

"Oh, Kipling? Well at least she won't have nightmares!"

Christina sat with Clarissa and Hannah on a custom made soft leather sofa over by the window next to the fire. Taking turns to read two pages at a time all three quickly became absorbed in The Jungle Book, so much so that she was late for her social event and her personal assistant, Alice was despatched to find her.

Clarissa spilt cocoa milk on her mother's lap and Alice fussed over her.

"Oh no! What a wonderful gown. Can I help you dress Christina?"

"No, he'll just complain if make him any later. Last time it was vomit which didn't mix at all well with Eau de Cologne. I'll just wipe it down with some carbonated water, thank you."

"But milk will pong when it dries."

"Oh stuff! At least it won't smell as bad as Hugh after the brandy and cigars." Christina hugged and kissed Clarissa, then to Hannah's amazement turned to embrace her and then Alice. She called into the bathroom annexe, "Eight o'clock bedtime, Helena, no later!" She blew a kiss to her eldest daughter and walked briskly to the door. The heady fragrance of French perfume hung in the air in Clarissa's crèche long after the late summer evening had turned to night.

When the girls were fast asleep Hannah went to play snooker with Alice, eager for a foil to help her match the skills of Sir Hugh who was competent and Lady Christina who was unbeatable.

A postcard showing the pier at Portobello came at the beginning of July, bringing an immediate smile to Hannah's lips. The message from Willie Proven was not the first correspondence she'd had since leaving but served to confirm the level of surprise as well the extent to which she was missed by one and all.

'We were all astounded at your leaving without a word. Thought perhaps it was something I'd said, or Walter dribbling all over you. Tell your people that I am planning to come for a weekend.

Aye,

Dr Richard Brane MD'

Isabella tried to persuade her to return, as did Harper, who promised her a place at Gillespie's, 'Come hell or high water,' Harper vowed, 'I know people who know people, who will get you in, despite the clamour over precious places for girls at what was traditionally a boy's school.'

Hannah wrote back saying she would not return to Edinburgh, or even discuss it further – she was adamant.

She intimated to Isabella in her first letter that she had, 'hit the ground running, to borrow an analogy from the world of rail commuters. Yesterday I was changing nappies. I asked to do it and they let me, although strictly speaking I'm not supposed to. Later in the evening I was reading bedtime stories. Within twenty four hours I began to feel at home but have not actually had a chance to catch my breath since. There are at least four people here who would talk the leg off a stool. I can't say who just yet but hopefully you will come and meet them.'

Three months had passed in the blink of an eye! Isabella broke her rail journey on the way to visit her dad in Paris and Willie and Walter came down for a weekend in late September. Jim was too busy and had no holiday entitlement but he sent his love. Lady Christina's enigmatic Personal Assistant, Alice, indulged them like long lost friends providing separate guest rooms and offering to arrange entertainments. Picking up on Scouse vernacular Willie told Hannah they were 'gob-smacked.' Walter demanded Hannah give them the full house tour, which she did with her eldest charge, Helena Leslie, toddling along in front as attendant courier.

In his own inimitable style Willie insisted on trying on a housemaid's uniform and Lady Christina's silk dressing gown. Luckily she was out visiting friends. Helena laughed fit to bust.

"Evidently Wull has not lost his touch with the girls," observed Walter.

"You try it on!" shouted Helena but Walter demurred thoughtfully, promising to give her a game of 'French tennis' instead, where the idea was to gently keep the ball in play.

On Saturday evening Hannah offered to take them into town to see a show Alice had been talking up, featuring an exceptional troupe of Jamaican singers but all they wanted to do was play snooker and walk around the lawned and wooded grounds. Willie wanted to find a fishing rod to angle for carp in the Japanese garden, which everyone but Helena felt was a very bad idea. Alice shook her head and claimed Hannah's ticket for a friend whom she discreetly avoided mention of by namen.

"It might be a long time till I save enough dough for a place like this," explained Willie, "I hope you don't mind, Alice. I want tae make the most o' it!"

"Maybe you could just rent in the meantime?" suggested Alice, quick to slip into his Edinburgh drollery.

On Sunday afternoon over a delicious five course meal of roast beef with fine wines freely offered despite their ages, Willie and Walter talked politely with Sir Hugh and Lady Christina about school and career prospects - respectively in the worlds of Medicine and Accountancy. All too soon it was time for them to head off to Allerton Station and travel north.

Taking coffee with Alice after the event, Lady Christina voiced the opinion, "They are fine boys, Hannah. You have some charming friends."

"Aye," thought Hannah, "Butter wouldn't melt in their mouths."

With a view to comparing notes with Elizabeth, Hannah wrote asking about their 'respective families', telling her in detail about her own situation.

'The Leslie's Mansion in West Allerton is discreetly charming in its veiled opulence. Superficially it is what I imagine to be described as 'Victorian Renaissance' - by which I mean reverentially Elizabethan retrospective in style – you know tiny yellow bricks; big exposed beams with peaked gables and multi-panelled glazing, lime plaster rendering. The house is triple-fronted with three separate entrances, each with their own stairways (front and back) and there are in total no less than fourteen bedrooms!

Unlike larger, more traditional houses, it has two fully equipped kitchens and four spacious bathrooms, if I include the en-suite in the Master Bedroom. In a way it's an ideal design for an extended group - in this case the Leslie family, plus staff. Allerton Grange is private without being rambling or cramped.

On the west side of the house (the back) are two tennis courts and a snooker room. I can't imagine what their country estates must run to but if I was wealthy I know I could imagine nothing finer than this harmoniously designed country house.

Wooded slopes run down to open country to the rear of the house, beyond the lawns. There are lovely walks through pasture land north and south. So much for the accommodation and setting.

In the centre of the building, playful concealment ends to reveal the most amazing double stairway, surrounding a grand entrance hall, with natural light streaming down from above, filtered through teasing coloured glass. Finely carved folding doors open or close in two semi-circles to reveal or partition off a sumptuous music room with glass dome above and grand piano in the corner. Beyond this traditional ballroom are two smaller sun rooms, flanking multiple French doors giving way onto patios and lawn. Then there are the usual adjacent spaces – library, dining room, study and drawing room.

And there is a railway station two minutes' walk away! Sir Hugh jokes about having made them build it for him personally, so he can get in to the office more quickly in the morning. It may well be true!'

Hannah felt the need for discretion where outsiders were concerned. Even Elizabeth cautioned her about giving too much private information away, in her return letter. Normally Elizabeth just adopted the fashionable convention, rarely giving advice about anything. But importantly Hannah too needed to tell someone that she felt unexpectedly happy. She wrote:

'Almost immediately after coming here I felt respected and needed. From the outset the Leslies and their staff recognised and approved of me, for what Alice Hughes has kindly described as 'competence and unselfishness.' I had to pinch myself. Was she talking about someone else? 'I must learn to be content with being happier than I deserve,' even though I'm too exhausted to read Jane Austen.

Elizabeth, how strange it feels to no longer be taken for granted or ignored, as was so often the case at school or at home! My little charges, Helena and Clarissa, aged three and eighteen months respectively, are even tempered and quite charming. Developing relationships promise so much. Above all it means, quite explicitly, at least five years of retention, during which time I will be expected to travel and interact with the children. I can study in my free time and begin to save up for the house I hope to buy in Portobello, when I finally return.

I have made a new friend in Alice, Lady Christina's Personal Assistant. Alice is no caricature of the norm. At twenty three she is serious minded, or at least tries very hard to sustain that impression, despite an iniquitous sense of humour. Alice is more than competent in a host of formal responsibilities, demanding interaction with the Leslies and all their staff.

Frankly I'm amazed to find a person of Alice's obvious quality and relative youth working in such a capacity but she obviously loves it here. Lady Christina indulges her, at times treating her more like a close friend and confidante than a personal assistant. Alice is a brilliant actress, musician, dancer and impresario. I suspect from bright hilarity which I regularly see around this place she is in fact Lady Christina's alter ego.'

Elizabeth wrote in her reply,

'Your long term intention to return home may dissipate when incentives of a career with such a noble family become more fully realised.'

To emphasise the point Elizabeth sent a package accompanying her letter. In the box was a piece of the most sumptuous fur - a ladies hand warmer of the most elegant style but despite Elizabeth's good intentions, Hannah was not in the least charmed by it.

She looked at the mink hand warmer but didn't touch – sniffing disdainfully to herself before returning to open and read her mail. The cardboard box from Elizabeth lay open all day on a Japanese lacquered table in Hannah's charming, spacious bedroom, as she went about routines with Helena and baby Clarissa. Eschewing consideration of the article, Hannah avoided touching or even looking at it, until her true thoughts had condensed.

When evening chill entered the room through windows on two sides it occurred to her that this might be a time to playfully test its efficacy. Lifting the long mink hand muff tentatively from watermarked crepe paper, Hannah slipped it over her hands then linked her wrists. It occurred to her that if the fur had been reversed to the inside it would certainly have worked as a hand warmer but failing such departure from convention in the world of high fashion, a lady with cold hands would still require matching fine gloves.

She laughed out loud, "Pah, ridiculous!" she said to herself, tossing the article back into the presentation box. Taking out her diary, confident for the first time in years that only she would re-evaluate its content in years ahead she wrote,

Wednesday, October 13th 1909.

Pelage

'Who decides such a thing? Were women who wear these furs ever consulted by men who produce them? Who defines what is desirable in the manufacture of such items in practical terms? Perhaps Sami women, sewing boots for their children with the skin on the outside? Evidently not. More likely some wealthy idiot wandering Oxford Street looking for a Christmas present for his doxy. He will pay hundreds for something Reindeer herders take for granted, if they can afford a carbine more readily than credit at the store in town. This reversal of logic characterises the strange ways in which the world can be turned on his head by convention and also the essential paradox of human personification. We *do* personify everything - from the phenomenon of Creation to our pets and stuffed Teddy Bears. This human weakness lends the emotive quality to fashion. It makes me smile to imagine ridicule aimed by humble Inuit at the wife of a visiting Canadian dignitary, stupidly wearing her warm coat inside out. I am baffled by the unimaginable wealth of a million notables in ten thousand cities and centuries past across the globe, who between them created this market imperative defining stupidity as appropriate. If all they want us to do is admire the magnificent coats of animals, why bother killing them? They might spend time training the creature . . . invest in a suitable lead.'

Imagining coarse woodsmen inspecting evil traps, Hannah shuddered and took off the muff. Pitching the scraped remains of several dead rodents back into the box, she placed it out of sight with walking shoes at the bottom of her wardrobe.

The Leslie family encouraged openness and individualism in interaction with all their employees. Hannah felt certain they were unique and soon realised she would never need a reference to work for another noble family. She'd already been spoilt. Work experience would never involve the transference of skills because no-one else would want her – and she would probably not want to work for them.

Sir Hugh Leslie was on the board of directors of a railway company based in Liverpool. He worked extremely hard on a daily basis, although he had no need of additional income. The wider family had estates in Scotland and Ireland and owned diverse investment properties around the globe including so Alice told her in India, Malaysia and the US. It seemed the Leslies were used to talking openly about almost everything, except the finer details of business and legal matters that involved vast corporate structure. 'Everything' included aspects of their personal lives Hannah supposed most members of high bourgeois elites would avoid speaking about entirely.

One evening a couple of months after she had settled in, Sir Hugh asked Hannah to return to the library when she had finished reading Helena her bedtime story. He was in his favourite niche by the fireside with a book and glass. Asking Hannah to sit he offered her a drink.

"No, thank you, Sir Hugh, I've not eaten yet."

"Ha, want to keep your wits about you," he said, more as a statement than a question, "Well sit down won't you? Take your ease."

Turning a chair towards her proprietor, Hannah sat beside a square mahogany writing table.

"Christina told me to speak to you. She says I'm far too busy to give the time of day. I'm on notice to chat with all the staff on a rotational basis. You've settled well Miss Harper, would you agree?"

"Please call me Hannah, Sir Hugh."

"Splendid, if you drop the Sir, I will call you by your first name as well."

"I'll find that difficult."

"Well practice . . . say it now."

Hannah smiled expansively, "I *will* find that difficult, Hugh."

"Excellent . . . so would you agree?"

"I am happier now than at any time in my entire life."

"I like that subtlety in a young person, especially a woman. You say 'happier now' rather than happier here." Hannah waited for Hugh to make his point. "You have no illusions Hannah do you?"

"I'm not entirely sure *everything* is not illusion Hugh, no *delusions* though."

"I'm not sure of the difference. I'd need to look it up but most certainly everything is illusion."

Hannah laughed, "You're right, I would need to look it up too, if there are any differences. The concept of delusion was something that pre-occupied me for a while."

"May I ask why?" Hannah lifted her right arm onto the padded antique table, opening up her shoulders as she warmed to Hugh.

"I wouldn't know where to begin explaining, but in a word – education; my own education."

"Ah, eureka! The solution to all problems. Why do you smile?"

"Oh . . ."

"Please Hannah don't say, 'Oh nothing'! That's the one thing I can't tolerate. It's probably why I married Christina, she never hesitates to say what's on her mind."

"There was a period of several weeks when the boys in my school ran around the place shouting 'eureka!' Their Classics teacher explained the word and they began to filter it into conversation. It was quite funny at first."

"You went to a co-ed school. Tell me, which contingent are more disruptive of good order in classes, boys or girls?"

"There was no disruption. There was dry humour and its counterpart, frustration, occasionally bursting out at the seams."

"Hmm, I'm a Trustee of the Liverpool Collegiate at Mossley Hill. I wish I could say the same about them."

"And you believe education is the solution to all problems?"

"I'd have to mull that over for a few days. You know the aphorism about horses and water. If it isn't, I can't imagine what else could be. Christina would have me raise the matter in the confessional."

"As a palliative for doubt?"

"Indeed – 'examine your conscience' is standard advice for Roman Catholics. I try very hard to keep a foot in both camps."

"If you don't mind me saying that seems historically rare."

"Not according to your sister Elizabeth. She says its common practice in Lothian for faith communities to share the upkeep and turn on the heating in winter." Hannah beamed with surprise.

"Oh, you met Elizabeth!"

"I thought she told you? You came highly recommended."

"Well thank you. Lady Christina has been more than kind to me. She helps me choose books and suggests play activities for your daughters. I can't imagine being any happier. I'm glad Elizabeth spoke up on my behalf."

Alice regularly invited Hannah to accompany her around the city, on days when the Leslies went out together as a family or on their evenings off, for which both had fairly regular scope, as neither Christina nor her daughters were particularly demanding after around 8pm.

There was a weekly Suffrage group meeting at a church in Bootle with popular appeal, which soon became a window for both into a new world. The young women found one another easy company and soon became firm friends. Both liked to talk. Alice and Hannah agreed that the most disarming people were those prepared to reveal a little of themselves, without raising obvious social pre-conditions.

"Maybe the Leslies have so much wealth that conventional barriers no longer serve a purpose," ventured Alice, as they walked briskly towards Allerton station one autumn evening.

"Most of my father's golfing elite would not deign to talk to anyone without first checking testimonials and credit worthiness, although background wouldn't matter so much," cautioned Hannah.

Alice laughed aloud, recognising someone of a similar nature in Hannah. Being older and longer established with the Leslies, the template of her routines meshed easily with Hannah's itinerary and status as Governess, allowing them to develop free-time activities of mutual interest. Whatever subtle chemistry was in play between Alice and Hannah, it worked like magic. Hannah quickly fell under Alice Hughes's spell and Alice for her part could not have been more appreciative of her devotee.

Most remarkable about Alice at that phase of her life was passionate condemnation of religious pomposity, although she frequently voiced the elastic claim of creed upon her own soul. Killing time between buses they strolled down to the esplanade facing the broad Mersey, Alice explained that her father was a Baptist Minister in Stamford and her mother ran a small but appealingly prominent woollen shop. The product of mother's endless hours of recumbent watchfulness as she took in a steady stream of coin from smiling, overweight farmer's wives translated into access for Alice to a renowned finishing school, some thirty miles south of her home in the folded greenery of saintly Cambridgeshire.

"Some of the girls would hop into bed with one another," Alice revealed, lowering her eyes for a guilty moment, then looking straight at her new friend. Hannah was sensitive enough not to comment, or ask what wasn't volunteered.

Alice the impresario was rehearsing for the part of Varya in The Cherry Orchard, to be staged during the festive season by Allerton Amateur Dramatic Society. She'd learned all the other female roles as well, for fun. Despite Producer Russell's entreaty that she employ the rich Home Counties English acquired at finishing school, Alice preferred to broaden her professional range by parodying a variety of optional voices. Naturally these included Russian, Liverpudlian, Irish and, for Hannah's benefit, Edinburgh Scots. Within a week or two of knowing Hannah, Alice had added Morayshire Scots to her repertoire of hilarious caricatures.

"Fair is foul, and foul is fair: Hover through fog and filthy air," Alice croaked with a Highland lilt, as they paraded down into an evening pea-souper licking between warehouses and tramp steamers.

"The villainy you teach me, I will execute, and it shall go hard but I will better the instruction," Hannah retorted in her best Mediterranean pidgin English.

"Ih, Whit the blue blazes are you on aboot hen?"

"Surely you know Alice? If you mention the 'Scottish Play' its bad luck. You need to quote The *Merchant of Venice* to ward off the witches curse on thespians!"

"Oh thanks pal, ah didnae ken. Us proddystunts dinnae believe thon Popish twaddle."

"So ye won't be making the pilgrimage tae Rome in the Kings's entourage?"

"No fear hen!"

The effect of Alice's mimicry on both women was electrically funny. Brown freckles Hannah hadn't noticed before seemed to appear from nowhere as veins in her tight skinned, pretty forehead distended with laughing. Hannah cautioned seriousness long before they approached the church hall but all eyes turned Alice's way as she stumbled through the door with a dizzy grin on her face.

Alice Hughes's disciplined performance as mysterious, deeply religious Varya, for the suburban elite of West Liverpool in the run up to the festive season of 1909, was nothing short of breath taking. For Hannah, Alice was Varya brought to life.

Awaiting an opportunity to repay kindness and encouragement Hannah told Alice after the opening night, "Revelatory events may be possible everywhere Alice, but this is one I will never forget. I'm certain

Dr Chekhov would be delighted if he could have seen your performance." Hannah Harper became Alice's second most avid fan - after Russell Evans.

The following Tuesday evening the NUWSS meeting was cancelled in the run up to Christmas but they decided to go into town anyway. Alice revealed a little more as they walked arm in arm down the lane from the house.

"They indoctrinated me. Did your family indoctrinate you?"

"Oh yes, as thoroughly as most: 'Think for yourself, question everything, believe nothing till they've built it and it hasn't fallen down for a few years!'"

Alice laughed as Hannah spoke, "Gawd . . . you blummin' Scots are radical mate," she blustered, trying out a fashionable Aussie persona to lighten the mood.

"Tell me about it?" prodded Hannah discreetly.

"Oh, you can't imagine. I feel guilty as soon as I start thinking about it."

"Well, if you're not ready to talk . . . I'll be there to listen when you are."

Stopping on the lane opposite the railway station Alice sat on a bench, closed her eyes and prayed silently. With fingers spread apart in piety, she reminded Hannah of Caravaggio's storyteller, from *Supper at Emmaus*. Hannah waited patiently. Moths flew madly into the angled glass of the street lamp behind the bench. At length Alice began to bare her dualistic soul.

"Supposedly faith is all about 'commitment' yes . . . but commitment to what? At first it was easy - when I was young and didn't have to think about morality and difficult choices. But every imponderable was answered indirectly from the Holy Bible, as a handbook of legalistic judgements." Hannah avoided comment as her friend became visibly perplexed at thoughts and images within.

"You see it's not just a question of 'The Leap of Faith' if what you are being told is plain bloody wrong. I mean, I believe in an All Seeing infinitely compassionate God. I also believe that Jesus was God

231

incarnate. But here's the thing - I do not accept the mores of an ancient culture which committed genocide and used women as servants. Somehow they lost me in the detail Hannah. I just can't sit there looking pious, pretending to be enraptured when there is so much obvious confusion and hypocrisy in this world. We are not put here to smile at our own salvation but do nothing."

Alice seemed to be petitioning Hannah, standing in front of her with hands thrust into coat pockets - demanding some kind of perspective on faith. Alice's pretty mouth hung open as though there was more to say that she dare not utter. Huge porcelain doll eyes glistened fiercely under tears of self-doubt. Despite being several years older, to Hannah she was the embodiment of moral rectitude and innocence. But even the lovely Alice was guilt ridden.

Hannah wondered for a moment if guilt somehow defined the human condition. Her answer, when it came, was floundering and hopeless, "Well, religion has its place and faith is faith. They are not necessarily one and the same. If you still have faith you will go back, when you decide how the Church can change . . . you know, become more relevant to the times. When you have reflected upon how, you may contribute. Maybe one day they will have women in positions of seniority."

"Oh no . . . they're blinkered. They take it all for granted. Their smugness drives people away. Pastors I know are so busy talking about sin and forgiveness that they never really listen to what anyone has to say, positive or otherwise, unless set within their chosen context. If they can't win every argument they simply avoid the discussion. I live by principles of my faith and I pray Hannah. I've been blessed with love and compassion for others less fortunate. I thank God for those gifts. But I am not constantly in need of forgiveness, nor do I have the desire to be imbued with folk tales from a millennium before Caesar invaded Britain - somehow intended to enlighten me as to my current shortcomings."

"Okay, let's find an all-male bar in town and demand to be served." Alice laughed like a back street battler, slipping back into the Aussie idiom, as if Hannah had thrown a switch, "But I don't drink beer Sheila, nor do you!"

"We'll ask for vino then, or sarsaparilla".

"Well okay cobber, jump on your mule!" intoned Alice - this time with a Russian accent, "But only if ve can play Billiards. You know I love play billiards in moral crisis? Huh?"

Disarmed by the sudden lightening of tone, Hannah laughed open mouthed at Alice's spontaneity. Her natural humour had turned the black mood round in an instant. In that sense at least it struck Hannah, Alice truly was blessed.

"I guess that about wraps it up for Old Religion, eh?" pleaded Alice thinly, still seeking forgiveness.

"Ne'r mind eh, Matilda? We can always paint our faces an' go walk about with the Abbos," retorted Hannah, proffering the crook of her left arm.

"Yeah Cobber, let's start our own Dream Time!"

That evening the women agreed to seek out the first dockside saloon that might tolerate their presence. Hannah was left with an over-riding impression that her delightful friend's crisis of conscience was not just about the strict moral code of being a practising Baptist.

As the train approached Hannah tentatively broached the subject for her, "This deep moral concern is about your affair with Russell Evans, isn't it? You've broken the mould." Alice looked at Hannah appreciatively, glad she was confirming her own perceptions.

"Shhh! I'm Dreaming!" she breathed, as a half a dozen carriage doors flew open.

Looking from her window a week or so earlier Hannah had registered a tender moment between Russell and Alice. Lady Christina had taken it into her head to organise the girls in pruning fruit trees in the orchard and break open the stored Bramleys as a reward. She had risen early to ask the Cook, Mrs Heap, to bake pies if she would. Alice had visited Hannah in her bedroom with a cup of tea and passed on the request for her to join Christina and the girls in the orchard just behind the northern end of the house. Hearing children's laughter and excited voices, Hannah dressed down for the occasion.

Looking through her gable window fifteen minutes later to check the weather, she peered through sheltering Yew trees to observe of the trio working excitedly beyond the brick wall of the orchard. Armed with a pole cutter and frame saw borrowed from the gardener Mr Selkirk, they were cutting back branches to sew into a mesh for a slow garden fire. Helena and Clarissa called to one another enthusiastically as Lady Christina stood on tip toes, to bring next year's fruiting branches back into reach.

Smiling as she turned away to find her winter boots, Hannah was surprised to catch a glimpse of two people at the far end of the long wooded driveway, near the north gate. One of them was unmistakeable for his sheer size and balding head with naturally black side hair. It was Russell Evans, Dramatic Society Producer and local Co-op Manager. A slightly built woman of average height was standing on tip toes just like Lady Christina in the orchard, only she wasn't reaching up to cut back an unwanted growth.

Although they were over a hundred yards away along the avenue of Cedars, Hannah knew by the hem of a dusky yellow dress showing under her coat, that this had been Alice having a tender moment with Russell. Remembering a story once told to her by Great Gran Han, concerning her parents, she turned away from the window, with a smile of hope for Alice and Russell.

If she chooses to tell me I will consider her dilemma, otherwise Alice's indiscretion is none of my business. I will neither think not speak about this.

As the locomotive began to slow down for the stop at Mossley Hill an elderly couple sitting opposite got up to get off. Alice chose the moment to re-materialise back into the real world.

"I'm not sure whether he's characterised more strongly among the household as The Gay Batchelor, or the Lonely Widower. We daren't even tell them the truth about him being the wolf in sheep's clothing." Hannah was shocked to hear Alice repeat the same Chamber Maid's caricature she had overheard. It meant that someone repeated

234

information only divulged by Russell to the Housekeeper who conducted business with him.

"Who could be the source of such gossip?"

"Mrs Mason, the person he spends ten minutes chatting with every other day when he makes his deliveries. She comes across as being such an agreeable lady - adding two or three new items to Mrs Heap's list every time he comes to take an order, as if he were the International Buyer for Harrods."

"Hmm, I've noticed him always standing in the kitchen vestibule, never invited to come in and sit. I think he's too polite Alice. She treats him like her own personal Butler."

"The truth is she's a pompous, two faced old wind bag who'd not think twice of destroying my reputation or his. One may smile and smile and be a villain."

"Well regardless of that, love for Russell is causing you anxiety isn't it?"

"Hmm, Spanish Castle Magic, Hannah. Don't worry, I'll figure it all out."

Finding a bar near the docks called The Raven, which Alice knew had a reputation for hospitality, they immediately found themselves welcomed by two men playing snooker. An acne covered road mender wearing an overcoat which it looked like he might actually sleep in, watched Hannah with hawkish blue eyes as she approached daringly to put a coin on the rim of the table. Tar stuck to the uppers of steel capped work boots and there was filth under his trimmed finger nails.

"Oh Dear Lord, not the Sally Army, or worse still the Temperance League?" The young man was clearly smart but heavily taciturn. Evidently he had money and was glad to spend freely on his opponent, judging from a tray with eight drinks he leant over the bar to pay for between shots.

His friend was dark and slender and much more relaxed. As he bantered with the disarming younger man buying the drinks, Hannah guessed he had a Polish accent.

"If they convert *you* man, they reduce drink problem in Liverpool ten percent overnight!" Both of them were smoking roll ups made from loose tobacco.

"No, we're rabid Suffragists actually, who hate being hung upside down with our knickers exposed," answered Hannah with a cool swagger. Alice let out a wild laugh, then drew more attention by mimicking the other man's accent.

"Why you say this? When you hung with knickers out? You don' even wear knickers!"

"Funny! Andy McGiffen," admitted the larger man, gracefully holding out a thick warm hand, "And yes, before you start an argument you're welcome to play snooker. On condition you join us and we buy all the drinks for the rest of the evening - unless of course you decide to abandon us for being too unwashed, or crude – in which case you pay for a round before you leave. He's Marek Zalewski by the way but don't tell anyone I said that," intimated McGiffen, leaning his cue in the direction of his associate.

"Unwashed in his case ladies, crude in mine," added Zalewski casually, "I eat like a pig and fart in bath."

"But that is *na-ice!* You are honest, good clean boy!" replied Alice, still in the vernacular. Hannah shook her head at her friend's challenging boldness.

"Take your shot big man! I'm too busy with introduction, making roll up. Sorry ladies, please, come sit! Join us, lovely Galician Suffragettes. We don' bite," he insisted, waving an arm at empty seating.

McGiffen laughed, looking across the table at his friend, "Unless someone sits on your head you mean."

"By the way ignore this man. I always do . . . he is gobby scouse bastard."

Hannah's first impression of Marek was that he was on the wrong stage, in the wrong theatre. Lank hair and a refined, innocent face with almond shaped eyes made him seem Latin American in appearance, never eastern European. Was he a marionette of witches, or a figment of the creative master of the Dreaming? For Hannah, Zalewski even had the wrong name. He was a victim straight out of the heinous diary of a

Conquistador – Maricanchi perhaps but not Marek. Hannah knew without needing to be told that this unusual looking man was probably on the run from his home country and that because of his unusual appearance he could never hide even among other Poles.

McGiffen played snooker tirelessly to curb enthusiasm for drinking too much, which he did despite himself. He accepted with alacrity Alice's bushwhacker caution, "We play regularly in the evening at home so watch out matey. Don't offer challenges unless you're prepared to take sandwiches to work for the next month."

"Orrite Judy. T'anks for the warnin'," he retorted sceptically, "By the way your Polish accent just slipped. I had a feeling you were from down under."

Between small sips of beer, Zalewski rolled and smoked attentively to avoid talking about himself, scrutinising the women with the frown of a Cattle Barons' agent, speculating about the value of breed stock. Alice gravitated to Andy with whom she felt safe. Hannah gravitated to the Pole, whom she guessed might need protection at some point, if only from Andy.

When a group of Irish Dockers came into the pub half an hour later more coin was placed on the rim of the table. Easy glances were exchanged between McGiffen and the quare fellows which if ignored at this early stage of the evening would lead to social impasse an hour later, after the first gallon of ale apiece had been consumed. Reluctantly Andy gave way, buying another round of drinks before coming to join Alice and Hannah, where they sat at a table with the inscrutable Pole.

McGiffen spent the rest of the evening talking serious politics, mainly diverting toward his own challenging opinions which they quickly realised were intellectually dogmatised. Nonetheless the self-styled 'communist' road mender was quietly impressed with the two young ladies, especially when they spoke openly about their employers.

"Noblesse oblige!" Andy jibed, with a smirk on his broad seborrheic face, "Come the revolution we'll just throw them in jail if they're that decent, after a fair trial of course. All the other local aristos will be lined up and shot against a friggin' wall." Hannah snorted convivially through her soft drink.

"You think I'm joking love. I'm not – I'd shoot the bastards myself," pledged McGiffen, "If it came right down to it, I would."

"If you expected it might change things for the better? Like Robespierre and the reign of terror in Paris?"

"Precisely! It's what governments do to stay in power. Why shouldn't revolutionaries do the same? In the two years following the failed Revolution in Russia, executions went up sixty fold."

As Hannah debated with McGiffen, his friend Zalewski was happy to chat up Alice but was essentially saying much about nothing. He seemed suspiciously paranoid. Hannah guessed his receptive understanding of English was much more advanced than he was letting on. She tolerated Andy because she was fascinated by Marek, hoping somehow they would become friends.

At first Hannah was guarded about her involvement with radical political groups but as the trips to play snooker became regular, she became increasingly confident in a wide range of public situations. In the dockland pubs where McGiffen and Zalewski arranged to meet, Hannah and Alice were introduced to a number of familial, mainly quite young people who sought to challenge them in a benignly informal manner. There were union officials, students, longshoremen, even a Catholic priest who told them to call him by his first name, then argued that he too was a communist.

Father Robert Jordan told them, "The Qumranian community, of the early Christian era were *communalist*, if not precisely communists according to the Manifesto, but for a religious man it amounts to the same thing."

Alice was amazed. Short and neatly ginger haired, with a rich Scottish accent, Robert seemed to complement Alice's probing with bookish abstraction. For a moment Hannah imagined temptations a man of the cloth might encounter day to day. He was everything Alice had been taught to admire but in black clerical clothing with a dog collar.

"I've heard of this community," she told him, "It's where my own Baptist faith sprang up I think."

238

"Oh yes, in a sense it did Alice. There is a Baptist group in Iraq, whose original community pre-dates the crucifixion."

Alice smiled timidly. "But how does that make you a communist?"

"Well, as a priest I have no personal property as such. I've dedicated my life to helping others. Also I believe the Holy Mother Church needs to move with the times. As a Christian I have to bear witness to the corruption in public life. In principle I agree with sharing everything – including the abstract notion that in a sinfully unequal society, property really *is* theft."

"Hmm it's easier for a camel to pass through the eye of a needle, than for a rich man to enter the kingdom of heaven," said Alice with enthusiasm.

McGiffen couldn't resist interrupting with a smile, "Father Rob, we all know fine you're just trying to convert people. You don't have to work on Marek but it's too late for me – I'm on the road to perdition! You're welcome to call on us for a smoke and a drink anytime . . . just don't expect to save my soul."

"Oh Andy, I think you are a lot closer to salvation than you think," pronounced Father Robert, from under his flat tonsure of red hair. He held the snooker cue with both hands joined, as if it was a blessed altar accoutrement. McGiffen smiled, a cigarette balancing on his lip, "Well maybe you can give me Last Rights when the Bluebottles storm the basement and kick me fuckin' head in."

Father Jordan laughed more easily than anyone at McGiffen's front, "Maybe you overestimate your importance in the scheme of things Andy. You're no terrorist!"

"Well, I'll tell ye now if I was rich you wouldn't catch me wearing' a camel hair shirt!"

Foremost amongst the fluid gathering of easy, laughing friends were trade union organisers with working class political affiliations, which seemed to Hannah to have grown naturally out of a close network of traditional dependencies.

Jim Brown, a Dock Worker's Shop Steward, mockingly stylised himself as 'poor but honest.' This tongue in cheek response to every greeting where friends asked after his health resonated with Hannah.

"Most of society are poor but honest Jim," she told him.

Jim joked that he would have taken Hannah home and thrown his wife in the street if she was willing, "Just say the word love. I'd rather walk down the street holding your hand than spend the night hoping for a fortune in an oyster bar!"

"Yeah, cos she's not as salty and your breath wouldn't stink when you got home!" Ribald laughter rose above McGiffen's vulgarity.

"Ow, ow! Steady on now, take that back Andy."

"Sorry love, you should know better than consort with a crew of rustic commoners like us!"

"I didn't say that, lar! I mean my breath doesn't smell! I'll have you know I brush my teeth twice a day, an' I carry a pack of Wrigley's Spearmint everywhere I go!"

Hannah observed Marek and Andy's wider circle to be typically sharp-witted, coarsely funny and indomitably proud. At first she permitted, then cautiously encouraged predictable questioning of her views and political leanings. Alice and Hannah had never been so challenged or alive as in the pubs and streets of industrial Liverpool with their new friends.

Invitations to political campaign meetings and demonstrations followed. Without thinking twice about it, Alice Hughes and Hannah Harper had stepped right into the centre of a loosely conjoined protest movement.

Despite the warmth and generosity of people they met, Alice felt growing restlessness at first then wanted to run for cover. Already traumatised by ideological dogma she decided nonetheless to remain loyal to her much younger comrade. For friendship's sake she decided to accompany Hannah, whenever duties allowed. But this was a far cry from 'improv' at West Allerton Dramatic Society.

Hannah found working with Helena and Clarissa generally easy, if a little tiring due to its intensity. According to Christina there were, "No rules, other than engage with them constantly wherever we go and permit me to take over when I need to. You'll know, because I'll give you a wink . . . like this," she said angling her head and winking with her left eye.

"And if you forget to wink?"

"I won't forget. No wink means, 'get them out of my hair fast!' Don't look so perplexed child! I jest constantly but I'm no hoaxer," explained Christina, reclining decorously with a glass of Sherry in the south summer room at the rear of Allerton Grange.

Hannah sat on the opposite side of a circular wrought iron table, which she imagined if polished regularly would outlive them all. Sipping warm tea, Hannah was dehydrated after eating a supper of roast chicken the previous evening. She hoped to drink it quickly then ask for a second cup. Maybe Mrs Heap the Cook had been too liberal with the salt, she thought idly as Christina waxed lyrical.

"One thing I would recommend is that you tire them out before meal times. Also as Clarissa is becoming more demanding, read with her after her supper rather than permit games. I will join you frequently as I regard bonding between a mother and child as essential. She will let you know when she's ready to go to bed."

"Yes milady, thank you so much for all your kindness. I plan to review books in the nursery and ask Alice for funds to buy more."

"Excellent – and there is no need to thank me. You are absolutely ideal. Incidentally, one thing before you go?" said Christina lowering the volume to the nearest her smoker's foxy rumble could get to a whisper.

"Yes milady?"

"No offence but you really have to drop the 'milady.' I recall asking before. We are not living in the Dark Ages. I don't wish to be constantly reminded of my fortuitous birth right. Please address me as Christina. If I may presume upon it, I'd prefer to call you by your first name too."

"Yes, certainly. Please call me Hannah."

"Well, that's settled. Would you like more tea dear? You look like you could do with another cup. I need to tell Angela not to put so much salt in the chicken baste." Hannah nodded with a knowing smile. Her throat was dry and Christina had already lifted the pot. "I'll play mother."

Head of the Liverpool based branch of the Leslie clan, Sir Hugh exemplified a class of eccentric philanthropist whom Hannah found it easy to imagine in the role of Kingmaker in a past era. It was her guess Sir Hugh was perhaps more circumspect than Edward the Fourth's Warwick. He was certainly more genial.

Half a dozen years older than Christina, Hugh was only in his late thirties but a clear reflection of past centuries shone out from under thickening ginger eyebrows. Thankfully he'd replaced carpet slippers for the silvered poniard. Despite his geniality, Leslie carried an indefinable quality of power in his leonine voice and broad, slightly stooping shoulders, although at five ten he wasn't tall.

When Hannah knew him well enough to speak tentatively of the Suffrage Movement and the role of women in post-industrial society, he warmed to her instantly.

"Good for you Hannah! Get involved in something meaningful and pursue it with all your heart. Set your own moral standards my dear and learn to live by 'em. That's the only real challenge in life, although there are constantly fiendish distractions from it. Sort that one out in your head and the rest is easy. Just don't set fire to any railway stations," he warned, levelling with her over his bifocals.

Then he added more thoughtfully, as if recalling a previous conversation, "Complex world we're in nowadays. Far too many bull headed Nationalists you know? Idiots shouting for war abroad, when they should be advocating justice at home. We certainly need more women in public life to strike a balance."

Like many English aristocrats she'd observed lately at Allerton Grange, Celtic or otherwise in origin, Sir Hugh seemed to speak with the dictional economy of a Surry horse trader.

Another subtle paradox, like the mink muff - sophisticates who think it disarming to emulate the clipped mannerisms of the venal bourgeoisie. I wonder how I appear to him. Does my speaking voice betray cultural prejudice, or inverted snobbery? No doubt it does.

"If that's all sir?" she asked politely.

"Indeed . . . Look I'm not keeping tabs on you but always tell Alice where you are going and when you'll be back." Hugh's tone flattened to the Monaghan lilt underlying his public school education and long association with English friends.

He wanted to say, 'I might have to bail you out of Edgehill Women's Penitentiary sometime,' but he wished to avoid patronising Hannah.

"We're meeting at St Francis Xavier's church hall in Everton, Sir. I'll be back by eleven."

"Oh ho, case in point Hannah Harper! Watch out for Spring Heel Jack!"

Smiling confidently at Sir Hugh's refreshing contradictions, Hannah spun off to her room to change out of work clothes. Ten minutes later she rushed out to an evening meeting with other Suffragists met through Zalewski and McGiffen. Their friend the 'communist' Catholic priest was happy to rent out the church annexe to members of his community, for a secular evening meeting with moral overtones.

Chapter Twelve   *Southenders*

Hannah saw the road ahead as the beginning of adult life, which she embraced wholeheartedly, without fear. That evening she was elected as Branch Secretary of the Women's Suffrage group, NUWSS – The National Union of Women's Suffrage Societies.

With direction from older initiates, especially women from textile mills, Hannah began to make acquaintances within the Trades Union Congress. She met shop stewards of the Dock, Wharf, Riverside and General Labourer's Union, listening to speeches by numerous others in what seemed to be a critical time of striving for improved pay and working conditions. Her union were non-aligned, "Unsurprisingly, men being men," she told Alice when reporting back, "we met with a mixture of both resistance and support from Liberal and Labour affiliates. Women being 'naturally conservative' in their view, they'd prefer not to extend us the vote!"

"Until the revolution comes and then we *all* get to vote for the same party?" Hannah laughed at Alice's quaint reductionism, "That's democracy for you Sheila!" she added with a grin.

McGiffen lived with his mother and much younger sister Irene in a brick terrace a stone's throw from the Mersey, neatly situated between the Leeds and Liverpool canal beyond the Stanley Docks. His father was an absentee navy man, who Andy promised to put in his grave if he ever appeared at the door again. When queried by Hannah he told her, "No, I don't wanna chuffin' talk about him. Suffice it say he's a cruel bastard, living up to the reputation of every old salt – 'never drunk at sea, never sober on land.'"

Aileen his mother came out from her darning to greet them in the hallway. Massively built and bursting out of her summer dress, she extended warm hospitality, trying to prevail upon them to have a cup of tea. Zalewski brushed past calling, "Hi ma!" to scoot downstairs to clear up the basement room where he lived and worked. Andy spoke for the others without politesse, declining on their behalf.

Hannah sat with Alice in the basement in a cloud of tobacco smoke, as they all sucked on bottled beer like they'd been nurtured on it. McGiffen the road mender came across loud and clear as a horse that had been led to water and chosen to drink his fill. Zalewski listened respectfully to his pupil, speaking only when invited to answer Hannah's objections.

"As a whole the political movements representing working men and women amount to a tenuous but potentially very powerful group. They have overlapping interests. Longshoremen and Merchant Sailors are often casually employed, or dismissed without good reason. They understand the plight of women who usually have the same issues. 'Hire and fire' suits the owners, because uncertain retention keeps wage bills down. These men have been victims in the past . . . but now they're beginning to organise – to flex their muscles."

"I find this fascinating! I want to get involved and I want you both to help me. Whenever possible, I will volunteer to attend union meetings as a delegate from NUWSS."

Zalewski answered for Andy, "Okay, Hannah what about your political credentials? You have to choose. One way or the other men will ask. A few *may* support you if you represent Con U but the majority will never again give you the time of day. Being Suffragist is not enough, you need broad political affiliation even to gradualist, male dominated shite. Excuse Liverpool vernacular. I never learn to curse until I come to this rough city, full of Irish bastards."

McGiffen laughed effusively for possibly the first time since the girls had met him. Pale blue eyes and wild ginger hair made him look like an enormous baby, a scaled up version of the ragged urchins playing within earshot in the crowded summer street.

"Okay Marek. Take me to political meetings of Socialist groups that you are involved with."

"Okay, I will gladly do that, but first you read Engles and Marx, I will give you books. Communist Manifesto; Condition of Working Class in England; Capital - critique of Political Economy," Zalewski tried to scowl at Hannah with his pleasant face, expecting signs of intellectual prejudice.

"That's Okay I've read Engels, but I'll borrow Das Capital if you'll lend it to me. I won't be visiting home for a while."

"You read 'Working Class?'"

"I had to. It was a condition of staying on at school."

"Your teacher was communist?"

"No-one was a communist. My father insisted. He said it was the most important book of the last century."

"Oh, I am impressed. I'd like to meet father."

"Feel free; come with me to Edinburgh. He'll sit up all night drinking with you, then teach you how to play golf the following morning."

"See, what did I tell you about Scotland McGiffen? Okay Poputchik, Andy will now brief you on fire drill . . ."

McGiffen swallowed deeply from his beer, looking at Zalewski in surprise. But he stood up and walked casually to the far end of the basement where he lifted a wrought iron grating and threw it onto a dusty old dining table, next to the Eddison Mimeograph printing machine that dominated the room.

"This is the coal chute we used before I put the locking concrete bunker in the yard. I only use it when the miners threaten to strike, cos the local scallys would be in there in two minutes. Ma keeps her coal in the scullery." Hannah did not ask what Andy kept in the coal bunker at other times. Perhaps sub-consciously she didn't want to know.

"So, listen carefully. What I'm telling you is, if the Bizzies come you'll have thirty seconds to climb out of here and leg it down to the canal."

"You think they're watching you?"

"Oh yes, and you too by now Alice."

"Oh, Good Lord. And what then? I mean if they do pay us a visit?" Alice looked like she expected to hear the door kicked in and Aileen pushed roughly aside at any minute.

"Good question. Come on, I'll show you. Drink up an' we'll go for a walk."

Helena learned to read, Clarissa to walk and talk. Both had hair as white as Norman butter, with cornflower blue eyes. The Leslie children were charming and Hannah was their best friend. Life was sunshine and flowers. Christina worked, organised and entertained but didn't dictate. West Allerton Grange was a well-run ship, on which Hannah rose to the discipline of accommodating others. From Christina she learned to open her ears and her heart at the same time. From Alice she learned to have a pocket diary to hand at all times and the fine art of prioritising commitments. Political activism had to be kept separate and secondary, or it could never be sustained.

When asked to a follow up meeting with her patron in the library Hannah told Sir Hugh that she wasn't angry; that she loved her job, seeing it as a challenge but was moved by an ethical spirit to get involved in the main issue of their time. She went on to say, "In every meaning of the word I have come to see myself as a benign custodian of your children, a mature big sister essentially."

"Splendid, I agree fully with that sentiment. This was precisely how Christina characterised the role to me when we first discussed the matter. You have a great deal of responsibility, as their first intermediary for the big bad world Hannah. Their bonding with you is entirely natural and acceptable. In time they will learn to love and trust others, without becoming overly reliant upon anyone but themselves. You are the perfect role model."

Hugh studied Hannah over his whisky tumbler. One side of his face was red from collar to hairline from sitting close to a blazing fire, the other as pale as a plucked chicken.

"Was there something else?"

"Yes, there is," he answered slowly, "I have a personal request and a gift for you if you will accept. One dependent ont t'other, if you'll pardon a Yorkshire-ism."

Hannah smiled to see the horse broker learning to relate to others outside of the Home Counties. "Don't be surprised, I hear you and Alice teaching the girls your comic routines. Clarissa called me 'cobber' when we were playing croquet last Sunday.'"

"Oh, I do apologise, we need to be more guarded how we talk to one another during the daytime!"

"On the contrary. A little natural freshness in a child is part of their experimenting with language. Don't change anything on my behalf but watch out for Mrs Mason." Hannah waited to hear the request.

"I would like you and Alice to take the children swimming at St George's Baths. I've arranged for an instructor there to teach them, if you are unsure how. She can teach you and Alice into the bargain, if there is a need. Christina picked these costumes out for you. The smaller one is for Alice, if you both agree. Christina has the receipt if you wish to change them, or take them back."

"That's a wonderful idea, thank you!"

"Don't thank me, thank Christina. She wants to go on an ocean cruise. In the meantime I plan to convert the north-wing conservatory into a heated pool room. Supervising it will require professional vigilance."

"And preparation."

"Precisely . . . speaking of hazards that we all learn to step around . . ."

"Yes, Hugh?"

"Be very careful what you commit to Hannah. They are watching you."

In the year that followed Hannah dragged Alice along to meetings with Fabian Society and nascent Labour Party affiliates. Marek encouraged her to study press cuttings he'd collected about activities of Bolsheviks in Russia. In turn Hannah and Alice invited McGiffen and Zalewski to NUWSS meetings.

After one such regular Tuesday evening meeting, Marek introduced Hannah and Alice to two émigrés sitting in the corner of a popular seaman's pub, The Baltic Fleet, opposite the Albert Docks. McGiffen explained, "The landlord at the Fleet is known for discretion and can help a fellow disappear as if by magic, if the Bizzies appear with the Battle Bus–which is normally cue for a brawl."

The bar offered Lobscouse, generous Norwegian fare favoured by the world's most respected seafarers, in turn enhancing Liverpool's reputation as home from home. Ale provided was usually in plentiful supply and allowed to stand for a week in a large cellar before being tapped and was normally of the highest quality. Hannah would have felt at ease in the place on any social occasion. She could hear at least four different languages being spoken at the same time, as they searched for Marek's friends. Men crowded around the bar looked proud and decent. They laughed easily and tolerated other groups they were unsure of. One man's face lit up as they approached.

"Marek! Dobry wieczor," said the younger, smaller of the two men smilingly, standing to hug Zalewski.

"Ladies, meet my brother Sigismund. Siggy, this is Hannah, and Alice."

"Very pleased to meet you both, at last."

"How interesting, he's been talking about us to his brother, Alice. I wonder if that's a good thing?" Hannah replied with a smile.

"No, really not much at all! In fact the less Marek says about a woman, the more likely it is he's fallen in love."

Hannah held out her hand to Marek's smiling brother. Siggy took her hand but instead of shaking it, he bowed with his left arm crooked behind his back, clicking heels together like a man of military background. Half a dozen knowing pairs of eyes instantly turned Siggy's way. Hannah smiled before glancing at his associate.

"This is our cousin Stan, also from Gdansk," asserted Siggy nervously. Hannah knew instantly the big man sitting watching from the corner was not Siggy's cousin, nor was he named Stan. Maybe Arkady or Dmitri if she had to guess.

Hannah noticed a down-dressed fellow with a one month beard, wearing a woollen hat and nursing a pint with both hands. Maybe he was waiting for someone but everyone in the friendly bar ignored him. The fellow had slid low to a nearby table to make himself small, staring into the middle distance with the crazed expression of an inmate of Moss Side House Psychiatric Hospital, with a hint of a Cheshire Cat smile that said nothing so clearly as, 'Fuck off an' mind yer bizzo if you don't want trouble lar.' Cheshire Cat studiously ignored their friendly banter.

Stan was equally impassive. Enormous and fair of complexion, mane and beard, the cousin from Gdansk was twice the size of Marek and clearly Russian or Ukrainian. Fear looking out from the good fellow's eyes spoke of need for refuge. Reluctance to speak and a closed face told Hannah instantly he hadn't come to Liverpool of his own volition. Looking at Marek with a pained smile, she asked a silent question.

"What is wrong?" he whispered. Hannah put her hand on Marek's shoulder. Leaning close to his ear and smiling casually like a young lover, she murmured below the hubbub and Alice's attempt to engage, "I'll tell you later. Your brother is very gracious . . . but he's an open book Marek, more vulnerable even than you are with your carefully faked passport. He should never try to lie. Let's get out of here!"

As they headed out past thirsty seamen onto the pavement Alice suddenly felt exposed, not to leering intentions of men eager for female company but from scantily clad prostitutes, who summed her up instantly as 'a hard-up posh, slapper.'

"Woz up luv? Daddy kick yer out coz ye gor preggers?" one of them called after her.

"Yez can bunk up wi' me if yer like, I'm not such a meff. A pretty arse like thar'll be good fer biz, an' we can share the rent."

"Yeh, wor about it gerls? My ma'll love you Southenders."

"Yeh, bring yer boyfriends back darlin'! We can have an orgy." A gale of high pitched laughter rippled across the street, to the delight of old familiars approaching from the docks to interrupt the ragging. It was early in the evening or the corner girls would certainly have given pretty, overdressed Alice a more hostile reception.

As the group of friends sauntered towards McGiffen's house near Stanley Dock, a filthy cloud of grey smoke billowed towards them.

"Chuffin' 'ell tha's comin' from near my gaff . . . look there's a blaze in the street!"

"I think they finally set fire to your tar truck Andy, like we planned. Maybe the riot started without us," joked Zalewski, for once hinting at their intentions. Half a dozen small boys ran in and out of the pall, lobbing bits of an old pallet onto whatever the source of the fire was in the middle of the street. Uniform in appearance despite differences in age, they were all emaciated. Despite running wild with excitement, the children were all probably older than they looked. Their hair was shorn to deter lice and nits - a privilege which Hannah noticed was not extended to three girls watching from a safe distance on the pavement opposite. They contemplated the game, stern faced like the Morrigan awaiting a time of redress. All of the girls and boys had something in common though - their clothes were grubby and tattered.

"Little bloomin' scally-wags, look, they've set light to a mattress right next to me wagon!"

One woman was busy reeling in washing as night fell, from a double pulley cord draped high above the street, where no-one could steal her laundry. Wild, howling laughter accompanied her strained effort to recover the hand washed clothes before they were thoroughly contaminated. The street kids' focus was evidently targeted with pride on a pair of worn out old gutties tied at the laces, flung up with great persistence to drape over her washing line. They swung suspended twenty feet up, above the middle of the street.

"Hey wash 'em for us missus will ya an' 'ang 'em out ter dry, there's a love?" shouted the ringleader, a skinny fellow with a flat cap and a waistcoat, "They were starting ter make me webs pong. I think ah must a stepped in a dog turd about a year ago!"

"Get lost you li'l gob shites. Go on . . . fuck off!" McGiffen ordered as the group of activists approached the blaze near his house. Half a dozen children retreated up the street, to carry on the banter from a safe distance.

"We've been lookin' after yer wagon for ye mister! Gie us a ha'peny fer a poke o' chips. Me stomach thinks me throat's been cut!"

"Put this fire out first. Youz'll get no'tin till ye do. Don' come knocking till this is all gone. And don't chuck that mattress in the canal!"

"You're too kind Andy! They set fire to that so you'd pay them to get rid of it."

"We all have ter earn a livin' somehow Marek! Welcome ter Stanley Villas, Siggy an' Stan, the only place in Northern England where the cockroaches hide in fear. When the dock is full an' the tide is in - the sewers back up. If it rains tonight the streets'll be runnin' wi' shite when we head off ter work in the mornin'."

It transpired that Stan and Siggy had worked in several sea ports across Northern Europe. In McGiffen's basement, amid piles of leaflets and flyers for meetings generated for meagre profit on behalf of affiliates, including the Catholic Church who kept Marek in rolling tobacco, Stan gave account of himself in muted tones. He described the awful living conditions of industrial workers and peasantry at home in St Petersburg.

"I leave my country nearly five years, after uprising. Terrible repression followed," they sat in silence more rapt than a trusted priest in a confessional box.

"They round up people like you. Good people, how you say," Stan pointed two fingers at his head. Alice let out a barely audible gasp but Stan realised she had misunderstood his meaning.

"Intelligentsia, same," said Siggy.

"Da, inteligentsja, all rounded up to rot in jail," he explained, smiling benignly at Alice.

They discussed nationalism in the Baltic States and Poland, how it is always used by brutal regimes to mislead and repress. Stan began to relax as he continued his exposition, "Police came to look for me in Gdansk, at Santa Anna Church because I help organise Straz against Imperial German bastards. They don't want Jews, hate Pomeranians; fear Russians; hunt down communists, like Okhrana. Instead they take people homes away, just because they are not Prussian. He knows, army officer," said Stan pointing at Siggy, "This will be same if you allow," grumbled Stan, "You organise now . . . to fight this thing here."

"What 'thing' Stan? Paint a picture for us," Andy demanded, "What exactly is the force at work here?"

Stan looked to Siggy for a more precise description. Sliding down in his chair the former soldier smiled indulgently, remembering what he'd learned before absconding, "Divide et impera, et divide ut regnes. One and the same thing Andy. If they cannot repress you, they will send you to war. Either way, elites constantly seek division." Observing Alice, Hannah could see she was sombre with apprehension.

Stan's accent sounds like Alice's impromptu Russian but for once she's not inclined to mock.

Marek, perhaps concerned with Hannah's rebuff in the Baltic Fleet, had been silent till now, "Secret Police watch Liverpool," he agreed, "They know what can happen if they are not ready. Poor people all round the world are angry, ready for revolution."

Despite Stan's successive flights from oppression, they encouraged him by degrees to speak freely, undaunted in their idealistic intentions to create a socialist forum. Andy brought the travellers plates of stew and a jug of ale.

Once they'd eaten they began to relax, guarded however about speaking too freely of home and family. What they did commit to was the broad intention of eventually returning to their respective homes. As the little group talked late into the evening the three émigrés seemed the more grim and resolute – utterly convinced that the way forward was 'continual revolution.'

Turning to Hannah and Alice, Marek said, "Now that Stan and Siggy are here we will advise Liverpool Dockers and Suffrage Unions on military action, with layered resistance, until we are caught and thrown in jail."

"By 'layered resistance' you mean acts of terrorism," stated Hannah.

"If you saw what I saw, you'd want to be ready," said Siggy, "They use soldiers against civilians. That is first step in creating division, why I am zdrajca - dezerter."

"It's our only hope for the future," added Marek, "We have suffered brutality first hand. Been driven away in fear for our lives. Capitalists respect only when trains do not run and ships are not unloaded. And armed resistance."

A knock came at the door and Alice visibly jumped. Andy loped upstairs with a purse in his hand in which he kept coins for betting at snooker. Voices could clearly be heard from the street above.

"No we dint piss on it mister, honest! We used water in a pale, dint we lar? We dumped it in the Stanley dock like you telled us."

"Ye daft bat lar, I din't tell ye that. Take that pale back where ye nicked it from. Here's a ha'penny each. Now go on, clear off. An' don' be windin' up thar ol' ma wit' her washin', or I'll come out there an' gi' yer a thick ear."

"Thanks mister! You're the boss!" came the chorus from half a dozen urchins in rags. In an instant they raced down the street like a flock of starlings at dusk, to make the chippie before it closed.

Strolling in confidence with Alice along green lanes of West Allerton towards the Leslie mansion, Hannah realised they had travelled in silence up from Lime Street. The magnitude of societal complacency that had to be overturned oppressed them both. Alice ceased her natural variety act, unable to step with confidence into a Vaudeville routine to raise a laugh.

"What are you thinking Alice?"

"Something you asked me about Russell, not long ago. I'd like to turn back on you."

"What's that?"

"Do you love him?"

"Russell? He's adorable! Why, do you see me as a rival?" Alice laughed so much she had to stop in the lane and Hannah turned to wait for her.

Alice shook her head and pointed. "You! You are incredible. No-one will ever outflank you."

"What? What did I say?"

"Stop pretending! You know damned well what I mean, Hannah. Do you love Marek?"

"Of course, as a human being. As a dear brother - an individual worthy of being loved as much as any other."

"Oh! As much as me?"

"Well, yes. And I love you very much Alice."

"Good Lord . . . I preach at you about frigging religion like you just climbed down out of the nearest tree . . . but you're the one with the living faith. Please forgive me Hannah, I have no right."

"Alice, tragedy closes some people off from the world. Take those girls on the street who shouted abuse at us. No doubt they are all just as worthy of respect as you or I. Under the ignominy and danger of their marginal existence, every one of them has feelings and personal dignity. They sell their bodies but their souls are somewhere beyond. Out of reach. Not unlike the grubby sailors they give comfort to."

"Go on, I'm listening . . . how does this relate to Marek?"

"Marek is devoted to redressing the ills in society, no doubt because of some great loss he finds it hard to speak of openly."

"But you can't fall in love with him!"

"If I did why would that be so wrong? You've broken the mould with Russell."

"Wake up and smell the cowshit cobber!"

"I am awake and I can smell it. In that field, just beyond the hedge."

Afraid that there wasn't time to say what she needed to say before reaching the house, Alice stopped again in the middle of the lane. Reclining against an ornate fence bordering fringes of the Allerton Grange woodland, Hannah waited, hands thrust in pockets of her unbuttoned coat.

"Okay get to the point."

"It's not just Marek. Andy has his own truck."

"He lays tar for a living. He makes money."

"That's precisely what I'm trying to tell you."

"What? They earn money and spend it on a wagon?"

"No, they *make* money. Andy is what, twenty three? Yet he runs a work crew, all living in the same cheap trinket boxes with outside dunnies. But with the wad he carries he could move his ma and the girls out to Freshfield."

"It's where he grew up. What would the residents of Victoria Road say about a truck with a tar boiler and rakes parked outside on the street?"

"He'd never have to look for work again. He could spend his time filling in pot holes in unadopted lanes. Like this one." Hannah was silenced. Alice really was older and wiser, even if she had been educated at a private boarding school.

Eventually she accepted the point, "Look, I apologise Alice. I see things too. And we may see both sides of the coin before long."

"The crates of beer in the basement?"

"Yes, and the printing press. Marek could have managed with a small mimeograph but that thing is an industrial quality press."

"Now we're talking. The day Andy took us for a walk down to the canal?"

"Sure, what about it?"

"More bottles stacked behind the outhouse next to the concrete coal bunker?"

"True but they drink all the time, when they're not working and Andy used them for topping the wall."

"You noticed? Smashed glass mortared all along the top of a six foot high yard wall. Does McGiffen hate the local scallys that much Hannah? I don't think so. They treat him like a God. The street kids flock around asking him for money. What does that tell you?"

"Tar smells like petrol, doesn't it?"

"Now you're thinking what I'm thinking?"

"Maybe . . . why is the coal bunker so far from the back door. If ma ran out on a winter's night, she'd need to take off her slippers and find a pair of wellies."

"Good question. And what does he keep in it instead of coal?"

"Why did they take us along the canal that day Alice?"

"Because if we get lifted by the Scuffers, we'll spill the beans."

"And it will double their chance of escape if Police are searching a hundred barges, back yards and boat sheds, while they head for miles of warehouses, with cargo steamers conveniently berthed alongside."

"So whaddya think cobber?"

"I think Andy and the Poles are a small part of a complex chain of socialist, republican cells. Perhaps someone is financing them who they know little about. I believe you are right Alice. They're not just printing leaflets and forging passports. They're preparing to man the barricades."

Relaxing now that Alice had managed to clear the air they walked on into the gentle summer night. Rounding into the avenue of trees leading to the house Alice lowered her voice, to avoid being overheard by anyone sleeping with a window open.

"The difference with a walk through the streets of Everton couldn't be more bluntly contrasted," laughed Alice nervously.

"No, I was just thinking something along the same lines. Everton's not too bad Alice, compared to the Derby Road area and houses backing onto the docklands."

"Yes, all that work going on next to all that poverty takes your breath away doesn't it?"

"I have no illusions. I've seen it all before Alice, in different parts of Edinburgh. I can also say I've seen urban development how it should be. Edinburgh has its slums but nothing like on this massive scale. At least there are green spaces to walk into, not just twelve miles of industry sustained by an army of the poor."

"Do you think the government will ever do anything about these squalid conditions?"

"I doubt it. I imagine the same pattern repeated in every major industrial city in the land."

"Look at this *modest* building before us – with Sir Hugh's attempt to enhance it with a heated pool," said Alice waving her hand at an excavator nestling in the trees beside the orchard, parked up ready for the family's imminent departure to Monaghan, "There is architectural ostentation in every Town Hall throughout the land that would make this house seem ordinary. Civic buildings, cathedrals and churches, opera houses, railway stations and public-parks – but it all gives the lie Hannah doesn't it? It's why I can never go to church anymore. There is just too much hypocrisy in public life. Who is all that ostentation for? All that dressed marble I mean? Why not start with the homeless and all those living in poverty?"

Hannah looked in amazement at her friend as they stopped below their own adjacent rooms at the end of the house, where they would not be overheard. Alice's eyes flooded with tears of disappointment. Like McGiffen she'd had her fill of learning life's hard lessons and it was breaking her heart.

"Well it has to start somewhere . . . You already know part of the answer Alice. It's right here in this wonderful family. What did you tell me about Christina's trust fund? How much does she give?"

"Oh, the charity?" said Alice, dabbing her eyes with a hanky, "Yes, she gave over ten thousand pounds last year. I know, because I sent the cheques for her. Hugh has his own fortune and gives even more."

"So where does it all go?"

"The Daughters of Charity of St Vincent de Paul; the General Synod of the Church of Ireland. I dunno, a host of others."

Hannah hooted like an owl, then remembering the late hour covered her mouth, "No, I mean they could rebuild the entire Central housing area with that amount of cash. I just can't imagine it being used, can you? In Ireland?" As Alice continued a perplexed debate with herself, Hannah's voice faded. Hannah was more concerned with finding practical solutions to dynamic issues than with venting her feelings. To her the issues were clear.

Reaching out a hand to Alice she gently squeezed her upper arm, "Are we agreed – we need action as well as principle? You mustn't be at odds with yourself Alice. We *have* to do something and we're already involved."

"I'll be alright Hannah but today has been more of a shock for me than anything I've seen in my life. I'm beginning to think the pursuit of excellence amounts to a barrier, which the male voters we envy can't see beyond. A kind of blinding conceit that stops them seeing the truth.

They ignore the stink of grubby children. Never see exhausted bag ladies working from dawn till dusk. Prostitutes selling all they have. Old vagrants sitting just around the corner in alleyways, just off their beaten track. If they did they would ask different questions. They'd ask your question, about where all the money goes."

"Oh, I'd say it goes into a ring of fine houses like this one. Dozens of them in Liverpool alone, Alice. Planted on wooded hillsides like the Calder stones, celebrating the elect of our grasping society."

258

"Time for bed," decided Alice, taking out her key to open one of the back doors on the north wing of the house.

"Yes, dream time," replied Hannah with weary detachment.

Lying in her room that soft summer night in July '11, Hannah found herself unable to sleep, instead she tried to meditate with the window cast wide to the night air. Two owls called to one another through a wide crescent of woodland to the front of the house. The more she thought about her own circumstances and things she wanted to change, the more Hannah felt cheated. As an ordinary person without academic qualifications she didn't feel equipped to contribute to society in any significant way. Nor did she believe for an instant the authorities were genuinely concerned to alleviate deprivation she witnessed far and wide.

In the distance thunder rolled as the smell of warm rain drifted on fragrant air through her window. Hannah rose to look out at the sky to the west. A wonderfully pungent aroma of salt air preceded a weather front breezing in off the Irish Sea, illuminated by distant flashes of lightning. Picking up her diary, Hannah found that there was enough illumination from lamps along the driveway and a full moon to scribble a few thoughts before sleep might lift trepidation to a subliminal plane,

'I find there is something mysteriously thrilling about the rotting seaweed smell of the ocean, carried by a weak Atlantic front. I wish with all my heart to wake up every morning and look out at the sea. If not on some tropical island, then at least in my beloved home town. Never in my nineteen years have I appreciated Edinburgh so completely. Who could know it and not fall in love with it? Today I visited a foreign country, in a Dark Age of hatred and rebellion, with virtuous fellows I've grown to love in contention. Allowing uneasy thoughts to wander back from events of the evening, I find accompanying reflections of recent weeks of growing activism floating to the surface. One persistent theme recurs through all these vital conversations - surely education has a crucial role to play in society. I wonder where it might take us over the next hundred years. Altruistic protests happening at home in Edinburgh will ensure no more tolerance by parents of selective schools. Demonstration against the old elitism led to riots and the new academy being destroyed by an act of arson. People are too smart not to see through such discriminatory offerings for general emancipation. An image persisting when I pause to think about home and demands expressed by a wise population demanding equality, is a scene from early this evening of urchins lighting a fire in the middle of the street near my friends' house. I doubt any of them have ever set foot in a school. Teachers wouldn't know what to do with them if they did. I wonder if there will be vestiges of such snobbery and desperate neglect in the Liverpool of 2011?'

When the conversation with Hugh about education resumed a couple of weeks later, Hannah told him she caught 'a prevailing sense of cold cynicism in government policy.' As they hiked around nearby woodlands and fields with Christina, Alice and the girls, Hugh ribbed her quietly about her views and how she'd arrived at them.

Clearing a field with sheep belonging to farmer Reynolds he let go of his pet Collie Oscar, folding the leash into a pocket of his waxed jacket. Remembering what Harper had said about the education industry constituting another self-serving bureaucracy, Hannah prepared to argue the point quite strongly as she listened to Hugh.

"We're on the brink of radical change, don't you think? More and more adult education classes are opening all over the country. The curriculum on offer for women is broadening. The Liberals want a compromise agenda and that means preparing women for having the vote. In the end they know it's an argument they can't win. Of course, fundamentally you are right Hannah. As I told you before, I perceive the same cold cynicism. Politicians only ever willingly accept change that is good for them."

"Thanks Daddy!" Hannah replied without thinking. She was flustered and embarrassed to talk about what she believed so fervently. In an important sense Sir Hugh Leslie had become a stand-in for Harper, "I beg your pardon sir that was a gaffe!"

"Please don't apologise. Freud calls it parapraxis – the expression of a subdued impression or wish. I'm flattered." Hannah smiled and blushed

260

with embarrassment at the same time. She had to admit a warm and deep affection for Hugh that went beyond reverence.

Such conversations helped Hannah rehearse for occasions when she had to speak in public and met with predictable resistance for her gender and relative youth. Transport Union members she and NUWSS colleagues had discussions with often spoke against extended education, especially for women. Now at last she was ready for them.

During a visit to Shipwrights, Evans and Co, in the midst of refinancing as they struggled to fill their order book, one plausible engineer in his fifties expressed the dilemma of reactionary politics most aptly for Hannah.

Convenor for the Confederation of Shipbuilding and Engineering Unions, George Barraclough had a voice respected by owners and ship smiths alike. He'd arranged the meeting reluctantly but briefly introduced Hannah and colleagues Mary and Arabella. They had no idea how exclusive this elite of skilled craftsmen were, or how conservative, as Hannah stood to deliver her plaintive address.

The men seemed indulgent, glad to down tools and convene for twenty minutes in the huge engineering shed but no-one had asked any questions. The smell of acrid smoke, the crack of sledge hammers and bright flashes of welding from across the vast yard told them this was by no means a full turnout of the workforce. Less qualified men were excluded from the Confederation and some recent affiliates were disenchanted with lack of action.

Knowing not to expect too much, Hannah cleared her throat and called to the men to gather to her. Drifting reluctantly in pairs and threes from their normal workstations they stood around awaiting her revelations. Hannah spoke tersely, seeking brief engagement rather than a platform for a lecture.

"I imagine you all know what this is about, so I'll get straight to the point gentlemen. We have come to ask your active support for women's Suffrage. Indirectly also, for your support in gaining equality of educational opportunity, pay, socially accepted birth-control and child allowances."

Sitting on the nearest steel worktable was the Shop Steward, a surly man with grey hair, wearing a washed out blue boiler suit. Raising a hand he volunteered his name, "Cyril Makepeace." One look gave Hannah the impression that nothing might be further from the truth. Cradling a massive adjustable spanner in both hands like a mediaeval bludgeon, Cyril took it upon himself to respond to a narrow aspect of the NUWSS appeal for affiliation.

"Why should we pay more taxes to provide an education for some twit who's gonna turn up here out of the blue on a Monday morning and start ordering us around. Much less some woman?" Makepeace seemed to be deliberately missing the purpose of the delegation, to focus on a gripe of his own. A murmur of approval ran through the men seated around the shipyard's engineering base.

"I've been doing this job for eighteen years and none of those suited pricks up in that office on the mezzanine has ever so much as passed the time a day wi' me."

"Who'd wanna pass the time o' day wi' you Cyril . . . ye miserable old bugger?" asked one of the men, a tall fellow standing with ankles crossed, as though leisure was a priority whenever he could grab it. Hard laughter rolled through the group of men.

"Er, excuse my rough colleagues' industrial language darlin' but ye said yer wanted equality wit' the men!" chipped in George, with a touch of vaudeville timing. A cacophony of coarse banter saved Hannah's embarrassment but when it died down Cyril continued to hammer home his point, which did not escape Hannah.

"Look, no disrespect to you lasses coming here mind, even though it is all pie in the sky," this to more intrusive laughter, "No, no - you girls stand up for what you think is right and personally I wish yous all the luck, I do really . . . But listen, listen . . . My wife died last October and they wouldn't even pay me for taking time off to arrange her funeral. Three kids at home Miss Harper – well, they should be at school actually," he said, laughing to himself while cueing up the next droll response for his mates, "But the idle sods won't ger out o' bed. Education just serves to strengthen injustice see? If I was educated would I spend the entire day hammering rivets? No-one would. And no ships would get built, or repaired. And don't tell me those heartless bastards up there behind the glass didn't have the education to sympathise with my plight when our lass died. So what good has it done them? If this company is running to catch up it's down to *their* financial mismanagement, *their* greed and stupidity," he said raising an arm to point as he raised his voice, "private owners and shareholders take the profits o' *my* labour. Change that first if yer gonna change somethin'. Then come back an' talk about educational opportunity."

Hannah glanced over her shoulder beyond the workshop to a glass walled Supervisor's office on the first floor. Sure enough, two men in suits stood watching at that very moment.

"Imagine one o' them toffees not gerrin' time off if their wife died," chimed in a slightly built fellow with long red hair. Cyril glanced at his friend respectfully, "It would never happen Ricky son, bur they're not hammering two thousand fickin' rivets a day. My point is, ladies, students don't have to work. They have time on their hands to think of ways o' rubbin' *our* faces in shit when they finally do come through. The bosses love that – havin' some wet behind the ears public school twit who doesn't know the job, winding us up. It reminds us all we're just a worthless bunch o' scallys." Cyril sat down to a ripple of applause.

Another old sage picked up the mantra, "Cyril's right! As long as owners make their fat profits, that's all that matters. They couldn't care less if we live or die."

Barraclough had the last word, "That's what makes me a back page philosopher lads. The on'y studyin' thar'll ge' me out a here, is if I bet me shirt on some rank outsider running in the three thirty at Haydock Park."

Hannah took the point amid a storm of sardonic hilarity. Living out the Historical Dialectic would inevitably involve strife. That night Hannah fell asleep laughing, wishing she could make peace for poor Cyril.

As months of campaigning for worker's and women's rights went by Hannah noticed that her dear friends Marek and Siggy would never sit together. But that wasn't all they did for discretion. When travelling on

263

buses one would go upstairs and the other sit near the front step. On arrival Siggy made a habit of circling the streets around a venue as Marek chatted to delegates. In meeting halls they avoided eye contact, sitting as far apart as possible and never left together.

If his brother entered wearing a hat, Marek would make an excuse and immediately slip out. Later they would meet behind a boat shed on the canal, where both would sleep rough until McGiffen strolled past and stamped out a cigarette. If he flicked it into the canal the brothers would be gone for days.

Stan stayed inside during the day in the shared basement quarters two hundred yards behind the docklands. Tainted slum urchins and tough Italian immigrants helped keep him safe. No-one could approach in a police uniform without starting a buzz. On rare occasions when the Russian came to the pub, nursing one of Marek's masterfully faked passports, he listened warily before speaking in front of strangers. Stan weighed up everyone and trusted no-one but he was purposive – he always had traces of printer's ink on his fingers.

On their way to the regular Tuesday meeting Alice told Hannah, "Stan says he was a beekeeper and that he would never clip the wing of a new Queen. Unlike our honey farmers in Monaghan he never uses smoke, yet the bees never sting him. Apparently he hangs basket hives in an orchard, not on the ground. He says nature is God's gift."

"You like him very much, don't you Alice?"

"Yes, I do. He's a lovely man, haunted by the brutality he has seen. I think his eyes are hardened, like someone who has foreseen his own doom."

Although all three émigrés habitually ignored strangers, they tended to become animated in any open discussion. The brothers were expert at prompting others like Hannah to speak up in meetings, by asking the right questions. As individuals Marek, Siggy and Stan seemed warm and generous – their eyes betraying this perception in a brief instant of kindly recognition whenever they encountered a known friend. But their developed identities remained hidden beneath caution and fear.

Hannah understood that 'the Poles' as her gregarious NUWSS associates referred to them, conveyed a dangerous sense that there would soon come a time for anyone with a conscience, even in glibly extrovert Liverpool, to make a stand against self-serving authority. She also knew with deepening dread that come the day, they were the most likely to get hurt.

Despite being uninitiated in struggle, Hannah was never naïve. Understanding the need for altruistic principle in political life, she came to believe, "That there can be no successful revolution – no dictatorship of the proletariat," so she told her friends, "Unless it is desired by a majority." Collecting leaflets with the intellectually refined Arabella Lister one early evening she quizzed Stan for his views on this crucial subject as he hastily whisked around McGiffen's basement tidying up. Since the Russian had set up home with Siggy and Marek had moved upstairs to share a room with Andy, the place looked almost shipshape.

"At the very least it requires the failure of the old system *and* education of the masses, to demand a more equable ordering of society. This is the only way to achieve true democracy within the organs of our state. Don't you agree?"

"In '05 Hannah, Tsarists blamed Revolution on 'too many educated people.' They were misguided in who to support but should love only Tsar, father of all good fortune. Government re-organised schools, universities syllabus. Greater, what you say teaching?"

"Emphasis?"

"Yes, emphasis . . . on patrie?"

"Patriotism?"

"Patriotism. We should both speak French. Would be easier."

"Hmm, that would be nice. But it wouldn't help you blend in here."

Stan offered hospitality and as they drank cheap Bulgarian wine in his vault, Arabella and Hannah concluded that the first part of her stipulation – the failure of the Old System - seemed possible at least.

"Otherwise Stan why is there an escalating arms race between Britain, US and Germany, if not to facilitate some imminent global land grab?" asked Arabella, "It's no longer Russia and Japan at odds, although that is the excuse they are using."

"Escalating?"

"Sorry! Expanding rapidly –mushrooming!"

"Ah, *mushrooms!* I will give you girls money. You bring me mushrooms. Also . . . kolbasa – salami. Zalewskis never eat, live on bread and cheese! Russia and Japan would be in arms race too, spending money on Dreadnoughts if not 'four furlongers', strapped fer cash lar!"

"Yes, yes you're right. I think this is what statists in Russia and elsewhere will always do Stan, to subdue workers and keep their grip on empire," agreed Hannah's blonde intellectual friend with a smile, "And don't worry about giving us money. We're glad to bring whatever you need."

"Well bring me another case of beer Arabella – McGiffen drinks it all! But Russia? . . . Russia is shit. Russia is its own empire, too big to control. Japan? . . . Japanese think *we* are all stupid. Pardon an angry man who swears too much ladies. They live in middle-ages, think Emperor is God. Meiji goes to cabinet, *never speaks!* Taisho demokurashii, is bluff for Americans, who they need but will always hate."

"Oh, my Lord, international politics seems so blatantly cynical," said Arabella. Tall and robust, the daughter of a publisher from St Anne's, studying Textile Science at the University, Arabella could not have looked less the liberal futurist Hannah knew her to be. Staid and middle class, she spoke with a plum in her mouth but was exactly the sort of person Hannah knew would eventually have influence, once she'd made her way in the world.

"But we have much in common ladies. We fight elites who benefit from creating conquest. Zalewski boys and I, on the run from home, we see ten thousand Suffragists and workers here. Same cynicism here in government. Pattern is same Arabella. History repeating."

Walking to their meeting hall in Everton with the leaflets, Arabella told Hannah she thought there were, "echoes of the past here in Liverpool, of England's Civil War."

Hannah mused for a minute upon a subject taught in Scotland from an entirely different perspective.

"Ha! England's short and bloody civil war led to a century of strife in other parts of the British Isles."

"I know that Hannah and in a way that's precisely what I'm trying to get at - despite the time scale. Parliament refused to grant King Charles Ist's military levy, isn't that right?"

"Uh huh, which led to him losing his token moral authority as Sovereign, along with his head," but how does that reflect on our situation?"

"Well, I don't imagine anything like that happening again. Not here at least. Maybe as Stan says in Japan or Russia, where the stakes of running an Empire aren't as high."

"By stakes do you mean profits?"

"Yes, exactly. The nice thing about having a Monarch as head of state is that they can be blamed for all the double dealing and pushed into the scrimmage to have their head lopped orf."

"So what do you think will happen here Arabella?"

"If there is an Arms Race, there will be a war."

"There already *is* an arms race . . ."

"Then you can thank God for the Gold standard Hannah dear, or it would have already kicked orf last month in Agadir. I will call at the delicatessen in Crosby before I meet you next week. What did he say he wanted again?"

"Kolbasa."

"Kolbasa, right! We can buy the crate of beer at the Raven."

During an interlude in a supremely happy time at Allerton Grange working with the Leslie children Hannah went home for a vacation, for the first time in almost three years. Purportedly visiting Harper and Margaret and their baby son John, she chose not to mention her planned activities there on behalf of women's suffrage, to her employer or the family. Having booked into a small hotel on Frederick Street for convenience, it seemed to her all that was required was to make appropriate connections around the city, simply by talking and listening to people. Hannah was relieved and inspired to find that her activism was a small part of a burning national debate.

In the morning after her arrival in the city she made her way over to Shandwick Place, to join a meeting of the Edinburgh branch of NUWSS. Hannah walked unannounced into a gathering of union delegates planning to support Dock workers at Leith in their industrial action. Organiser Chrystal Macmillan, just returned from an international conference on women's suffrage in Stockholm, was speaking calmly about how to extend national membership, with over half a million members and several hundred branches already established across the UK.

"Throughout 1911 there has been a tremendous feeling of agitation abroad – not just in Liverpool, which is a hotbed of left wing politics. Alongside this growing militancy of the national workforce, the refusal of women's suffrage has provoked the worst acts of terror this country has ever seen. It may seem certain to some of you that change will come soon, ultimately benefitting all. This common demand for social justice is giving momentum to a new, unifying Labour movement, already very popular in here in Edinburgh.

At every opportunity from now on, we have to recruit men. Support the reasoned basis of their causes and they in turn will listen to us and support ours. In so doing we insinuate ourselves into their argument, which ought to be collaborative, not insular. We establish a basis for challenging employer's abuses and at the same time chauvinism which victimises women. We're not going to break windows ladies – we're going to break resistance to our legal rights."

Hannah introduced herself and was greatly impressed by Macmillan's warmth and determination, not least because she was a pacifist, as well as a democrat. Chrystal was obviously smart – she explained to Hannah that she'd studied Moral Philosophy, as well as Mathematics and had a degree in Natural Science.

"Part of the problem for me personally Miss Harper, is that although I sit on the University Board, I have no voting right to propose a candidate for election as Member of Parliament. But you're here from Liverpool? I didn't see your name on the list."

Hannah laughed lightly, "Yes, I came home for a holiday! But there are delegates here I know from Liverpool."

"Of course, they've been given funds to pay for their visit. The movement is gathering momentum, despite the harmful bombing campaign." Hannah wanted to tell Chrystal something personal but just smiled and kept her mouth shut.

The Zalewski brothers' 'layers of action' is thankfully nothing to do with me. At last I have the right direction. I know we will win.

For Hannah it was vital to discriminate between violent and non-violent action, no matter how much attention the Pankhursts generated. Feeling insincere for what she knew but could never say, Hannah nervously offered around a bag of nectarines she'd bought in the Market. Most of the thirty or so delegates at the Saturday morning meeting declined but Chrystal took one. They were soft and smelled of summer ripeness. Hannah's antidote for dread indiscretion was to show enthusiasm and get involved – here as much as in Liverpool. Macmillan was glad to give Hannah a lead role for her local knowledge.

"How do we open the discussion Chrystal – assuming the Dockers allow us an audience at their meeting?" Hannah asked, recalling the stinging ridicule of Evan's CSEU Shop Steward.

"It's important to create an ideological bridge with affiliated Trade Unionists - under the banner of recognised principles of fairness and equality," answered the middle aged academic. She wiped her chin as juice from the moist fruit ran from the corner of her mouth, "the more so because their industry is an all-male preserve. Two or three miles to the south, so you should remind them, are fishwives' sheds where their women folk toil in stinking slime, with fingers freezing from the ice."

For a local girl that connection was never hard to make but hearing it from a skilled barrister made the argument sound simple. Hannah loved to be challenged or heckled – always having a convincing answer ready. Thoughtful engagement inspired her best work.

"Assertiveness consists in quietly saying the same thing over and over again, until they get the point," said Chrystal evenly, smiling with her eyes. Hannah knew she had found her spiritual mentor at last.

Three of the women present at the meeting invited Hannah to accompany them. Two were delegates up from Liverpool – Mary Randall and Victoria Wilmington. The third, a local teacher named Fiona McGregor, was reluctant to take on the role as spokeswoman, so Hannah volunteered. Between them they agreed to let Hannah address the Dockers, who were to meet at the end of their shift at six pm, in the Seamen's Mission.

Having learned her lesson at Evans and Co, each time she had addressed a meeting since then Hannah had politely asked the convener to, "Add a little momentum for me – make an introductory plea on behalf of the Suffragist movement, if you will." They never let her down, sometimes expressing opinions they never knew they had. She was a rolling rock, finding the conversion of malcontents easy. Usually a simple vote for mutual support was a massive 'Yes.'

Mr Matheson of the Scottish Union of Dock Labourers didn't let her down either, "Thanks fer a decent turnoot lads," he began, "This brief meeting is all about solidarity with NUWSS, supporting women in their demand for basic civil rights. They are already in support of our motion tae strike. If you show a simple majority, I will tak' a Branch resolution tae Region. Put yer hands up if ye want tae speak. Tell the girls yer names. Be nice tae them either way, regardless o' personal opinions. An' let's avoid casual profanities, even though yis are normally a set o' foul mouthed bastards." Laughter set the scene for success.

Anticipating the mood of tired, brusque men Hannah explained to the fifty or so Dockers who had stopped by for no other reason than it was on their way home, "I intend to convince you to support women's Suffrage at the very top of your political agenda – not just as a side issue." There was a murmur of contention with smiles across the room, as they picked up on her local accent.

"Good luck wi' that lassie," said one moderate fellow, younger and less taciturn than the rest. Hannah reckoned she might have five minutes until thirst got the better of pragmatism.

"Your women work every bit as hard each day as you do - when they put in a shift skinning haddock, or firing bottles and," she paused for emphasis, "then they go home to make *your* suppers and scrub the dirt out o' *your* collars. They take responsibility for getting *your* bairns off to school. They make time to lay in enough food for the week. Quite apart from the issue of 'a fair day's pay for a fair day's work' . . . can any of you tell me why *you* think they should not be allowed to vote in a general election?'

The response when it came after general approval of the arguments made so far was as usual off the point, typically perhaps from one of the least intellectually endowed individuals in the room. His objection was as hackneyed as a worn church step, polished by a hundred thousand dour supplicants.

"I think a woman's place is in the home an' I don't want *my* wife out tae work. She should be at home looking after the bairns," came a thick voice from the back of the room. Hannah didn't see the man who spoke up, so she stalled.

"Sorry, may I ask your name sir?"

"You may . . . but I'm no' sure I'm ready tae gi'e it. I dinnae want ma windaes put through in the middle o' the night!"

"That's perfectly okay. You prefaced that observation with, "*I think,*" then you said, "*I don't want,*" but that is entirely her choice to make, Mrs whatever your name is, I mean *never yours*. Your wife is *not* your bond slave and is therefore entitled to her own opinions."

"What about the marriage vows, "Love, honour and obey?" came the same ecclesiastical sounding sage from the back. Hannah moved gently to the right of men standing rudely in front of her, like full backs intentionally harrying a goalie.

Glowering at them pointedly Hannah took her time responding, waiting until she had line of sight to the objector. Looking directly at the man to weigh him up, it appeared that although sitting on a table he was very tall with aquiline features. Tight calculating strength was woven like dried basketwork into every pull and tuck of a middle aged frame. A hooked nose and shoulders stooped with work, lent him accipidridan austerity.

"Again, that's entirely a matter of *her* choice. I think you'll find the rites in the church in which you were married do not extend to the issue of the political state barring women from voting in elections. So can we stick to the point please?"

Hannah looked around the loose assembly of tough looking men with a challenging manner. There was always a reactionary fool. Hannah knew that well-rehearsed, deadpan responses usually led to their embarrassment and ridicule. As she carried on speaking Hannah was not strident, but equally refused to be cowed.

"The best example of what I can tell you is in respect to Edinburgh's own Chrystal Macmillan. I was privileged to meet her today along with my colleagues here, Mary, Victoria and Fiona, who some of you know. Chrystal is a highly skilled legal advocate – a barrister. If, God forbid, any of you good men was accused of a serious crime, or needed open access because you were sacked unfairly from your job – I have no doubt at all she could help you as well as any man. And you wouldn't care about her gender. So for what earthly reason is she not allowed to vote to elect the MP who represents the University for which she sits as an academic board member, other than the fact that she discriminated against as a woman?"

Hannah could see and feel them gradually changing their attitude as she spoke. Fiona McGregor couldn't suppress a broad smile. These Dockers were worthy, strong minded men for the most part. Having become more confident each day at citing inequalities between women and men the cooler Hannah was in silencing and controlling even the most antipathetic crowd. The more tension she felt when they refused to listen, the longer she waited for a voice of harmony to speak from the crowd. Now Hannah felt it about to come.

"Slavery was abolished in 1807 - but without fundamental rights under the law, women have no higher status than chattel, *property* owned by men. In that sense we are glorified slaves - at the mercy of the state to whom we pay our taxes; at the mercy of employers who deny us fairness and recognition; at the mercy of men generally - who wrongly imagine they are free to ignore, ridicule, or abuse us."

Pitching her voice just above the murmur, then lowering it when they began to respond, Hannah showed maturity and great patience. Patience lent her credibility. Developed understanding of the issues and her rapier wit brought mastery.

"I think you make some good points," said a fellow sitting near the front, "Sorry hen, Davy Robertson. In fact - I'm amazed women have put up with being second class citizens for so long."

"But we are not *second class citizens,* Davy and we don't put up with it. Women have been fighting for their rights as citizens for the past five or six decades. It's only with civil disobedience – fire bombings every other day – which we denounce entirely, that government is at last paying attention.

So gentlemen, what do you say? Can we achieve a *peaceful* change that is so long overdue? Will you accept our proposal for affiliation?"

Matheson's proposal for a vote for mutual support, put to a show of hands, met with a massive, 'Yes.' Hannah noticed that the man with the eagle face was one of the first to raise his hand to vote in favour.

Later that evening, after cheers and felicitations from union colleagues, Hannah walked proudly across to Lilly Hill Terrace. At last deep enmity towards her step mother for balking her higher education was in the past. Coming to terms with disappointment felt towards Margaret as an individual would take a little longer. At nineteen Hannah knew that Margaret represented everything she herself wished to avoid becoming in life – the little kept woman, devoting all her attention to controlling the purse strings. For Hannah the sexual metaphor could not have been more precise.

Equally Hannah couldn't resist comparison between Margaret and some of the rebel women of Huddersfield and Leeds whom she'd heard speaking on behalf of the Women's Social and Political Union. Strolling up the hill from Parson's Green she wondered idly if Margaret was even fully aware of their clamorous issues - let alone their desperate, quite flagrant attitude to forcing political change.

Margaret twinkled brightly in her blissful domestic firmament while they raced and smouldered often to explode in bright flashes of light - languishing in jail and blackballed by local employers. For Hannah the trick was to ply a middle course between extremes. In a time of desperate trouble she planned to keep her feet planted firmly on the ground.

Her half-brother stood in the hallway, searching the stranger's face with big uncertain eyes. Crouching down at the threshold Hannah rummaged in her coat pocket for two sticks of Edinburgh rock which she proffered in her left hand. The melt-in-your-mouth confections were spontaneously purloined by a playful bendy parrot named Hamish, who suddenly flew swooping in from the right.

"Aaawww, Edinburgh Rock c c c c c caw!" crowed Hamish.

"What . . . stop now! That's for John Harper . . . Hamish, you silly bird! Give me that rock back," she began, acting out a rainforest canopy conflict, wrestling around the hallway after the heinous avian who was trying to make off with the goodies.

Little John ran squealing with laughter straight to her assistance and between them they managed to restrain the wild glove puppet. Carefully opening the wrapper half removed by Hamish, she broke a piece off and handed it to the little man to taste. With one hand folded casually behind his back, John popped the raspberry flavoured spice into his mouth like an expert.

Kneeling on the floor Hannah offered her hand, addressing the toddler with gleeful eyes and loose hair, "Hello John, I'm your step sister Hannah. Later you can give me a proper hug and a kiss if you wouldn't mind, though I know boys don't usually kiss girls."

Little John stepped forward dutifully to plant a skim of partly masticated rock onto her right cheek, as an advance on a proper kiss.

Margaret giggled in delight, something Hannah realised with surprise she'd never heard before. The little man stepped from one foot to the other and back. Unable to speak he waved his mummy away with one hand, chewing the mouthful with a full set of milk teeth. Swallowing it promptly, John moved immediately to hug the still attentively crouching Hannah.

"Sorry Hannah, Mag says never speak with your mouth full." Barely three he was clearly university material. The child's posh accent hinted at the kind of transformation which follows a family in the wake of aspiration and success. Throwing arms around Hannah's neck he gave her a proper but very wet, sugary kiss, planted squarely on her lips. An unexpectedly easy connection had been cast with an important little agent in the family.

"You are delightful," said Hannah. John draped his right arm around Hannah. Looking up at Margaret, Hannah saw all the woman had ever wished for shining back with pride.

"Congratulations Margaret! I can see at a glance you've rediscovered your youth. He will repair all the years of hurt."

"Thank you," answered Margaret vapidly, unsure whether to be delighted or offended.

"I know from experience the demands of having little ones around makes a body unselfish. And you will be the best mother of all for him."

Margaret recognised the fact that she was looking at a different person to the child she'd raised, someone never fully recognised before. Her limited appreciation of 'Duff' did not quite correspond to the vibrantly confident adult now standing in her hallway. Harper had not yet returned from playing golf, so they had tea and Hannah read John a bed time story. Agreeing to return for dinner on Sunday afternoon before catching her train back to Liverpool, she hugged Margaret warmly for the first time in fourteen years, before stepping out over the threshold. Lillyhill was no longer home but somehow that didn't matter.

Margaret made a great effort for Hannah, inviting her parents and making a Sunday roast. She bought wine and put out her finest table wear. At the age of thirty six, long constrained nest-building instincts had come to the fore. She set up Little John's high chair between herself and Hannah so the child could engage with the new friend in his life.

A wonderfully primeval aroma of roasting vegetables and beef filled the house and the adults chattered loudly as the feast was set before them. Hannah took little John's portion to cut into smaller pieces.

Despite the upsurge of the motor vehicle, Anthony Kemp was a coachman so conversation seemed naturally to swing towards chaotic changes he saw all around, as the old man consciously tried to compensate for his granddaughter's discomfiture after so many years of estrangement. Anthony was delighted to see Hannah, yet sorrowful that it had been so long.

"Practically no-one requires the services of a horse drawn carriage any longer," he complained, "Forward looking Edinburgh City Council have dispensed with the last of their horse drawn trams," he added with a sense of irony, "Now all the toffs have shiny new motor cars. I'm fifty eight years old," Tony Kemp reminded her, "Too old to enlist, or I'd join the Army Transportation Corps."

"Don't be an old fool Tony!" Teresa railed, "What happened to your anti-war sentiments? Anyway you love my home cooking more than your stinking horses!"

Little John laughed raucously, "Stinking horses giddyappin and gilloper gallopering along Gramps!" Hannah spooned John up a mouthful of potato, to interrupt his flow.

"Don't count on it, don't count on it!" Tony repeated, trying to think of a response to Teresa that might stop short of affront, "Your cooking was never as good as your eldest daughter's," he threw back with a wry smile. Chewing his roast beef he winked at Margaret as if to confirm the judgement, "Anyway my point is: the army are the only people who value the tradition of keeping large stables of horses. Everything is speeding up you see," he grumbled, addressing Hannah, his chosen audience.

Tony spoke with the polite Southern accent reserved for what remained of his posh clientele, as he unselfconsciously spooned out more roast potatoes from the serving dish at his end of the table, "It's like the telegraphs and phones, Hannah Dear – a public display of modernisation happening for over a century in factories and fields."

"You mean mechanisation, Tony," put in Harper, "We had the world's most up to date threshing machines in Aberdeenshire when I was a lad. You'd be surprised what stingy farmers take for granted when there's extra money to be made."

"That's true John – but I'm talking about what is essentially *a luxury* – the motor car." Swinging around in his seat at the end of the table he looked incredulously at Hannah and Margaret sitting to his left. Teresa wasn't concerned to be left out of Tony's appeal to reason, concentrating instead on enjoying her meal – she'd heard it all before.

"The owners don't really need them," Tony opined between slurps of Claret, "But what does this 'urban elite' do? They spend a fortune buying one, then another bigger fortune keeping them from falling in bits. Isn't that true John?" Grunting affirmation, Harper raised his knife in the air, "So in order to justify the unreasonable outlay, they wave goodbye to the neighbours and trek off to the Highlands, where they end up in a ditch somewhere. Then they join some expensive motoring organisation, to get breakdown insurance." Little John laughed freely at Tony's scornful tone, while the others pretended to sympathise.

"Ah well now, that kind of change strikes me favourably Da," Harper affirmed.

"Oh sure, it would, because of the ridiculous 'free market economy' you keep talking about. It's free to those who live only to make a profit. The rest of us pay through the nose."

"Well I admit, I do talk about it and why not? It pays my wages!"

"Because the market economy is like the machines people drive around in John - it can't think and it's dangerous when it runs out of control."

"Don't you two ever get fed up of talking politics?" Tere demanded of Tony, "He knows all your stories and you know all his. Clearly you spend too long lounging around in my pub." Tony ignored Tere's barbed comment, even though it was true. He was a rolling rock.

"The government is spending millions laying roads that immediately clog up with vehicles - when for over a century people and goods have arrived at their destination in half the time by rail." Anthony looked pleadingly at Hannah, apparently the only one listening seriously to his rant. "Absolute madness," he concluded, smiling at her and quietly shaking his head.

"Yes, Gramps I agree, especially when you consider the increase in accidents each year."

No-one picked up Hannah's point but for a moment she seemed to be seeing something in her mind's eye. Fundamentally things at home had not changed and never would.

Having done his bit to break the ice, Anthony resumed attention to his delicious topside, working at it gently with a silver plated Sheffield knife and fork. Hannah turned her eyes to the ceiling, ruminating silently over Tony's point about life speeding up, "Perhaps the allure of motor vehicles lies in the illusion of rapid individual movement? Maybe they're an expression of the desire for social change, which ordinary folk can't see happening." Hannah didn't want to imply that any of the present company was stuck in a rut – so she didn't labour the point.

There was a degree of rapprochement between Margaret and Hannah, extending to promises of more frequent contact. Harper suggested Hannah occupy the spare bedroom if she returned to Edinburgh – at least until she found alternative accommodation.

"I just might take you up on that, Daddy. I have a plan I need to discuss with you some time in the near future."

There were postcards and a letter for Hannah too, which Margaret had not found time to forward to Liverpool. One was from Elizabeth and another from Willie who was studying Medicine at Glasgow University. Opening it with a smile Hannah read aloud,

'I lost my address book along with my briefcase and two thousand words of my second year undergraduate dissertation written on 'The Divergence of Taxonomic Groups from their Common Ancestor.' Ironically it was stolen whilst I was immersed in what became a fiercely personal, slightly drunken argument with a railway official about what day it was, and whether or not my train ticket to Edinburgh was transferable after midnight. Please forgive my oversight at not memorising your address,

Yours ever,
M Barrass Esq,
Pugilist.'

Harper tried to offer a perspective, "According to your mutual friend
Walter Chalmers, who was with him at the time but denies being drunk,
Willie put the briefcase down in order to punch a Railway Inspector. By
the time they finished their altercation and Police had arrived to
formally caution him, Willie turned around to look for the briefcase and
it was gone. Walter said he remembers an opportunistic vagrant bowling
along in the direction of the Argyle Street exit."

Hannah laughed merrily throughout Harper's explanation, thinking
how little Willie had changed.

"It wouldn't surprise me, there are plenty of opportunistic vagrants
in Glasgow," Hannah granted.

"No doubt the individual responsible will turn up at lectures, in
disguise as the Professor of Anatomy," ventured Harper.

"Yes, and if he reeks enough of alcohol and disnae trim his beard
they'll never catch on," said Hannah, stung into sarcasm by recollection
of precisely how dense Willie Proven really was.

"He's a fine lad," declared Harper, disregarding Willie's spat with the
Railway Inspector.

"Yes, he will be a doctor soon!" crooned Margaret, "You should write
to him. Maybe invite him down to see you again at Allerton Grange,"
suggested Margaret, glancing at Harper questioningly. Hannah looked
at her father but his face was closed. She smiled warmly, hugging them
all goodbye in turn. Turning left at the gate Hannah headed back to her
hotel in town, through Holyrood Park.

Extraneous to holidays which she was always invited to spend with the
Leslie family, Hannah accumulated time off from her charges.
Membership of NUWSS took her on wonderfully challenging weekends
of adventure. It was a legendary time of mass political involvement,
unprecedented in the history of modern civilization and Hannah knew

that women were the leaven in the dough of rising democracy. She and her colleagues were dedicated and fearless.

Regular evening meetings in town were rounded with stimulating, impassioned conversation ranging over every important topic. Hannah was too young to have been swept away on the controversial tide of violent dissension but felt privileged instead to be riding the crest of the NUWSS wave, with strong insight into pacifism exemplified by Chrystal Macmillan. A campaign that had been gathering momentum for over fifty years was now irresistible.

Sitting in the south summer house with Alice on a mid-summer evening, in response to predictable concerns voiced again before a weekend jaunt, Hannah told her, "I know full well had I been nineteen instead of seventeen on joining the suffrage movement, I would have found my way into Holloway by now." Alice's mouth hung slightly open, always a bad sign, meaning she was at a loss for words. "No doubt if I'd been in Edinburgh in '09 when the 'Guid Cause' marchers protested, I might have felt angry enough to break a few windows. More to the point if poor Jim Birnie hadn't been run over on the day of my trip to visit Queen Victoria's statue, my life could have taken another route, involving a reputation for defacement."

"Hannah we both have to accept that with increasing numbers of arrests at demonstrations, detention at some point seems more than likely," said Alice, for once not acting anything other than herself as she studied Hannah over her coffee cup.

"I suppose you're right Alice. I'm content to know I've benefited from both the mistakes and the wisdom of others. Our trips to Manchester and Yorkshire have been more than educational. They leave me with a deep sense of injustice and outrage. My body feels tense and my mind fills with images of struggle," Hannah explained, lowering her voice. Thirty feet away Christina was listening discreetly, wrapped in a summer short coat amid favourite lilies, smoking by the French doors.

Early on Tuesday afternoon of the following week Christina approached Hannah working with the girls in the west facing walled garden, "They seem fully absorbed, as ever. Tell me the activity for today."

"I'd like to say I planned to make it layered for the different level of understanding of each, as well as appealing to all their senses. Helena has instructions from me which she has to explain to Clarissa, when they finish independent tasks. Then Clarissa gets first chance to explain to me what they shared and learned together. That way I can gauge how well each of them has learned what I hope they will discover."

"Alice tells me Clarissa is quite the prodigy, beginning multiplication tables?"

"Well it's not quite that simple but yes, she is beginning to apply rote counting she has learned."

"She counts to one hundred?"

"Yes, and in fives, tens, twenties and fifties."

"So what's the current plan?"

"Sets of things. She estimates a number of objects, ideally below one hundred. Helena writes the number down for later reference. Clarissa remembers the set number, starting with twos and goes to work. Right now they're counting petals and flower heads."

At that moment there was a furore from a dense, multi-coloured bank of hydrangeas that Clarissa had fallen into.

"Stop laughing Helena! You have to help me! Hannah says you have to help me!" came the petulant shriek.

"I am silly, just don't trip over yourself!" Christina laughed aloud but linked arms, to draw Hannah away so the girls would not appeal for intervention or become distracted from their activity.

"Look here, these are interesting plants we should all investigate."

"Oh yes, quite imposing against the brick but it seems prolific. Perhaps they need more room. What is it?"

"Aunt Cornelia's hemp garden my dear, the low growing ones are a mixture of Cannabis Indica from Nepal and Hindu Kush, the taller ones Sativa she brought back from Egypt."

"Tell me about her, was she your aunt?"

"Oh no, Hugh's . . . on his mother's side. His father owned a string of forest plantations throughout the Far East and India, producing every imaginable chemical and quite a range of raw materials, mainly for rope making and the newspaper industry."

"But this is also used as a narcotic yes, or a sedative?"

"Yes, she said they saw it growing everywhere. The farmers smoke it for different purposes. A little of the lower plant during the day when they're working for hours in the fields. The taller one to relax at the end of the day."

"And Cornelia . . . I mean did she?"

"Oh, I imagine she did, on a regular basis. When in Rome . . . According to Hugh, Briggs the gardener got involved in hanging and sousing them in wine for Auntie. Helped her arthritis, so she said."

"And?"

"Me? Good heavens no," said Christina with a bright laugh, "but Hugh insists it improves the appreciation of his VSOP . . . as well as other things I won't mention while the children are within earshot."

"But is that all it does? My mother was addicted to laudanum for a while before her cancer went into remission." Christina looked askance at Hannah as if to say 'how would I know?' But the look was also one of eternal complicity. Christina was becoming very fond of her children's governess. Without thinking of her own role in Hannah's evolution, it was plain to see the bright girl had metamorphosed into an exceptional woman.

"They seem very well organised. What else do they have to do?" she asked, nodding towards her children.

"Count flowers on at least three types of plants, use the illustrated books by Grant and Oliver to identify them or ask. Then draw and colour. As they get older children resist art activities involving coloured pencils, or paint. That is such a shame. It's part of a wider more insidious process." Christina waited for more but Hannah was not about to elaborate.

"Can we have the paint now Hannah?" asked Helena.

"Yes but only if we have finished. Painting can take a long time and needs full concentration."

"Well, I did five plants and counted petals on three flowers of each plant," said Helena, reflexively bending her right arm with her left hand wrapped over it above the elbow, as if constraining impatience, "Clarry knows exactly what to do Hannah, she's just finishing off. I did help her, a little, just a little," Helena added pinching fingers together.

"Okay, I'll look at what you've noted. Put your pad on the work table and fetch paints and brushes from the conservatory. Then I will trust you to bring water in jam jars if you agree not to run."

Helena sprinted off, enthusiastically calling over her shoulder, "I won't run with the water!" As the smile faded from Christina's face she placed a hand on Hannah's arm.

"I owe you an apology."

"Whatever for!"

"For not getting involved."

"Involved in what? You help with everything the girls do!"

"No, NUWSS I mean. Will you allow me to accompany you tonight, if I promise not to probe into your Polish revolutionaries?"

Christina signed up with the union on Tuesday, wrote a substantial cheque for Alice to bank for them on Wednesday and got up out of bed early for the campaign briefing over breakfast on Saturday. Alice explained that they were heading for a lunchtime meeting at Shires' factory in a small industrial town north of Leeds.

"You say you want to learn from *them* because they are the most effective strategists?"

"No, not learn from them," answered Alice, "share ideas and experiences. Offer solidarity maybe."

"Is that because NUWSS believe civil disobedience to be wrong? I'm not at all sure where I stand but Hughie has thoroughly indoctrinated me about trying to maintain 'dialogue and balance.' By the way Hannah, you need to scotch rumours that he is descended from Jesus, before Clarissa and Helena tell our entire circle of friends. Clarissa prides herself on being able to repeat the word 'great' eighty times, followed by the word Grandpa." Alice almost shouted with laughter and Christina shook her head in dismay.

"Oh, that's my fault! Now it's me that should apologise. They must have overheard our discussion concerning the intertwining of the Leslie and Sinclair family histories. We wanted to tell them a little, like Hugh suggested . . . not the whole thing. But they ask so many questions. Harper taught me all about the Earl of Orkney and Templar knights when we visited Roslyn Chapel."

"And you were explaining it all to Alice when the girls were listening?"

"And Hannah was explaining it all to me!" said Alice in the overstated tone of a perfect six year old.

"Your problem, not mine Hannah," declared Christina, "Although I suppose a trip to Provence to put folklore into perspective might be due. For now tell me about these Lancashire militants."

Alice looked at Hannah who felt she'd rather give way. After all, briefing Christina was her role in life. "Civil disobedience you asked about? It can't be wrong really, if it doesn't hurt people physically. Lancashire mill girls we talk to appear long-suffering. They are pretty forthright in condemning employers and the government, wouldn't you agree Hannah?"

"Yes, they're remarkable. At first meeting they seem poles apart from the Lady Balfours and Chrystal Macmillans of this world. I would say what characterises them is a kind of earthy disillusionment."

"It's not surprising you think that Hannah, with your refinement and intellect," remarked Alice.

"Thank you but it's not just a matter of background or intelligence. Christina, the mill girls understand the issues better than we do, despite their lack of eloquence. Because they struggle to earn a living every day they've become more direct and physical in their outrage. They express themselves in ways I find astonishing."

Christina combed back hair still wet from her early morning swim as Alice and Hannah studied her for a response. The Butler, Laine, came to announce the girls were leaving with Hugh for races at Cartmel and to enquire if Christina wished to see them off.

"Thank you Sutherland, I'll be there in a moment," Christina answered, keen to maintain professional standards if not convention.

"So these tough women have strong little hands on the thrapple of our National Economy and we think that's good?"

Alice went first again, "Basically, yes. The mill girls are simple and hilarious. Often they're self-deprecating with their biting sarcasm." She looked at Hannah, inviting her to take over.

"What I've learned from them Christina, are shrewd answers for any unthinking Dockers or Miners still dragging their feet on the issue of women's suffrage. Their anger and cynicism gives the lie to right wing press images of 'the long coat and shawl brigade' – you know the type, emerging from their local institute with greengage preserves and floral painted porcelain, 'to raise money for the cause.'"

"Well noy, I suppose I'd better lard up my old shillelagh," declared Christina, slipping into Monaghan brogue.

"Oy'd fill the knob end wit' lead if oy wuz you missus," Alice advised, in instant repartee. The moment perfectly exemplified the reason Christina employed Alice. Outrageous cries of laughter from the three women echoed through the house as Sir Hugh entered with the children to say cheerio.

At Shires' factory in Guiseley they were greeted by Production Floor Manager, Ken Davis who was anxious to ensure work was not interrupted until the belt conveyor stopped. Walking them out the front gate round to the delivery entrance he began the guided tour, gradually raising his voice and finally having to shout to make himself heard above the din.

"We get the ceramic bowls made for us under licence at Johnson's factory across the road. Here we make flushing cisterns for export around the world," he explained. At one end of the production line piles of coal slack were being tipped from a succession of delivery trucks onto a vast yard. Tired, filthy men propped themselves against sliding doors as they smoked, watching one of the trucks dump its dusty load. Others waited at a distance, ready to shovel barrow loads to men working a dozen small furnaces. Inside the factory three or four engineering supervisors wandered between crews and their presses, checking sand box castings before baking, as well as the cooling cisterns for integrity. If in doubt they poured water in, adding to humidity in the hellish miasma of dust, sweat and fumes.

In another hall, closed off to prevent unnecessary conversation from outsiders, women worked at incredible speed putting together weights, floats, rubber seals and flushing handles which were thrown into trays for the assembly line. There cistern carcasses were trimmed by a man cutting around a template with a steam powered saw. The next individual, a woman not qualified to operate power tools, applied polish and worked it around the smooth exterior of the shell. Then another man whisked a padded, steam powered polishing machine over them quickly buffing the coal pitch tanks and lids on all six surfaces. Finally, flush assembly components were packed by a woman into the cisterns along with the measured pipe lengths. Men with a pallet truck rolled them, stacked by the dozen, across to a loading bay where each item was matched to a standard, white ceramic bowl.

At last the klaxon blared. Steam valves were vented and closed and the shimmering sound of steel rollers turning on a hundred thousand tiny ball bearings gave way to aching human bodies and expressions of mental exhaustion.

Ever the natural aristocrat, Christina settled herself on a toilet bowl unpacked for inspection. Hannah and her NUWSS colleagues paced up and down as the factory ladies brought chairs from the canteen.

At last Rebecca Deurden, their branch stewardess, stood up to open the meeting, "I, we, work piece-work rates that are an insult bordering on the criminal. In't that right ladies? I also know damn fine, no man can stand alongside us. Mr Davis was bangin' on about some book he read by a yank called Taylor . . . supposed ter mek us all work faster. I'd love ter see him come 'ere an' try, cos Mr Davis couldn't. He sat in wi' us an hour a day for a month but couldn't get near us. He even told us ter stop talking so as not to distract him!" All the women present laughed.

"What wor it he said to you Edith? We wus *lightning fast?*"

"I must say he was very complimentary Becky, he said, 'you all have lightning fast, clever fingers.'"

"But what else?"

"Yer, in his estimation we could turn out half as much again as the quickest men employed here, 'while spending the entire shift talking through every family affair under the sun.' "

"Does that mean gossip Rebecca?" asked Alice. Laughter echoed up to the thirty foot high roof and the ice was broken.

"Men simply cannot engage their brains and bodies at t' same time. I'nt that a fact girls?"

"'specially on a sat'day neet after a few pints o' Tetley's!" came the agreement from a middle-aged blonde lady. With hair tucked in curlers under a neat blue headscarf, the attractive woman looked like Saturday night was still important to her.

"Aye they tek it much too serious Nellie! I think it'd be romantic if a man chatted wi' ye while they were swimming up the beach!"

Whispered explanations and hamming followed, leading to general hilarity. Hannah and her colleagues had heard the same mantra everywhere they'd campaigned across the north of England. Invariably the institutional prejudice of men against women met with the same concluding round of derisive sarcasm and hilarity.

Alice had warned Christina what to expect. But underneath the self-effacing mockery she caught an impression that these women would actually fight to improve their circumstances. One or two faces were familiar from front pages of the national fish and chip press – girls from Leeds and Manchester being dragged off their feet by London Bobbies.

Their personal accounts, shamefully grave yet individually compelling sounded like stories from the front line of a distant war. Taken out of the wider context of 'the movement' they felt awful to Hannah.

"Bloomin' police were a discredit to't uniform," inveighed one of the younger girls, "These are British men-folk . . . oo' kick and punch their own women! I came 'ome wi' a black eye, an' mind I've on'y just discovered I wor pregnant. If I'd 'ad a miscarriage our Nathaniel woulda found that bastard and pur 'im six feet in 'is grave."

Another earnest face backed her version, "Ah tell ya - theys dogs ont friggin' street wi' more decent character than those big rough twats!"

Nothing could have brought home the division in society as clearly as such accounts of the systematic abuse of women.

"It's policy and procedure," declared Becky, "Unofficial and deniable of course but us Yorkshire girls don't lie."

Pausing after condemnation of the Police, the quorum searched their visitor's faces for objections or disbelief, offering personal details to mitigate any doubt,

"If you beautiful ladies go on a demonstration to London make sure you wear your best bloomers," cautioned one wiseacre, "They lift you by yer ankles and carry you upside down!" No-one laughed.

"They'll ger a shock if they arrest me. I'm planning not to wear any!" put in another.

"Oh, you dirty clart, you never do," accused a third.

"Many times," Hannah told Christina as they walked to Guiseley Station, "I've seen this coarse hilarity spun in circles through the community of mill girls - like hands on the clock; like market forces of supply and demand, goods-in and goods-out."

Christina smiled warmly in conciliation, "Then you've seen the best of human nature, brought out by the worst. That is poetic Hannah. And it's in your nature to honour them."

On the way home from Leeds, rumbling through glowering alpine townships – Huddersfield, Brighouse and Mytholmroyd - conversation between Christina and branch associates Alma Hartwood, Betty Watson and the ever present Alice Hughes died with rocking of the train. In her mind Hannah returned to the same imponderable questions.

What is the essential value of education? Does knowledge empower us by reinforcing some definable moral quality? Is a relatively more educated society necessarily a better one?

This enigma had gnawed at Hannah during years of working, while surrounded by understated opulence and refinement taken for granted. In contrast to life with the delightful Leslie family, everywhere she went in Liverpool there were despondent people with no sense of belonging – no real aspiration for the future.

For the lucky ones there's work and more work. Occasionally horse racing and football, seasonal jaunts to Llandudno, or St Anne's. But grubby urchins are everywhere. What choice have they? Become a pickpocket, sporting a cheap suit and jaunty cravat, a spring loaded knife hidden up a sleeve waiting opportunity from dark corners.

Worst of all Hannah remembered a flippant conversation with Margaret and Harper about sectarianism, not long before fleeing their complacency. McGiffen had told her recently he was afraid to walk unaccompanied into Everton without a tar hatchet nestling in his overcoat pocket. Hannah realised that outwardly welcoming Liverpool was as culturally divided as Glasgow, or Belfast.

More than once the friends witnessed brawls starting in a pub and spilling out onto the street, usually over someone inadvertently whistling a snippet from a song. With dismay Hannah noted that the recently popularised 'Sash my Father Wore' seemed to cause more indignation in its banal commemoration of historical schism than any Church Synod or Papal Bull, aimed at heresy in modern times.

For decades football supporters on both sides claimed the tune with different, equally contemptible lyrics, reworked by frivolous thugs on a Friday night before a game.

"I was just there for the crack officer," went the standard plea, "They've got the best ale an' best snooker table. If I dared to sing it aloud they'd a sent me home in a pine box. It's just a song! After all it's a free country. That's what *we* fought for at the battle of the Boyne."

Everyone knew that story and others equally pathetic. Yet every Saturday night the same streets were despoiled with blood and broken glass, over the same trite affiliation to being either *Catholic* or *Protestant*. Then blood had flowed for freedom, now it was drawn in the name of puerile intolerance.

Meanwhile the Ulster fashion of casually stirring animosity with shameful bravura offensive to Catholics caught on in towns all over Southern Scotland, with young people inducted into marching bands for want of something worthwhile to do with their time. Hannah was thinking of the lawyer Gandhi and his struggle against racial apartheid in South Africa, when Alice disturbed her reverie.

"Why so glum? We did well today."

"Oh, just pondering the interminable stupidity of men. Certain of our favourite pubs in Liverpool," she complained, "might as well put a sign over the saloon door saying, "No Protestants!" as well as, "No Women.""

"I'm easy, you liberal minded old crow, just don't put RIP on my gravestone," joked Alice, deliberately misconstruing her point, "Why not suggest it to McGiffen? I'm sure he could get the landlord to agree." Hannah laughed aloud at Alice's distorted logic. It was the casual reminder she needed to stop thinking.

Chapter Fourteen *Vingt et Un*

Vacuum assisted breaking of six jolting carriages and the squeal of studded brakes on cast iron wheels brought Hannah back from irresistible slumber. Tight faces of Union colleagues smiled back across the carriage as the commuter train rumbled down another Pennine gradient.

Alma Hartwoods, generously proportioned and almost as attractive as glorious Christina, was a nurse and midwife of great experience. Betty Watson, bespectacled and diminutive, an old hand in the world of domestic service. Since meeting Christina she blatantly curried favour, clearly hoping for an opening at Allerton Grange. Both delegates had grown up families and relative financial security.

Although the old campaigners were tough minded, redoubtable women with much in common, it seemed to Hannah they lacked passion. Indifferent to outsiders, they sometimes found difficulty generating trust in women half their age. Despite the wisdom of years their uncertainty seemed to deny the future. Perhaps their imagining moral flaws in the motivation of any individual deemed militant, reflected deep caution. In turn that caution invited failure.

Alma and Betty were talkers, not fighters. They represented a new breed of professional activist - in it for the longer run and praying each night they would be on the right side of history. Hungry for the controlling authority of political power, they really had no idea what they might do with it if it ever came.

This common tendency of unimaginative, indecisive and often reactionary people seeking status as union officials fascinated Hannah. She knew that any mention of McGiffen's sleeper cell would be enough to cause Alma to scold and sulk. Betty would be so cross she'd get hypertension, probably resulting in a sleepless night. Hannah understood their fears and wanted to say something positive, "You know what Alma, Betty, I am so grateful to eat well. I'm always warm in my bedroom. Luxury for me is having a scuttle full of coal and some dry kindling to throw on at eleven o'clock at night in winter time." Alice laughed and Christina's mouth almost dropped open. "Extravagance is the knowledge that there are always cuts of meat and a fresh loaf to slice for sandwiches. Tomatoes and fresh lettuce. Milk and tea available without so much as a groan from the Cook, at any time of day or night."

"That's right," chimed Alice, turning to Betty, "'Food is there to be consumed,' Mrs Heap says, 'not rationed. It helps my meal planning if you use it up – so help yourselves if I'm not here to get it for you. I go off at nine but don't hold back on my account,'" said Alice, laughingly mimicking Iris Heap's easy tone.

Christina burned with embarrassment but said not a single word. Indirectly this was the highest compliment anyone had ever paid her in her life because these were *her* instructions by proxy. Alice continued unabated in her flow, "Mrs Heap actually said that to all fourteen of our assembled domestic retinue, Betty, 'Just use your discretion. Always keep me informed if something runs out. Don't cook up the Sunday joint if you come in after midnight from the Argyll Music Hall and fancy a little snack!'" Betty was speechless. Christina took out a handkerchief to dab her eyes and blow her nose, her hands trembling with emotion.

At St Helen's a teenage boy clambered aboard briskly, followed by a well-dressed gentleman in a town coat and suit. With a rounded head, short neck, low set ears and creased eyes giving the appearance of oriental ethnicity the boy had visible characteristics of John Landon Down's syndrome. Clearly he was also overweight and breathing heavily. Parking himself opposite Alma he moved along the padded couch to let the gentleman accompanying sit down beside him.

"Hi, I'm Josh," he said with a smile.

"Oh, hello Josh," replied Alma, a little reluctant to reciprocate.

"This is Terry, he's my dad," Josh intimated, "We're on our way to Liverpool. We're staying with friends and I'm going to see my specialist on Monday morning at t . . ten thirty." Josh evidently had word-finding problems when speaking quickly.

"Oh really, nothing too bad I hope?"

"No, I try not to think about it, but I'm duff. Worst is not sleeping at night 'cos I can't breathe *and* I keep farting . . . all, all the time, but really not on purpose."

There was a brief hiatus as the train pulled out of the station. Alice was bursting with delight. Hannah and Christina knew she wanted to mimic Josh and make some characteristically funny observation about his farting. Prudence held her back for the moment but Josh clearly rang her bell. Josh's dad whispered a caution about his language, overheard by Betty who could not help smiling.

"Oh it's alright Josh. I have exactly the same problem," she said, smiling at the man as if it was also his problem by proxy, "I just keep a straight face and look the other way, pretending it wasn't me." Josh laughed easily, unselfconsciously wiping the corner of his moist lips with his sleeve.

"Yeah, I try not to worry about my problems," he stated graciously, "I can read you . . . you know. I c . . can say all my times tables up to twelve. I speak French."

"Joshua, it strikes me you are a very fine gentleman and we are all delighted to meet you," said Christina, "I am Lady Christina Leslie and I live in Liverpool. These are my colleagues Alice and Hannah and these two ladies are Alma and Betty. They are our friends."

"Can I practice my French on you? I can count to thirty," he asked Betty, visibly happy with Christina's putting him at ease but unable to process an impression of all the faces quickly.

"Okay, go ahead."

Josh sat on the edge of his seat with hands apart and fingers spread – his head leaning forward slightly as he focussed full attention on the feat of memory he was about to perform. Hannah watched gleefully from the far side of the compartment.

"Un, deux, trios, quatre; cinq; six; sept; huit; neuf; dix; onze; douze; trieze; quatorze; quanze; seize," he paused "– seize – seize- seize", he repeated mechanically without stopping. His delivery of the counting, like his normal speaking tempo, speeded up and slowed down as Josh tried to pace himself through laboured breathing.

Josh's dad leaned his head to the side smiling effusively, holding up a hand against the ladies' intervention, "Pardon me, this is all part of the show," he explained.

With understated comic timing, Josh raced ahead with the uncompleted task before his dad might try to stop him, "dix-sept; dix-huit, dix-neuf; vinqt." He looked up at the smiling faces of Betty and Alma opposite, before deciding to carry on with the show, "vinqt-et-un; vinqt-deux - Oh figgulsticks . . . I forget the rest! I'll sing you a couple of songs in French later if you want?"

"Oh that'd be lovely," said Alma warming to the entertainment.

"He pretends to get stuck on sixteen," explained dad mildly, "He does it in English too." Hannah observed that Josh's dad had a look of sheer delight on his face.

Josh is no burden to his devoted father – he's a joy to behold. And this is the answer to my life's riddle! Knowledge is nothing without love!

"Where are you going?" asked Josh, having successfully broken the ice.

"Back to Liverpool," answered Alma, speaking easily now that she could see Josh didn't bite.

"Do you live there then?" inquired Josh, intent on maintaining dialogue.

"Yes."

"And do you live there?" he asked turning politely to Betty, "I, I know these three do."

"Indeed."

"And, and where have you been?" Betty and Alma looked guiltily at one another.

"We've been to a women's Suffrage meeting, with some trade unionists," stated Hannah for them, leaning forward closer to Josh.

"Uh . . ? Uh?" intoned Josh, turning his head to the left towards Hannah and pressing his ear.

"Hi Josh," she said gently, holding her hand out to touch his, lightly, "I'm Hannah. All five of us have been to a meeting in Leeds with some

294

women who want better pay for their work. Also, we all want to be able to vote."

"Yeah, yeah – in an election!" verified Josh, "I like Lloyd George and Asquith," he admitted disarmingly. His dad's proud smile slipped into slight embarrassment, "When I'm vinqt-et-un ans, I'm gonna vote for the Liberals."

"Oh, so would I, if they'd give us the vote," agreed Betty.

"What is your view of the government's proposed Conciliation Act?" enquired Josh's father. He was a large, intense looking fellow with very dark, slightly unkempt hair, "Sorry, Terence Lightowler," he confessed, extending his hand to each of them in turn. Well dressed, with the bronzed hands and face of a farmer, Lightowler conveyed an impression that work took care of itself.

"Manipulation of the electorate," all five of them chorused with variations, almost in perfect time.

"And what are you going to do when you get back to Liverpool?" resumed the delightfully sage Josh.

"I have a job interview at the Children's Hospital I work at. I hope to become a Matron," said Alma.

"Well you'll *get it*, I hope!"

"Thank you Josh. You are very kind."

"I work at the 'questrian . . . *e* questrian stables, for my dad with the horses." Josh pointed at his father, who smiled as his son praised him openly, "My dad is good. He pays me lots of money but you know what I, I have to get up early every day. Terry makes me pay rent so he doesn't have to pay no bloomin' taxes. He built a house for my sister Rachel and another one for my brother Jez on our farm. I have my own horse!" Hannah tuned out her tired mind, as Josh continued entertaining exchanges with Alma and Betty, including a mix of personal details with interesting information about likes and dislikes.

"I really don't like getting up in the morning. And I shouldn't have to work if, if I do not *feel* like it!" Josh rounded off his edifying dialogue by singing a couple of songs in French. At one point Alma became quite stirred by his engaging style.

"Can I say that I think you are the most pleasant individual I have met all day Joshua Lightowler. I can't believe you are only seventeen," she told him.

It occurred to Hannah with quite a shock that in reality there was very little material difference between success or failure, poverty or plenty, except in a notional sense.

Deprivation, like the money that can alleviate it, is another mechanism of control.

An open, easy relationship with Christina Leslie had revealed to Hannah the fact that wealthy individuals don't necessarily consume a great deal more than the poor, if prudent in their lifestyle. The Leslies suffered the same daily vicissitudes of weather and health; mood and routine; failed expectation, broken transactions and sorrow. Essentially they had the same basic needs for clothing, food and shelter, health care - not to mention love and respect, which Terence Lightowler and his family clearly bestowed upon poor Josh.

Josh wished Alma good luck with her interview, waved to the others in turn with eye contact normally spared, then turned to leap with both feet together onto the platform. Lightowler smiled at the women as his son sped off towards the ticket barrier. Alice handed him a card from Christina and asked him to write if he would, regarding the outcome of Joshua's hospital visit.

"Perhaps you'd both care to come for tea, some time when it's more convenient," she added circumspectly, "It's been a pleasure meeting you and your son."

"Please let us know when you might come over again," added Christina.

"Indeed I will your Ladyship, Ladies. Thank you all. Sorry I have to dash!" Terence raised his hat then turned to race after Joshua.

Strikes and labour disputes over unionisation had gathered impetus during the years Hannah was in Liverpool, now in the summer of 1911 they spread like wildfire through ships, docklands and railways.

Sprawling in an armchair with feet spread out in front of him in the school staff room adjacent St Alexander's Church in Bootle, Andy looked like a hobo version of The Christ hanging above on the wall. Father Jordan had put in a word with the Headteacher, since Siggy mentioned unwelcome attention from strangers at their last meeting in Everton. With a cigarette in mouth, ever the man of action, McGiffen complained of a bad back from splitting up five sixty-gallon drums of tar. His audience waited indulgently for him to begin addressing them.

"Things are movin' to a head," he warned. A dozen NUWSS members, five community leaders and a handful of teachers from the school stared at Andy in disbelief. "Every evening for the past two months Orange Order scabs have pressed areas they think of as leaning Republican, or just Catholic, with insults, bricks and bottles. Every borderline chippy, public house and general store wakes up to the chore of boarding windows and grimly sweeping up broken glass. But as bad as it sounds, these are just skirmishes before the battle. I can tell you fer sure its gonna kick off before the end o' the summer guys and gals, so dig out your battle boots, or stay off the streets! It's been great fun workin' wi' all youz bu' I can never be sure we'll meet again."

"So no meeting in Huyton next Tuesday?" asked Alice.

"You might be able to get to Huyton from your leafy lane next Tuesday Alice but not from here you won't and yer won't be goin' on the train."

"Why here? Why now?" asked Father Conlon, one of six full time priests who helped manage the flourishing parish.

"Yer 'ave ter understand Father, Liverpool's a base for well over ten million tons of shipping annually. Workers in this city meet demands of an increasing global market - for every imaginable kind of food and raw material. Our shipbuilding an' engineerin' yards, all the miles of warehousin' indirectly benefits a hundred armies of similar workers worldwide. What we send out, they thrive on, and vice-versa."

"And what discriminates Liverpool from all the other seaports around the world Andy?"

"Nothin' in particular, just more resentment and solidarity, Father. Over a quarter of all ships plying the oceans and trading throughout the

Empire are registered here in the UK. Glasgow, Tyneside, Hull, London, Dublin or Leith. All the deck officers and crews, *everyone* knows the same story. Non-white seamen are damned good but they're fed up wi' being pushed around too. Wages, conditions, medical care and provisioning are all shite. Pardon my ecclesiastical Latin."

"You're suggesting that as resentment swells, our Dockers and Merchant Seamen will hold a knife to the jugular of the universal supply of commodities. That's it, isn't it?"

"Couldn't have pur it better myself Father Conlon. But we learned the lesson from invisible money men, brokers and bankers who buy and sell wholesale cargoes, plying the oceans of the world. Every food shortage and famine, the high cost of living - right down to the price of a barrel of tar, is controlled by money grabbing middle men. What they tap off each day could house and feed a nation of starving urchins. The richest hundred and twenty thousand people in this country own two thirds of the nation's wealth. If that's not injustice, tell me whar is?"

"Well, as a priest I'd have to say it is logical to want to see the wealth of nations distributed for the benefit of all mankind."

"Not only logical father, moral," put in Mr Holden the History teacher.

Another voice came in from a stern faced, dignified little woman at the back of the staffroom.

"The Liverpool of fifty years ago was a hell hole of Cholera, Tuberculosis and Scarletina, not to forget poverty. Starving Irish came here in their thousands." McGiffen wasn't sure what her point was, so he shut up.

In silence that followed a roomful of diverse souls more or less pious and well-meaning glanced at one another for cues, or clues. Hannah stared at Marek, wondering when he would finally come out from the shadows to show his hand.

Tilting forward on his school chair, his friends were surprised to see Zalewski stand up and introduce himself to anyone he'd not met before. Pacing forward slowly, he looked at each individual around the room before speaking.

"I am Catholic first, will always be so, because as a child, first I was Catholic. Now I am Socialist but in my heart and actions I seek peace and redemption, which we know comes with Holy Communion. Let me tell you where the problem lies, very simple. Measurement of an abstraction is the problem - of all manufacturing and trade activity on some . . . *relative* . . . monetary scale. This gives us nothing more than a crude framework – an account book for profit and loss. Achievement of tremendous human endeavour creates only irritating, dirty little coins. Grubby pieces of paper. Currency. Pointless - yet indispensable to those making the profit. Never so to those suffering loss who go without."

A ripple of appreciative laughter ran around the room as the group relaxed, seeing some common ground. None but McGiffen had any inkling of Marek's activity as a philanthropic millionaire.

"You're advocating a return to barter?" asked Alma.

"No, listen to what I say! It *is* indispensable – and *why* indispensable? For *whose* benefit? What purpose, this cause of all injustice and suffering Alma? Because, I tell you, glut of money drives this *damning* human weakness," Zalewski sniffed the musty air in the school room as he paused to let the point sink in, "Greedy elite in every country creates discrimination, hatred and warfare. Money causes this. Capitalism. We need ownership by all for all. Land, railways, docks. Everything that can be produced. "

Father Conlon and the lady at the back flipped down padded boards thoughtfully attached to the back of chairs for Friday assemblies and knelt to pray in silence. Most of all the priest was disturbed by what Robert Jordan had told him about 'sectarianism marring the spiritual progress of the wider community.' Conlon, the Redemptorist, loved everyone equally, notwithstanding the impenetrable illusions of History.

Hannah and Alice planned to be in the crowd on 13th August when union leader Tom Mann was due to address the strikers. On their three mile walk into the city they saw hundreds of Mounted Police and armed soldiers, including elite Cameron Highlanders, who bantered with them as they dismounted from an impounded bus.

"Is this how you normally travel tae work?" demanded Hannah of one of the three squaddies blocking the pavement.

"On'y if naeb'dy else is using it hen. We'd 'a' gied yis a lift if ye'd stuck oot a thumb."

"You're a long way frae home lassie," said the Sergeant, a wry smile on his face, "I hope ye've no come here tae stir up trouble."

"No, but one look and I can tell that's why you're here."

"Oh, dinnae be too hard on us hen. We've orders tae protect the population when the riot starts."

"I'm glad tae hear it, what time do you plan tae start it?"

"That's privy tae the Chief Constable hen, but Colonel's Stewart's gone tae see 'im the noo."

"Well maybe if you hang around in the back streets long enough you'll miss it!" suggested Alice, clearly charmed by the friendly RSM. In turn he laughed warmly at her cheek, a glint of the serial womaniser in his eye.

"Aye, ye'd hope so. They ne'er tell us any'hin lassie. Stops us worryin' afore they sen' us intae action."

Wandering around for two hours amid tens of thousands of demonstrators, they looked for people whom they knew would be in the vast crowd but saw no-one familiar. Their experience as activists in the heartland of Stanley, Everton and Bootle with the boys they loved had been nothing more than a microcosm of revolution – a pebble on the strand of discontent. Alice had brought sandwiches and a flask, or they would have had to go without. Even catering staff at the Station Hotel had walked out in sympathy with the National Strike. Liverpool was a seething mass of angry humanity, with a TUC committee running everything from the movement of goods to the posting of mail. For a few weeks there had been echoes of Robespierre's Parisian Committee of Public safety, during the mother of all Revolutions - but now there was a battle cruiser on alert in the bay and hundreds of armed Police and soldiers hiding inside St George's Hall, waiting for the signal to attack the crowd and break the strike.

Tom Mann had a microphone rigged to a loudspeaker system, which he used to bring attention back from the carnival atmosphere. For weeks there had been a breakdown of the nominal structure and functioning of finely nuanced, conditional capitalism but amazingly these dissenters knew how to organise themselves without controlling authority. The crowd hushed and settled as the public address system echoed Mann's terse message across the square.

"A hundred thousand people have come to the centre of Liverpool this afternoon. The authorities have allowed us to 'police' this hundred thousand ourselves. Why? Because they enjoy surrendering their power? Or because they're afraid of being trampled underfoot. There's a thin line between order and chaos. The police force of Liverpool may tread it this afternoon. A step wrong and the Mersey will rise a foot by nightfall, with largely innocent blood.

We're gathered here today, peacefully, to demonstrate our determination to win this long and terrible battle against the employing classes and the state. What does that mean? Only this. All the transport workers of Liverpool are arm-in-arm against the enemy class.

We have sent a letter to the employers asking for an early settlement and a speedy return to work. If that brings no reply, if they ignore us, The Strike Committee advises a general strike.

In the face of the military and the police drafted into this city - and of the threat to bring gunboats into the Mersey - we can see nothing except a challenge. A challenge to every worker who values his job. A challenge to every claim each worker makes of his employer. A challenge to every right a worker should expect under common decency. Brothers, we rise to this challenge. And we meet it, head on."

This was justification the authorities were waiting for. Within a matter of seconds the orderly expression of communal solidarity soured under a deluge of sadism. Mann had put up his dukes but no-one had rung the bell before the knockout punch was landed. Mounted Police in their hundreds charged into the fringes of the crowd as a second line drew batons and assaulted people trying to disperse, brutally cracking their heads open as they ran from the horses. Union officials on the podium were quickly swamped by men pouring out of the vast building behind, beaten and pushed aside for the magistrate to step into their place. Guarded by armed and disciplined soldiers with an officer holding up the microphone for him, Stipendiary Magistrate Stuart Deacon 'read the riot act.'

Hannah and Alice were astonished to hear the words being brusquely read out, amid a sudden roar of anger from eighty thousand incensed voices around the plateaux.

"Our sovereign Lord the King chargeth and commandeth all persons, being assembled, immediately to disperse themselves, and peaceably to depart to their habitations, or to their lawful business, upon the pains contained in the act made in the first year of King George, for preventing tumults and riotous assemblies. God save the King."

In spite of all the warnings and preparation Hannah and Alice could not believe their eyes or ears. The peaceful meeting was being deliberately turned into a pitched battle, not a hundred paces from where they stood. Hannah realised with a shout of adrenalin that Marek's perspicacity could never have been more starkly cast in its wisdom.

The seasoned campaigner had told them, "If they cannot rule they will divide. They set women against men. Force girls into prostitution. Juveniles to borstal. Make neighbours hate one another for emblems of a pope or foreign king. If they cannot create enough fear at home they will start a foreign war, intended to repress and kill *you* - agents of change threatening *their* interests!"

"Hannah we have to go," Alice pleaded, as fighting began to spread around the podium area. Dozens of horse drawn vehicles emerged from side streets in every direction: St John's, William Brown Lane, The Old Haymarket and Lime Street, dispersing hundreds more Police who waded into the defenceless crowd with batons flailing. Armed soldiers from out of town were emerging from trams, buses and trucks. Unfamiliar cracking of warning shots could be heard above angry voices.

Men around them began arming themselves with cobbles and coping stones before moving forward into the fray. Hannah was unexpectedly distracted, not by the violence but something Alice had no intuition about. The Police would let the crowd disperse to the north where most had come from and she was looking that way.

"Solidarity is one thing but I do not intend to become a casualty today," snapped Alice peevishly, as though Hannah might have objected to that caveat. In panic Alice took Hannah's hand, to head over towards the south end of St George's Hall and Lime Street Station beyond. Hannah held the smaller woman back.

"They're on strike remember, Alice! That's why we walked here."

"Well we'll walk home, come on let's go."

"Fine but not in that direction we won't."

"Well where then?"

"Marek, I want to see Marek. We should head for McGiffen's house, we'll sit it out, then order a cab later."

"Well let's go, quickly!"

Stan had got up late as it was a Sunday and Andy's ma objected to the sound of a printing machine being worked on the Sabbath, even in the name of a good cause. He cooked some eggs on his single burner portable stove, then went to borrow the newspaper McGiffen had smuggled in. Ma obliged Stan but told him the others had gone to the demonstration. A light of affection shone in her eyes for the gallant Russian whom she'd grown to love and respect. Ma knew in her water things were about to change for ever, if not for better. From the front window she could see four funnelled HMS Antrim turning over her engines in the estuary. She knew that one salvo from her six inch guns would erase her entire street and every poor soul living in it from existence. She wondered idly if Jack McGiffen might be aboard and if he was asked to shell his old street, would he think of her and his family.

"Marek said to tell you to lie low and wait for Andy to come back, Stan – they're expecting trouble."

"Hmm, trouble every day ma. Life is trouble. If I was not here to see it, trouble would be over too!"

"Stan if ye wern 'ere t' see it, trouble ud follow yer, lar. Read yer paper an' feel free ter use it for wiping you know what, especially the front page wit' all the politicians talking' shite."

"Ma yer a star, thanks! I got printer's ink everywhere else . . . may as well have it on me 'you know what.'"

"If yer mean yer bum crack Stan, just tell it like it is – I'm not easily offended!"

"Ma, I love you!"

Heading out to the brick outhouse Stan did not think twice about the strong smell of petroleum fractions permeating the McGiffen residence. Andy was a road mender and always carried barrels of tar on his wagon. After nearly a year Stan was used to it, as were all the neighbours. A dab of petrol was the only thing to remove it from axe handles or grubby hands. It had never occurred to Stan to ask Andy what he would do if there was likely to be a police raid, although he knew the Zalewski brothers were not only involved with unions.

Occasionally there had been drunken discussions about the use of petrol or paraffin as an accelerant in arson attacks. These analytical examinations of effective acts of sabotage ventured speculatively into relative merits of destroying the country home of a wealthy colonialist; a lodge frequented by top masons, or a warehouse employing bag ladies at less than subsistence wages. In one instance McGiffen argued in favour of targeting a cargo vessel 'that everyone will see burning.' Due to his tenuous émigré status Stan knew better than to ask what conclusions they had reached. Also he had completely overlooked the fact that the tide was in and the sewers backed up, as ever.

The night before the demonstration McGiffen had panicked. Marek had better contacts than Andy's Irish republican socialists and stayed calm. The Irishmen anticipated conflict with relish, making a point of saying nothing to people on the ground, whereas Polish communists hankering toward national unity at home looked for middle ground and would risk an occasional warning. In the event both men foresaw what was coming, on the back of police and army contingents pouring into the city. Despite Marek's assurance that they had already won, McGiffen was terrified of what the day ahead might hold for him, his family and his crew.

Andy waited until 2am on Sunday morning to finally wake Marek and ask for help in pouring 120 gallons of high octane petrol locked in his coal bunker into the pan of the outside lavatory. Being lighter than water, the fraction made its way successively up the hill into pipe bends of every one of fifty vintage water closets. In the intermediate twelve hours none of it had gone where Andy intended. Almost two and a half gallons of immiscible, highly flammable fluid had made its way into the ceramic bowl drain of each and every toilet backing two parallel rows of terraced houses.

Hannah and Alice headed away from Lime Street in the direction of Stanley Dock and McGiffen's house, through a crowd consisting of mainly striking men. The maze of slum land dwellings they were headed for were by now the scene of running battles. Tom Mann had declared war on the employers ten weeks before and now, following Police and Army action directed by the authorities, Liverpool was on the verge of revolution.

Unless someone backed off soon, insurrection was a nailed on certainty. Everywhere the women went to avoid Police baton charges, angry men were moving in the opposite direction prepared to defended slums that Jim Larkin described as 'not fit for swine' with their lives. Many were slightly drunk and armed with half bricks or empty bottles. In their faces Hannah read a sense of equanimity - of dark consternation fulfilled at last.

Drafted-in Police with no local sympathies were moving into fringes of the dockland areas to make token arrests. Risking life and limb to grab a handful of scallys too daft to run, they were not particular about who they brutalised in turn. But no-one molested Alice or Hannah as they picked their way along the police cordon into the rabbit warren of the docklands.

By the time they approached the bolthole of McGiffen's house they had witnessed dozens of unwarranted and merciless acts of violence but very few arrests. Police had a free hand under the riot act and court authorities were not happy to be involved. If the strikers didn't get that wicked message in the next few hours, the army would help to clarify.

Stan finished taking care of business and selected a photograph of 245 peers voting in the upper chamber to wipe his bottom on. Folding the newspaper he tucked it under his arm and bent down to hitch up his pants. Balancing a smouldering roll up between his lips, he buttoned his fly, buckled his belt and flushed the toilet. Before turning to go he flicked the burning dog end into the pan.

Fifty ceramic bowls instantly and neatly snapped at the fluid level as below their bends pipework was blown asunder. Fifty wooden seats cantilevered upwards on metal fixings and ripped free on a fierce thermal wave, propelling them with massive shards of white porcelain through fifty corrugated asbestos roofs. Fifty heavy ceramic pans took flight over short distances only to dash onto concrete floors, or against brickwork resistant to venting flame.

Thankfully only Stan was blown through the door of an outhouse. Predictably everyone else living along the two streets was too busy at that precise moment fighting with the Police. The fact that no-one else had dropped a lighted butt into a toilet since 2am the previous morning was nothing short of miraculous, given the temptations of mixing business with pleasure.

Amid sounds of chaotic movement and skirmishes came a returning ambulance followed by an army fire crew who had briefly visited the area under a hail of missiles and abuse. The tar truck was gone. The front door was open but there was no-one at home.

"Hello? Mrs McGiffen, hello?" Alice called through the house. She was met with only silence. Hannah led the way down into the basement room where she gasped as she stepped through the threshold.

"Oh my God, Andy was right . . . just look at this!"

Warm tea and a frying pan had been knocked onto the floor and Marek's printing press was buckled beyond repair, lying amid a thousand leaflets. More concerning was the fact that the Zalewski brothers and Stan had evidently vacated the premises. Personal effects such as they'd had were nowhere to be seen and the basement had been ransacked.

"We should go," exhorted Alice.

"No, no. At some point Andy will come home with his family. And I want to find Marek."

"Oh, dear Lord! Why didn't you tell him you were smitten?"

"Alice did I ever give any indication that I am *smitten?*"

"Not until now, but you clearly are." Tears welled in Hannah's eyes, as if to confirm Alice's keen observation.

"Some concerns go beyond intimacy and affection."

"Oh . . . altruism, integrity, dedication to a benign cause?"

"Yes!" Hannah shouted, "Sorry Alice, yes." Alice watched Hannah in the silent, failing light where for once even the rats seemed scared to intrude.

I'm not *in* love with him, although I do *love* him."

"Devotion?"

"Maybe, if there had been an opportunity."

"And why do you feel the need to find him any more than Siggy, or Stan or Andy? We all knew this cruel ending was written in the stars."

"Because right now Siggy and Stan will be slipping out of a nearby harbour on a Norwegian trawler and Andy will be offering Lord Leverhume a bargain he can't refuse on a new tarmac driveway, while planning to torch his mansion. Marek was always the risk taker. He's the one they came here looking for – whoever did this . . . and because there has to be something more." Hannah sat still in the half-light with her hand over her brow for several minutes without speaking.

"I needed to see him again one more time. The good and great lead relatively simple lives Alice, making big decisions forced upon them by circumstance and privilege. Who to elevate and what to bury under the foundations of the newest cathedral to hypocrisy. Marek's is a more tortuous path, but . . ."

"But what Hannah?"

"He is nobler than any of them."

As evening descended, sounds of the rioting drifted back into the centre of town where it had started. Angry Trade Unionists, Protestants from Everton and Catholics from Bootle, now with acknowledged common ground between them - reassembled for a return match with the scuffers, Riot Act or no Riot Act. Hannah suggested to Alice they walk back along the canal towards Kingsway and Scotland Road.

Closing the front door they went around the side of the house where Urchins were burning three mattresses in the street.

"Don't yous throw dat in the canal when you're done barricading against the Bizzies," called Alice, "ye'll block the bleedin' sewer again!"

"Sewer? The whole street's a fuckin' sewer, Southend! Some mad gobbshite blew up the fuckin' carzies!" called a skinny lad wearing a flat cap as a sign of status.

Turning the corner Hannah and Alice picked their way through chunks of a smashed lavatory and pieces of corrugated asbestos, strewn all over the ginnel.

"Oh blood and sand, hold your breath Judy!" warned Alice, stepping around the foul debris. Two hundred and forty five peers of the realm smiled back at her as she avoided treading on their creased image.

They waited outside the boathouse for over an hour but there was no sign of movement. With a sinking heart Hannah followed Alice along the tow path, still searching the shadows for her friend.

Eventually they did manage to find a cabbie prepared to take them home to West Allerton - via Old Swan and Mossley Hill, making it more worth his while - on the understanding they were 'not toffs,' or strike breakers.

"How do we know *you're* not?" demanded Hannah, with the front of a fully qualified survivor.

"We're Suffragists," said Alice, "So show some friggin' respect lar!"

When ma had seen the barely conscious and badly burned Stan off into the ambulance she took her daughter, Irene, by the hand and made swiftly off to report to her son at a builder's yard in a back street half a mile north of the house. Sean Toner, the discreetly confident proprietor, politely vacated his 'office' space – a pornography lined store room full of sand and cement bags, for the family to talk privately.

Sigismund sat smoking silently in a corner with a dismantled truck's gear box on the floor in front of him. His hands were covered in finely grained swarf and he stank of hypoid-gear oil, coating his hands and clothing. Today he was Toner's mechanic. Tomorrow he might be a deck hand on a trawler.

Andy knew he wouldn't have time to alert his crew and they would despise him for looking out for himself. He knew from ma's report of the demolished outhouses that it was only a matter of time before word got out and the Bizzies moved in to look for him.

"Friggin' blocked sewers! I said they'd be the death 'o us all ma!"

"Don' be frettin' on tha' lar. Think yersel' lucky it's din't blow Stan's arse 'alf way up is friggin back! Or me! Or bloomin' Irene . . . ye big daft sod!"

"When did Irene start smokin' ma? 'Ave you started bloody smokin' Irene? Yer only bloomin twelve an' yer smokin'?" cried Andy, turning to his tight faced sister. Irene was small, rotund and gentle in her mannerisms but behind crystal blue eyes was the same sharp intelligence of her revered big brother.

"That'll ruin yer health. Don't yer know there's an American study that links smokin' wi' cancer!"

"I'll take my chances wi' tha' any day, rather than risk being around you . . . blowin' up half the ruddy street!"

"Watch yer cheek Irene. And don't be repeatin' that, or I'll end up a fond friggin' memory like our da!" said Andy pointing a tar stained finger at ma's little angel.

"For the love of Mike, can we not argue! I've had to give up my goods and chattels for your brave adventure into the world o' Republicanism and Labour unions. You know I can't werk cos o' me back. We rely on you Andy!"

"Sorry ma. Come here you," said Andy, hugging Irene and extending an arm to ma for a bear hug.

Two hours later Andy pulled up at the new fishing wharf at Fleetwood. He went alone to chat with Captain Granville Ineson, master of a state of the art steam powered deep sea trawler. Siggy watched from his space between the tar barrels on the back of the flatbed truck as Andy sub-consciously reached his big, generous hand into a trouser pocket. But somehow Siggy knew this time money couldn't buy it.

Ineson looked at the truck, puckered his lips and shook his head once to the left side only, internalising doubt. He had plenty of money and wasn't about to risk drawing attention from the Harbourmaster by lifting the truck onto the stern of his boat, especially if it compromised buoyancy or stressed his derrick.

Siggy thought of upping the ante but knew the fisherman would suspect that the heat was not far behind them or worse, the dubious provenance of currency offered and the possibility of a Treasury reward.

McGiffen paid extra for Ineson to arrange a rare cargo Master visiting the fishing port to deliver his truck to Dublin for him, when he returned with his next load of cod.

Andy shouted across at Siggy, "Get the tarp out *cousin Seamus!* We're gonna have ter live hand ter mouth for a week or two in Eire, while these gentry get around ter deliverin' the tools of our trade!"

When the ropes were tied and the magneto removed, Andy handed over his ignition keys with the money, scowling at the tough captain. "Take off the hand brake and push the bugger," he snarled "Ye've been paid enough!"

"Of course!" agreed the genial conspirator with a smirk, "You look out for me Andy, and I'll look out for you!" As he ushered the friends towards his ship Captain Ineson shook his head, surprised that a man on the run should be so mistrusting of an Old Salt. After all this was Fleetwood. Where else was he going to be if a fellow was looking for him?

Stan was under for forty eight hours and when he woke found himself bathed in a sea of fire, with his right hand cuffed to the frame of the bed. Visitors came and went. He talked to them, but was so deeply sedated that he could not remember one day from the next, or what had been discussed the last time he was awake, without prompting. Friends and well-wishers came, including Alice and Hannah but no Siggy and no Marek. All the time there was a question lit in Stan's nerves, which in truth had followed him for the past seven years. It manifested in the awkward questions asked by doctors, nurses, and friends and of Stan to himself. He groaned when thinking of it, 'Eto pizdets! Kak yebat? How in the fuck am I going to get out of here?' he asked himself, turning into the darkness. When dull consciousness was at last restored and the effect of formidable opiates finally began to wear off, the answer to his dilemma was found sitting in a chair near the end of the ward. A policeman in uniform, briefed to ensure Stan went nowhere.

"That's 'im in there Sarge, sleeping in my bloomin' glasshouse!" said Archibold Winstanley, pointing at the recumbent Zalewski. In an instant Marek was awake and in another instant rose to look around and see that the game was up. He had planned to talk himself out of just such an unfortunate discovery by the local police, but a glance towards the top of the allotment confirmed the approach of a squad of armed soldiers. Marek knew they weren't looking for vagrants. They were looking for communist insurgents on the run from Liverpool, where the Police had a free hand following the riots. Marek intended to act the wag; stall them until they brought in a professional interrogator. But he knew it was only a matter of time before they handed him back to his own government.

In truth, despite three hundred and fifty with split heads and two shot dead in cold blood, Asquith's cabinet had already decided to concede to the strikers, as Marek had told Andy – the authorities were simply taking their pound of flesh. But in turn the unions strengthened one another. Seamen and Dockers assisted Transport Workers and Railwaymen. Speakers of every political stripe flocked to Liverpool from all over the country. The message and method learned there quickly spread to Belfast and London, Southampton, Glasgow and Edinburgh.

Hannah had observed how within two years Tom Mann's method of bringing in diverse supporting voices - religious and liberal, trades unionist and socialist - to support rights of affiliation and improved working conditions, spread to Ireland, Europe, America and back to the Antipodes where he'd cut his teeth. At home transport workers, miners and warehouse operatives all benefitted from national negotiations, extracting concessions from a bankrupt government. Indirectly mill workers and factory hands across the country benefitted too, gradually restoring reduced wages to where they'd been ten years before. Yet flagrant abuses continued.

Part Four

Chapter Fifteen   *Fire in the Sky*

On a clear pre-dawn Saturday morning in the autumn of '13 when
Liverpool was at its flourishing best, Hannah was still trying to get
women to support the Suffrage movement. She parted company with
Alice and a small coterie of campaigners at the corner of Regent Road, as
the women dispersed along miles of wharves lining the Mersey. Walking
briskly with a bundle of campaign leaflets and newsletters, she braved
familiar territory along the dock side. Hannah had been warned as a
child that docks were traditionally a no go area for women – at least in
superstitious Scotland. She shuddered 'as if someone was walking over
her grave.'

The morning air was heavy with the fishy damp smell of rotting
hemp. Beneath the pungent aroma was a sooty fragrance of burning
slack hanging in the air that caught in her throat. From beyond dozens
of cargo vessels lining the wharves, came the cry of gulls. Every few
minutes there was the hoot of a pompous tug boat pilot. Coarse
exchanges between crane-men, grafters and delivery drivers, falling
despondently in the dry cold of a November morning, could be heard in
the near distance.

Standing in a pool of arc light beneath a sign reading NO
SMOKING BEYOND THIS POINT Hannah watched the loading of
a grain carrier as she smoked a cigarette in a silvered ebony holder, given
her as a Christmas present by Christina. Hannah quietly marvelled at
how little attention was paid to her by the handful of watching Dockers,
gratified to note their indifference amounted to a new kind of grudging
acceptance. Propping her cigarette on the edge of an empty pallet she
began handing out leaflets to sack makers on their way in to the early
shift at EH Darby Ltd.

For the most part the women demurred politely as they hurried on,
but a few did stop to talk. There was a lull between the start of the day
shift and the release of the night shift. From where she waited, Hannah

could hear the spring-loaded stamping of an expensive CTR time recorder as poorly paid women scurried in through the entrance.

As the women poured out of the factory she moved forward boldly, to hand out leaflets encouraging union affiliation and support of NUWSS. Working briskly, she chatted lightly with the women, taking full advantage of the queue at the time clock that slowed their leaving. Like the girls she'd met at Shires, Hannah's hands never stopped for fear one of the bag ladies might escape.

Catching sight of her shapely behind and obvious determination, a man driving a small, motorised forklift truck stopped for a moment to wolf whistle at her. Hannah responded in the conditioned manner, with a scowl and turn of her shoulder, but three successively louder attempts came from the warehouse crane-landing behind the fork truck. When she finally looked in their direction, a man with a profusion of freckles, straw-coloured cropped hair and a gypsy ear ring waved down at her.

"Hey Judy, I'm Mick but I'm not gonna say 'is name cos 'es a waste o' space." Mick paused momentarily before shouting an apology, "Sorry for my mate not having a big enough gap in his teeth. I promise to give him lessons. I mean if yer gonna wolf whistle a gerl ye should do it proper like – don't ye think love?" he said by way of an excuse.

Hannah cracked a smile, full of warmth and recognition, shaking her head rather than trying to scold the man. His generous blue eyes were all cheeky innocence under the cold arc lighting. The pallet truck driver said, "Go steady smilin' at that pervert love . . . you'll make him fall to his death!"

"You two vote for solidarity with these bag makers, understand! Vote in support of women's Suffrage!" she called back with firmness in her voice, looking in turn at both men.

"I never thought twice abour it!" said the pallet truck driver disarmingly, "my old gal threatened to stop feedin' me if ah dint."

"Absolutely no question about it gal," said Mick's mate, "You scratch my back, I'll drive your Rolls."

"Bloody good – but don't forget! And stop your colleagues referring to women as, 'hey Judy' and dark skinned people as, 'smoked Paddys.'

Learn respect and teach respect!" she nipped out her cigarette like a seasoned smoker and marched off briskly back towards the town.

Hannah reflected upon the knowledge that she'd be back there in a week but not as part of her challenging education in political activism. It would be the White Star jetty she'd be coming to with her little charges, as an employee of the Leslies' embarking on a voyage to the Mediterranean and New York. But first she had a week's leave which she intended to take at home in Edinburgh, "If Sir Hugh's Board of Directors coughs up enough of a pay increase for the Railwaymen," she told Alice, "And we won't be going on holiday if they don't! Not with Hugh at least."

The Board did pay up, just in the nick of time. Reduced services and wildcat strikes in every sector of industry made long distance travel unpredictable that week but Hannah managed to get home, with a change at Glasgow.

Looking back, it felt a time of healing in all aspects of her life. Harper insisted that she stay with them and Hannah was glad to – in her old room. Time seemed to pass quickly, with familiar harmony that could exist nowhere else but in her childhood home. Hannah realised that she missed Edinburgh, recording that impression in her diary after a pleasant weekend.

On Monday she shopped for a winter outfit and borrowed items from Margaret's extensive wardrobe suitable for the warmer Mediterranean climate.

On Tuesday, with a little prompting, Walter took her to the Opera to see Ernst Denhof's Company performing Tristan and Isolde.

Finding time between gossiping with Margaret, who was now at home full time with little John, she walked alone along the beach front at Portobello on Wednesday afternoon. Wondering where so much time and worry had gone since childhood days spent there, Hannah began to feel a little blue.

Thinking of her first family – the one she liked to remember best – the Wilsons and Robertsons, Great Gran Han, Jessie, Elsie and her mum, Hannah tried to recapture what was lost. In the evening she picked up her pen again after bedtime and wrote,

'It's so long ago that it no longer hurts to think of what I've lost. Maybe I just hurt so much that I'm inured to sorrow and can't feel the difference. So much living has distracted me in the meantime, mostly joyous in superficial ways but also full of struggle. But this was the place I was happiest in my youth. There were holiday jaunts with my family to Portobello and Rothiemay and time I spent with Isabella, Willie, Walter and Jim. We had the gang hideout in the park, impromptu picnics with fig rolls and smuggled beer on the beach. There were galas and water fights in the surf and we went every day when the weather was warm. Whatever happened to those simple but glorious days? How I always longed to share them with my mum.'

At Jenners, Hannah spotted a leather valise almost matching tooled luggage provided for her by the Leslies, "To avoid embarrassment Margaret, though they offered to give me a case."

"You must accept, or they will be offended. Here is some face cream," suggested Margaret, "Put a little on before going out in the sun."

"The Italians put olive oil on their skin."

"Oh well, when in Rome. Oh, I forgot to tell you," announced Margaret as if still on the same subject of cosmetics, "these letters came for you. We forgot the last time you were here – I do apologise," she added, delving into her handbag. After handing them over she moved quickly through the store with little John before Hannah had time to object.

"What? When did these come Margaret?" asked Hannah thinly, pursuing several paces behind as she examined the envelopes. Margaret turned to look at Hannah with a carefully prepared speech, "There are three posted from Portobello, with the same gentleman's copperplate, sent some time apart but the latest date stamped a few months ago."

On this account Hannah had nothing to say, suddenly falling silent. Somehow she knew who they were from and what they were about. She even felt guilty without knowing why, imagining being observed from a distance.

"I wonder who they are from?" ventured Margaret limply, "Maybe that bus driver, what's his name?"

Hannah felt blood pulsing in her forehead as a vision of William Macdonald jumped into her mind's eye. This was why Alice was wrong about Marek.

"Next time you are up you should invite him over for supper," chimed Margaret. Hannah was speechless with rage.

Aye, if he's still interested. Why did you not forward these to me, you callous little bitch? You decided he was too old!

At nine o'clock on Friday morning as Hannah said goodbye, Margaret, who had been much more amenable lately, looked concerned. Scowling at Harper disapprovingly, she put a finger to her lips as he joined them in the hall. Hannah saw it yet despite barely contained fury she smiled warmly, hugging all three of them goodbye in turn.

Turning left at the gate she headed back to Waverley through the park. Like the black cat she'd seen on the wall staring at the moon over rooftops, Hannah felt the world flying again into the endless universe beyond.

Preoccupied by the still unopened letters, she remembered a fleeting glimpse of something unconfirmed at the time of her previous visit. Walking through the bluebell woods alone she mumbled to herself, "Harper! The old bastard doesn't approve of my bus driver."

Sir Hugh arranged with London and North Western Railway for collection of all their goods and chattels, which were taken to his own privately booked freight car. He also had his own carriage for those accompanying him to London. A similar arrangement had been made for the onward rail journey from Waterloo to Southampton, on the London and South-Western Railway. They stayed overnight at the Savoy.

Hannah had to be on guard constantly as Helena and Clarissa wanted to explore the vast hotel. After supper they insisted on seeing Cuban musicians they'd overheard playing in the ballroom. Alice accompanied them to relieve the pressure of constant vigilance on Hannah.

Around two in the afternoon of the second day they boarded a grand Union Castle liner, due to sail that evening for Alexandria. At last Hannah had time to think without worrying. She would have opportunity to read and write on their voyages around The Mediterranean and across the Atlantic. There was an extensive library on board RMS Balmoral Castle. When Hannah was not pre-occupied with taking Helena and Clarissa off their mother's hands, Alice could find her there with her nose in a book.

Over the years Hannah had made a friend and ally in Lady Christina, with whom she conducted a close professional relationship. Christina was from an entrepreneurial Irish Catholic family but had clearly married for love, not title. Sir Hugh worshipped her but no doubt could have had his pick of the venal aristocratic bunch. A man of intellect who loved a good argument, he nonetheless conceded every minor issue raised by his exquisite wife without contest.

Despite the great falling away, religion had always been and still was in Christina's mind at least a major issue. Consequently Hannah Harper's views were of interest to her. At last in the bright twenty one year old she had found a foil for discourse - given that Hugh tended to agree with her too easily.

Sitting on the open patio of their suite, sipping cocktails as the sun painted terracotta clouds over the Bay of Biscay, Christina tentatively broached the subject again, "Who could witness such beauty and not believe in God?"

Hugh was relaxed but a little taciturn in response, "If you were a Protestant dear, you'd be seen as a religious fanatic."

"I'm not though, I'm Roman Catholic which means I can discover other people's thoughts, safe in the knowledge they cannot taint me."

"Hmm, 'Forgive me father for I have sinned – I read a book about French Somnambulists,' said Hugh mimicking the regular sinner in the

317

confessional box, "'Well my child I'm not sure what that might be,'" he continued, now playing the doughty Irish priest, "'But if ye'll give me the len' o' it I'll tell ye the next time ye come to confession if it's a sin or not. For now ye'd better say tree Hail Marys . . . just in case it's the work o' the devil.'"

"Oh Hugh, just because men are pre-occupied with wars over territory doesn't mean no-one should waste time thinking about matters of faith. This book I'm reading is about Emmanuel Swedenborg, a tremendously gifted visionary."

"Religious affiliation," mumbled Sir Hugh, with the reluctant tone of a benign patron revealing details of a bill in an exclusive restaurant, "caused deep division within our family in the past. In the end our forebears acted judiciously. On more than one occasion they chose the right time to defend Sovereign and Union. Quite frankly from then on religion has tended to take a back seat for the Leslies. Not that we don't daily thank God for all our blessings," he added approvingly, after a sip of his drink, "It's just that religion has its place - in the Church. It should never be argued about, or discussed in front of children. Especially not when a person is sober."

"At least when you're not, you have an excuse for indulging in nonsense?"

"Precisely!"

Over where Helena and Clarissa were finishing their supper, Hannah laughed aloud at Sir Hugh's casual irony. He winked at her as he sipped his drink, feet stretched out on a deck chair under a Provencal crocheted blanket.

Seven year old Helena was not interested in the banter between her parents. Instead she was giving attention to Clarissa, who was taking her time over supper, "Eat your fois gras Clarissa," it's really very nice."

"Ugh! I hate it . . . chopped bird livers. You can have it but you'll get fat like Daddy." Five year old Clarissa laughed aloud, carried away by her own discourtesy.

"Sssh! He'll hear you," warned Helena.

"Well? He was talking about us," whispered Clarissa, leaning over to Helena with crumbs stuck around her pretty mouth.

"Well, perhaps you shouldn't eavesdrop. There might be things you are too young to know," answered Helena, who was far too much of a lady to leave traces of food around her lips when she'd finished eating.

"They're going to get drunk and talk about religion," said Clarissa resolutely. She'd discovered that the more she listened the better was her chance of having the last word – essential when dealing with Helena, the boss of her life. Both of Christina's lovely girls were miniaturised versions of the noble lady – Clarissa in fact more vigorously Nordic in appearance than her elder sister. Now both listened in to the adult conversation.

"Well there's definitely more to life than stocks and bonds and railway timetables Hugh," reasoned Christina.

"Oh, no doubt but whatever it is the Vatican will never encourage you to look into it in any detail."

Christina inclined her head towards Hannah, "He's talking about my ghosts. It always comes back to this," she murmured, below the hearing of her children.

"Ghosts!" whispered Helena in Clarissa's ear.

"I hope there are none on our ship!" whispered Clarissa in return.

"They'll send Bishop Clary with his exorcist and we'll all have to rub ashes into our hair as penance," cautioned Hugh. Hannah was surprised by such directness but smiled thinly at his mockery.

"Oh don't worry Hannah there are no ghosts in the house in Liverpool, as far as I'm aware. Just some of the ancestral homes in Antrim, Donegal . . . Kintyre."

"Monaghan," stated Christina.

"Monaghan," Hugh added casually, like an echo along a cavernous corridor. Hannah was bubbling under with restrained laughter.

"Bedtime now darlings," advised Christina, bending over to kiss her daughters, "I shall return to tuck you in, once you are settled. Go with Abigail. Make sure they brush their hair and teeth," she said turning to the nervous looking aide de camp.

As the girls left, Christina moved across to where Hannah was sitting. Reaching out she took her by the hand, "Come on Hannah, let's go for a walk. I've had enough of being ridiculed. After all, they're his ancestors who come back to haunt the living. Life was so easy for successive generations of Leslies that they just can't get enough of it," she declared with casual irony.

Although she had no university degree, Christina Leslie was a cultured, well-educated woman by contemporary standards. 'She speaks four languages: Irish, Spanish, French and Italian fluently and a fifth badly – English,' Hugh liked to say mockingly. Christina also had enough finishing school Latin and Greek not to appear foolish in serious minded male company, when they were too fuddled with drink to avoid argument with the girls they loved.

Not that a passing knowledge of Homer flattered, nor particularly interested her. One of her most notable preferences was to baldly insist on staying when the men were passing the Brandy, at least until they lit the cigars. Rounded in her talents and character, Christina was open minded and eager to learn. Men who met her tended to fall for her charms completely and without exception.

A hint of mannish athleticism to her tall frame showed up in particular on the golf course. Strong lines of a clever face, combined with creamy voice and azure eyes flecked with white, afforded her the illusion of confidence in any company – from thoughtfully compacted crèche to chandeliered court. Intuitively, Lady Christina Leslie saw in Hannah Harper more than a little of herself.

She witnessed imposed limitations and frustration buried deep. Long familiar with her Governesses' searching intelligence, she also caught the flash of quixotic green eyes and her humorous, reassuring tone as Hannah worked with her daughters. This young woman had an inner light, suggestive of confident discernment. The fact that Hannah respected and approved of Christina in return was also clear to her.

Linking Hannah's arm Christina confided some of this impression to her as they toured the upper deck of the fine ship. Half way along the first class port rail Christina stopped. Turning to look in Hannah's eyes, she spoke in a tone of disarming lightness with humour in her voice, "May I ask you a personal question?" Hannah smiled her assent. "What, in the most general terms of course . . . What in life would you say you are looking for?"

Hannah gazed at Christina, wondering if there was some unspoken motive behind the question. For a moment her smile faded, then quickly returned.

"Well, speak of it, if you can!" urged Christina.

"No, I wouldn't like to say, because if I did it would be gone in an instant." A play of humorous engagement ran over Hannah's face. Christina tilted her head an inch to the left as if to appraise her and at last a beatific smile of acceptance spread over her handsome face. She turned to walk on, "I understand . . . you have a dream? I'm going to probe you more deeply, Hannah Harper. We all want Spanish Castle Magic but you are an enigma."

"I suspect we all have to make compromises to find the perfect balance in life."

"Ha! Isn't *that* the truth?"

They stood together at the rail, perusing distant lights along the Galician coastline. Hannah waited in silence as warm breeze raced with the seagulls over the ship's white wake, "Do you have everything you want now? Or perhaps you know precisely what you need? Tell me how you see it."

Hannah turned to look at Christina, noticing her claret silk attire for the first time since shifting focus away from Helena and Clarissa. Christina was everything Hannah would never be – wealthy and beautiful, without being gladly rooted as an individual. Secure for life financially, barring the unimaginable, but without her friend's stoical assurance - Christina conveyed a sense of undefined potential that might never be realised.

"Things in themselves can never be enough, Christina. Approval; recognition; success, are relative conceptions – gone in an instant – buried along with a name. We all strive for things that pass through our fingers, like sand."

"Go on, I would ask more questions but I suspect you have more to say."

"You know much more than me. It's not my place to lecture you."

"Aw, you are coy. You're teasing. Well then . . . what about love; marriage; family, children - the tangible manifestations of all our striving?"

"I'm sure those things define most people, even by their lack. Nonetheless, there is always a need for us to see behind the veil."

"Even in our most fulfilled moments? What do you think is *there* - 'behind the veil?'"

"Wonderment, Christina . . . Devine compassion for every lost soul. Recognition, for every child in a wrinkled old body when it comes back to open understanding, annealed by the half-forgotten amazement of youth. I believe sorrow shapes us, when love no longer can."

"So you too are a believer!"

"Not a believer – an observer. If you will, these lessons are commonplace. All we have to do is look."

"Do you disapprove of people like my husband? The day to day rationalists who clamber over one another in their headlong rat race? Feel free to speak openly, I won't be offended."

"Why are you asking these questions Christina, because of my political affiliations?"

"I'm sorry if I'm encroaching on your privately held beliefs but you've made no secret of them have you?" Christina countered with surprise.

Regardless of her twenty-one summers Hannah still looked innocent. Wind whipped at her buttoned coat, picking at curls of tied up hair. Reflected highlights of the safety lamp above played in her moist, dark eyes. Hannah was beautiful, in fulsome innocence but her face was tight with concern. Pondering these soul searching questions, she looked past Christina's shoulder into the darkness above the ocean. Breathing in deeply, Hannah's chest shuddered as though some heavy burden was leaving her. Resigned to their trusting relationship, with no reason for inhibition she decided to open up, "You know, I can't be like *them*."

"Who can't you be like? The socialists, or the TGWU?"

"No actually, I meant Suffragettes. They are impassioned and desperate because the struggle has been so long. But they've gone too far. I *can* see a point in them planting a bomb at the Bank of England as a gesture, even though I'm a pacifist," Hannah turned to look up at her friend, "But Lime Street Station in Liverpool? For God's sake! They alienate people by their extremism. They've become terrorists. And they've set back the women's movement twenty years. Oh, they'll get token concessions from the government of course . . . but in turn lose the mass support they need." Hannah looked at Christina with genuine sorrow in her eyes.

"In other words, they'll win the battle but lose the war?"

"Yes. Its men we need on our side, not martyrs. But it'll all be the same in a hundred years!"

"Ha! Don't lose heart. We can always limit their sexual activities. That would guarantee their support," Christina smiled roguishly, placing a hand over Hannah's arm and they giggled like schoolgirls.

Opening her silver cigarette case Christina proffered it to Hannah, who accepted, since she was off duty and not around the children. Christina inserted a fashionable Gauloise into an ostentatiously crafted Parisian fashion-house holder, as much a symbol of autonomy as an accoutrement of wealth. Hannah searched for an equally fine holder, given to her as a Christmas gift by the Leslies.

Leaning on the safety rail, Christina's dreamy eyes scanned a stunning westerly skyline. Rubbing high cheeks with her long, lacquered fingers she spoke quietly above the ship's humming vibration as it plied the exuberant Atlantic.

"Are the WSPU strongly against the old institutions then? Monarchy and the banks? Or do they simply see them as a bastion of male intolerance and conceit?" Holding up her hand, a cigarette lighter snapped open. Christina cupped its flame as Hannah's cigarette hissed, then she lit her own. The Ronson clanked shut with industrial surety as she turned to look at Hannah for an answer to her question, again with a playful smile around her eyes assuring goodwill.

"Purportedly, they are just a women's army in the field but clearly their challenge goes beyond City financiers to the Masonic inner circle who control everything, don't you agree? I mean . . . they targeted Roslyn Chapel."

Christina drew on her cigarette, smiling benignly as she thought about Hannah's assertion, "You're sure it's not simply another random act of spite, against whatever is held in esteem by The Establishment – like Kew Garden's tea pavilion, or Manchester Art Gallery?"

"No, I don't agree. It's inspired - in a malicious sort of way. In Scotland they talk about nothing else but the Masons. Every mother's son is a member of the so called elite - even bus drivers and green keepers. The *real* secret society is surrounded by a not-so-secret-society. At home they love all that obscure, ritualised nonsense. It's a natural replacement for the failed clan system."

"So this campaign of violence is guided by people who know how to convey a real sense of menace?"

"I would say so. They see no boundaries in targets they select, or in sympathisers with whom they associate to make their plans. They don't care if people get hurt . . . and they do, get hurt."

"Yes, they are quite flagrant. The bomb under the Coronation Throne for instance? What did you make of that? Did that amount to High Treason?"

"Exactly, the bomb under the Coronation Throne was a clear message to the Royal Family - 'keep out of the debate.' That the campaign will become more extreme the longer our fundamental right to vote is delayed. In the meantime, anyone of influence speaking out against votes for women will become a target for violence, from a section of the community with no other voice. There is a conscious link to the 'rebel girls' called to book, refusing to recognise the jurisdiction of courts and judges. I suppose their case rests on the basis that they have a natural right to be judged by a jury of their peers."

"Other women, yes of course! And why not?" acknowledged Christina, with an expressively lifted brow and a warm smile.

Hannah looked over the rail into the warm night, indicating she had said enough. Two women from opposite ends of the social spectrum stood easily in each other's company.

"So dear Hannah, as we steal an out of season holiday through a Europe about to immerse itself in another round of destructive warfare, how do you see this matter of WSPU's approach turning out? Will

Asquith throw Pankhurst's Lipstick Marxists in jail, or will there be a little dance shuffle in which the opponents compromise, for the sake of national unity? Can you see Emmeline becoming the first woman Prime Minister?"

Hannah stood perplexed, choosing to ignore the rhetoric about Pankhurst selling out, to focus instead on why Christina was suggesting this would happen in the first place. This smart lady pretended to be naïve, when in fact she was merely disarming and indulgent.

"*You* are tutoring *me* Christina, not asking me."

"Hannah, don't be coy! The Police came to Hugh over two years ago. I know you know because he told me he'd spoken to you. I completely approve, or I would never have joined the movement. Just because I never quizzed you before doesn't mean we're at odds. Perhaps I should have declared my support for you and Alice more explicitly."

"Thank you. I always felt secure speaking with Hugh. I know he was worried about me but since some of my activist friends disappeared after the Police started the riot, I've restricted myself to campaigning for NUWSS. But I don't understand what you mean by 'another round of warfare.' I'm sorry; I just don't know what you're implying. You refer to events in Russia perhaps? I judge myself reasonably well informed but wouldn't like to say, Christina . . . I mean . . . you've clearly thought about this a great deal more than I. Tell me what *you* think will happen."

Christina smiled again with her sensational dark blue eyes, lowering her voice as though imparting deeply intimate, startling information.

"There *will* be war Hannah and it is likely to be terrible. Hugh says it will be started by the Germans 'running to schedule, like an express leaving as soon as the stationmaster blows his whistle.' Which I suppose is the one thing Hugh really does know about. He says their invasion plans are already printed and distributed. All it lacks is some little confrontation to give them an excuse to set it all off and . . . there will be no turning back."

Hannah stared at Christina, lips parted slightly, still hesitating in confusion. At last she responded tentatively, her voice trembling in light of Christina's incredible revelation.

325

"My God. You're serious! You know people who decide such things over the Brandy and cigars don't you? Winnie is a relative, isn't he?"

Christina lifted her eyebrows in a gesture of sultry aristocratic eloquence, "Oh, please allow me some credit. I'm an educated woman Hannah! Read August Nieman: *Der Weltkreig: Deutshe Traume*. Sorry – that translates into Scouse as, *The Coming Conquest of England* . . . Published about eight, or nine years ago. Never popular in our country beyond the gutter press but still available I imagine, if you place an order with a decent book shop."

"'World War – German Dream?' Yes, I vaguely recall the furore at the time but I was only a bairn. I remember Anthony and Harper were pleased when Chancellor Bulow said this was not Germany's plan at all."

"Anthony?"

"Sorry, my grandfather."

"Your father and grandfather openly discussed politics in front of you as a child?"

"Every time we went riding, or when they came for Sunday dinner. My Gran would tell them to shut up."

"Oh no! How important that is for young people. School will never teach that kind of insight. It needs to come from parents, don't you agree?"

"Absolutely, but people were talking about World War again, when Agadir caused the run on the stock market a couple of years ago."

"Okay, no doubt they were, but mainly in your Liverpool branch of NUWSS I'd wager. Broadly speaking, Nieman said Germany needs to attempt what Napoleon failed to achieve, a kind of Central European dominion that subjugates and takes territory from weaker dependencies to the east – you know Ottoman and Russian states they see as backward and rebellious," said Christina, with tongue in cheek. Hannah wondered idly how many Martinis she'd had but resisted the temptation to tell her she should be lecturing at Trinity. "France can chip in Alsace and Lorraine. Belgium and the Netherlands need to fall into line too."

"Why does that have to involve us, Christina?"

"Because it will involve Russia. And we will run guns and grain to sustain their cities, like we did a hundred years ago. Not that they should need it, but the Tsar's regime is unsteady. All this is necessary to preserve the balance of power, you understand."

"How ghastly politics is! It's too complex to unpick all this . . . What about the Third Republic? And where do you think the USA will be in all of this? Surely they don't want war in Europe?"

"What I understand from debating the twisted logic with Hugh and his cronies is that the cooperation of thriving western states simply reinforces the German Dream. They admire France and Britain, Hannah dear. They certainly don't seek to destroy us – merely break up easy trading arrangements allowing us to cooperate with our colonies and thrive."

"While Europeans fight amongst themselves?"

"Indeed, inspired by romantic notions of true cultural identity."

"Oh dear, how despicably banal . . . I can't help wonder what the world might be like now, if Napoleon had won."

Christina laughed at Hannah's simplistic reflection, flicking ringlets back from her lovely neck as she stood up from the guard rail to her full height.

"It would be exactly the same as it is now Hannah – governed by greedy men, exploiting every kind of human weakness – as it always has been."

"But *why* Christina?" asked Hannah beseechingly. "How can war serve any purpose other evil and injustice?"

"That's what I wanted to ask you. Undeniably all war *is* wicked. But for better or worse the world *will* be a different place when it is over."

Hannah suddenly felt alone, despite the warmth of Christina's friendliness towards her. Surrounded by dread, dark Atlantic and cold infinite sky so far from home, the desperate politics of Nationalism, Empire and warfare staggered Hannah's mind.

She appealed to compassionate hope beyond Christina's insight, into the world of men, "In what way will the World be different?" she pleaded like a child, "It will be less wealthy, certainly. Much sadder.

Bereft of continuity across generations and burdened by a legion of cripples. Who will benefit?"

"Oh my dear, please don't weep. I wish I'd said nothing."

"But you didn't, so tell me what *you* want to say."

Christina looked out into rolling whitecaps defining a thousand yards of glowering visibility. She blew a large cloud of pungent cigarette smoke before composing her thoughts for Hannah's edification, "Every war in history has been about suppliers making money and the exercise of power across international markets. This one will be about the competition for trading opportunities on a global scale. Conan Doyle insists important battles will be fought at sea. Again my dear, an all-male preserve," she added, touching the back of Hannah's hand, "Ultimately of course their planned expansionist war is also a way of deflecting Democrats and ideologues of every flavour - whether Independent Labour, Suffragist or Marxist. But I warn you child, so mark my words, Hughie tells me the impending disaster will make the American Civil War seem like a domestic tiff."

Hannah gazed down at Christina leaning on the rail, trying to comprehend the enormity revealed to her.

"After all he's the entrepreneur – he says 'it will be industrial warfare – with enormous siege guns and naval blockades, battleships and submarines attacking merchantmen, liners and so on.'"

Christina wanted to hug Hannah as she stood to her full height but seeing her eyes had filled with tears, smiled gently at her instead.

"Come on, let's find Alice and get you both an aperitif, or Hughie will order dinner without us!"

"Thanks for warning me Christina. I realise now this is why you asked me about my future." Hannah managed to speak without a tremor in her voice, "So few will be prepared for this abomination. The Poles tried to warn us."

Hannah felt there was something fundamentally important in the relationship between a child and its parent. For a week she had observed this realisation, emerging in each shining new backdrop they visited - Santander, Gibraltar, Barcelona and Toulon. The Leslie children depended upon her and loved her much too much, so she confided in Alice. Increasingly Hannah felt like their mother, as opposed to simply 'their elder sister' as advocated by Christina.

Clarissa especially had become demanding, now that she approached Preparatory School age. The innocent set of her head with delicate features and golden tresses gift-wrapped the lie that Clarissa's future was sublimely assured. Unlike her elder sister Helena, now used to routines outside of home at Belevedere School - attendance at which seemed to make her not only furtive but sometimes inexplicably provocative - Clarissa was still at an age where she offered everything and hid nothing.

Hannah was her favourite, evidently more so than her own mother, since Clarissa chose to spend more time with her. Attachment had been natural of course, in the sense that adaptive human nature is extraordinarily social and dynamic. When the girls returned excitedly from exploring Toulon with Hannah, the perspicacious Hughie alluded to the problem head on, "We have to ensure this dear girl never escapes the clutches of the Leslie dynasty, Christina. Also we must parade a file of suitably groomed and flush young men for her approval. Can't have her going to waste on some bearded union convener, on the run from his thresher factory in Minsk now can we?"

"Must politics enter every damn conversation Hugh? Let Hannah simply enjoy being on holiday without thinking too much! Or for that matter you doing her thinking for her."

"Oh Lord, I can't win! You women demand work alongside men but then won't allow us any say in domestic affairs. D'you know if there was a golf club on board I think I'd go and join it!"

"There *is* a tennis court Hugh – go and play with Alice! Get her advice about finding a man for Hannah. She's a better match-maker than you."

Christina was feeling magnanimous after two Martini's when Hannah re-joined her on their private observation deck, after an hour reading to the girls. Christina was smiling across the stretch of rippling, greasy water to the semi-circle of hotels sweeping around the harbour of Toulon. Hannah was conscious of the fact that Christina spent most of her time at home in Liverpool organising soirees for Sir Hugh's friends and associates, with charitable organisations or her beloved theatrical committee. In Hannah's mind was an emerging rationale of parenthood which she felt obliged to offer in challenge, "Don't you think each successive generation owes their little ones more than their parents offered?" she asked.

Christina responded by saying she had her own very personal recollections, of a very happy childhood - her own framework to place any impression of Hannah's into, "But yes, yes. You are so right. At first I was afraid of being a mother, reluctant to have them. But from now on I intend to be at home as much as possible, especially if we do have a another. Hugh wants a big family, so he says. Which is his way of saying, 'I want a son and heir please.' Boys need more nurturing, don't you feel? At least until they're old enough to find food in the larder."

Lady Christina was warming to Hannah's chosen topic of conversation. Wine with dinner might help her forget entirely her own experience of relative neglect. She was working positively on her own guilt, freely voicing her feelings, "And every child needs siblings to teach them the harsh realities of the world. Family is the most important thing in life, don't you think Hannah?"

A sweet Irish brogue had crept into Christina's speech as the second cocktail interfered with her synapses. The more lit-up she became with the refreshing herbal wine the faster she tended to talk. Hannah smiled at a vision she fleetingly caught in her imagination, of the same lovely woman as an innocent teenager, maybe ten or twelve years earlier.

Several hours later Hannah was trying to read in her room but could not concentrate. Excited cries from booted and blanket-wrapped passengers lying flat on deck chairs and benches in the small hours of the morning transmitted first to Clarissa, then after she had returned from exploration with Hannah to her elder sister. Who could have denied them, amid gasps of wonderment reminiscent of applause for Pansy Chinery and the flying Zedoras? Helena had appeared at two thirty in the morning, aroused by loud acclaim for a galactic firework display more engaging than any circus act. Disciplined and polite, she in turn had come to seek Hannah's permission, "Oh do please let us go up on deck. We can't see them properly through port holes. We'll wrap up warm and keep quiet!"

By then Christina and Hugh, who had not quite finished their hand of Bridge, received word of the general furore and decided to break and resume when the spectacle had been witnessed by all. The Purser agreed to ensure cards would be left where they were, promising to secure the first class lounge until asked to unlock it. With a borrowed pair of binoculars and a half bottle of Napoleon's favourite Cognac to ward off night chills, Hugh gave full support to the star gazing adventure. Hannah explained that he needed a cushion beneath his head and to lie full stretch like a sunbather.

Meteorites came so frequently that Clarissa soon counted well into the forties. Hannah herself gave up counting when her tally reached fifteen within the first twenty minutes. There were smoky trails near the zenith of the Milky Way which evaporated in seconds. But some seemed to come in low and vertical, to erupt or bifurcate violently with sidewinder trails of white stardust, wafting in the winds of the high ether. There were two or three explosions of light like camera flashes, leaping across hundreds of miles of star strewn sky in a breath taking instant, causing gasps and murmuring. Shooting stars came from all directions, as the iron superstructure of Balmoral Castle marched against the wheeling Milky Way above the star gazers. Some tore across the horizon from south to north, splitting a second later into multiple fragments with meandering trails of flaring dust. Bridge-party members called and pointed in awe to the indigo sky surrounding the brave lights of Toulon.

"What is that release of energy that races across the entire sky?" asked Christina.

"Well my dear, I'd like nothing better than to be able to explain but I fear I'd make a fool of myself. You'd need the word of an astronomer, or perhaps Madame Curie at the Sorbonne, for a proper explanation."

A band of stars slashing the zenith of the clement autumn night twisted gently across silhouetted davits and rails of the great ship lapping at anchor off the seaway into Toulon.

Hannah's young heart filled with romance as the teeming sky smiled down on her, dwarfing pitch black Mont Faron. With its royal mantle of bright stars, the silhouette to the north east whispered remembrance of timely deeds by the hand of a brave Lieutenant of infantry, at a fortress not a mile away across the sea. Hannah knew the legend and was not surprised to overhear murmurings about 'signs and omens in the heavens.' People loved to scare themselves.

As Cognac soaked into his tired mind, Sir Hugh waxed lyrical on behalf of the star gazers, "Tolstoy's hero, Pierre, believed Napoleon to be the anti-Christ of Revelations. Events as momentous as any in Homeric legend were played out on these waters. On that shoreline just there, to the left of that pretty little town, Bonaparte stormed the fort to take it back from the British. It led to a cataclysm across Europe, like the one Sir Arthur Conan Doyle predicts. When did it all culminate? Just over a hundred years ago."

"Be quiet you old fool, you'll give us all nightmares!" growled Christina, to a chorus of acquainted laughter.

When at last she retreated to her room, Hannah thought about what she'd read in the press of the seemingly gratuitous naval arms race. Christina's prophetic version of Hugh's deliberations about war on the continent made her shudder. Pushing cruel absurdity from her mind, Hannah tucked frozen feet up under the middle of her blankets. As she turned onto her side to sleep, she knew with almost unbearable urgency that it was time to start thinking about her own future.

At dawn Balmoral Castle weighed anchor to set sail for Roma but the children slept half the morning, exhausted after excitement of the previous night. When they did emerge they were difficult to entertain so Hannah walked them around every inch of deck and stairway, until they were ready to drop. Following their exertions she deliberately read them two chapters of *Uncle Tom's Cabin* to instil in them a sense of reality.

Later that evening, Helena and Clarissa ate heartily and slept early. After dining Hannah made polite excuses, retiring early to her dormitory inboard of the Leslie's suite of rooms, for once hoping not to be disturbed by the two excited girls. The meteor shower proved to have been unrepeatable as well as tiring entertainment. Even the Bridge School broke up early, dulled perhaps by after effects of too little sleep and too much familiarity with Napoleon.

Hannah reflected on awareness that the Leslie's had become a second family for her. They treated everyone working for them with the same undiscriminating kindness and indulgence. It had been easy to fit in at the house in West Allerton, easy to discover a greater sense of self. Wider issues of past years, 'What might have been if I'd stayed on at school, then gone to university?' no longer seemed to matter. Working for Hugh and Christina had provided a unique framework for personal moral growth, which felt neither radical nor parochial. Hannah was aware of the fact that almost fifteen percent of people in employment in '13 were in domestic service. She could not imagine many who might have had as wonderful an experience as she'd had with the Leslie family. Hannah didn't just admire them, she loved them.

Politics mattered to Hugh and Christina, because people mattered to them. Her patrons were neither afraid to speak, nor under pressure to act in any pre-determined manner. They were not nouveau riche, yet ancient and elevated social status somehow divested them of the arrogant smugness of the very wealthy, making them progressive. Rooted in historical culture, the mildly eccentric Leslies were happy with their balanced lives. Both could see beyond discrimination engendered by wealth. In many ways the Leslies were as artless as Chrystal Macmillan, Alma and Betty, or indeed some of the thoughtful, hardworking mill girls.

Christina had much in common with the middle and upper class wives met with Hannah through NUWSS – cultured and sensitive people in the main, dedicated to justice and equality for women. Many of these people were larger than life characters, self-assured and ultimately decent. Issues of basic human rights had that potential to cut across arbitrary divisions of social class.

Hannah had a plan to extend this fundamental happiness into her own sphere of control, now she had sufficient funds for a deposit on a small house. In her heart of hearts she hoped that there might be something suitable in Portobello, because she'd always loved the sea.

Above all it was now time to explore her own ideas, committing to whatever principles she saw fit. That step forward might bring new direction to her life. She could become independent and make her own decisions – this transition would be vital for her. The purpose of education, for so long a burning issue in her time under the tutelage of the inimitable Christina Leslie now appeared simple for Hannah – it was to teach oneself how to think. In fact she had learned more of autonomous thinking than any degree course might have offered.

Lying on her bed Hannah's attention turned to the one imponderable condition that might bear upon all her vague plans - in fact an ulterior reason making the prospect of homecoming still more attractive. There were three unopened letters she guessed had been sent by the enigmatic bus driver. Four and a half years had passed since she'd met William Macdonald under bizarrely shocking circumstances. Hannah had been too pre-occupied with travelling to look at his letters with a clear mind, or without the imminent prospect of interruption. If there was one major reason to leave Christina Leslie's service other than the duality of her bonding with Clarissa and Helena, it was the fact that she rarely had time to herself. Hannah read,

'20, High Street,
Portobello,
East Lothian.
28/11/1909

Dear Hannah,

I hope my writing does not too bring too much embarrassment for you, or disapproving attention from your parents. I feel relieved to have put pen to paper at last, as I said I would. It gives strange comfort to me to simply write your name. I telephoned your home and spoke to Margaret who said your father would not mind if I made myself better known to you and your family. If this is not disagreeable, perhaps you'll write back and let me know if I have your permission,

Yours,

William M. Macdonald.'

She clamped the letter under her hand and tried to recall a perspective on the timing of his phone call. He'd written shortly after her leaving home and had clearly telephoned prior to that, asking Harper's permission through Margaret.

Conventional but not so conventional he couldn't recognise the power behind the throne. William Macdonald miscalculated if he thought Margaret would care either way – she didn't care enough to forward his letters.

"Damn, he'll have given up on me by now," murmured Hannah to herself.

If he hasn't married some other girl half his age, or been hog tied by red haired Morgana le Fey, he'll be too angry to even talk to me! Poor man!

Slightly disappointed with Harper's high handed vetting, Hannah opened the second letter. She reminded herself that this was clearly an individual of a certain energetically conservative type – someone she barely knew and owed absolutely nothing to. Why should he anticipate mutual interest on her part?

Someone a little too presumptuous perhaps, in need of re-education like so many men?

Immediately bemused by the fact that the second letter ran to three pages of standard bonded notepaper, she shuffled over in bed towards the table lamp. What could he possibly have wished to write so much about? With a charmed feeling of temporal detachment, Hannah began reading a letter written over eighteen months before.

'19th April 1912

Hello again Hannah,
I wonder how you are. Margaret said you don't write or telephone,
due to a strong grievance against her. You may be surprised that I
know a little about your good people. They have been kind enough
to speak openly to me. It turns out my cousin Ali and his wife
Marion are close friends of your father. It's only fair I say this openly,
in case you think I'm using unfair influence to spy on you, or inform
myself gratuitously about your affairs or activities – though given the
opportunity I would be keen to share my interests with you.

The fact is that because of former closeness between Ali and
John they invited me to their home at Hogmanay and the
Christening of their little boy John Jnr. He really is quite something
to see and both your parents are walking on air.

Your father confided that he misses you greatly, wishing you
would write more often. He is worried about your situation in
Liverpool, not that it's any of my business but strikes emanating
from there virtually brought the country to its knees last summer. It
was dreadful to see photos of baton charges, knowing many
demonstrators were hurt and some shot dead, as it was to read about
organisers locked up and policemen injured.

If it is of interest to you to know it, I am a Steward of the United
Vehicle Workers, and a long-standing member of the Fabian
Society. My father Malcolm was also, before he passed away last
year. I know you campaign for women's Rights and political
representation. Perhaps you'd care to know that I fully support you
in that. For my part I wish only to hear that you thrive and are
happy. It seems this is a time of great uncertainty, when even 'the
Ship of State' might founder.

Pardon a topical analogy to the over confident builders of ill-
fated Titanic, shocked to the core I'm certain as they recover from
their trauma in New York hotel rooms, or the Belfast Boardroom. In
that context, don't you think it fiendishly playful how financiers

speak of 'Confidence' controlling the political economy of the world, not just the fortunes of Harland and Wolf? Its sad counterpart of course, is fearful destitution for many. I hope the company survives, as so much of the Northern Irish Economy depends upon it. Events such as this dreadful sinking prompt us to think of those we would wish to protect, though they are far from home. God rest their souls, poor people!

Your friend aye,

W M Macdonald.'

Having read his letter twice Hannah lay back, reminiscing about the momentous time of the strikes. She thought about people she and Alice had met, or heard speaking: Dick Stocker the TUC delegate from the Lancashire Mills; awesomely inspirational Jim Larkin from the Irish docklands; gregarious Marxists, Gertrude Tuckwell and Tom Mann, who had been speaking on the day the police started the riot.

Above all there had been Mary Bamber for whom Alice, Hannah, Christina and many of their friends campaigned alongside to elevate the status of the most ruthlessly exploited women workers.

Hannah smiled to remember uncertainty as to whether Sir Hugh might be annoyed with their political activities, when strike action throughout the city led to a mass walk out of his railway workers. In the event Hugh responded to the momentous news of Asquith's intervention in the National Strike by reviewing wages of all his domestic staff and giving them a pay increase too.

Hannah remembered him saying, "I feel a little guilty for being a capitalist, for putting rolling stock and steel rails before the families of my good men. Don't repeat that, or they will take it as a sure sign of weakness. Then they'll come out in support of someone else," never once cracking a smile. Sir Hugh was joking, as ever, but they believed him. He also explained to his staff that he fully supported his railway workers and the Fabian's demand for a minimum wage. Hugh was only

337

too happy to respond to government direction, to order his Board of Directors to negotiate.

For over four years Hannah had been in the midst of a massed labour campaign which spurred a new level of highly effective mutual support in political campaigning. On the back of it the Labour Party was now organizing apace in Liverpool. It seemed the best hope for everybody longing for justice and social reform as a way of life – not just Suffragists like herself barred from the political process. All in all it had been a time of great hope, as well as great strife.

It was around that time Christina made it known she was glad to retain the services of her personal assistant despite the fact that Alice had fallen pregnant. Some of the staff were scandalised. Christina's private counselling sessions with Alice, in which she advocated a very Catholic pro-life decision regarding the unborn child, added fuel to the fire. When the question of Alice's accommodation and availability for work routines were raised by Mrs Mason as Alice approached full term, Christina responded characteristically by offering her a larger bedroom, adjacent to the creche.

Alice had spurned anxious counselling that sought to implicate the man involved, disdaining Mason's presumption that the father was Russell Evans the delivery manager from the local Co-op. The fact that Russell also happened to try his hand at theatrical production from time to time didn't merit Mason's assertion that Alice had, 'Shamed the Leslie family through her *goings on* up at Allerton Amateur Dramatic Society.'

Christina coldly asked Mrs Mason to explain the euphemism, "Did they have sex on the stage, or *anywhere* in the theatre, Janice?" Mrs Mason didn't see the funny side. Having threatened to resign she subsequently affected rapprochement with Alice, bear hugging her in an embrace that avoided eye contact but only when it was clear Christina would never fail to support her personal assistant.

Hannah recalled a whispered conference in Alice's room over a smuggled bottle of Cabernet, "The jealous old gossip cast aspersions in an attempt to get me sacked! What unwritten law pertaining to the status of women dictates that Russ should marry me, or that I must abandon my career in the household of Lady Christina Leslie?"

"The same one that dictates your unworthiness to vote?"

"Hmm, precisely! Why shouldn't the intensity of a wonderful performance of Shakespeare or Chekhov foster true love between two members of a production team? Why must a mature and sensitive man be valued more for standing at the back door of a mansion, ticking off grocery items delivered on a weekly account?"

"Well Alice, who else but you really knows Russell Evans?"

"Precisely! She can keep her piggy, snub nose out of my affairs!"

It had been a pathetic clash of egos leading to a dreadful farce but thanks to the prevailing sentiments of the time and Christina's good graces as a liberal minded employer, Alice survived. Learning late in life to contain her hostility, the Housekeeper survived too.

The last few years had been a very strange time of social and political upheaval in Liverpool. It seemed ironic to Hannah in retrospect that there was a continual melding of new interests and alliances between ordinary people who were just trying to live life in a sensible way. She remembered being inside the homes of organisers and prominent leaders, observing chaos in their ordinary lives. She drank their tea, smiled at their children and patted their dogs. They argued lightly whether it was appropriate to 'own a car in time of stringencies, when wages had dropped ten percent over ten years' or 'buy an ornate lacquered table imported from Japan' or 'submit to an education system indoctrinating children en masse, with readings from The Collect or Psalms each morning.'

Everything was moot for discussion in the tidal upwelling of social change. The most crucial debate shaping the future of Britain took place in the streets and suburbs of Liverpool, not in the House of Commons. It seemed incredible to Hannah that, in parallel to countless days of tired legs and print-covered fingers standing on gloomy street corners beating her gums with a thousand diffident women - the National Strike really did begin with the Transport Workers Federation in Liverpool backing industrial action of a seamen's union over degrading medical inspections.

"Dignity!" Alice pronounced, "People rebel when their personal dignity is transgressed, like I did with Mason!"

"Yes Alice but it only works if individuals organise on points of principle . . . if they join a union and the union is well run for its members." That summer dock workers finally flocked to join the NUDL.

Hannah began to wonder what Alice and Christina might make of William's missives. The reference to strikes was unpredictable, given his activity as a Baptist Lay Preacher. That in turn didn't sit with involvement as a Freemason. Alice would definitely have a lot to say about such polyglot, enigmatic interests. In a time of communist priests, union supporting owners and a socialist King, nothing was certified – apart from continuing strife. William's third letter was perhaps the least predictable but reading it would close the circle for Hannah.

'13th June 1913

Hello again Hannah,

I saw John at a Lodge meeting last week. He told me that you had not been home and seemed vague as to whether you received my previous letters, so assuming the worst I didn't press the matter. Surmising that you have read them, I will venture this last attempt to communicate with you. Oh hell, that sounds maudlin! I certainly don't wish to pester you.

There is something I worry about that I have never discussed with anyone, even Moira, whose pity I avoid more than her fearsome ridicule so couldn't abide. I suppose it comes down to the significance of any particular action or event, taken at random out the sea of events we call living. But I can't leave it alone, Hannah. On the day of James Birnie's last ride to Leith (I wonder where the poor old stick was going, what vague plans had he for that final day), Moira and I were running late. I was delayed at the depot, after 'rollin' oot o' bed wi' a sair heid' – my own stupid fault, as I am no serious kind of drinker. My team Craigmillar had won at the fitba' on the Wednesday night and that was my excuse. I don't play anymore but they call me their Coach – so I take it to heart, even more than I used to when I could play. Moira forgot her extra ticket roll, which she does all the time and went scootering back for one. They don't just give them out – she had to queue and sign it out, like they were season tickets to the Empire Theatre. This is an indication of just how much they trust us. Then we encountered Dougie Peel, the most fearsome Inspector on the team – which annoyed Moira, who delayed us even further by arguing with the old cud. He cited us for running late and accused her of 'raising the length of her uniform dresses' – always guaranteed to provoke.

All this may sound extremely mundane - which it was - but I couldn't resist the temptation to speed up between stops. I was glad when your contingent from Bellevue got on because that meant we were running to capacity. I skipped a couple of stops running down the hill to Leith. I knew you would all get off quickly as a group and a large queue would stream on if the delivery man took more than a minute, which I guessed he would. I guessed wrong.

I was already signalling traffic behind of my intention to pull over when I heard the thud and breaking glass from behind. I should have told Moira to block passengers alighting from the platform, even though most of them were off by then. The delivery driver had moved away, so for safety I should have pulled in towards the pavement immediately. What I mean to say is, by not waiting behind that truck, I gave the idiot a chance to come inside of me.

The accident was as much my fault as his. If I had not been impatient to get back to the depot dead on time for the turnaround – if I hadn't let that old jobsworth Dougie Peel get under my skin – poor old Jim might still be around. Who is to say that the continuance of his daily battle with elements, finding comfort and filling his belly was any less significant than mine, with its stop-go round of trivialities? I mean, where is true dignity in all of this life?

Aye,

William.'

'Dignity' - there it was again. A bell had rung in Hannah's head. Suddenly her heart felt lighter. Strange luminosity came into the room as she meditated on William's profound words, more than was shed by the screened reading lamp above her head she felt sure. Lying back to listen for the grumbling drone of the ship's mighty engines, the humming resonances they set up in thirteen thousand tons of creaking steelwork, Hannah's mind became a blank page free of worry and doubt for the first time since she was a three year old back in Rothiemay.

For a time out of mind she rested in reflection, her mind washed clean of ambition and need. Old chimeras, satisfied for now, faded from her notice. No-one had moral claim on her. Hannah's mind was crystal clear. Half an hour later, as meditation rose again into thought, she found herself strangely alert given the time of night.

Reaching for her diary she wrote –

'How essentially human is this strange, floating hotel - defined by transient modernity and the million passengers that will live aboard her for a brief period of happiness, or distraction, as she plies the ocean. How grandiose yet unnatural. From the moment of her launch she is predestined for obsolescence and the scrap yard. How might I personify Balmoral Castle's cumbersome beauty? She is an evanescent window into a half perceived universe of confused expectation – a plethora of personal ambitions, indistinguishable from the passengers she sustains. How sad and at the same time how bravely beautiful. Only through fleeting acts of will do we reify our existence, living each mindful moment in a discreetly narrowed eddy within the endless flow of time.'

Hannah rose silently from her bed and went over to the wardrobe where her case was lodged. There she found writing paper, envelopes and pen. Checking the first of William's letters to confirm his address, she wrote briskly, because of the hour and stiffness in her back from sitting up in bed to read for so long.

'24th November 1913

Dear William,

I finally received your three letters and read them just this evening-aboard RMS Balmoral Castle, sailing through the Mediterranean between Toulon and Rome!

Guilt is not entirely a bad thing, for it serves to keep good men honest and wary of impulse. It is also a commonly used tool for repression, of which the naïve and weak minded among us seem to carry the greater burden. Just pick up any newspaper to see community leaders write about 'mentally sick Suffragists' and 'strikers holding the country to ransom,' not to mention moralising letters meant to represent 'the law abiding majority'. It's not my law if made by people who don't recognise my fundamental rights, especially when enforced to keep me silent.

James Birnie's passing certainly left an impression of his individuality with you William, which you generalise into a sense of responsibility for other homeless people like him. It's a pity we can't do more for them when they're living, yet in the kindness you showed Jim, you did all anyone reasonably could.

Today we anchored at Toulon, a gloriously pretty pink and white town, nestling under a fearsomely steep mountain where a lighter went to pick up the detoured post. According to the Chief Steward, Balmoral had been displaced from her scheduled visit to Marseilles by 'provisioning requirements of half of the US Navy.' Word is that there are no less than seven battleships moored there! Earlier in the week, sailing out from Palma we passed close by two of these monstrous ships - Arkansas and Florida, with their supply tenders - heading for Suez perhaps, then on to the Gulf of Arabia?

One cannot help wondering if the Americans are merely flag-waving to cut a dash for European friends and allies, or cynically preparing for a war in which Africa and the Middle East will figure as contested territories. Judging from all the talk in Liverpool about Churchill's oil burning Super Dreadnoughts and the number of motor vehicles we now have to dodge crossing the street, Coal is No Longer King. Sorry, I wrote this without thinking. *Honni soit qui mal y pense.* I apologise – for my uneasy talk of war, as for Harper's strange behaviour!

Tomorrow we will have a short stay at Rome, where I will find a Postal or Union Castle Office, to leave this letter for a vessel going the other way. Then it's on to Alexandria and the Pyramids of the Nile. On our return the plan is to pick up a Hapag Lloyd vessel bound for New York. There the Leslie family plan to lodge us in a hotel for two weeks, while they sojourn with relatives and friends somewhere out of town. My understanding is that their friend's house is enormous, even by Leslie standards but they don't want to impose by arriving with too much of an entourage.

Sir Hugh says we have all earned a holiday. My friend Alice has planned an entertainment schedule for us all, on Lady Christina's behalf. On the other hand, I have a growing sense of not always being needed by my employer even though that is part of the plan. It will be all-found, so I plan to enjoy this opportunity to the full. Lady Christina's personal assistant Alice and I have our evenings planned in fine detail in, 'The City that Never Sleeps.' I will write again on return to Liverpool at which time I may have a better idea of when I next plan to visit Auld Reekie. Hopefully we will meet up then. Incidentally, there is no need to be formal with respect to my family. I regard myself as independent from them in all major respects. The only person you will ever need permission from is me William.

Your friend,

Hannah   x

Chapter Sixteen   *Freeborn Son*

William Macdonald arrived early for his meeting with Hannah at Portobello Pier tearoom. Knowing that a Saturday morning in early June would be busy, especially with the promise of warm summer sunshine, he'd decided to stake claim on a table rather than wait outside at the entrance. Now he searched the gathering crowd of distant promenaders in the hope that he might spot her coming. The plan was to leave his coat and hat over the back of a chair and dash out to greet her half way along the pier. Disarming nonchalance was key to creating the right impression, rather than thinking too much about paying her entrance fee. He would buy her breakfast instead.

I will act naturally. She's not a creature of convention and might object to stuffiness and propriety. I'll just be friendly, put her at ease.

The more William assured himself of this strategy, the more uneasy he felt about the whole damned thing. Perhaps he was letting too much ride on an impression made by a thin slice of a girl when he was still in his late twenties.

That's how I still think of her but I'm thirty three. She must have changed in appearance in five years. What if she has a man?

In their correspondences neither had broached the subject. William looked around self-consciously on the off chance she might have arrived before him, smiling stupidly at a group of young women chatting in the far corner of the pavilion. Their conversation immediately rose, buzzing with gentle competition to speak with approval of what they imagined the look to mean, although they were largely out of earshot. William looked so smart that he did merit their approval.

Of slightly above average height, he appeared dark and dapper in his well filled suit. The breadth of his shoulders made him appear a little overweight and short, but close inspection revealed he was neither. A neatly trimmed beard and level gaze lent him the appearance of an émigré Russian novelist. Sombre eyes in a large open face told a story at a glance to anyone interested in physiognomy – this man was thoughtfully intense, whilst perhaps a little unhappy and vulnerable. From any angle he looked like a very solid gentleman, someone a fellow might ask to borrow money from in a tight fix.

A pleasure steamer full of tourists pulled up at the end of the old pier and William congratulated himself with a brief smile, realising he'd made the correct decision in grabbing a table. Relaxing, he welcomed distraction as sightseers filed off the little boat and came chattering through the tearoom. He felt so nervous he could barely contain anticipation.

William had corresponded with Hannah in a light hearted, playful manner, since her reply to his forgotten letters of lost hope. Having been forlorn for years, since last winter he'd been full of romantic expectation again. Although strong minded and extremely determined in nature, Macdonald was anything but obsessive. But he knew himself to have been moonstruck that day back in June '09 by the maternal schoolgirl in the black and white uniform.

An exchange of pleasantries was one thing but meeting again face to face was altogether different. This day would either confirm or destroy the myth of the cynosure he'd nurtured for five years. William held a vision of dark green eyes, with chestnut hair falling loose as she leant over the old man. Fresh smelling rose water and soap still drifted unsolicited into his mind, in close-up no camera could capture in such sensory detail. Since Hannah had finally replied to his letters, every time William turned his face to the pillow after a long shift, her self-assured comforting of old Jim jumped back into his mind.

Maybe Hannah Harper symbolised William's need for escape from a lifestyle serving only to limit his soul. He had no claim on her and virtually no shared experience. If anything, her obvious intelligence and what he'd learned of her since intimidated him a little. But that tantalising awareness made the obscurity of his desire all the more challenging and subtle. Comforting himself with the thought that there were a few strong, graceful women in his wider family to act as a potential lightning rod, William deliberated on the reality that he was experienced in listening and learning from them. Maybe the girl reminded him in a subliminal way of his mother Christina. It struck him suddenly that they *were* similar in appearance. Both were quite tall and easy in their movements. There had been a familiar openness in Hannah's expression not unlike his ma's.

Perhaps that was what I glimpsed in our brief encounter.

Whatever the reason for his fascination, William knew that the impression made upon him by Hannah Harper was what in folklore amounted to love at first sight.

Oh cripes, that dog-leech Freud again!

William turned his attention self-consciously to his newspaper, to avoid eye contact with girls now watching him with interest.

Silently lowering herself onto the steam-bent ash chair Hannah considered punching her fist through the broadsheet. Taking care not to move legs which would give away her presence she lent her chin on her hand like a bored society girl, pretending to look out of the window at the south bay. Hannah always had two modes - both of which seemed to present unshakeable confidence. Although at times daring, a contrastingly delicate, precautionary sorrow was forever just below the surface.

Absorbed with a fascinating article entitled 'Electric Super Weapons of the Future,' by Professor Aleksander Servisa – a topical science contributor to the Scotsman, extrapolating on discoveries of Tesla and Marconi – it was some while before William glanced over the top of the broadsheet to see the disinterested nymph sitting opposite. His surprised expression seemed extremely comical, yet Hannah didn't laugh – she just looked at him with her chin still propped on her hand, saying nothing. The incredible image defying his imagination moments before, of 'an atom bomb that could instantly sink a super dreadnought,' suddenly became an irrelevance the world could never need. Even folding the paper seemed unnecessary. Words were unnecessary. Here was all William needed sitting in front of him - all he would ever need.

Looking at one another in a long moment of silent recognition, averring every benign thought each had had about the other for so long, they both smiled with hearts shining playfully through their eyes.

"What? What's wrong, do I not live up to expectation William Macdonald?"

"No, no . . . it had just struck me that you remind me of someone."

"Let me guess – your younger sister Euphemia?"

"Naw."

"Naw!" they both said again together.

"Your mother?" suggested Hannah, at the same moment he said, "My mother." Both smiled and laughed effusively. Reaching across the table Hannah took William's hand, and he stood up to bow as he kissed hers. Turning her head askance, Hannah beamed at his mock gallantry. Girls at the corner table chattered intensely, like sparrows fighting over a crust.

"Well that goes some way towards making up for the entrance fee to the pier and the nonchalance of the newspaper."

"But at least I got us a table!"

"True, not easy with today's wall to wall sunshine. Well . . . I suppose you'd better get it off your chest right away– tell me about your mother."

"Oh God, no . . ."

"No? Well that might confirm my suspicions, making me think the worst. You've let it out now, so let's have the full details. How am I like her?"

"You have a certain look perhaps, just my impression." Watching intently, Hannah waited for him to say more. A waitress came to take their order and William was glad of the interruption.

Finally he resumed, "I'm not going to say too much and make a fool of myself. You'll just have to meet her and judge for yourself. I think you could be easily mistaken as a close relative. Shall we say her daughter, for sake of argument? My mother has deep set eyes, a strong brow and forehead. And she often ties back her hair."

"I'll bet she's as skinny as a bean pole too? Tell me about her. Where is she from originally? What does she do? What's her maiden name? Maybe it will turn out we're related," Hannah suggested, with a hint of irony in her voice.

"My mother's a McSween, latterly from Dunbar. Her family were crofters and drovers. My forebears have been intermarrying with McSweens for generations. Originally her family came to East Lothian from Skye – like the Macdonalds. My dad and his brothers and of course our grandparents."

"What is her name . . . it's not Hannah by any chance?"

"Christina."

"Ah, Roman Catholic. My employer is Christina also. Quite the most wonderfully enigmatic woman I've met in my sweet short life. I believe if I had a daughter I would name her after her. Incidentally my mother and Great Grandmother both had exactly the same name as me – Hannah Wilson Drummond – imagine the confusion that led to at meal times! 'Hannah, this is yours . . . No, dinnae eat that silly it's for Great Gran!"

"We're Baptists actually – perhaps no' the most predictable conversion in the history of religious intolerance – but you're right about traditional associations with Catholic Spain. It's a small world though, I imagine we are all interbred many times over." Hannah laughed deliciously at William's disarming candour. "My father played a bowls knockout round agin a team frae Inverkeithing, four guys and four gals and every one of them was called either Jimmy or Maggie."

"Yeah, especially that lot from the Highlands. William the Conqueror had the biggest problem though." William stopped talking to look at Hannah in confusion. They had both been so eager to talk that the conversation had rapidly but unintentionally degenerated into an overlapping script line for a summer season vaudeville sketch. Was she making a point about interbreeding, or people having the same name? Glancing at his newspaper Hannah waited patiently for his response.

"Come again?"

"William the Conqueror – he had an army of Normans."

349

William laughed out loud – a rich, deep laugh corresponding to the curve of massively powerful shoulders and shiny black beard. The noise level in the pavilion seemed to rise along with his elevated mood. Women in the corner were chattering loudly now and people queuing for snacks looked around smilingly.

Sunlight raced across a perfect, cobalt blue sea as the slowly rotating tide of humanity began to wheel again around the hub of Portobello's promenade and narrow streets. The flux of joy was energised imperceptibly but incrementally by mutual attraction, blossoming in the hearts of Hannah and William.

"Tell me what you read in addition to the Scotsman, William."

"You name it Hannah, I'll read it, even if I don't particularly like it, or want to read it. Burns, Stevenson, Hume, Sir Walter Scott of course - all of that traditional Scottish foundation."

Looking at her suitor with a bemused smile, Hannah felt a sudden charge of energy running through her. Despite their long acquaintance and infrequent correspondence, it was not until now that she had begun to appreciate William's breadth of experience and intelligence. In taking so long to respond to his interest, she had put herself in a position of impartial influence. She'd underestimated him but now he had her full attention. Catching a look of evident surprise William began to feel slightly embarrassed.

Wishing to give a serious account of himself he tried to explain, "The truth is, I have been thoroughly indoctrinated by my beloved mother. She didn't learn to read properly until the age of twenty five, after meeting Flora Stevenson. In the years that followed, I not only had to teach Christina the mechanics but supervise progression, guiding all her studies. She demanded it and I have to admit she inspired me. In fact she would inspire anyone doubting the value of formal education." Deciding whether to reveal an intimate truth William paused for a moment in his explanation, somehow knowing his future was tied to this delightful young woman.

"You know we have a kind of beautiful rivalry – all above board, ken? Now it's my mother who tells me what tae read! I'm required tae keep up, afore we incur library fines." Hannah wanted to laugh out loud but caught a look of sorrow in William's expression.

"What is it?" she asked cautiously.

William looked away for a moment, then smiled again before replying. "Christina would have shared the entire vista of her developing mind with Angus, my pa - if he'd ever had the same education. Dye ken, the chance to sit by the fireside in the evening and read a book? He would have loved it. All their lives they were of one mind. His existence was one short, harmonious exertion, devoted to eight bairns." William stopped himself from saying, "Angus only ever had time to work himself into an early grave."

"So it's not just Arthur Conan Doyle that appeals to you?" she asked teasingly. William smiled broadly, seeing that Hannah not only recalled his preferences but was certainly going to have much in common with his mother. He was on safe territory talking about his mother, Christina. Clearly Hannah was listening and making notes.

"Years ago she joined the Women's Guild – they have monthly Literary Society meetings. She writes poetry."

"Who does she like?"

"She loves it all – especially women poets like Mary McPherson but also Wordsworth, Blake and Byron. Her favourites are Dickens and Hardy."

"Hmm not McGonagall or Milne then?" Hannah asked teasingly, "I need to look up something in the Property Advertising section," she added quickly, picking up his Saturday morning edition. Hannah's quick footwork to hide intellectual snobbery landed her in an even bigger gaffe than the sudden change of subject.

"Well, ah must say yer in an awfu' hurry hen . . . looking for a huis so soon! I hinnae even asked ye tae marry me yet!" Hannah's merry laughter bubbled through the overcrowded tearoom. The more she tried to give a straight account of her intention to prospect houses in Porty, the more William ventured scurrilous notions. Her attempt at defence was matched by his disarming pretence at gullibility.

"Well, it wis no me got ye pregnant woman, so I shouldna ha'e tae buy us a three bedrooms huis!"

Hannah briskly skimmed across his long hair with the folded newspaper. When their laughter subsided she tried again to give him her account, "I saw something for sale on the way down here from town William, which I want to go after if I can."

Pausing from her search of the property section to look straight at him Hannah stated clearly, "I have the money you know and plan to invest it. I expect to return here in the next year or so, when Clarissa Leslie goes to school. I'll be looking for a job, preferably one allowing me to study as well. I will no longer have the luxury of living rent free with no bills, nor be able to bank wages each week while watching them grow."

"They won't give a mortgage to a single woman Hannah, with or without a job. Unless you take out a Bond, or maybe you have a guarantor?"

"I have over £150 saved William, enough to buy a house here outright and that's what I intend to do. I always loved Porty. The long beach with the huge sky and this amazing pier with the boat trips! The busy wee town with crowds of people in the summer. When I was a teenager Isabella Stuart and I used to mitch off school when we were bored with Needlework, or Domestic Science. When the weather was fine we'd come down every weekend to swim in the sea, or earn pocket money working in a tearoom. There was always something to do."

"Oh, well," William murmured thoughtfully, "that's very good. I've been saving for the past twelve years but have nowhere near that amount. Maybe I *will* admit to being the father."

Tight lipped, she rolled the paper and skited him over the head again, this time with vigour. He pretended to flinch with an exaggerated scowl.

"Yes, well, I'm sure you could contribute to the rent and bills," she mused, trying to steer the conversation in a serious direction, "Even at thrupence a pint the social round must be major outlay, huh? Especially if you regularly work up a thirst playing bowls and soccer. Not to mention visiting the Masonic Lodge every Tuesday, isn't that what you told me?" William grunted in vague acknowledgement, so she pressed home the point, "All those boring discussions about the historical precedence of affiliated lodges? Commissioning stained glass windows to the immortal Hiram Abif? Charitable fundraising for poor widows of men who worked all their lives for a pittance? That would drive any weak-minded man to the bottle."

"Naturally!"

"Aye, *naturally* you're expected to stand your round when you retire to the Three Monkeys," she baited smilingly, but he ignored it. In a way she was setting a precedent for all that might follow. Hannah's smile faded but her searching look remained. Clearly she was correct in her assertions about William's 'social commitments.' Also it was apparent that any activity surrounding 'The Lodge' was unimpeachable.

"Don't worry William, I'm used to being stonewalled. Anything probed into in the wrong drift with Harper becomes unmentionable by default. Including matters of rumour abounding in popular myth that any minister would denounce from the pulpit."

"I cannae imagine hen. Nothing involving the abuse o' animals I hope?"

It was clear to Hannah that William Macdonald had knelt beneath the throne, been raised up and clasped to the bosom of the Right Worshipful Master as a freeborn son. And his lips were sealed as tightly as Isaiah's.

"I really don't know where it all goes," agreed William vacantly. In trying resolutely to avoid Hannah's assertions about the Lodge and by sticking to the former subject, William remembered his sense of humour, "Onyways, wi' you in the state you're in hen, I'm gonny hae' tae gi' up the charitable life an' work double shifts."

She hit him firmly over the head a third time with the folded newspaper. William laughed at her appreciatively, like they'd been happily married for twenty years.

Having finished their lunch William offered his arm to link with hers, taking care to make sure she walked on his right side as they set off along the pier. Hannah knew the Highland tradition. Smiling askance for the roguish effrontery, yet giving unspoken assent she placed her fine hand inside his elbow.

Turning right at the end of the pier they walked in the direction of 5, Bath Street, former residence of Sir James Grant, Inspector General of Army Hospitals. The pretty little house situated off the High Street, a short stroll from Portobello beach was offered for sale at an advisory price of £75 Sterling.

On Monday evening Harper came to view the property with Hannah, William and Margaret. John junior explored the house hand in hand with William, whom he'd instantly latched on to, showing particular interest in his émigré novelist's beard. Number five was a tiny haven of peace in a bustling hive of activity. When John ran into the garden at the rear Hannah exchanged a sultry, knowing look with William that burned into the poor man's soul. Every inch of his tailored, forty four inch town coat seemed to fill with willing potential as he shepherded the little man around the overgrown garden. Margaret hummed and hawed about work that was needed but Hannah stressed the ideal location.

"It fits Harper's criteria – of being the worst house on the best street. You should take a walk down to the prom and check out the fine architecture near the bottom of the street."

"Okay Duff, no need right now. I think I know what you mean but let's do that later Harper, yes?"

"Of course Margaret, but she's right. I can tell you that now. This will be a wise investment."

The following morning Harper made arrangements for Hannah's purchase through his solicitors, with a reduced offer of £70 cash. He advised her on obscure but important matters of conducting a building survey and necessary insurances and she allowed him to make appointments for her. Within three days a bid for the house was delivered formally to the owner's solicitor. If it went through, so Hannah told her parents, she planned to offer it for let until she moved back to the area.

Margaret was delighted of course. Duff had turned out to be 'the wise one,' in the long term absence of Elizabeth, now living temporarily with her charges in South Africa. It was she whom Margaret most wished to patronise. Margaret was as strong in showing favour now as she had been in unmoving lack of interest for her education five years earlier. And she openly advocated accord between her and William. Yet for some reason Hannah was intractable. The more Margaret voiced unsolicited opinions about how she should live her life, or with whom, the more resolute Hannah was not to discuss it.

On the afternoon of 12th of July 1914, as the matriarch waxed lyrical over Sunday roast, it no longer mattered what the man's prospects were, "The fact that he drives a tram for a living is in no way demeaning."

"Hm, hm," agreed Harper, between mouthfuls of food, "A proud occupation for anyone so *visibly* a cog in the modern machine."

"Will is a *very* active Mason, John. His father Malcolm was farm Grieve for *Lord Balfour* . . . all his working life. At one point he was *Grand Master* of the Haddington Lodge." Harper was more interested in his Sunday roast which he ate with appreciation, smiling at his delightful partner with accepting eyes.

"Word is that there was money in the wider family. William's mother still lives in a *fine house* on Brighton Place, even though her husband passed away three years ago." Harper nodded, which she took as a cue to keep banging on in Will's favour.

"There are *two brothers* who own farms, Duff says – Angus and John. Another brother, James, is training as an *architect*. Two uncles, on Will's mother's side, own *a slaughterhouse* and meat packing business in Haddington." Knowing he would have difficulty remembering all this unless he resorted to his client note pad, Harper decided not to ask questions.

"Will is a Lay Preacher, devoted in his Ministry to charitable works. And he organises a football team. Like all *good Masons*, I think Will Macdonald amounts tae a lot more than the sum o' his parts."

"Hmm, he disnae play golf, even though his faither was a green keeper," Harper objected lamely, through a mouthful of beef, "I'll ha'e tae teach him."

Rubbing her foot on Harper's leg under the table Margaret chided, "Don't you agree? You're a good Mason and you amount to more than the sum of your parts!"

"Maybe John would like to take a nap after dinner?" ventured Harper. Leaning over to Margaret he whispered, "Then I can show you the sum of my parts!" Margaret returned his affection with a knowing, promissory smile.

'Will' as Margaret began to fondly refer to him, was implicitly recognised as a member of the secret urban elite which cut across class barriers. She romantically imagined him a kind of modern day Templar knight - a humble but most visible cornerstone of the Lothian social pyramid. Nothing more needed to be said in his favour.

"But their engagement might ha'e tae be a long one Harper, if there really is war in Europe." Margaret spoke her mind with alacrity, even though the couple had not made any announcement.

The two Johns, father and son, silently considered the sobering rider to Margaret's enthusiastic monologue as they munched their food. Suddenly the permanent smile that had been on her face since Hannah brought Will to supper back in early June began to wane. The boys looked at Margaret, wondering if they should ask what was wrong, but her dawning realisation was clear enough to Harper. Privately, he was glad that at forty four he was only eligible for a year of the impending fiasco.

"Mammy, why are you not talking?" asked John.

"Oh, dear son! I just ran out of things to say for a minute."

"Where is Europe Mammy?"

"Oh, a long way from here. Finish your dinner and you can have some ice-cream." Harper gave her a dubious look.

"Will daddy and William have to go?"

"Go where son?"

"To the war in Europe."

"No, there's not going to be war in Europe. Everyone says they don't want it." Affectionate flapping and contradiction from Margaret served only to reinforce her five year old son's perception of what the adults kept talking about. She went to help slice up his man sized portion of roast beef.

"Anyway no son, Daddy's not going anywhere."

"He's going to play golf with William," little John remarked, pointing an accusatory middle finger at Daddy at the head of the table. Margaret was glad to change the subject.

Complexities of the Old Alliance System, the rashness of Austria and Germany had brought about a grim diplomatic impasse over Serbia. Everyone visiting the Harper home over the past couple of weeks had been talking about it. Anthony was incensed at Austria's ebullient posturing, railing on against nationalism of one stripe being as shallow as another. The threat of European war was like terminal illness in a neighbouring home - utterly inexplicable under a long summer sky.

Margaret decided to avoid being too specific in front of her child. Instead she continued her diatribe about intrusive political events more elliptically, "John, mad things have been happening for years that make a sane person just stop and shake their head. Suffragettes attacking Whitekirk Church and Roslyn Abbey! What were they thinking?"

"They want a national holocaust of pious memorials because men control religion," censured Harper, "Bloody idiots they are! Some o' these sacred places date back to Saxon and Celtic times," he added despairingly.

"Well it appears to me these Suffragettes want tae destroy the very symbols o' traditional Scotland - morality itself - tae ha'e their equality! Men and women always had different roles fer God's sake. I mean . . . can men ha'e babies and raise bairns?"

"How *do* you make babies mammy?" asked John, "How did you make me?"

"What a smart fellow to ask that! You just popped out of your Mammy's tummy," declared Harper artlessly. Margaret was on a roll and not ready to talk about babies.

"Ask me again in about ten years son," she said blowing a kiss. Little John blew a kiss back. "The day I read about the firebomb at Roslyn, I had tae hide my dander in the kitchen. I took it out on the stuffed chicken!" Smiling irresistibly in recollection of thoughtful antagonism with Duff, she sipped her wine.

"How could I forget? You ordered me to broach the subject when she arrived remember, so you'd no' ha'e tae confront her openly by voicing an opinion."

Convenient revival of the sobriquet 'Duff' offered a code for use in the presence of their brilliantly observant child.

"No, no John," said Margaret holding up her right hand, "I ha'e tae concede she's right – women *should* ha'e the vote – provided o' course they've had a decent education to prepare them!" Harper spluttered some of his wine and had to dab his mouth on his serviette.

Margaret looked at him askance but her seriousness made it worse. She wasn't sure how to justify this but it seemed to make sense to her. Harper had to place his hand over his mouth to prevent its contents flying across the dining table, his body rocking violently with suppressed laughter. At last he swallowed, then he could laugh freely. Little John and then Margaret joined in Harper's infectious mirth. All three members of the tight, supportive little family laughed lovingly together.

"Ha ha! You look so funny daddy!" little John told him, letting gravy drip off his fork as he pointed with the implement. Harper waved back at his son with his left hand. Leaning forward he took a mouthful of wine to irrigate his mouth and give it something to do other than yield to Margaret's absurdity.

"I'm sorry, I'm sorry," he pleaded, "Don't ask!" Harper beamed at Margaret for half a minute before explaining, "It was so charming . . . the way that you said that. You're right of course, I'm sorry! Women should ha'e a decent education first. Dinnae say that in front of Duff for God's sake. Everyone knows women have smaller brains than men – perhaps some kind of intelligence test could be arranged before they vote?" Margaret still wasn't sure what she'd said that seemed so ridiculous to Harper.

After a pause where both thought of ways to approach concerns about Hannah without offending the other, Margaret mentioned what she thought was a moral victory, "When she came to help me last Sunday with the washing up, I let her know what I thought, you know."

"Oh yes – how so?"

"Well, I avoided the negative word Suffragette, that might ha'e tainted oor wee campaigner by association," she assured Harper, "Dinnae fret . . . I'd calmed doon by then John. I just told her I felt *very strongly* that the Pankhursts shouldnae be blowing fingers affy Postmen and setting fire tae fitba groonds."

"And what did she say?"

"She didnae say anything. She produced a form from her handbag for the NUWSS and made me fill it in."

Harper laughed again incredulously, "You joined the suffrage movement?"

"Of *course* I did – Duff said it's the only way to stop that bitch Pankhurst!"

"Oh mammy, 'stop that bitch Pankhurst!'" repeated Little John with a broad smile. Harper roared with sweet laughter, "Well I'm so glad the rift between my adorable wife and youngest daughter is healed at last! Talking about the outbreak of war has put other events of recent years into perspective," he concluded without intended irony.

Harper knew fine that unresolved animosity between his wife and daughter had deflected Margaret's best intention - of match making an engagement between Hannah and William, with an open house party to celebrate.

"Hmm, well I suppose my joining actually meant more to her than it did to me."

"Was that all you broached with Duff?" asked Harper again, implying the delicate subject of William Macdonald.

"Why do you keep calling Hannah 'Duff'?" asked little John. Harper went to fetch him some apple pie and ice-cream. With a smile on her face Margaret answered very much in the manner learned from Harper. Lowering her voice to a whisper she said, "Because we don't want you to know we're gossiping about her!"

"What's gossiping mammy?"

"If you never do it, you never need to know," proclaimed Margaret, "Now eat your pie before the ice cream melts."

"It's what the blethering old wifeys do when they're out putting that red stuff on their doorsteps son," Harper stated with bluff humour.

"No! Is that right daddy?"

"Yeah, in fact that's why they do it – the *only* reason John – so they can watch passers-by and start gossiping about them. See, if they gossip too long in the shops, the butcher and the Co-op grocer would tell them tae *move on*."

"Move on ye old . . .?"

"Gossip."

"Gossip! Ha ha, yes!"

Margaret slapped Harper playfully on the shoulder. He waited expectantly for her reply to his question.

"Yes, I probed but she didnae bite. William was here, so she might ha'e felt a little embarrassed."

"Maybe he's no' popped the question?"

"Regardless, look at how they laugh in each other's company. See, I'm a great romantic. Look how long I waited for you, John. An' consider how long Will has waited for her. They must be aching fer one another by now. Twenty one is an ideal age tae marry, or certainly tae make a commitment. So, I will admit tae being mildly disappointed they've made no announcement."

Harper laughed again at his burgeoning little firebrand. In age he was idling down from the top of the highest hill, but Margaret was guaranteed to keep his pulse racing for many long years.

"Perhaps they need more time together tae consolidate their courtship," he offered over a raised spoonful of ice cream. He rubbed his ankle against hers as if to confirm the point. Lowering her head she smiled discreetly to herself. There was a dark, unspoken shadow in the affairs of men that Margaret felt but could not define, lying beneath all the laughter and happy talk of the future.

"It's this ridiculous war they're threatening. It might cause years of waiting for Hannah and William." Margaret looked at Harper and smiled compassionately. He said nothing but in truth was amazed as always by her directness. She really had influenced his daughters in a righteous manner.

"It will all been worth it of course. I loved you more deeply for my own years o' longing."

Pensively watching the boys eating, Margaret tuned out of their desultory conversation about whether 'apple pie was nicer hot or cold.' In trying to recall some of the events of that time without Harper, hindsight allowed her to reflect momentarily upon what she might have done differently – in particular how she might have handled her own feelings, acted with sensibility if there had been an intrusion, like a rift with her family, or war had intervened. Like a pitchfork springing off a hidden stone Margaret's mind deflected from the remembered pain of wanting for so long what she could not have.

I dealt with the secret guilt of envying a dying woman. Perhaps not everyone is so certain of love as I've been with John. Yet what might have been if his wife had lived?

Margaret's mind reeled away from the thought. Without a word, she rose from the table to take empty plates through to the kitchen.

William Macdonald had no intention of proposing, so he told his brother Jim as he placed a pint in front of him, in a front corner of the Three Monkeys, "I respect Hannah too much to show my hand under these circumstances." Jim looked at William with incredulity on his face.

"She's flush, while I've become increasingly complacent over the years about the use of money."

"Whit! You're bloomin' minted man. I suppose you want the twenty-five bob I borrowed affy ye tae buy thon divider set?" protested Jim, thinking the evening's fun was about to be curtailed before it had begun.

"No Jim! That's ma investment in your career boy. I get a percentage of every commission ye do after ye qualify. Jim, I ha'e enough saved tae buy her little house outright just the same but she never asked."

"So how is that 'complacent' big man?"

"Well a few years back I bought eighty quids worth o' Bank of Scotland shares wi' ma savings. It's aw tied up. And due tae the financial markets shrinking, they're probably worth less than when I bought them."

Lowering his voice Jim vented on a popular theme, "It's the bloody arms race! That fat prick Churchill wi' his Super Dreadnoughts," he muttered, "It's ordinary workin' men like us who pay for it aw!"

"Most of that money - fifty quid no less you may recall, came as compensation frae The North British Railway, for ma injury."

"Aye, bad luck that Wull, some pain nae doot, losing four toes? Its damn near happened tae me – some shunter kisses the buffers on a truck wi'oot hitching up properly - an' seconds later the bastard starts tae roll."

William sucked deeply at his pint before resuming the explanation, "Much as I'd like tae have asked her - now that she's buying that house on Bath Street Jim - it would put me tae shame."

"How so? That would be an incentive for most men, especially wi' a crackin' wee Jessie like that! Dae a straw poll roon' the Three Monkeys if ye want a considered opinion on the matter. Some o' the boys'll go callin' on her tonight. Then ye'll change yer tune."

"No! Shut yer rag box!" William demanded, looking over at a group of old familiars quietly perusing a broadsheet, as two younger friends finished off a game of 501.

"Why not then?"

"I cannae explain why not Jim. What I *do* think is – and you can confirm this for me – if, hypothetically mind, we had been buying a house together, doubling the money would ha'e more than doubled the set of accommodation it would offer?"

"Oh aye. Porty is expensive for first time buyers, wi' all the rich Hectors moving down from overcrowding in town. You'd get better value for a hundred and fifty, than for seventy five, nae question."

"Well look Jim – either way I'm no' put out," William concluded finishing his first pint, "It just wasn't my place tae raise the matter," he added, standing up from their table.

When William returned with four more pints, Jim queried Hannah's jibing assertion that he drank too much, "Yeah, yeah that's whit I need . . . you start on me too!"

"Sorry but you shared the information wi' me pal. An' it happens tae be true."

"Okay, I admit that . . . in private moments of reflection I've felt . . . that *occasionally*, drinking led to instances of profligacy . . . and disgrace," William confessed, lowering his voice.

"I can cite a number of instances where I've had tae . . ." William interrupted Jim with a raised hand.

"It has always been outwardly convivial . . . and no-one ever got hurt. An' I still work it aff, *twice a week* on the fitba field training wi' the lads at Craigmillar."

"No-one that didnae ask fer it ye mean!" mused Jim, referring to William's previous point, "Christina and Marion ha'e been on aboot reducing your drinking for years. They see it as a barrier to marrying ye off." Jim smirked before taking a hypocritical suck on his second pint.

William went on the defensive, "Jim, you know I ha'e a very wide circle of friends. I've always been regular in Sunday observances and prayer meetings. I'm active in the Kirk *and* Lodge, as well as Union and Labour associations."

"But?"

"But . . . I agree to a measure o' remorse fer no' moving forward in life, or career. An' I ken people whisper aboot 'why at the age of thirty three has he never married?'

"Is that what they say?"

"Oh come on, the hell! You've heard gossip aboot me Jim, 'This lad is handsome and always popular with the women, clearly he's no' a big Jessie.'"

"Aye well, there *was* speculation."

"Concerning?"

"Oh, there's a few roun' here might ha' played their hand for 'Morgana le Fey' – yer red-head divorcee conductress, if they hadnae thought she was dotty aboot you big brother."

"Moira Rae?"

Jim looked guiltily into the middle distance, confirming William's impression that he too had heard the gossip.

"'I've been listening to their aspersions for years, Jim – 'The lad is simply ha'in too much o' a good time. Ho, ho ho! You can read it in his eyes – he's too versatile no' tae grasp an opportunity when it arises.' So aw ma friends and family assume I've been playing both ends against the middle?"

"Ye mean getting in a clinch wi' Moira on the back seat every time the bus reaches the terminus?"

"Precisely! All but my closest friends, you and Ronnie, assume the worst about me!"

Jim tilted his head, raising both eyebrows in a gesture of doubt, "Well you *can* understand William – Moira's a stunner, even if she is in her fifties."

"Not you too! What do I have to do to convince people? Moira turned me down, Jim."

"Oh aye, nine years ago, on the rebound after her bastard o' a husband came home frae South Africa and beat the living shit oot o' her. An' as we aw ken, you're too proud tae ask her ever again."

"By that I take it ye mean Christina; Marion who will no' believe me an' young Ronnie and 'Phemie, who by way of contrast accept anything I tell them. Jim, I knew Moira long before my accident on the railway. I had already waited for years for her to resolve her situation. When the rat who spawned her two kids finally moved oot o' her life and the youngest of them was grown up and settled, Moira finally achieved the thing she prized most in the world – her independence."

Jim narrowed his eyes before daring to speak his mind, "An' so it came to pass the cardinal rule was broken, in the case o' Will Macdonald and Moira Rae becoming, 'You *can* ha'e your cake and eat it too.'"

William glowered at Jim but his younger brother simply laughed. A minute later he broke the silence again, speaking softly so others in the bar would not pick up on any tension, "But naebody spoke too loudly aboot their impression, nor dared offer unsolicited advice or unwelcome opinion. Wullie Mac has a gentle good nature - until provoked, eh? Then the hoons o' hell would whimper and press to be first through the door."

"Ye wee shite! Yer too clever for yer ain guid!"

"Dinnae deny you've been there. What d'ye say tae that boy?"

"I say it's your roon'. Double up and get the same fer Peter. He's due any time. An' dinnae you listen to a word Sergeant Snap has tae say boy – or ye'll both hae me tae answer tae."

"Dinnae worry big brother. I'm an architect, no a ruddy so'djer!"

"Aye, you're telling me . . . nearly the architect o' yer own doom," William growled, piqued by Jim's razor tongue.

"Sorry Wull, nae offence pal. I overstepped the mark. Clearly you love the girl an' she's delightful man. When's her return to Auld Reekie?"

"There are documents for her tae sign – I imagine she'll come the week o' the August Bank Holiday. Hopefully the week before, if her employer allows."

"Oh well – by then we could be a nation at war . . . if the German's dinnae agree to keep oot o' Belgium."

At that moment the door opened and a cry of recognition went up all around the bar. A Regimental Sergeant Major of the much vaunted Cameron Highlanders walked boldly up to the two men sitting in the corner, "Well, there's nae holdin' you boys back! Looks like I've some catching up tae dae," observed Peter Macdonald, nodding at the table covered with full glasses of beer.

In the quiet turmoil of the summer of '14 equilibrium was fleetingly restored in the lives of Hannah and William. Exultant in their loving friendship, each had returned to familiar routines and favourite friends. And now William had been offered a clear perspective by Jim, regarding the breadth of what he wrongly imagined to be a discreet reputation, taking into account skeletons in the cupboard Hannah was deemed not quite ready to hear of. One look at Moira back in '09 had been enough to give her a pointer though.

Hannah set off for Liverpool, intent on seeking a perspective on affairs of the heart without fear of contradiction. Pensively looking out of the window of the carriage rolling west towards Glasgow, she anticipated an evaluation from Alice. It was her advice Hannah valued more than any other - even her mentor Christina, or childhood friend Isabella. Isabella was resident in Paris, completing her MA in modern languages at the

Sorbonne and Hannah missed her greatly. But they would have tailored advice to Hannah's perceived temperament – whereas Alice would look candidly at circumstances as well as risks.

Alice Hughes had acquired some of Christina's sage objectivity. Her thinking would certainly be something like, 'Never rush into anything without a plan. It's important to be realistic about the future, to actually decide what *you* want before jumping in.' Hannah imagined she could hear her confident voice. And of course Alice could talk more of the needs of a small child, how they drag upon the energies of their mother. Hannah tried to recall a little of what Alice had said in the middle of a bitter quandary involving her Co-op manager less than three years before. At her eloquent best Alice could be as forthright as an urban Cleopatra.

"This is the essential conundrum of female dependency Hannah," she railed, "Men think of love and romance as the ultimate prize and can't get enough of it. Women however are left in servitude to squalling brats, who just appear as a by-product of that romance. An annoying quirk of nature!"

After making the Liverpool connection at Glasgow, Hannah opened her valise to find her diary. Settling down in a compartment that would probably remain empty until Dumfries, she planned to scribble down some of her thoughts in advance of resuming dialogue with Alice at the first opportunity. Smiling in anticipation she began to write the first insightful paragraph,

'Militant feminists express the view that the world is a selfish greedy hive because of men with their destructive attributes. Additionally because of irresponsible, complacent women. I know this first hand from years of involvement in the Suffrage movement. This world view is hedged about with ethical contentions, defying easy analysis. Seemingly iconoclastic convictions, growing in popularity, may be a reaction to 'original sin' concepts of Old Religion – the Adamic texts of the Old Testament are still shoved down every primary school child's throat, before they are even able to read.'

Sitting back from her diary Hannah looked out at the lowering hills of Strathclyde. Willie Proven would be annoyed to hear she'd been in town but not visited. Re-reading her diary entry she imagined a dialogue, with him saying, "So what? Who cares? . . . Make love while the sun shines!" Taking up the pen again, she recorded an imaginary response,

'So what? So this . . . men blame women for the sins of the world. Yet in a woman they will seek rescue when they find themselves without faith, or belief. And *I* care! The part about making love, I'd agree with old friend, but presently I'm trying to establish my own set of conditions. I need *proof* Willie . . . *Willie* proof!' Hannah laughed out loud at the imagined vulgarity, before resuming her diary entry,

'How should my strong religious and spiritual beliefs inform action, especially when they are judged by so many women as 'mind control'? Conversely can 'morally accepted standards' be drawn from the random actions of individuals, William Macdonald included? After all, it is William I am trying to think about.

People act in a certain way for particular reasons which may not be well perceived, or even explicit. They do what they think they are supposed to do – without ever really deciding anything. The underlying issue, it seems to me, is always attachment. Attachment to parents, family, home. Attachment at one remove, to work and employers, friends, community, church and state. Attachment . . . *always* at a price.

In a sense, living is engagement in a web of economic activity that we buy into as individuals. What will any of it amount to, when weighed and measured with the soulful distance of a hundred years? Does anything really matter, other than how we avoid suffering while serving our own ends?'

Arriving late at Allerton Grange, Hannah was surprised to find that Hugh and Christina were nowhere to be seen. Mrs Mason told Hannah, 'Sir Hugh and Lady Christina are visiting with family friends. The girls are upset about a private matter, details of which I am not inclined to divulge." Hannah turned to go, thinking Mrs Mason had finished, "Oh and perhaps I should tell you, Miss Hughes has a trainee." Mrs Mason seemed a little perplexed. Despite her normal composure she was actually at a loss as to why the Leslies were choosing to harbour a potential enemy infiltrator.

"She's a Miss Visconti, newly arrived from Milan," the Housekeeper explained scornfully, "I understand her father works for the Italian Embassy in London although in what capacity I'm not clear. In any event, Alice will explain your role in helping the young lady adjust to her duties."

Sitting in her room that night, Hannah read mail then wrote letters in reply to family and friends. Jessie had alarmed her by mentioning the illness of her namesake and niece, Kate and Ewan's daughter, Hannah Wilson Robertson Harper, sick with Tuberculosis. Willie Proven, whom she'd neglected far too long, was intent on heading abroad with the Army, even though he'd not completed his degree. Then she wrote to Isabella and Elizabeth - but not to William.

In the late evening half-light she undressed and drew the curtains back to let air into the sultry room. Her naked body felt moist in the summer heat. Sitting at her bureaux, Hannah came back in meditation to something brewing all day, 'the sanctity of the individual' - the principle of autonomous thought and action being of paramount importance.

Looking across at her own reflection in the dressing table on the far side of the darkening room, she resisted the urge to light a gas lamp. At this time of year Hannah enjoyed sitting in the failing light – finding it easier to relax, or meditate with a degree of discipline. There was a soft knocking on the bedroom door. Hannah threw on her dressing gown and moved eagerly to open it.

Alice stood in the light of the stair way lamp, leaning nonchalantly against the flock wallpaper with a knowing smile. She held aloft two ostentatiously large red wine glasses and a bottle of Chateau-Neuf-du Pape. Hannah was tired and had missed supper. It was a bad idea but she decided the wine might revive her flagging spirits.

"I won't stay long. Do tell how you're feeling about this dreadful news," Alice entreated, moving swiftly into the room, before one of Mason's drones spotted her.

"I just don't know, Alice. I'm up and down you know? With this ridiculous war and the news of the Suffragettes selling out."

"But you – how do you feel in yourself?"

"I've felt myself becoming duller, more stupid as time goes by for years," said Hannah with self-mocking wit. Screwing the opener into the cork, Alice handed the bottle to Hannah to pull out.

"Odd times I've been nettled by loud-mouthed, oppositional men. But never as much as recently by the dangerous smugness of my step-mother. I hate being angry Alice. Maybe it's a sign of the times that I can't avoid it."

"It sounds like she tested your patience?"

"I will summarise: Margaret's advice confirms that the adult world is full of compromise."

In her heart Hannah knew that she longed to be a child again. Now she vented with a child's impulsiveness, "For me the world has lost its innocence. Maybe it never had any. So called civilization is a web of unthinking deceit. The truth behind all the politics is that everywhere humans walk this Earth, we ruthlessly and endlessly exploit one another. We are more deadly to our own species than mosquitos, or poisonous reptiles." She pulled out the cork and handed the bottle back to Alice.

"Oh my Lord. You're not yourself! Have some glug, see if that will repair it. Hannah went on with her rant, as Alice poured out two full glasses of wine.

"It seems that behind every momentous act is someone's personal gain – usually though not always one man, or a small coterie. The impending war with Austria is about this."

Pulling up an armchair Alice smiled and clinked her glass against Hannah's.

"Oh yes Han, it's all about 'colonial expansion, competition for spheres of influence abroad, flexing of industrial muscle.' I read that today in the Times."

Hannah sipped her wine to see if it was ready to drink. The foretaste ran bitterly around the edge of her tongue. Alice ran on with her theme, "This is the predictable outcome of a childish race, to see who could build the biggest fleet of Dreadnoughts. And a meaningless system of outmoded alliances."

Hannah threw sticks and coal into the grate as she listened to Alice in amazement. She continued to paraphrase the editorial, "The widespread economic subjugation of men to machines," Alice drank deeply, satisfied with her own eloquence. Hannah looked at her askance, not entirely sure what she meant by the last point. She sat down, pulling her gown tighter before responding to her friend's vituperation.

"What irks *me* is talk of the Pankhursts suspending their campaign, until this fiasco is all over. Alice, after all the damage they've done alienating men from our cause, now they're supporting war! Violence only ever begets violence. So for them I suppose it reduces to a matter of which enemy they hate more. In this case Austrians and Germans."

"I agree! I see it in perspective now – those callous harpies never did have the moral high ground. They never represented me, or any of the good people I met!"

"Absolutely not!" agreed Hannah, also drinking deeply, "Now the hypocrites have sold everyone out . . . men and women alike, for the sake of this stupid war!" Alice grinned broadly at Hannah's righteous annoyance.

"Exactly, it's a compromise to salvage reputations and paper over cracks in their organisation."

"Christina tried to warn me last year that this war was coming," murmured Hannah gloomily, "She was right."

Alice's tiny face, reminiscent of Millais' *Cherry Ripe,* peered through indigo sky reflected from Hannah's dressing mirror. Large lumps of high quality coal smoked and hissed in the fire grate.

"They sold out on the women's political movement years ago with their hateful firebombing," prompted Alice, telling Hannah what she wanted to hear.

"I know. This latest compromise is entirely predictable for them," grumbled Hannah in exasperation. Alice wanted to feel Hannah's contempt, though fear dulled her judgement. She was after all her one true friend. Whatever her deepest sentiment was, Alice would agree in principle, observing with relish bright intellect ranging free with the effusion of alcohol rushing through Hannah's brain.

"Yeah - the Establishment bought them over, like Sir Hugh's railway company buying up some badly run branch line," said Alice with the flourish of a well-rehearsed line in a drama. With a brilliant flash of prescience she added with contempt, "One day they'll probably build a statue to Pankhurst, like Queen Victoria's in Leith. When they do, you can vandalise it for everyone she has let down!" Hannah laughed at the recollection of her own diverted moment of sabotage. Then her face darkened with memory of another, more personal betrayal.

"They were probably infiltrated by Russian communists at some point. Or even statists in the pay of our government. Bomb makers playing a double game, to discredit the Suffrage movement. The Zalewski brothers were involved locally somehow. I suppose we knew it all along, didn't we Alice? That's why they encouraged us, amongst all the others. We were with the wrong union for them to show their hand. They were always furtive, defensive somehow. The more so when they were friendly towards us."

"Sugar it! You're ragging me. You think they were stringing us along, all that time?"

"I want to share a little secret with you. Despite my friendship with Marek, his brother Sigi knew that I had a real shine for him. I could tell that he liked me too - by the gentle way he spoke. We had a connection, Alice. He could never easily lie about anything, right from the start. He seemed to relax visibly whenever we met."

"And your point is?"

"My point is there was fervour in his eyes which I soon realised was not for me. I doubt it was for another woman, or any individual."

"Look Hannah – they were lovely guys – but they were not communists. They were left wing . . . but like you said at the time, they had other loyalties." Darkness thickened as the afterglow of the mid-summer sun finally disappeared with their naïveté. Shadows in the room seemed to dance with another kind of energy.

"I can read people Alice."

"What do you mean?"

"They were decent, whoever they owed allegiance to. Whoever was using them - they were loyal and faithful to their own ideals."

"Oh Lord. Are we all so easily deceived?" pleaded Alice, "What exactly happened to our gallant Poles?"

"Marek was arrested by armed police and soldiers. Remember, I read you the article from the paper. The authorities were alerted by a local pensioner who found him sleeping in an allotment in Parbold. It said in the paper he'd spent three nights walking along the canal."

"He was deported. And Siggy disappeared on the same day as the McGiffen family."

"Correct. Father Jordan told me they both found work in Dublin but it was best not to contact them directly."

"And as you know, I visited Stan several times in hospital . . . until he was well enough to travel back to languish in a Siberian katorga. He said ma was with him until the ambulance came."

"Then they upped sticks and left before the dust settled."

"Dare we smoke?" asked Alice, "I always get a yen if I have a drink. It's like an alarm bell going off in my head."

"Fine, we're at the far end of the house. There's no-one nearby to smell it. Lift the sash though. Let's move our chairs over by the window."

They sat facing one another with legs propped up on each other's armchair. On the window ledge was a Caithness Crystal ash tray and the remainder of the bottle of wine. Warm scented air mixed comfortingly with the dankness of Hannah's unused bedroom. Pale blue light from the northerly edge of the world combined with whitish gaslight glow of the conurbation to the north-west. Only a scattering of bright stars shone overhead. Alice blew smoke out of the window where it drifted with the moths.

"'Suffragettes' – I use that word pejoratively now, Hannah," she said with fiercely virtuous eyes, "needed organisers to conduct a nationwide terror campaign for so many years. Pankhurst said, 'we have no such apparatus. No constitution, no internal democracy, no formal meetings. Just an army in the field.'"

"Unaffiliated bomb makers," Hannah conceded quietly.

"Bomb makers," repeated Alice, "Where would you even start?" She peered at Hannah, her face pinched in uncertainty.

"I suppose with great discretion at first, Alice. To develop technical know-how. Then experimentation out in the wilds somewhere I'd guess. More crucial would be planning and development of a secret organization up and down the country, to make and plant bombs. They would all have to be trained," Hannah looked pensive. Terrorism was not her forte but logic was, "They must have put out feelers to paramilitary groups and armies abroad. Irish, or Polish republicans perhaps," she added doubtfully.

"So the bomb makers must have been secretly funded from start to finish. Protected and unseen, because anyone arrested would crack under police investigation within days, revealing the extent of the invisible organisation they were part of," Alice was on a roll. She had always been opposed to WSPU, "I don't believe there were many spontaneous acts of violence, and people get caught too easily doing that kind of thing."

"No, I'm sure you're right. They were undemocratic. Dictators easily find excuses for the use of force – as long as somebody else commits the act of violence for them. I'm not surprised Pankhurst's daughter Sylvia defected last summer. No more than by Emmeline backing our government's response to the 'German Peril.'"

"So you agree with me? The government played it down for years? I mean the whole issue of Suffrage – ignoring and mocking women?"

Hannah internalised Alice's question as she did every fierce contention beyond her experience. Snorting smoke from her nostrils into the room, Alice stubbed her cigarette out then promptly lit another. She was on edge. Hannah knew her mood had something indirectly to do with information withheld by the housekeeper, as well as her own tenuous status within Christina's bounteous domain now that the girls were due to attend boarding school. In turn Alice guessed that her friend and confidante would soon be leaving.

Hannah sipped her drink as she considered all that Alice had been saying. Alice was blustering. She'd never been strong enough to stand by her own principles and now was a little drunk, "I think men have been consistent in patronising women as they always have done."

"Ha! You're beginning to sound a little like the Pankhursts," said Hannah, tiring of her friend's invective.

"Between them the bastards subverted the women's movement of this country! Don't you see that was the intention all along? Softening prison sentences and allowing a network of bombers to thrive. They conspired to make the mass movement seem more extreme! That, at least, is my assumption."

"Yes Alice, I have no doubt the Pankhursts were presented with a mass of irrefutable evidence by the Police, then offered a compromise. One that promises amnesty to close associates, while restoring WSPU's reputation in the eyes of the public. It's a selective use of justice, allowing more people to sleep well at night once the stray lambs are back in the fold."

"Yes, and suitably rewarding Pankhurst in the longer term, as if the misuse of union funds hadn't already done so," spat out Alice.

Hannah laughed sardonically as alcohol buzzed into her brain, "My God you're really on form tonight," she observed, finishing off her glass of wine. Alice leant towards her with the bottle. She still hadn't finished exploring the conspiracy theory. Stripped of her defences, Hannah shook her head and smiled, "Oh Alice, don't you get it. Nothing . . . nothing in this world, is ever black and white. All we can ever do is refuse to let someone else pull our strings!"

In indignation Hannah decided two things which she went on to scribe into her memoir at around one o'clock that morning,

'I am the true feminist. It is my nature *not* to commit acts of violence. Nor will I sponsor or condone them in any degree. This war our nation is about to engage in is a collaborative act of criminal stupidity. Decadent, drunken men are placing bets on an arm wrestling bout in a noisy charnel house. There is no clear underlying moral precept – just an injudicious reaction, tinged with racial hatred – ludicrous fear of the 'Hun'. Leaders of the Central Powers are equally to blame - stupid men conspiring to act unjustly for ambition and personal gain. Additionally - from now on I will remain a committed pacifist. In reference to legalistic double talk I am now a 'conscientious objector' - by extension of my heartfelt disapproval of systematised violence. I will not support this war in any way.'

Staring out of the window into shimmering darkness, Hannah prayed for Alice and for her family. Unsure how to personify intelligent reality she sought to connect with, Hannah knew for sure it did not correspond to the dualistic god of war used as a timeless patron for the brutality of mankind. And if life had no apparent meaning, she would imbue it with her own. Hannah decided that the mind behind time and matter bore characteristic qualities of transcendent motherhood - serenity, reconciliation and accord.

When she dropped into bed the wine put Hannah's light out as swiftly as a verger's candle pole. But her dreams were all too real. The entire Earth with all its people was suspended in an intermediate state between living and dying. Wild animals surrounded her. A black leopard turned to face her, snarling. With nowhere to run she surrendered to the beast, imagining herself reborn with a suckling child at her breast.

Awakening with the first glorious light striking through branches of a magnificent cedar across the wide driveway on the verge of the front lawn, Hannah realised her curtains were still open. But she was glad to wake early, as the back of her head throbbed and she was stiff from sleeping too long in one position. Removing the pillow from under her head to restore blood flow, she soon became fully alert.

Thankfully the fine wine left no hangover, so she rose a little after six to bathe. Hannah was brewing tea in the kitchen when Mrs Heap arrived to prepare meals for the day. They hugged and chatted as Hannah made the Cook a cup of her favourite Earl Grey.

Returning to her room with a mysterious feeling of happiness Hannah sat down to meditate on the incredible events of that summer. She opened her diary again to record deeply concerned reflections about the person who troubled her most in life. After re-reading the affirmations of the previous day she added,

'Bearing upon the related matter of my true affections for William Macdonald, I will not answer yes or no if he asks me to 'jump over the broom.' I will consider in my own time whether to commit, or turn him down flat. I do love him but that does not construe into my *needing* to marry, or accept him as a life partner to the exclusion of others. I owe him that honesty. Right now I realise that I would not have welcomed being put in this position recently. I would have said no had he asked me. Initially I imagined William needed time to mature a little. Now it is I who find the adult world perplexing - yet the last thing I want is a parental substitute.

Freedom of thought. Freedom of expression. Responsible, autonomous action. These are my life aspirations. Everywhere women are subjugated, making these ideals seem vague. Yet in many ways we compromise too easily - prostituting ourselves. I pray to God for strength and clarity of mind never to do this.'

Great Sophia how I miss my mammy!

Hannah lay back on her bed fully clothed, still slightly drunk and feeling bilious after drinking milky tea. The girls would not rise until eight am or later. Soft fragrant air, heralding a glorious summer morning, wafted into her room with songs of competing blackbirds and cooing of doves.

Listening to squeals and rumble of freight traffic from a distant railway line beyond the open sash she imagined the dolorous, combined thinking of a world of men waking up to impending disaster. The female population of Edinburgh was already fifteen or twenty per cent greater in number than their menfolk.

We have been duped into having the wrong argument. Civil strife at home was always going to lead to war abroad. Everyone involved in democratic socialism predicted this. At least William is thirty three - and unfit, if his missing toes are taken into account.

When she thought of love as she did now, Hannah mused upon a higher realm where issues of possession, ownership, demands and expectations of marriage were transcended. She tried to imagine a place where there was no sorrow. Drying a lonely tear from the outside corner of her eye she turned to rest her face on the pillow, dreaming of summer days in Rothiemay when it had been possible to stop thinking.

Four generations of women folk, drinking tea among scent-dripping roses in an emerald garden. Swinging in a hammock, I reach down to brush daisies with my hand as others chatter idly. We are family. Conversation and laughter fertilise our souls. There is one mind, one feeling, one resolution under a life-giving, gathering sun. There are no human shadows, or shuffling feet in the cold, silent kirk in the Milltown. No saw miller works in the forest. It is a holiday for all, with time to waste in the long grass. In turn I embrace each member of my extended family.

In loneliness Hannah Harper mourned the death of poor happiness – always so fleeting, so rare and abused.

Hannah planned to seek out Alice to discuss her views about William but had dozed off despite getting up early. In the event it was Alice who came to see her. While sitting at her dressing table there came a gentle knock on the bedroom door. Half expecting one of the girls, Hannah called, "Enter!" as politely and pleasantly as she could, in an attempt to model the command for Helena and Clarissa. But it was Alice who popped her head round the door, eager to talk without intruding.

"You've not finished dressing. Mrs Heap sent your breakfast. I'll just leave it and come back later."

"No, come in Alice. Sit, while I brush my hair." Alice put the tray down on a coffee table near the fireplace.

"Here let me do this, it will be quicker. You keep it so soft! How do you manage it?"

"I just wash it every day in clean, warm water. No soap." Alice worked gently but swiftly, glancing at the clock on the mantelpiece. Hannah wondered if it had run down. Then she remembered that she had wound and set it on arrival the previous night. Something had happened. The place was too quiet and Alice seemed nervous in her movements.

"Tell me the news, Alice. Something unusual has happened, something bad."

"God, you are a witch Harper!"

"What about you? You project your thoughts telepathically! You've been naughty and you're bursting to let me in on the scandal – or else you're scheming something up and need an accomplice?"

"Well, how about this - they're gone and Christina has left me in charge. They left an hour ago. She felt it was inappropriate to ask you to accompany them at such short notice since you'd just got back and told me not to wake you."

"Oh! This was Mrs Mason's dark secret when I came home late. We shouldn't have got spluddery. Why on earth didn't you tell me?"

"Because there was a lot of tension and Christina wanted to talk him out of it. I was sworn to secrecy."

"Oh, I see. I don't like the sound of this. Anyway, gone where? They can't just 'go' without us! Where to and for how long? Stop teasing me. Spill the beans woman! You must know the details."

"Well, yes and no. I heard raised voices . . . which I never heard the like of before, something about him being the Director of Operations for the railway. I know the War Office want Sir Hugh to join the Army. And I know Lady Christina will not have it. So that's how the rift began when you were in Edinburgh. The girls were upset because you were not here. And before you quiz me, they said, 'Mummy and Daddy are not talking,' but that was all. They have no idea what this is about. That's your job, for when they come back."

"I feel guilty for not being here. Where have they gone?"

"Christina and the girls have gone to Castle Leslie in Monaghan. I think Hugh went off to London to help organise the mobilisation. He's an army reservist, so there's talk of him being offered a commission. He told me they are more likely to listen to his advice if he wears a uniform. Christina told me Hugh is expected to go to Moore Park in Cork, for some sort of officer training. She wants to be that bit nearer to him if he comes home at any time."

"Does Hugh they think there will be trouble in Liverpool - that we may be a target for anti-war demonstrations here?"

"No, they think there will be trouble in Ireland, silly! You know the Leslie folklore – how quintessentially 'British' they are and how they unfailingly respond to 'the call to arms.'"

Alice gave Hannah the brush. Hannah pulled hair from between its bristles with her comb, then handed it back for her to continue brushing but first she turned to face Alice.

"Ireland? How will that figure?"

"Oh God, you're so naïve for such a dedicated politico! Don't you know your 'working class hero' has them all fired up . . . whatsisname . . . Larkin?"

"Jim Larkin. How can trade unionism affect the war?"

"Search me . . . I'd have thought he'd be happy – you know, plenty of jobs for the boys. Russell says for once the Irish are against it all, so trouble is brewing. Sit still please, so I can finish your hair."

"Oh, I don't think they need to worry about the Revolution just yet – the British Army relies on volunteers, not conscripts - even if the Irish are always Britain's mercenaries. Don't you think it all sounds a bit like a boy's adventure comic – 'British *Expeditionary* Force'?" Hannah ventured sceptically.

"Yes, I know. Perhaps they're off to collect butterflies, or find the South Pole."

"Hmm, or make first contact with Belgian cowgirls, wandering helplessly through the Ardennes forest." Both laughed boisterously, but knew such scepticism could never be voiced in the open. A shadow fell slowly over Hannah's face.

"They killed millions you know?" she said, looking at Alice standing by the ornate fireplace.

"Who killed millions, the Irish? What are you talking about Hannah?"

Alice's perplexity was genuine – she had no idea what Hannah was referring to. Rising from the upholstered buffet, Hannah slid it under her dressing table. Picking up a lightly woven, cream coloured cardigan from the bed she draped it over her shoulders. Waiting for Alice's attention Hannah chose her words thoughtfully, "Poor little defenceless Belgium . . . whom our small but elite BEF are rushing to defend against Germanic imperialists, threatening their security? Tie my hair up for me. It's easier for you if I stand."

"Explain!" squealed one of Alice's tempestuous Russian characters, stamping her foot on the thick Axminster.

"Sorry dear . . . King Leopold's trading company, purportedly. But its employees were in fact Belgian soldiers and trained mercenaries. They *murdered* half the native population of the Congo valley."

Looking at Hannah in dismay, Alice voiced uncertainty, "Natives?"

"That makes a difference does it?" asked Hannah disputatiously, waiting for an answer before offering more information.

"No, certainly not," conceded Alice, petulant now rather than tempestuous.

"They *welcomed* Christianity, helping the first explorers. They naïvely led prospectors to diamonds and gold, offering hospitality to European traders. As always, religion helped to disarm them in preparation for the butcher's knife."

"As always?" demanded Alice.

"Yes, as always - like Spanish Jesuits accompanying Conquistadores, helping them burn the books of an unknown civilization. Ottomans and Moors. Moghuls eradicating Hinduism - I don't know Alice, read your history!"

"Sounds complicated," said 'Cherry Ripe', returned to her most vapid, natural persona. In between sips of tea Hannah laughed involuntarily down through her nose at Alice's tongue in cheek unworldliness.

"Strip away the politics behind any war in history, Alice. You'll find an explosive mix of murderous stupidity and human greed."

"Hannah, it's too early in the morning for you to be lecturing me – dastardly old King Leopold or not!"

"Sorry, I won't say another word."

Alice gave Hannah a sidelong glance as she poured herself a cup of tea, hoping to make up for her ignorance of recent history, "Anyway, Christina's gone, so I'm in charge," she reminded Hannah, with a petulant tilt of her pretty blonde head. Alice's hair was tightly wrapped and pierced in a bun with a blue enamelled slide. With her Merino cardigan, yellow floral calico dress and fine shoes, she looked the picture of modernity. Dynamic and accessible, Alice was in every way that it was possible for her to contrive, the closest replica of unique Lady Christina.

"She told me, 'keep the cleaners out my smalls and don't lose any of my jewellery if you go out dancing.'" Both women roared with delight, their serious anti-war mood suddenly forgotten.

"Well I've heard some outrageous things recently Alice but that's definitely quote of the week!" After roaring with laughter again Alice thoughtfully cautioned, "be careful with the 'Bag Lady' patter Hannah, Mason will be spying on us more than ever."

Alice stood back from Hannah with a mock-questioning look - evaluating her lightweight, cream summer cardigan – a curling brush in her right hand and Hannah's Spanish ebony and silver hair slide caught between her lips. Alice spun her friend back around, gently scooping a wide tress of long hair, clipping it in a high loop with one deft movement.

"You think I'm joking don't you? Christina gave me fifty pounds for 'extraneous household expenditures.' Ha, ha!"

"In other words, keep the home fires burning?"

"In other words, 'have a party, like I would if I was in town Alice, only with your own select group of friends. And I'll foot the bill.'"

Hannah turned round to smile at Alice, "They're great aren't they? Their generosity is prodigious. I'm going to miss them."

Alice paused before replying, "I love her like a sister. I've never know anyone so kind." Then continuing despondently, her voice trembling with emotion, "Christina trusts me, even though she knows what I'm like. I'm gonna keep account of every penny, whether they want me to or not."

Smiling softly and shaking her head, Hannah said, "She'll never ask."

They went downstairs to the breakfast room to have their meal together and on the way Alice asked Mrs Heap for poached eggs with toast. Over their meal Alice resumed her story.

"Hughie wants us to check over the *entire house,* morning and evening. We are to keep lights on and I quote, 'deter opportunistic burglars and breakaway factions of the Suffrage movement, present company excepted.'" Hannah stared at her, refusing to rise to the bait, "His choice of words, not mine. Oh, come on silly – you know what he's like!" Hannah smiled, imagining she could hear his voice in her head, "Yes, I know exactly what he's like, the old wag."

"Well, I'm having Russell junior and his daddy move into the house for the duration. It's all above board. I asked Christina and she approves. She said, 'the requirement for you to remain on duty in my absence would be unreasonable otherwise.'

We have hell on avoiding that hag Russell is burdened with. If it wasn't for his seniority with the Co-op, he'd have divorced her years ago," Alice levelled at Hannah, with spiteful determination in her eyes and voice. Hannah nodded her agreement.

"I didn't want to pry."

"You are amazing Hannah. This is why you're my best friend. You are so honourable. I thought everyone knew!"

"I don't gossip."

"What are we doing now?"

"I don't know. We're being honest with one another, as friends should – not mercilessly speculating about someone's personal affairs. When people divulge information of that nature about another, I tend *not* to ask questions."

"So none of the other staff tell you their scandalous little secrets?"

"In a single word, no. Like you Alice, I am too close to the family for them to be sure I won't repeat what they say. I hear confidences because they trust me – but they are not opinions. They are facts. I just don't repeat them. Ironically, I'm aware of lies others have spread about you. But not the truth."

Alice laughed heartily, "Well don't worry! Now that it's all resolved and I've retained my dignity with career intact, I'll fill you in on all the sordid details about Russell and his blackmailing harridan. Preferably up in your corner annexe, over another bottle of Sir Hugh's finest claret."

"Hmm, I can't wait! You bring the fags."

"And, you should get that man you are always writing to down here for the weekend. It's about time you lost your virginity. I can't give you any better advice than that!"

Hannah had the answer to unasked concerns about the Leslies and felt great relief for Alice, Russell and their son. She paused with her tea cup hovering in front of her mouth but didn't know where to begin expressing her love. As usual Alice said it for her, "Well hell, life has to go on, in amongst the bloody struggle for survival! Doesn't it?" Hannah's face was a picture of ironic, good humour.

"Alice Hughes – you are a force of nature! What happened to your sermon on spiritual guidance? Maintaining of moral standards? Or was that just your Daddy speaking. What was it he said? 'Once you lower them, they can never be raised again,' that one?"

"Hannah, the death rate is about to rise suddenly and exponentially. People of all ages and from all walks of life instinctively feel this. The Grim Reaper is about to have a street party in every town throughout Europe, indeed all around the world. Everyone is invited. Boys over eighteen will provide the main entertainment but no-one will be permitted to escape the raillery, or charades."

"Alright, you've lost me Alice – what's your point?"

"My prediction is that the birth rate will rise along with it."

"What? You think we should start doing our bit for king and country? Produce a fresh generation of canaille, for deployment sometime in the mid nineteen thirties? Hughes have you been at Christina's Old Bushmills."

"No, Hannah. That might be nice stuff but it's Protestant whiskey. Hughie drinks the Bushmills, Christina prefers Jameson."

"If you're hell bent on laying in for a wild party, you need to know that all Irish whisky is paraffin, Alice. Folks up in Morayshire use fractions of that quality as interior lighting fuel."

"You're helping to make my point for me, Hannah. Why is an appreciation of the finest liquor a traditionally male preserve?"

"Well, Hughie seems to have missed the point, drinking that awful Irish stuff."

"No, that's just expediency. He'd sup the devil's brew if it kept him in favour with his tenants back home in Monaghan."

"I'm at a disadvantage Alice. I've never stayed at the Leslie family home for any significant length of time," Alice ignored Hannah's objection, assuming it would soon be rectified with an extended visit, "And I fear she'd drink anything to forget her own feelings of inadequacy," ventured Hannah, with an expression of concern for both Christina and backsliding Alice.

"Good point. I'll try some of that too hen . . . hoos aboot you ih?" said Alice, in her most refined Sauchiehall Street drawl, lifting her china tea cup with a shuddering hand, pretending it was a slug of meths. Alice missed the point as ever, but Hannah's heart went out to her noble friend, retreating with her daughters into the sanatorium of magical Ireland.

Ten minutes later Maria Visconti, Alice's roomy eyed Italian understudy, stuck her head round the door to see what the cause of loud raucous laughter might be. At that precise instant, Alice and Hannah were chinking cut crystal whisky glasses before downing a taste of Christina's medicine with scrupulous salutations to their mentor, "That's beautiful! It's smoother than Bourbon and certainly not as sickly as that blended Scottish stuff," ventured Alice.

"I'll get you a bottle of Macallan the next time I'm near a spirit grocer in Edinburgh," promised Hannah with an indulgent smile.

At that moment they both looked up to see a leer of manifest disapproval in the line of Maria's lips. At sixteen, too young for finishing school but too precocious and elegantly lovely to remain at home in Northern Italy, she had been accommodated at her mother's behest by the ever indulgent Christina. Maria was to learn English from Hannah, and everything else pertaining to becoming a modern day 'lady in waiting' for an aristocratic family from Alice. Between them they had even conspired to find a housemaid's uniform, ostensibly so Maria would fit in while observing each job role, but also to deflect Mason from probing too deeply into her need to train abroad. Alice had scurrilously proposed that Maria might overhear gossip and act as a conduit for her mentor. In the girl's bright, calculating eyes was enough of misjudgement for Alice to want to face her down with a flea in her ear, despite Christina's caution that Maria was from, 'an extremely well connected, wealthy family.'

"What on earth do you think you're doing? Standing there looking like some disapproving Mother Superior? This is the urban home of a titled British family, not a convent in Lombardy. You should know better than to judge, Maria. Today is the National August Bank Holiday . . . and in case you didn't know, war has broken out with Austria and Germany."

"But not Italy!" retorted the still smiling Maria.

"And Alice Hughes has started on the road to perdition early," whispered Hannah.

Turning her face away to avoid giggling and giving further offence to Maria, Hannah felt she was committing a betrayal of good grace. Alice tried to suppress an explosion of laughter as Maria spun away. Hastily swallowing a sip of tea and a mouthful of the delicately flavoured, orange Gran Surtido that the child had brought in her trunk all the way from her palazzina overlooking the Ticino, Alice's veins stood out in warning on her forehead once again.

As Maria marched off briskly towards the kitchen to order another pot and more toast from Mrs Heap, arms swinging purposively with a glorious smile on her exquisite face, she was followed by peals of outrageous laughter. What Maria could not see as the heat of embarrassment rose in her chest was that Alice had spluttered tea and fruit cake all over the fine linen table cloth.

"Christina would certainly *not* approve of you eating and drinking in the same mouthful," challenged Hannah, "Invite Maria to join us and explain your outburst, as soon as she comes back!"

"I will, I will!" cried Alice, gasping for air as she fought hysterics, "She's just so *deliciously* forward. I think she's going to teach us!"

As Maria neared the safety of the kitchen she shook her head and laughed aloud, trying to recall the translation of a French proverb

When the cat's away . . .

After apologising profusely to Maria over breakfast and offering her a glass of whisky which she wisely declined, the women set off on a tour of the building with three year old Russell junior in tow. He pulled away from his mother at the top of the north wing corridor as they approached the stairs. Russell was missing the girls – especially his beloved mentor, Clarissa.

"Go wake 'issa Han! Mummy 'issa!" he kept saying, tugging at their skirts.

"Russell darling, Clarissa has gone with Helena and their mummy, for a little holiday on their own," explained Hannah.

Maria took Russell by the hand, "Come on Russell, you give me visita guidata!"

"Visita guidata!" parroted Russell and they sped off along the corridor to open all the vacant rooms and dive on the beds.

Hannah promised Alice that she would continue routines with Russell.

"Thanks Hannah, he needs structured activity. But I've already explained about them leaving," conferred Alice in an undertone, "He's just so used to them being around."

"I hope my absence didn't put too much pressure on?"

"No, not at all. Maria stepped in straight away. She really is an angel, even if she does think herself superior to us all. And I did my bit too. Now I have nothing much to think about apart from forwarding their letters, although Christina told me to open everything. After the contretemps between her and Hugh I kept out of the way. The girls didn't want to go to Ireland though." Alice stopped on the upper floor hallway to look up at Hannah. "I tried to help Christina turn it into 'an adventure' but she was extremely distraught."

"Was it that awful?"

Alice stared into Hannah's eyes, unable to describe the depth of what she had witnessed. "She collapsed on the floor, Hannah, begging him not to go. I never imagined such piteous heartbreak for a soul this side of the grave. Her howling must have shattered his confidence. She disappeared somewhere on her own all afternoon, after she'd roasted him. Helena knows of course."

"Helena knows everything. My only wish is I had been here to stick my oar in."

"Indeed she does. But no, some things are too intimate to get involved in. I suppose there was the incentive of them all travelling together as a family for the last time. It really is too sad Hannah, all of it."

"Last time? What are you implying Hughes?" Hannah stood rooted to the spot – her face as rigid in perplexity as the weathered side of a galvanised water tank, "Oh Jesus, Lord of my heart – not again!" Hannah's expression appeared set in place to meet an eternity of suffering. Alice was afraid her friend had stopped breathing. She was three years old again, looking out of a train window at receding forests of her beloved Morayshire homeland, although now able to meticulously recall how badly young children accept bereavement and radical change in their family life.

"Christina just knows. They both know," was all Alice could bring herself to say. Hannah realised that this was a revelation of the truth too enormous for Alice to broach, even with a bottle of finest Cote du Rhone to loosen her tongue.

Turning attention to mutable smiles of her little boy as he returned with Maria, Alice declared gaily, "We might be going over Ireland to live with them soon! You're going to love living in a castle, Russell."

"Can daddy come too?" he asked without hesitation, understanding imperatives of familial operation that war and occupation tend to trample across.

"Well, maybe he could visit but he has the Co-op to run don't forget, otherwise people like Mrs Heap wouldn't have enough food to make all our nice meals," Alice glanced at Hannah with pain in her eyes, "Okay . . . let's check up for Hughie that there's no burglars hiding in the bedrooms!"

Russell Junior led the way down the generous north stairway, two paces to each tread, still holding tightly to his mother's hand as Maria and Hannah skipped after them.

They checked all three main stairways to three floors, each with branches East and West. Then with nothing better to do than idly discuss plans for a party, they wandered around, inspecting eight entrances and all of twenty or more rooms and basements.

"I swear I've never seen the interior of half of these rooms!" objected Hannah, "I need a diagram. Look, there's even a first floor laundry room! Did you ever come up here?"

"Yes and there's a galley kitchen, buts sssh keep your voice low, or Mason will hear us! We don't want *her* offering Maria the guided tour, with her bunch of keys jangling like a prison warden. After all this is really her job."

As sunlight shafted through an east facing bedroom window, Hannah felt a prevailing, indefinable sense of temporal shift. Good intentions were already trapped in lost moments in this harmonious house. The sounds of a generation of brave, happy voices had already fallen to silence with an accretion of endless dust no-one noticed. Forgotten and cold, charitable love would soon be forever fossilised in wood, stone and glass.

Fascinated, they dwelt in the crèche suite of bedrooms, marvelling at a customised range of scaled-down furniture - divans; wardrobes; desks and chairs as well as custom made bathroom fitments provided for the Leslie girls - as if they had never had time to look at them properly until this very moment. The crèche was in fact a suite of graduated smaller and larger rooms with both east and westward aspects. Opposite, looking out on the front of the house was a large playroom and classroom equipped for art and drama. Smaller dormitory rooms, including Russell's, were thoughtfully equipped with heavy drapes which would allow an infant to sleep at any time during the day.

"Remarkable really," suggested Hannah, "These drapes are double faced and lined! This could be an amateur photographer's dark room."

In each of the crèche rooms they visited, Russell sped across the floor to jump onto the bed.

"Should I stop him?" asked Alice.

"There's a moment for that I think, Alice. But not now. This is his child's exuberance. If he does it when Clarissa is here *she* will tell him off."

Alice laughed teasingly, "But you'll tell me when to draw the line? You were sent by Gaia, the Earth Mother! Even Christina looks to you for advice."

While checking security of windows in the children's en-suite bathroom they laughed uproariously about personal recollections of perching on a porcelain rim in a freezing outhouse, as 'trainee bog users.' Maria and Russell laughed flamboyantly along with them. As a trainee himself the child knew the score.

With a little poetic licence, Alice asserted that both she and Hannah were 'broken in' to adult self-care routines with use of the 'Ideal Standard' pan – still a modern day luxury.

"Thees is signorile, il lusso! In Lombardy they have hole in the floor!" said Maria with a wry smile, "Jou are molto fortunato!"

Alice had another opportunity to rail against convention, whilst speculating about change, "Who the heck decides these things Hannah? Some national plumber's convention? Or a specialist team in a back room at Whitehall? I mean what *is* the standard size of a citizen's BTM?"

"I don't know Alice. I'd hazard that duty falls to the British Standards Association. Maybe Thomas Crapper himself was co-opted onto the board at some time – no pun intended."

"Roughly how large was Crappers bum?" asked Alice in a scurrilous undertone, glancing over to check that Russell was still playing with Clarissa's dolls in the bedroom.

"Slightly larger than average, I think."

"That would explain a lot! But why is there no apparent choice in such matters?" demanded Alice vehemently, "I mean a seat is a seat, large, or small but no-one wants to fall down a big hole as a child."

"Hmm, true enough Alice, especially if the hole is full of ordure."

"My point precisely . . . or roll off the edge, as an overgrown adult could in a moment of urgent need."

"God forbid! Or slide into the bowl in the dark after the man of the house has left the seat up."

"Yes, terrifying! But as a mother that's not my main concern. I mean, why don't they make them with two different sized swivel seats on top of the pan? Top one with a high sided, small circumference, shaped for little botties?"

"Yes, dead simple! And make the whole dratted thing lower?"

"Right but like you say that could present problems for going in the dark after too many sloe gins. Maybe it should be on an adjustable plinth? Or have removable steps leading up to it, for wee doots like Russell Junior to rest their feet on?"

"At least you no have caviglia rota, how you say, nel buio?" asked Maria, lifting her black-stockinged leg and pointing to a shapely ankle.

Hannah translated, "We don't have the hazard of breaking a leg in the dark, she says." Alice laughed deliciously at the image but accused her new friend of exaggerating.

"Draw some working diagrams Alice. Russell can help. Send them to Mr Davis at Shires in Guiseley. You remember - the factory where the women on piece-work regaled us with stories of how slowly men work?"

"Oh yes, and the bullying tactics of Police in London. How vivid their stories were!"

"I read in the business column that Shires have a mission to civilise the colonies by bringing conveniences into the Twentieth Century. They may well be interested in your design suggestions."

"Yes, so they should be. Being young is purgatory. No-one really cares how you feel."

Linking arms they wandered down into the suite of dining rooms: family and functional, morning and evening. Russell raced ahead buzzing his lips to make the sound of his model 20 horse power Daimler. Maria followed excitedly, happy to build on the false assumption that she was pre-occupied by children. He invited her out onto the lawn to show her the Japanese carp pond, recently stocked with brightly coloured Nishikigoi.

"Well that was a far cry from talking about Shakespeare," sighed Alice, her face drawn tight after laughing so much.

"Yeah, and you never mentioned the Scottish play! No, Alice, no! Enough foreboding for one day."

They opened huge Canadian Maple sliding partitions, opening onto a magnificent, matching parquet floored ballroom. Strong summer light flooded down from a glorious domed atrium above the east side entrance of the house. The pillared, marble-floored lobby gave way through the ballroom onto a huge glass walled summer room with gentle lawns beyond.

The effect of being able to see right through the vast house from vestibule to gardens, with its mixture of colours and textures from the entrance to the woodland below the lawns, was invariably stunning. No medieval castle or baroque palace expressed this combination of harmonious entreaties to the eye within such a relatively human scale. Alice told Maria, "Allerton Grange rivals the finest houses of the modern era around the world, including the USA." She knew first hand, because she had been inside dozens of them.

In the reception hall blue-grey Sienna wall panelling contrasted onyx and white tiles, framing half a dozen Carrera marble carvings of classical provenance, inviting the visitor away from stairways left and right. Warmth of wood and flashing brilliance of glass chandeliers glimpsed in the adjacent ballroom, led the eye to Naiads protecting fountains flanking greens and yellows of the central summer room.

Decorative foliage of magnificent trees, young and old, surrounding a natural lake visible through the house bestowed an overriding presence of Mother Nature, tangible just beyond ten panel French doors. Allerton Grange was permeated with a magical, joyous harmony, uniquely conversant with the understated Leslie family and everyone privileged to know or work with them. It was testimony to the playful, accommodating mind of its brilliant young architect – the now middle-aged, Sir Hugh Leslie.

Alice went straight to the piano and started to hammer out a clipped and strident excerpt from Beethoven's Fifth Symphony and Hannah's laughter echoed in harmony with the gallant attempt. Russell stopped his car engine noises to look back and laugh at his mother too. The ostentatious, patterned floor - relieved of rugs in readiness for stripping and polishing while rain held off - helped to flatten Alice's slack resonances. For once exquisite woodblock with its deadening acoustics, was winning a token battle in its lost war with musical soirees and stilettos.

Alice stopped playing to look pensively across the immense space at Hannah, sprawled across a leather couch beneath the coloured glass dome. The cupola above bridged Romanesque stonework, atop curving walls of four adjacent rooms. Alice could see beyond her friend to the palatial lobby with curving stairways, embracing Odysseus returned from his voyages. She could also see Il Spinario in white Carrara, Ming Dynasty porcelain vases and mediaeval Arabian fruit bowls, resonantly attractive against blue veined Italian marble cladding. A priceless and revered twelfth century golden Shiva danced opposite a fifty year old Shibata Zeshin lacquered table. Above the wall-panels, frameless Japanese cranes kissed the sky in adulation as they flew over mountain peaks.

Alice was awed by the subtle effectiveness of Lady Christina's inclusive artistic vision – hers was Cheruit's Paris Belle, on the front cover of Bon Ton Gazette - in bluff contrast to a Yorkshire millionaire's self-styled mediaeval castle that she'd accompanied her to a few years before.

"A bugger to heat in winter," both intoned at roughly the same moment, gloomily quoting Sir Hugh whenever Christina asked for the partition to be opened. Complementary laughter rose softly, as early August sun offered enticement above the glass dome between fluffy white clouds.

"I could fit my entire house in here, gardens an' all," observed Hannah, gesturing only to dimensions of the ballroom.

"I'll never be rich," Alice resolved, with a tinge of regret.

"Nope, neither will I," concurred Hannah, "But you never need to be Alice, as long as you reconcile your personal life with Christina's itinerary."

"Hey, I've got an idea. Let's go into town tonight and pick up a couple of soldiers before they leave for France. Wouldn't that be exciting?" Shaking her head Hannah laughed, as though Alice was a younger sister in need of confinement. With moribund green eyes gazing and voice echoing as in a well, reminiscent of the out of tune piano, Hannah counselled, "Be careful what you wish for Alice Hughes . . . it may just come true!"

"Oh Hannah! You miss the point, I'm talking about giving, not taking!"

In a moment of silence they stared earnestly across the vast space - each young woman reading a different kind of compassion in the other. Then at last Hannah cracked a smile and gales of laughter resumed, echoing through the living heart of the house, under cold breath from an armorial stained glass emblem bearing the family motto - *Grip Fast.*

Sir Hugh Leslie took his young family to the Castle in Monaghan. He ordered fires lit, then called on the butcher and grocer to arrange deliveries. He discreetly gave gratuities to several village residents, to discourage them from leaving. Then after a dozen terse conversations, he went by car overnight to Moore Park in Cork.

Unresolved arguments with Christina had been fixed, temporarily at least, when he explained his strategic role in ensuring the movement of men and materiel. But Hughie knew he was buying her off with his sad, loyalist gallantry. Driving south through misty, winding lanes north of Dublin with his chauffeur Ackroyd dozing beside him, Hugh saw again the downward curl of Christina's open lips warning him that she felt let down.

At Moore Park there was refresher training on logistics and command structure, to go with his field commission. Hugh wrote to Christina saying, "My soul is in suspension to the most awful nonsense of my adult life but I really have no alternative. They need me!"

When the doctrinaire business of commanding regiments of Royal Engineers in the field was over, Sir Hugh caught a train to Dublin and the ferry to Liverpool, at the end of the first week in September. He had a few personal effects to collect at home, before finishing business on Monday morning with his Board of Directors and family Trustees in Liverpool.

Thus it was that on a Saturday night, or early Sunday morning - neither Alice nor Hannah thought too much about details at the time - six weeks after the family's departure to Ireland, they saw Hughie for the last time.

Alice had found the gramophone, one of Hughie's new toys and set it up in the drawing room at the front of the house. A small group of smiling couples danced energetically over near the doors from the atrium, open in welcoming embrace to the main entrance hall. Several wine glasses were carelessly arranged across the priceless Japanese table.

In dismay Hughie told his Orderly to wait in the car. Inviting Lieutenant Whitaker his Adjutant into the library to wait, he pointed to the drinks cabinet and told the lad to help himself.

"Don't be shy, Paul. You've been here before, so make yourself at home. Clearly there is some sort of celebration going on, so there may well be supper available."

"Oh no, Sir Hugh, thank you anyhow. I ate well before you picked me up."

Whitaker was a Traffic Manager from L&NWR, whom Hugh knew to be reliable and confident if still a little green. He had asked Corps HQ at Chatham for someone who understood operational priorities and when they threw the request back at Sir Hugh, Whitaker was the obvious choice. Both men shared a commitment to the Territorials, who allowed them to re-train together in preparation for the 'real thing'. A lot would depend on lads like Paul, and Hugh planned to keep him close. After all, if Whitaker survived the war it would help his career.

Hugh strode through the crowd of chattering, laughing revellers without a glance. Russell was hammering out a stirring human cavalry charge from Offenbach on the gratefully retuned Steinway. A scattering of friends and acquaintances the evening had thrown up were comfortably, if not quite decorously, spread around the ballroom. People smoked and chatted outside on broad patios flanking a pair of illuminated fountains, to left and right of the conservatory opposite the sun rooms. A warm hubbub of conversation underlying the music was infrequently punctuated by shrill laughter from two or three overstated women.

Food was laid out on a large table, between islands of cane and wrought-iron garden room furniture and, as ever, Mrs Heap had been generous on Alice's instruction. The spread looked and smelled good to Hughie. He picked up a slice of quiche Lorraine which he ate as he searched the diverse crowd for sight of Hannah Harper. Outside he found more revellers spread out across pleasantly floodlit acres of lawn. Some had found their way into various other, more private parts of the house. In that instant Hannah appeared at his side.

"Sir Hugh! I wish we'd known you were coming. I hope you don't find this too much of an intrusion. Do you want me to ask them all to leave?"

"Oh! Hannah! Good Lord, why ever would you? No! I was looking for you. I have letters from Christina and the girls. There is one for Alice, which I will oblige you to give her when she is less pre-occupied. My only concern is that I'm clearly missing out on a damned good party. Christina will be jealous. D'you know, to my detriment I never realised you had so many fine friends," confessed Hugh with a conspiratorial smile.

Speaking quietly he instructed Hannah to investigate occupancy of his bedroom, as a prelude to collecting certain personal effects prior to departure for Chatham.

"Do that small thing first, then come back and I will tell you what I need. Go now, thank you Hannah."

Hughie was too much of a gentleman to mention the couple he'd glimpsed ten minutes earlier, copulating languidly in front of a blazing fire in the master bedroom.

Brevet Colonel Sir Hugh Leslie stood anonymously amid swirls of raucous party laughter in his rough, demeaning field uniform. Sitting on a decorative low stone wall rather than finding a party chair, Hugh left his hat on to avoid giving the wrong impression that he might indeed be planning to stay for a time in his own house. He looked and felt like a walk-on minor in one of Russell's more ambitious costume dramas.

Everyone ignored Hugh, apart from Alice whom he felt it best to avoid speaking to at this precise moment in order to save her obvious embarrassment. For once Alice was both mortified and speechless. With fingers held over her mouth in shock, she looked every inch a fallen angel in her sky blue chiffon frock. Russell, the creditable love of her life, played on obliviously beside her at the keys. Alice rose to approach Sir Hugh but he shook his head, holding up his right hand like a policeman at a busy junction, warning her away. Alice's embarrassment could wait until his own had been resolved.

Hughie fumed silently at the unfortunate turn of events in Europe, exasperated at the undue pressure it put upon him and his railway company, L&NWR. Britain's participation in the war couldn't really happen without him and a very small handful of similar entrepreneurs. He needed to get there quickly to organise it, or both France and Belgium would be lost.

Alice's party was interesting to see nonetheless, seemingly more of a carnival than an 'at home' evening. Her guests were clearly enjoying themselves, despite the informality. It needed something more however

– a professional dance band and fireworks on the lawn, Hugh imagined. He was used to moving in every type of loose social setting - after hunts; with local families and with dozens of servants during the festive season; at never ending baptismal celebrations and wakes in relatively more traditional Ireland. But right now he had no time for small talk about Alice's party planning.

Christina will scold me for sure for my lack of social graces but I don't care.

Rising briskly he turned a stolid shoulder on Alice's worried look, marching off through the drawing room towards the library. He hadn't time to indulge in imagining Christina's predictable objections.

'Does Alice have enough money for overheads?' Clearly she does. 'How's baby Russell? Is the little chap missing my girls? Are the household staff happy? Oh and by the way, get Mr Laine to check there are no stains left on the Indian rug in our bedroom.'

When Hannah finally re-appeared from tucking in Russell Junior, who had been disturbed by all the noise, Hugh ushered her into the library. Having introduced her to Whitaker, he tersely explained what he had to do.

"I have some business in town, possibly today if I can crash in uninvited on certain Board members. First thing Monday morning at the latest. So tonight I will stay at the Railway Hotel. We have already booked in there Hannah, so don't imagine for one moment that I am put out by your wonderful soiree. Following those meetings, I head south to the Corps of Royal Engineers HQ at Chatham. There I will collect orders for my posting, with the General Staff or one of the railway companies."

"Have you any idea of where?"

"No dear girl, not as such, but thank you for asking. I half expect to be sent to building works at Richborough in Kent, or hopefully Paris."

Without being asked Hannah took a crystal tumbler from the drinks cabinet, "Would you care to join the Lieutenant?" she asked rhetorically. Hugh nodded and she sloshed the glass full of fine, vintage malt hidden from Christina's view at the back of the cabinet where he always secreted it behind the Bushmills. Sir Hugh took it from her gratefully without comment and Hannah left the decanter out. Whitaker was plainly astounded.

Taking a step back Hannah curtseyed in respect, like a traditional Highland dancer – something taught at school that was never expected by Christina. Hugh pretended not to notice but the strangeness of that enduring image burned through his animus more surely than all the whisky he eagerly consumed that evening. He smiled affectionately at Hannah. Hughie was momentarily back to himself again, despite the unpleasantly inimical turn his life had taken over recent weeks.

With precise and diplomatic instruction on what to say, Hannah scurried off again in the direction of the Leslie's bedroom. Hugh stood like a pillar of stone. Mind and Body singing with the atomic patience of aeons he gazed out over treetops past the warm lights of Liverpool to the black Mersey Estuary beyond. He sucked hard at the rich brandy-like Rosebank Hannah had poured for him.

I will need to pull myself together. That poor child sees me as a man in shock.

In sorrow and confusion Hugh resolutely ignored people wandering in and out looking for a bathroom to clean themselves up after coitus or be sick from too much drink. At last he turned to Whitaker, whose brow was knit into a defensive ridge. Clearly the revelry irked Paul. Large round ears jutting out from a large and fair-mopped head gave him the look of a rugby player. Whitaker was going to be an ideal second wife – at least in the platonic, celibate dimensions upon which any good relationship depended.

Hughie initiated an urgent monologue that might teach Paul something of logistics, "Richborough will be no good for us Lieutenant. The CRE can plan that without me. That's not the main event as such.

It's just a way of sorting the predictable traffic jam. I shall ask for HQ liaison in France, where I might make a difference."

"Yes sir. Sounds good to me!"

"There's a war on but nobody here wants it. They can't relate to this damned fiasco over bloody Serbia. I can't understand why the Austrians are doing this, Whitaker can you?"

"No sir, I mean who would start a war when they are sure to lose it? Same with the Germans – I really don't know what they stand to gain."

"I think you'll find *their* motives have something to do with internal politics old chap. Forty Socialist MP's elected to the Reichstag no less. That and their sabre-rattling idiot of a Kaiser."

"Well it seems to have kicked off slowly while you've been away - I was told by our senior management that we can't get men through the assembly areas fast enough, Sir - in either direction, as it happens."

Whitaker walked over to Sir Hugh, imagining proximity might reassure him in his unambiguously distraught state. Hugh sat down on a leather bound armchair by the fire and poked fading embers to stir some heat. Whitaker bent over slowly, like a man three times his age, as he sat on a chair at the other side of the hearth. Hugh realised the lad was depressed too.

"There is still a latent misconception, especially amongst military men, that wars are fought and won by individuals on battlefields; as opposed to the reality that battlefields are forward defences for key resource areas where men and all the essential materiel are stockpiled."

"Yes, I know it Sir . . . Without preparation no satisfactory outcome will be achieved."

Hugh looked at Whitaker approvingly and took a swig of his Rosebank. Whitaker, who had been nursing his drink while waiting for the boss, knocked his back in one. Hugh motioned to offer a refill so the lad reached gladly for the decanter to do the honours, smiling as he sat back at his first sniff of the glorious malt. Hugh stretched his legs out in front of him.

"War is analogous to direct competition between large industries. In principle it all reduces to the dynamics of flow - the science of commercial distribution with an additional layer of violence; relabelled 'warfare' – nothing more."

"There *are* the dynamics of the conflict on the battlefield to consider Sir, don't you think? I mean, the comparative quality of opposing forces, and so on?"

"Yes, to some degree of course Paul, but unless one side is overcommitted battles are rarely decisive. Caesar and Cromwell understood this precept well. Napoleon never quite accepted the reality," mused Hughie, stirring his topped up tumbler to warm it in his hands, "He neglected his navy then failed to consolidate Prussia and Poland as way-stations for the Grande Armee's assault on Moscow. How long do you think it will take for the notion to crystallise this time?"

"I don't know sir, I'd hate to be critical without the ribbons to go with the opinions." Hughie laughed at Whitaker's sense of fealty, before continuing the interrogative.

"I mean specifically, how long for half-hearted time servers in their braided uniforms to admit that such basic concepts of logistics have eluded them thus far and consider stepping aside?"

Whitaker looked considerately at his Director of Operations, who coincidentally happened to be commander of his notional but not yet fully commissioned Railway Company. Paul decided to keep his mouth shut – thinking of the braid.

"Good Christ help us, Whitaker! We need a new organisation man!" Sir Hugh growled forlornly.

"You mean the 8th Railway Company Sir?"

"No, Whitaker. I mean the entire British Army."

When Hannah appeared back in the library she touched Sir Hugh's shoulder gently in order not to interrupt his diatribe against the Old Contemptibles. When he'd run out of steam he turned to look up at her. "The lovers have gone for a smoke in the woods," she informed him softly.

"Oh good! Thank you for doing that. They must be exhausted. Come on lad . . . you can help me carry some of this stuff."

Both men drained their glasses, offering one another a knowing half smile. With few opportunities left to imbibe, they might resume later in the hotel bar. Sir Hugh and Whitaker followed Hannah silently upstairs and she asked them over her shoulder what they would like from the kitchen. When both declined, she skipped away to get them each a plate regardless and to make sandwiches for the train. Hannah had the impression that Hugh's board members and legal advisors might actually meet with him at his hotel, outside of normal business hours as there would be Trust matters to clarify contingent upon his failure to return. In any event the reluctant hero seemed hard pressed with changing horses in mid-stream. She could see that Hugh was suffering the most forlorn detachment.

Sir Hugh stared out of the bedroom window that Hannah had opened to allow the room to air. Fresh sheets had been hastily put on the bed on the off chance he might change his mind about leaving. Indifferent to squeals and calls of revellers enjoying the scented air of his lawns and private woodlands, in fearful anticipation Hugh's scattered vision was precisely where Right and Glory might lead.

Seeing the imagined horror in his eyes, Lieutenant Whitaker asked, "Can I help in any way, Sir?"

"Just give me a moment lad," he replied softly, "I had this place built you know . . . after I inherited my father's title in ninety nine. It was my first major architectural project," Hugh turned to look at Whitaker with a smile, "I'm rather proud of it you know . . . Sit!" commanded Hugh, politely ushering his Adjutant to a chair across the other side of the vast bedroom.

Hugh propped his backside on the radiator in front of the window ledge, waiting as Hannah whisked in with a tray for them and departed as quickly without a word.

"What do you make of this insightful statement, Whitaker?" He spoke as if quoting from a handbook, 'Medical evacuees and troop trains are the opposing soccer fans, swapping ends at half time in the Cup Final.'"

"Who said that Sir?"

"One sage EO, appropriately enough named Marshall, made this apt declaration at my initial briefing at Chatham."

"I think he knew his stuff sir. Did he spell his name with an s – h?"

"Ha ha, yes of course! 'No-one is going anywhere in a hurry!' he told them, 'We are the well-meaning stewards, charged with keeping them apart.' What worries me is the sheer inspirational depth of Marshall's understatement. If it was the Cup Final, there would not be thousands of men bleeding to death."

"Unless it was Shelbourne versus Bohemians."

"Ha! Most apt Whitaker . . . But there *would* be thousands of extra Bobbies and a fleet of special trains and buses. This whole damned affair needs organising properly you see - from timetables to track laying, tunnels, trains. Hospital trains, troop trains, armoured trains. L&NWR have had sixty eight years to develop our level of understanding and expertise on handling such requirements. The BEF expect us to put our knowledge into practice in an equivalent number of days."

"Where do you see the biggest problem lying Sir?" Paul's eager eyes betrayed the false notion that Hugh might be talking about something that was actually within the realms of the possible.

"I'm not sure who presents the greater difficulty for us in meeting this challenge – parochial French rail authorities, or the professionally asinine BEF. What I do know, is that this feels like the most important task of my life."

"I imagine so, Sir. Men will die in their thousands if we fail to provide the distribution support."

"The word is already out man. The press latched on to it as soon as it finally became clear that 'war' meant men would actually get hurt. Targeting the French railways was their way of doing something for the war effort, which everyone at home would support."

Sir Hugh reached into his briefcase to hand Whitaker a newspaper cartoon showing skeletons stretched out in a railway station waiting room. One brave soul gasping his last breath was murmuring a little recently acquired Francais, in his flat Bradford drawl,

'Pardonay mwa Mushoor, a quelle heur arrive le chemin prochaine a Dunkirk?' An exasperated fellow wearing a railway inspector's cap pushed back on his head replied, 'I am sorry mon ami, zat was ze last train twelve hours ago!' There had really been no need for a caption –

sardonically glaring bones, draped in uniforms and bandages told the story.

Hugh explained to Whitaker that he wasn't sure what personal effects he was looking for – he hadn't time to think deeply about it, "After all it's just a prolonged business trip with restricted bar and restaurant service."

"You sound optimistic, Sir."

"Optimism is good Paul. Now where are the riding boots Christina had made for me? Damn, I took them to Ireland! What else? The silver framed photo of Christina and the one of the girls. Pity there's not a family group shot instead. Hell, is that too sentimental, Paul? We might have to share a billet with some fluffy faced public school oik from the Home Counties. They'll laugh at me for an old fool. You're a family man aren't you?"

"Yes sir. Two ankle biters. Joe aged four and Nathaniel fifteen months."

Sir Hugh held up the ostentatious silver frame, "Do I take this?" He vacillated, trying to imagine life near the front. Then without waiting for an answer he fumbled with the back of the frame, tearing the card to get at the picture of his wife which he stuffed into his wallet. Hugh realised with a jolt that he'd subliminally absorbed stories read and heard from the first wounded men returning from the front.

There can be no doubt – it's going to be hell.

Sir Hugh noticed his own hands shaking. He looked again at the photo of Helena and Clarissa, forever blinking in summer light, hesitating as he wondered what the girls would say if they witnessed his unseemly behaviour. Like a transient invader, Hugh ripped through the cardboard backing of that framed picture too. He patted the edge of the photograph to make it fit in his wallet.

Opening the wall safe he took out a clutch of bills of varying denominations which he slid into the pocket of his uniform jacket, "Money is ammunition Lieutenant. Always have it ready for use."

"Quite so Sir, I shall."

403

Bush . . . Where can I get a bottle of Old Bushmills without encountering Alice or a member of her retinue? The guest room next door – in the hospitality bureau! I must remember to keep one in our bedroom in future.

"Excuse me lad . . . I've just thought of something important, pertaining to our mutual comfort on the journey. I'll be back in a jiffy."

Thinking in circles of indeterminate need that could not be specified, Hugh felt like a child missing his mother. Opening the bottle he held it to his lips to gulp down some of the oily whiskey, then reached for a glass and immediately poured himself another. Sitting down heavily on the compliant mattress in the empty room, he allowed his racing mind to slow. Images continued to bubble to the surface for attention but Hugh could not get to what lay beneath it all.

In a long moment of agonising prescience came a vision of faces and voices of people he knew, places he had been. Foremost was Christina, the love of his life, whom he missed so desperately. Christina, joyous and effete; fulfilled yet without true ambition - definable only in the most subtle of romantic terms, like a masterpiece by a great artist. Hugh's dear family and gentle friends came flooding into his mind in turn. How good it had all been!

"And how bloody sad it all has to end like this. I drink to you all!" he murmured.

Hugh raised his glass to swallow again, then poured another for the road. Taking the bottle back to his bedroom he handed it to Whitaker to pack in the valise next to him where he sat near the bed. They went to find Hannah, sitting at a discreet distance on a lovers chair in an alcove at the bottom of the stairway. Beside her on the floor was a hamper she'd found in the kitchen, filled with randomly amassed items of food for two, all wrapped in greaseproof paper. There was also a bottle of claret and one of Brandy she doubted would ever be repatriated to France.

Hannah stood to offer her hand but Hugh ignored it, hugging her instead and kissing her gently on the forehead. Folding her arms, she whispered an apology for the raucous party and stilted farewell, "I'm

404

sure Mrs Heap and all the staff will be annoyed, knowing that they missed you," she warned.

Hughie shook his head, "Can't be helped Hannah! Be sure to tell Alice she has done nothing wrong at all – this is merely bloody awful timing. She can hold me responsible for not telephoning, or writing. For my part, I blame the Wheels of Fate and the Ministry for War."

"Not Gavrilo Princip?"

"No, certainly not Gavrilo Princip. Now go back to your guests Hannah and make sure they are properly fed and watered. Offer them breakfast, or patent medicines as required in the morning. Can't have any of them decrying Leslie hospitality can we?"

Hughie looked in her eyes and smiled wistfully one last time, before skipping off through the reception hall like a public school boy obliged to join a much vaunted team game. Hannah noticed his attaché case flapping in his fist and Whitaker, eager to impress, racing ahead carrying the wicker hamper. In the absence of Laine the Butler, given the night off by Alice, Hannah skipped ahead lightly to hold the front door open for them.

Oblivious to the sad melodrama unwinding within earshot, Russell Evans was hammering out a version of the dramatic overture from Tchaikovsky's 1812 overture. Hannah was sure the world had gone completely mad and that the devil walked abroad in the night.

Whitaker whistled to alert the waiting orderly, who was leaning against the car smoking. The driver had judiciously parked twenty yards away from the unwelcome attention of drunken people drifting in and out of the front portico. Hannah heard a clipped formal exchange and the crunch of Sir Hugh's short legs moving rapidly across the gravel. There was the banging of car doors, the cough of a gigantic Humber engine and the whine of gears. She waved but Hughie did not look back; he'd already kissed her and said farewell.

The Autumn of '14 in Monaghan was fraught with a kind of glorious indigence for Hannah. She wasn't so much at the mercy of Christina's listlessness given the absence of three members of her family, as the bureaucrats handling her house purchase in Edinburgh. Clarissa had gone to Dublin to join Helena at a preparatory school, although both returned home every weekend. But the already sombre atmosphere of Castle Leslie suddenly turned leaden for Hannah with arrival of the post on Saturday, 28th November.

Alice handed her the letter with familiar fine handwriting and she tore it open casually, not imagining sorrowful news would come from William's quarter.

"Nothing gloomy from home I trust?" cautioned Alice, "A boy from the village was killed at Ypres, so the community here will be in mourning. Also there is bad news within the Leslie family. Christina told me Hugh's brother Edgar is missing. His unit were cut off at a place called Neuve Chapelle. Hugh promises to give an update on whether they were relieved."

"Well Alice, I hope he's rescued okay," Hannah replied starkly. Reading her stunned expression as she looked up from William's letter, Alice said, "Oh, I'm sorry . . . you have bad news too?"

Hannah didn't speak. Instead she handed Alice the letter from William, detailing bad news from his brother Peter stationed at Nonne Boschen Wood near Ypres, "So Peter is okay? He says they cut down thousands of the enemy's best troops."

"Read on!"

"'. . . my brother Jim's squad was lost without trace,' Oh Hannah! I imagine they will spend winter in some freezing compound in the Black Forest. No doubt with thousands of poor French and Belgian captives. But at least he's alive. Always remain optimistic - it really works!"

"Yes, of course Alice. I agree, in principle. I'll tell William what you said."

Hannah was glad of an excuse to return home in advance of the Winter Festival, purportedly to sign papers for the solicitor authenticating the source of her funds and confirming she had paid tax on her income. Margaret was cutting up tinsel with little John in the living room when Hannah emerged from a Monday morning lie–in.

"I've been looking forward to the holiday since transferring to General Nursing last September," Margaret explained, "They need all the trained medical staff they can get in the convalescent wards and . . .

it hasn't been easy I can tell you. Harper collected this for me in the car," she added, nodding at a partially decorated Christmas tree adorning the front room near the window. It was something given in to, primarily because they'd seen a massive one in Jenners which her dear son was captivated by, she explained with the casual grace of someone used to an excess of income.

"Anyway, I think this is a lovely tradition."

"Yes, it's just a pity the trees don't have a root ball. Then you could plant it in a tub for next year."

"Well, even if it does die, the English all do it – and as you know my dad is English, so . . . I quite like the idea. Although it will create a mess on the carpet!"

"You'll just have to get Harper to buy you a Hoover vacuum cleaner!"

John Junior was so full of expectation he even had a letter of request penned for Santa Claus.

The bulletin concerning Hugh's brother Edgar had come that morning, on the third day of Hannah's visit home, along with a flurry of seasonal cards in the run up to Christmas and Hogmanay. Weeping silently, Hannah sat down on a chair unable to find words to express her sorrow. Margaret wisely directed her child back to compiling his list for Santa. Hannah sucked in a gulp of air to compose herself.

"The mail came late," she whispered thinly, shaking her head and holding up a hand, intent on starting her explanation again. Margaret stood mystified in the doorway, wiping fingers on her apron.

John was eager to continue baking ginger men with his ma, but went with Margaret's whispered prompt to add something to his list for Hannah.

"Our mail d'you mean? He's always late because we're on top of the hill."

Hannah cleared her throat and started again with a stronger voice, "Sorry, Margaret, I meant their mail. I only met Edgar a couple of times because he was studying in Dublin but he was charming," Hannah's explanation tailed off as she wiped her tearful eyes with a handkerchief. Margaret waited patiently for her to resume.

"They were expecting him home on leave the very day the sad news arrived in the post."

"Aaaw that's terrible! How heartrending." It seemed to Hannah that Margaret had never appeared so shocked. Clearly reports of Hugh and Christina's magnanimous character had captured her imagination. In fact Margaret told everyone she knew all about the pre-eminent Anglo-Irish family. The Leslies were not just three dimensional celebrities - they were luminaries, greater than any star of stage or screen. As a General Nurse Margaret's compassionate heart was now open to the sky. Even in a moment of mutual distress, Hannah was amazed to witness that soft centre. Margaret sat down on a chair as if all life's energy had been snatched from her heart, her eyes filling with tears. She hunched her shoulders in a moment of empathy for Hugh and Christina.

Without realising it, in that moment of humility the energetically dowdy Margaret had never been as attractive as an individual. Silent attentions from Harper when he drifted into the room served to confirm the impression as he reached down to caress Margaret's head. Pent up sorrow from five months of oppression in her daily routines was released in a gasp of momentary, quite frightening grief. She looked up appealingly to Hannah, who stood up to huddle with her and Harper. Harper looked at his daughter questioningly to explain Margaret's distress . . . so Hannah read Alice's letter aloud with a stumbling voice.

"Staff working for the family swear they saw Sir Edgar arrive home, waving and smiling as he walked up the lane with kit bag slung over a shoulder. They say he headed straight for the pub in the village, presumably to slake his thirst after such a long journey. Word came up to the house from the Head Gardener and there was a tremendous buzz of excitement. Stoves were lit and a fire built in his room. Late blossoms were ordered from the greenhouse – Irises, Daphne and Honeysuckle cut and arranged. Helena and Clarissa ran into the village to greet their uncle and get him to buy them a cream soda."

The room seemed to darken momentarily with the silence as Hannah's voice slowed to a halt and she gazed in astonishment at the letter in her hand. Harper spoke up to make it a little easier for Hannah to relate Christina's story, "But he never came? Is that it? Lord, how woefully disappointing!"

"He wasn't ready to go," observed Margaret, "He had his whole life in front of him!"

"Then the telegram was delivered," said Hannah. Sitting in stunned silence, all three paid dread deference to the imperious telegram.

When little John ran in with his Christmas list conversation suddenly energised, as if nothing bad had happened.

"Why ever did he join? He didn't need to. No-one should join!" said Margaret fiercely, thinking of her volunteer work at the Royal Infirmary.

"Tradition," mumbled Hannah.

"Say again?" requested Harper, for once needing clarification.

"Tradition, Daddy. Leslies always lead. Christina told me so. Sir Hugh and his brother Edgar felt obliged to set an example to local people, in volunteering for King and Country. Not that Hugh wanted any of *them* to go. Christina told me he went round the cottages expressly forbidding it. Hugh always plays both ends against the middle. On the other hand, I imagine he managed to persuade himself that expertese in running a rail network was indispensable. But he is no soldier." Hannah looked up at Harper who could see an old familiar pride, sparking again in his daughter's eyes, "They don't realise what they are committing to – none of them. They set off to war as though it's a game."

Hannah's assertion struck a chord for Margaret, who had sat on the end of the sofa to read her son's letter to Santa. Elevation made her appear larger than the limits of her petite frame but she spoke with molten iron, in a plain expression of contempt.

"Oh! You *are* so right Duff. You should see the poor beggars we have to treat! We haven't enough bandages or supplies to cope with the overspill here, bearing in mind we are a two day voyage from France. Imagine what all the other hospitals are like."

Hannah and Harper stared at Margaret, affording her respect not always demanded in the past. Little John forgot his letter to look at his mother in surprise, but Margaret knew some things are too important to withhold from the young, "None of them are short term injuries, Duff. They send us no hopers – then patronise us by complimenting us for 'advanced surgical standards.'"

They all looked at Margaret with rapt attention, not envying the manner in which she had come by this insight. Yet they realised that in a sense she was the only one among their wide circle who had seen the net effects of war up-close. Hardening her voice as she tried to shake off grasping sorrow, Margaret clothed herself again in the artificial mantle of professionalism.

Lifting her head she looked each of the adults in the eye as she spoke, "Let me tell you - there are no standards. They went out of the window when the first hospital ship arrived."

Margaret uncrossed her legs and moved to a carved mahogany dining chair, breathing deep and visibly steeling herself for what she needed to say. All three listened in silence although she could not bear to look at her son. Instead she caressed him gently with her left hand as he leant against her.

"There are no' enough operating teams tae meet the demand for what we call 'blunt trauma surgeries' – men with bullet and shrapnel wounds. We keep them sedated and let them die. There is a round the clock service in amputations, tae simplify matters and speed up the process. Though I'm no' sure that it helps. It just means more intensive care, bandaging and bed baths. There is constant pressure tae evaluate men who can be saved and rush them intae theatre. There are dozens in that category at any one time. The vast majority never get seen by a surgeon because there just aren't enough. You always think they can maybe wait *a wee while longer* . . . but they die of shock, or infection. Many poor fellows start to recover from post op then lose another leg tae gangrene. Any with deep, or complex wounds just never make the surgical roster, because they would take too long." Hannah and Harper were stunned into silence, not daring to ask for fear of the answer. Little John was transfixed, his innocent eyes bulging in his face.

"Worst of all are the effects of shrapnel. Men riddled wi' wounds too deeply infected to be excised," Margaret's voice trailed as she uttered the final execration, "who we just hope will die for their own sake. They

410

seem to hang on forever. Perhaps to remind us to question what we read in the papers," she cautioned finally, turning her pretty nose up in defiance.

Margaret's blue eyes had welled up with moisture. When Hannah rose to hug her again, she broke down in hopeless misery.

"Poor mammy!" said Little John, "We willnae let Daddy go tae Flanders!"

Harper went to Margaret also, mutely holding her hand in solidarity.

"Perhaps you should get out of it?" suggested Hannah, stunned by her alacrity, yet knowing Margaret could never raise this subject again.

"Naw, naw I cannae do that," burbled Margaret pathetically, gulping air as she tried to rationalise her situation in simple terms, "Someone has tae do this love. Wee John goes to his Granny and I come home for him at the end of ma shifts. He keeps me going, don't you son!" she added ruffling his hair, "I'm only part time Duff - forty hours. I've realised that's a great opportunity! I can save lives - and often do. Every day I save some poor boy who'd otherwise be lost – because there are so many in need of attention. It puts new light on what you were telling me about women who do piece work!" she added bravely with a forced laugh.

"We love you Margaret," said Harper, sounding a little like Marconi speaking through a transatlantic microphone.

"Yes and I love you Margaret," agreed Hannah with warmth in her voice.

"And I love you Mammy," said Little John, brandishing his list, "We can write to Santa for more nurses for the men!" he added strongly.

Hannah stood up and turned to Harper, "Daddy, you are taking us to the bar at Duddingston Golf Club tonight in the Brass Eyed Monster, as soon as my house purchase is complete. Book a dinner table for six adults and a child, for seven thirty - and be clear Harper, I am paying! On our way to the bank we'll call in on Margaret's mum and dad to invite them, so they'll have plenty of time to get ready. I'll ring the bus garage now and ask if they will let William know."

411

Chapter Eighteen   *Avatar*

Will sat on steps below the winding house smoking a Black Cat - a newly fashionable factory rolled cigarette. He was waiting for his conductor, killing the remaining few minutes of his turn-around when the phone message came. He'd heard the outside bell against the susurration of cables but otherwise ignored it. Increasingly passengers rang to ask conductors to check items they had left behind – purses and shopping bags mainly, occasionally a folding push chair forgotten in the rush, once even a small child. Having a phone and responding to public need was all part of the service.

Hailed through an observation window by the Shift Supervisor but informed as he approached that the caller had rung off, William went inside the terminus office anyhow, braced for the inevitable ribbing. Sandy Woodward was known by all and sundry for a gossiping jobsworth. William considered his manager to have the deepest inferiority complex. Anyone who knew Sandy eventually realised he had great unrealised potential, despite some deficiency of personal history that twisted his character. At best Woodward was smilingly garrulous, charming while provocative. At worst, especially when drunk, he could be anarchic, or spitefully pugilistic. Sandy made it his business to know every other buddy's business, in order to find opportunity to mercilessly rip the pish out of them. Failing that he would confute in whispers until sufficient information about their most human foibles had been gleaned. Then he would casually misconstrue their deeds, or intentions.

William knew Sandy for a self-medicating, openly declared sociopath with a life-long speciality in character assassination. He was opposed to the union and had locked horns many times with former friends on the crews when they had worked to rule or taken strike action, as they had several times in recent years. The man lived for his work and worked in order to stay permanently semi-stoned. Woodward's breath, skin and clothing bubbled with the percolating floral decay of cheap homogenised alcohol. In this sense Sandy was quite literally a product of modern industrial Lothian – a walking, man-sized bottle of Fowler's Wee Heavy.

"Eff off Sandy," William suggested, in the manner of a routine greeting, walking briskly into the warm office, "Ya wee knobstick – ye should ha'e been born a woman, the amount o' gossiping ye do!"

"Oh! G'day to you an' aw Willie Mac," replied Sandy with sardonic alacrity, "Ye fat, lazy bastard!" he muttered under his breath.

"Whit was that?"

"I said - we must'a forgot te mention, the phone is intended fer public use only William, no' fae personal messages. Even incoming requests fer your attendance frae members o' the Royal Family."

"Okay Sandy, I'll bear that in mind pal," acknowledged Will, the total absence of irony in his voice conveying the exact opposite intent in the discreetly coded double talk of 'the Lothian.'

For an instant William thought of ringing Harper's number in defiance of Woodward but due to the demands of mechanical winding gear, in theory at least trams had to always run to schedule and there wouldn't be enough time to talk. Any delay would cause an overload elsewhere in the network although in practice the system was as prone to mechanical and human failings as any other. Crew logic went, 'If a body misses a tram they just wait for the next one. So what does it matter if wu'r delayed? It might even be a pleasant surprise fer the man who got out o' bed late!' The mythology of custom and practice determined that Inspectors were unnecessary. Runs per day and passenger averages invariably balanced out in the end. Anyone fed up waiting could either walk, thereby improving personal fitness, or toddle off back home and save their fare. Where institutional logic and service standards failed, sage humour filled in.

Nonetheless, Will decided he would pick another day for a showdown with edgy but pugilistic Sandy. Getting one of the office clerks or engineers to telephone Hannah to leave a message would also play into the Supervisor's hands. Judging from his smug smile he was hanging around watching Will to see if he might do this, not that Woodward really minded. It would however be grist to his mill for contention at some future time. Will knew that if he challenged his superior it would never result in a sacking – since Woodward was in fact the worst kind of Manager. Instead he would make it his business to discover the precise content of William's message and use it down the line to insinuate himself rudely into his affairs. William didn't hate Woodward – he just knew him too well and had come to despise the scornful attitude. In the distant past they'd shared too much shameful boys own history. Too many pubs they'd been thrown out of. Too many women they'd gratuitously offended, or simply failed to impress.

"Ah know you Willie Macdonald! Dinnae be gearing in early at the end o' yer shift tae use ma phone. An' nae jumping aff at thon public box on Porty High Street. Wur aw on a timetable here!" shouted Woodward, with a smirk at Will's resolute back. Two fingers came up as Will skipped down the ramp to join his conductor, Davy Brockett, with a smile of jubilation on his face.

"Whassup mate, you finally jined the army?"

"Naw Davy son, better still – ah've been summoned by Royalty!" The two men worked as they talked, Davy checking between seats for drunks or lost bags as Will readied the vehicle for joining traffic below the winding house. Both men spoke loudly, not caring if they were overheard, "Well fer Chrissakes remember no' tae skoosh Old Spice on yer John Thomas, even if ye do smell like a farmer's dug."

"God no! Ye ony ever dae that once in yer life pal! I had tae stand wi ma balls in the sink for ten minutes – made me late fer ma first date at the age o' fourteen. An' watch yer cheek Davy. I had a bath just last night."

Davy shook his head, tutting sardonically, "Fourteen ye say? So ye were a late starter then Will?"

"Aye true, but am thinking o' settlin' doon at last Davy son – it's either that or she spurns me an' I'll sign up fer three years."

"Oh – blow me! Now that's a serious subject. Ye'd be better aff marriet an' up tae yer eyes in debt here at home son."

"Aye, but no marriet tae the job like Sandy Woodward."

"Oh no, sod him!"

"Aye, sod him. Davy I'm gonny make a phone call like the man suggested, at the box on Porty High Street. Keep an eye oot fer Dougie Peel an' dinnae let some drunken bastard drive aff wi' the tram."

"What, at this time o' day Wull? It's on'y four o'clock."

"Stranger things have happened earlier in the day involving drunks Davy!"

"Speakin' o' Sandy . . . Moira telt me youse had a history."

"Oh, is that so? History o' the Four Kings did she say? I was good at Poker years ago Davy, afore I found the Lord."

"Ha! You're telling me, ye cheatin' dog. Word is Sandy played the hoaxer back in the day, no?"

"You mean he has a warped sense o' humour. Silly old fool insisted on placing our pot on a hot tip frae an old toff in a town coat, we met in the bar at Musselburgh races. I'd on'y picked *five winners* in a row, on the basis o' recent form and studying handicaps Davy. We had nineteen bob but stood tae make that intae nineteen quid. I had the next one picked oot – 'Avatar' . . . I remember the bloomin' horse's name tae this day," said William with a generous laugh, "Well I *would* because we stood tae win a small fortune and the colt won. But we never backed it! Sandy was taken in by the fastidious cove because he'd been a Colour Sergeant in the RSG, or some such. You'd never ha'e credited what that man knew, or where he'd been. If you'd ever doubted that us Scots are a nation o' smart arses *he'da* convinced ye within five minutes."

"I hope yer no' includin' Sandy Woodward an' yersel' in that cooperative," Davy edged in, with a guffaw.

"No, right enough! He'd spent ten years building railway bridges in the States, he telt us - reeling aff quotes frae Mark Twain and Emerson, like they were close family."

"Now yev lost me son. I wis warned off Emerson, through the Kirk mind – but who the Hell's Mark Twain? Is he that retired jockey writing for the Pink Un?"

"Aye that's 'im Davy . . . So being a late liquid lunch hour and us getting pertish, d'y'ken, buyin' rounds fer one another?"

"Oh aye, I could ha'e guessed that part."

"The dapper wee cavalry non-com, giving advice to the two flush-in-the-pocket day trippers. The wee codder could ha' sold pea canes tae bloomin' Eskimos. So, Sandy the booze-shunter places our accumulated winnings on the cuddy that's supposedly taken the fancy o' Cock Sure Harry Soph in the tailored town coat."

William waited for Davy to see the picture, still perplexed at the annoying recollection of his most recent day at the races with Sandy. Davy laughed at William's predictable misfortune, before proposing the logical outcome, "Dinnae tell me son . . . Avatar by a sheepskin nose band?"

"Avatar by three lengths Davy. Of course the tipster's heavily backed choice never left the stall!"

"Smarter men than us ha' fallen fer that ruse at the races Will. N'er hit the same bookie more than twice, let alone five times in a row! Sounds tae me the old bastard was trained as a dragoon to rob people on the run. He con-diddled ye out o' yer winnings. Nae doot ye'd bet it aw wi' the same Joe Rooks?"

"Aye Davy, we did just that. Onyway there's a moral to the tale, if ye'd like tae hear it."

"Oh aye an whit's that Will: 'Dinnae mix business wi' pleasure?'"

"No, always bet each way!"

"Aye, or dinnae bet at aw!"

The maroon and buff coloured tram car jolted as Will engaged the drive gear. A clamp fell onto one of the oiled cables running the length of the massive shed and they pulled out of their bay in the garage, shuttling behind another tram car towards the street.

"Then there was that old Florence he used tae shag occasionally, lived up in the Old Town?"

"Oh aye, the witch wi' the long curly hair? She had a bairn but the coonsel took it affy her?"

"Right they did and it was very sad too. Ken, he tried te get me stotious on moonshine and bunk up wi' her fer a night," Will's voice was raised in an indignant wail – though Davy suspected this may have alluded more to the memory of wormwood knocked off from a rail yard by Sandy, rather than the tired old hen.

"Ah'll no ask whit happened. Ye'll ha made the moral choice Will, ah ken that fine!"

"You mean never drink whisky that's no' been checked oot o' the Bond by a customs man. Too right pal."

"So, seeing the ginger haired numpty get preferment, inspires ye te seek gainful employment elsewhere Wull?"

"Och, Sandy's okay . . . when he's sleeping. I dinnae want an office job anyhow. But mebbe I'll look around for something new . . . I hear there's assured work for drivers overseas."

"Aye, but they're aw low paid, temporary contracts!"

Amid echoes of whistling men, clanging tools and the whine of massive electric winding engines, the friends chatted freely about a wider world lately less certain and less assured than their combined experience of life in dear Auld Reekie. William declined Davy's kind suggestion of a rendezvous at the Three Monkeys, for pies and pints after their shift. He was determined to make the best impression possible that evening, so keen was he on Hannah Harper.

Winter sunshine played deceptively over meadows surrounding Duddingston Club House, as William strolled down the lane. He was pensive about what he might admit about his obvious interest in the larger than life girl who illuminated all his dreams. Her folks were all there waiting for him, occupying a large circular table by the long window. The moment of arrival could not have been better timed to herald William's presence or break the ice. A group of young men about to leave encountered him at the door. They showered him with hearty banter, solicitations and promises to meet up mid-week for bowling at the Sheep Heid to which he smiled and demurred.

Usually no-one at Duddingston Golf Club cared who you were, as long as you knew at least one other person in the room. If you didn't then it might be necessary to give a full account of yourself because some worthy soul would be deployed to have you weighed, measured, categorised and labelled - more eagerly than a post graduate anatomical researcher working in a basement lab at the University. People here had known William and his family for years – brothers, uncles and women folk. In part, familiarity was due to the fact that Malcolm, his father, had been talked out of retirement to work there as a green keeper. Also because the good fellow had been active in the Masons and for a time was Grand Wizard of his lodge. There was a social network on the fringes of rural Edinburgh, promoting the deception that it might actually be a small world. If it really was, William simply itched for a chance to meet the old soldier from the Royal Scots Greys again, to give him a tip in return, 'Don't ever cross my path in the bookies again old flower.' But right now that was forgotten, and he felt only a flush of happiness, as deceptive as the failing winter light.

When Harper spotted him approaching and murmured something to Hannah, she stood up to beam a smile at William. Throwing off examination of the base accoutrements of his little life, he stepped up with alacrity to admit the dream. There was a simple warmth of acceptance in Hannah's kind family for him to relish. It was easy to talk to any of them. Easy to steer conversation wherever, or away from whatever he wished.

Little John stole the show - temporarily engaged by Hannah, then each of the adults vying for his attention in turn. Uniquely, his 'generation' was a minority of one. Consequently he had the prevailing attribute of all single children, which effectively he was - Little John sought to consolidate the mutual love of both parents. Stuck in the middle of their harmonious double-act he was already a scaled down adult with good attitude.

Constantly reassured by the gushing tones of his adoring mother, the lad responded with guileless warmth instead of the cheek expected from children with elder siblings. Little John's correctness earned him open praise from all the adults, although occasionally he came out with moral pronouncements baldly echoing his mother's world view.

"You're no shirker William – even though you've not got a pot to piss in!" John stated with equanimity across the table to his new ally, shaking his head in confirmation. Everyone laughed except Margaret who coloured with embarrassment.

418

"You can borrow mine William, it's under my bed."

"Oh thank you, I'll collect it next time I'm passing!"

"I never use it anymore!" he added, forking a mouthful of breaded plaice with a child's erratic hand as William laughed softly at the bairn's innocence. Wriggling his backside on folded coats serving as an adapted high chair, he studied his new friend. Then pointing with a free hand, "I like your beard William. It's all shiny."

Gently taking hold of the boy's finger William leant forward to silently scrutinise it up close with a naturalist's straight browed, rigorous appraisal. Taking out reading glasses he compared the back of the hand thoughtfully with his own, musing like Darwin on some distant shore. Then he turned it over, unfolded the digits to count them off slowly, wishing to avoid the wrong conclusion. John tolerated the play, smiling rapturously, his fork held aloft in the other hand. Then shaking his head and lowering it slowly, William blew a mighty raspberry onto Little John's open palm. Harper watched in fascination as everyone around the table laughed cheerily – never having seen such playfulness between two males a generation apart.

William introduced a florin that he flipped and spun on the tablecloth, then made disappear before finding it again behind John's ear. Finally he dropped the large coin into the pocket of the little boy's jacket – which he patted with a clowning smile. When John retrieved it, flicking the coin awry in a poor attempt to copy William's spinning technique, a gentleman at an adjacent table retrieved it from the floor with the kind remonstrance that the boy was 'too young to be buying a round of drinks.' They all laughed generously, at entertainment only naïveté can inspire.

Margaret took the florin to look after and once again the focus was back on her. She talked endlessly about the marvellous discoveries made by her delightful son and heartfelt ambition for his success in future. After the main course, sweets came with a second round of drinks. Conversation became desultory as each of the adults tried to think of something to say of remote interest to the others. Everyone stepped around what worried them most.

Unable to resist what was big news for him, Anthony touched indirectly on the subject William dreaded and the root cause of his indecision regarding Hannah – the conduct of the war. William noticed Teresa Kemp kick her husband under the table, as Tony railed on about 'the Army finally admitting they needed horses by the million and farmers being offered top penny for their animals.'

William felt his temperature slowly rise with embarrassment tightening under his collar. He had managed to spare Margaret's feelings but couldn't hide his own.

Is my predicament so obvious to them?

Teresa's kick under the table had been for Hannah's benefit of course, not William's, but he felt there was no choice other than to steer away from the subject entirely. So embarrassed was William that when he did speak he almost choked on his meringue. Aware that his own words rang with hollowness bordering on deceit, he addressed a spurious question to Harper to avoid further talk about 'poor horses dragging artillery through the mud.'

"What do you think will happen to all the golf clubs up and down the country, now that cricket and football have been stopped? Do you imagine some of them may have to close down for lack of support?" William sank down in his chair like a drunk in a Police interview room as he prattled loudly to Harper about needing 'something to replace the fitba.' In truth he'd missed it badly since the government announcement on the 7th September recommending it cease.

"No William, golf is predominantly an old man's game – probably due to the cost of equipment and green fees. Most members here are either unfit for active service; family men or too old. The game is not a target for the press either way. In fact there are quite a few patriotic journalists who regularly play here, after they've written their articles encouraging football players to join up. There has been some falling off, but not so as you'd notice. You should play more often, William. In fact I'll give you a game next Saturday if you're up for it."

Even though he was thirty three years old with the toes of his right foot missing, William was extremely self-conscious about patriotic duty. He was also sensitive about his commitment to discussing future options with Hannah before voicing them casually in conversation. So much in love with her was he that any future without Hannah began to seem inconceivable - especially the one where he unthinkingly committed himself to the witches' cauldron of Flanders - the place where most of his amateur football side were presently learning that patriotism is a virtue bought cheaper than newsprint.

With Little John as a chaperone, the couple visited Edinburgh Zoo together. In truth the chaperone acted more as matchmaker. He talked about Uncle William at every cut's turn when he wasn't around. Uncle William was always a step ahead in planning some fun aspect of an adventurous day out involving the wee man. But William didn't need to play to the gallery. He needed a lot of time with Hannah to let the breach of her absence over five long years begin to close. Each knew the other's history without being familiar and the truth of it was that William was less easy in Hannah's company than she was in his. After the zoo they walked hand in hand on the beach at Portobello, gazing long with smiles of reassurance into each other's eyes at every pause, or turn.

When he took her shopping in town for house wares and linen, this time without his little side-kick, Hannah moved up a gear to lead through flea markets and auctions – impressively spotting items of greatly reduced value from the four corners of the globe. William was glad to be educated by Hannah on subtleties of a perfectly inlaid Japanese lacquered table; of Indian rosewood marquetry - women reaching into a tree designed to gracefully support the finest crystal fruit bowl and a hand woven vanity screen made of reeds from the Orinoco estuary.

Best of all was Il Spinario - a present from the Leslies which they collected together from the freight depot. Ordered from an Italian fine art dealer in London, it was a replica of the one standing in the lobby of Allerton Grange. The exquisite marble carving was of a naked runner, drawing a thorn from his foot – a forgotten classical theme executed by an unknown sculptor – small enough to place in the entrance lobby of a municipal building or a fine country mansion.

"It might always seem out of place in a porch, or a landing of a small house but however much visitors mock my delusions of grandeur," Hannah predicted, "No-one will walk past without touching it."

The more romantic time he spent with Hannah during the festive season of '14 the more difficult the subject of his intention to join up became for William. The more singular and positive in her outspoken views Hannah became, the more he returned in his mind to the need to make a decision independently.

Lying on his bed after a long shift, thinking of turmoil surrounding his affairs, William had to be honest with himself – he was stuck in a rut. Torn between lost friends from his beloved football team and broken-hearted Christina Macdonald, still missing his dad, Will found the prospect of arguing with Hannah - the declared pacifist - unfeasible. Above all, the thought of three younger brothers, Peter, Jim and Ronnie who had all gone to Flanders, burned William with embarrassment.

It wasn't just a question of how to manage his affair of the heart with Hannah. Over nearly twenty years more women had chased him than he cared to count. Each of those women, more in number than the total of the intervening years since his teens, had in turn inspired a spell of forgotten ardour. Commitment had always seemed a step too far for William. He knew with complete confidence how to play the game but over recent years the game no longer held interest for him.

"I will wait, until she's ready to voice her commitment to me," he told Davy at work the following day, "I'll not push, nor allow her to think I've lost interest. She's lovely man, I believe she understands. In fact the courting part seems straightforward – yet . . ."

"Yet they're advertising fer a new wave o' recruits in the New Year. Nae doot tae bolster the sad remnant of what used tae be the World's finest army."

William drove in silence as Davy took a couple of fares. Both men had read the morning editorial in the Scotsman. The BEF had been shattered within four months, holding off human wave attacks of a desperately retreating enemy. There was also the predictable need to contain a likely German Spring offensive on the western front. Kaiser Bill's future was staked upon that. Prussian militarists surrounding him had underestimated the Belgians and French but were not about to give up. Despite this situation on the ground, predictions that 'it will be all over by Christmas' were not unreasonable. The Kaiser and two or three of his inner circle were unreasonable.

Peter Macdonald was a career soldier – it had been his job for over a dozen years - which for the most part had not been too bad until now. Jim however had been talked into volunteering against his better instincts by Peter, joining the 'fiercer than fierce' Cameron Highlanders, during their summer recruitment drive. Then Jim's fiancé who had promptly broken off their engagement, told Christina of a rapprochement between them. His firm had been awarded a big contract overseas on the back of Jim's architectural drawings and were prepared to buy him out, if the Colonel agreed. Now, judging from peter's terse letter he'd have to sit the rest of the game out on the side-line - but at least the lad would have 'done his bit for King and country.'

Many of William's friends had also gone in the first wave, five of the Craigmillar amateur football side volunteering on the back of a nationally driven press campaign. All had been young, unmarried lads. They were committed, energetic volunteers, joining a professionally raised army - with supposedly the best of every kind of equipment and training. News that two of them had been killed at Ypres made the whole damned issue of joining more poignant. William was spurred to envision a precise range of talents he could offer the army, and how those skills might help lads at the front.

When Davy returned from collecting fares, William spoke just above the road noise to avoid attention, "I could pick my own regiment – maybe even the Camerons or Royal Scot's, even the CRE, like young Ronnie. I can drive a lorry, or a railway locomotive, lay track and do welding. If they prefer, I can use my skill with horses – even down to vetinerary experience and first aid, Davy. I could ferry wounded men, or horses, from behind the battle lines."

"Dae it if ye think yer up tae it Wull, wi' yer gammy foot. Ye wouldnae want tae be left ahint when all the other boys run intae battle though!"

"I wouldnae want tae be left ahint when the boys leg it the other way, mair like. Dinnae forget, I used to earn money as a sprinter, Davy. Once I'm up tae speed naebody'd catch me. Basic army training will be a doddle – I'm as fit and tough as most men ten years younger."

"You keep on telling yersel' that son - it'll tak' years affy yer life."

"Gowan, ye sarky we fudger!" muttered William, reaching for the newspaper to whack Davy. William was not afraid of living, nor dying.

Terrified of the animosity an open discussion of this nature might provoke with Hannah, William considered allowing her to go back to Monaghan and writing to her after volunteering. That way he could rehearse what needed to be said and lay out his thoughts explicitly for her consideration. At least then there would be no argument. In the meantime William knew he had to stop short of an explicit commitment to Hannah, whether promissory or sexual - until his mind was made up and she accepted his decision. The last thing he wanted to do was leave her with a fatherless child.

Hannah told William heatedly as they walked along the prom at Portobello, "I despise the most common everyday transaction, William, where an ordinary trooper offers his life for *one shilling and a penny a day*. If I had to risk everything, I like to think I'd do it on my own terms."

"Dear girl, how can we ever know the best course of action given all the circumstances?" he answered sheepishly, "The risk isn't the same for everyone and I imagine they pay them what they can afford to pay."

"William, I am not that easily fooled. The habit of independent thinking allows me the advantage of believing I *generally* do the right thing, given all the wider often confusing circumstances. I simply do not approve of this war." She looked at him in dismay, seeing through his misguided loyalty. Both felt like diplomats of estranged nations, communicating by encrypted bulletin.

Hannah had a choice to make herself. She knew Christina Leslie would probably not return to West Allerton from Ireland with Clarissa and Helena. Her family and staff were shocked by the loss of Edgar and were missing Hugh. The decision when it finally came would leave her with a difficult choice, but by now Hannah knew exactly what to expect.

Castle Leslie was a self-contained Elysian paradise, sitting within endless days of happy distraction. There, nature worked her constant miracle, with energetic assistance from wood sprites, leprechauns and a small army of retainers with scrubbed hands and leathery, smiling faces. Resident in the big house with its numerous annexes were a scattering of maiden aunts; titled and tenured widows; loud talking uncles - nebulously spread over a family tree which even when inscribed on Dutch Vatman paper resembled something akin to espaliered Bramleys pinned to the wall of a traditional orchard. Labradors, Collies and Terriers, given greater than normal attention in what was otherwise a community of differentially remunerated equals, acquired the exalted status of children and angels.

Although Helena and Clarissa would eventually attend boarding school in Dublin full time, their letters to Hannah made it clear she was already sorely missed. There would be a job for her for life, if Hannah accepted. But hurting from the realisation that Hugh's sense of duty to King and Country outweighed even his love for her and his abhorrence of war, Christina was hurting and her behaviour had become unpredictable. For now, in Hannah's estimation, her employer was more likely to stay close to her parents and appreciative in-laws than return to Allerton Grange.

Liverpool on the other hand represented the heart of the political life of the nation more so than cultured, much vaunted Edinburgh. Liverpool was where the real fight was. Events in Europe were a manufactured side issue. The docklands with their industry was the essential forum that had given meaning to Hannah's political activism. In a sense she had been distracted by William and purchasing of the house on Bath Street, which she now planned to let.

Privately Hannah agonised about the stalled women's movement, the disgusting brutality of war and the arbitrary manner in which

Christina's family life had been overturned by Hugh's spurious notions of duty. They had all been happy at West Allerton, and if Christina returned permanently Hannah would stay. She wondered about Stan, Marek, Andy and Sigi, although there was no way of contacting them without putting herself and Alice in the frame. At least in Liverpool there was a chance of hearing of them through one of Father Jordan's network of visiting Redemptorists, or one of the union officials.

Hannah also worried deeply about the happiness of her dear friend Alice, now separated from Russell. This was the down side of having such an indulgent employer. Lady Christina was impulsive, as well as faultlessly generous. She had no requirement to justify her actions to anyone. Hannah saw the big picture better than most – the insecurity and loneliness of ordinary individuals and partisan compromises made in the name of personal dignity, or national security – and she hated all the sham.

A week before the end of her winter holiday a telegram came from Alice in Monaghan that made Hannah's mind up for her.

I FEAR THE WORST HAS HAPPENED CONCERNING OUR PATRON. RETURN TO MONAGHAN IMMEDIATELY IF POSSIBLE. ALL EXPENSES PAID.

Chapter Nineteen   *Solace*

The most extraordinarily gracious man Hannah knew had stepped out of family life into the widest enormity vulgar death had ever spread in the history of conflict. Within three hectic months of his fleeting visit to West Allerton in the first week of September '14, dear Hughie's dynamic warmth was no more than a desperately forlorn memory. For most people who cared to know how he lost his life the circumstances were vague, but according to the discreet official word, 'he certainly didn't suffer.'

Hannah arrived back in Liverpool in late January to find Christina in temporary residence with the girls, patiently awaiting her return from a business meeting in Edinburgh arranged prior to the tragic news. All the permanent staff had been offered accommodation in Monaghan or retention payments if they remained in Liverpool. It was the first time they'd met since Sir Hugh's funeral in Monaghan almost two weeks earlier.

Alice remained at Castle Leslie where correspondence would arrive and staffing continuity was demanded. Christina expressed her intention to return there 'in due course' – meaning when she felt robust enough to accept unsolicited interference. She explained to Hannah that there had already been one difficult family conference with her parents, who had determinedly expressed their views, then another of a different sort with the eccentric Leslies. In the aftermath of Hugh's passing she had taken the girls out of school for a few weeks, with the specific intent of 'seeking solace in more neutral, familiar territory.'

The girls were vocal, especially regarding their delightful new Italian friend who, inspired by Glaslough Lake had invited them on holiday to visit Lago di Como with her. But they were clearly broken hearted, not wanting to return to their Catholic prep school for high-brow young ladies.

"It was cold!" chorused Helena and Clarissa in perfect time, "An' the foowd was yugh!" howled Clarissa, in hopeful past tense, with an insidious hint of Dublin brogue. Hannah could see their fair faces were

427

bursting with incoherent pain. She hugged them like they were her own. Wrapping up warm against winter chill, they took the car and headed out to Prestatyn. Having passed on the option of a scramble over Flint Castle, fog and tide were kind to them, affording instead a gentle walk in wan sunshine over the enormous beach. Moist sand sucking tremendously at bare feet begged them to dig down looking for treasure, to stay and play. After weeks of oppression the girls were only too happy to comply. Every shell, every slime varnished pebble was a source of unanswered fascination. Progress was slow yet they walked for miles - with support from Ackroyd, unstintingly shadowing their movement along the shore road with sandwiches and tea in the Rolls.

Madly flocking Dunlin swirled back and forth along the littoral, searching for a briefly revealed bonanza under the retreating tide, watching the sky above for mean predators. Warm breath rolling off thawing pastures of Clwyd mixed with the moist shrug of the sleepy Irish Sea. Unseasonably mild air blustered refreshing swirls around Christina's grief-stretched face.

In the distance a Royal Navy destroyer could be glimpsed, ranging in mad tacking sweeps between open sea and the Crosby Channel to the north east. Its white bow wave and uncharacteristic lack of filthy smoke gave a clue to the ship's modernity and grim purpose. These were sea trials with a spirited purpose, perhaps cautiously observed by eyes more devious than Hannah's. German submarines were known to patrol the Irish Sea and were apt to despatch an inshore fishing boat if nothing of greater value could be found. It was a dolorous reminder of a war that right now neither of them wished to think about.

"So, talk about your man, William isn't he? . . . Only if you wish, sorry, it was Alice who spilled the beans."

This is typical of Christina lately - an apology on the back of an assertion that begun life as an honest question. Where is the certitude of the brilliant individual I first met back in '09?

Hannah watched patiently as Christina carefully withdrew a sporting canteen from her shoulder bag, unplugged the stopper and drew gratefully on the aromatic sweetness of its solution. Hannah could see the glaze of pain in Christina's eyes soften, to reveal a will bent out of true from life's purpose. She'd seen that look as a child in the eyes of Harper and knew it reflected the stamp of evil in this world.

"Jameson?"

"Napoleon, VSOP darling. Only the best from now on. I'm making up for lost time. Drinking for two!"

"You don't mean?"

Christina paused to look questioningly at Hannah for half a second, then laughed sardonically. "Oh, Good Lord no! – I only wish! Then there might be something to look forward to."

She tilted the strapped flask with an offer to Hannah, who moved her head an inch to the left to decline. Christina threw her head back, shook wild hair free and opened her gullet for an unrestrained plunge into the tide of forgetfulness. Hannah was weeping inside for Christina and her daughters but forced herself to talk about William.

Life must go on. We have that much in common at least - in attitude, if not circumstance. Christina has given me so much. Tolerated so much.

But first Hannah hugged her. Tears turned readily to laughter as Helena chased Clarissa across the beach with the remains of a dead crab they had been throwing at one another.

"He's not my man. Although I *would* say we've grown very close."

"So, which of you is unsure?"

"Oh given the 'circumstances' probably him more than me, Christina. Everyone has inner secrets. It takes time to offer all that life has thrown up, on the pyre of affection. Not everything cancels out. He's thirty three, so you can expect him to have a history."

Christina waited for more. Linking arms they paraded after the girls, who were squealing and giggling as they raced across the sand.

"I think it takes a couple of years to really get to know anyone – don't you?" asked Hannah tentatively.

"Oh yes, I agree. 'Fools rush in' and all that."

"But I've missed talking to you. I need to decide where I may settle too. You know that I will stay as long as the girls need me, as long as you need me. But in as far my future plans have regard to William, there is certainly something holding him back. In fact, something he has opened his mouth to say then closed it just as sharply a dozen times. Some folk are eloquent Christina, even when at a loss for words. Will on the other hand is normally so forthright that he becomes eloquent in consternation. Silence speaks for him."

"I get the impression he is a man not easily deterred."

"Yes exactly, with all the charming enthusiasm of a tame farm dog."

"So, d'you think it's another woman?" Christina ventured with a teasing smile.

"Yes, several probably – or maybe a secret love child," conceded Hannah, in an instant revealing naiveté despite all her assumed political astuteness. Christina found it impossible to say what she knew.

How can such enormity stand before us yet not be seen by both? Dear Hannah has not transferred diamond clear insight for women's Suffrage and the Labour movement to this wartime scenario.

The only debate in Whitehall was how to shepherd enough canaille to Belgium without passing an act of general conscription. She knew Winston and whilst reluctant to gossip about a friend and distant relative of her late husband, Christina knew this war to be all the aspiring politician was thinking about. Even Winnie was on the brink of forfeiting a career in politics, albeit as First Lord of the Admiralty, to get in on the action.

At a loss to find a diplomatic way of saying what she assumed was the cause of William's reticence to marry such an exceptional girl, Christina was tempted to broach the subject indirectly by blurting out something about Sir Hugh. Circumstances surrounding his death had brought her nothing but torment, since the unexpected occurrence miles behind the front at Ypres. Instead Christina did neither. Gulping the chillingly dank air she tried to sound casual in making conversation, "You can't force the issue. Let William reach his own verdict. Just don't accept his ring without putting your devotee on the spot. The worst thing that can happen is a man takes you for a fool! Once they start lying they can't stop."

The girls had stopped to watch an inshore trawler landing its catch behind the headland of Kinmel Bay. On an island of sand at the grudging curve of the river three hundred yards from the sea were a dozen small craft, confident of both the lee and the tide. A stocky man wearing a green waxed coat with a bush-hat, bulked at his neck with a grey woollen scarf sat painting the hull of his upturned smack. The fisherman, keen to finish a repair while the weather held, stood up to greet a friendly Collie approaching over the headland brow with a walker trailing. Recognising a friend the dog raced down a steep embankment to greet the fisherman, leaping into fast moving water to swim confidently against the flow. Putting down the paintbrush in anticipation of furious shaking and spray that would surely follow, the man moved stiffly toward the dog.

Christina gasped aloud, standing rooted to the spot between curving pillars half way across the splendid iron road bridge. Something in the man's casual attire - the curve of strong shoulders; his apparent age and stature; the way he moved perhaps, was reminiscent of Hughie. But it was the unrestrained glee of the dog that confirmed the impression. Having avoided the subject of her husband's passing now Christina's hand went up to her mouth as her beautiful brow creased in perplexity, "Oh Sweet Jesus, that man looks just like Hughie with Oscar," she croaked, "Why is this happening to me? I see him everywhere! Sean Curran, the gardener, thought *he* came home too. He swears he spoke to Edgar the day his telegram came, the silly old fool! Hughie knew what would happen, Hannah. Somehow he *knew* he would never come back, yet he still went."

Neither woman could find an appropriate word in that moment, yet Christina built herself up to addressing the horror she needed to share with someone else. Hannah shuddered in anticipation of her friend's release of dark, emotive energy, "You know how come he looked so perfect . . . lying in state in the church at Monaghan, with just a tiny red mark on his forehead to spoil his beatific smile?"

Hannah felt it best not to respond, but turned to look briefly at Christina. Clenching body and mind she listened in silence, walking more quickly now, half a pace ahead on the narrow pavement. The girls had raced across the bridge to greet the dog that looked so like Oscar. The smart collie noticed them coming and was loping up the embankment to meet them half way.

Christina stopped to light a cigarette, sucking hard on her elegant ebony holder. Hannah stopped to face her. Glaring at her children's governess through moist eyes and a cloud of fragrant white smoke, she tilted her head slightly to the left to lean on the steel framework. Christina's pained expression said, 'Isn't it clear? I need your help!'

Hannah recalled a time fourteen months before when they had looked out across the Bay of Biscay. Then it had been she who'd been the recipient of much needed advice. Christina had been consummate in her mentoring of Hannah, but now their roles were reversed. Hannah still felt like a child though, as she looked down distractedly at a swirl of sand left at the end of the bridge by a thousand beach combers. A lorry swished past, disturbing the impatient air. She resisted the urge to rub her shoe in the sand, recalling the first time of walking unaided along the prom at Porty as a child.

Hannah listened in awe as Christina imparted a dark vision of hell on earth, all the while holding an image of Bishop Daly giving out communion bread in the vivid candlelight as Hughie attended his last Church of Ireland ceremony – his mind as ever elsewhere, "He only had part of his right side remaining you know - his shoulder and arm, the remains of his right hip and leg. All the rest of his chest and torso was gone. Nine tenths of his body had been scooped out like ice-cream. Incredible really, that it left his face and head untouched, apart from the splinter that went through his brain.

Halstead at the war office was afraid I'd get French to sack him if he didn't spill the beans. I did threaten him Hannah and I meant it at the time. Like a fool I demanded details and the little bastard must have gone right to the Field Marshall, to obtain authorisation to get them for me."

Hannah thrust her cold hands into her coat pockets, knowing from Christina's hard tone there was more to come, "Why shouldn't we know the truth? This kind of thing happens all day every day. It's what they mean by the euphemism 'missing in action' . . . there is literally nothing left to bury."

"How grisly that is for those who see it and survive!"

"'Pressure wave,' Halstead told me, 'Apparently that's what kills most of them,' he reassured me. Evidently their bodies are blown apart like rose petals in a storm."

"But how did this happen to Hugh? Wasn't he supposed to be away from all that - organising the railway?"

Christina sucked laconically on her cigarette holder, as if to say 'what difference does it make now?' She blew smoke out of her nose, shifting her weight on cold feet before answering, "Clever German bastards. Apparently they spied out the forward head-quarters from the edge of some elevated woodlands a few miles away. They dropped a shell right on the front steps as they were all coming out together. Anyway it saved Clery the undertaker a lot of work. He just borrowed a tailor's dummy from a shop in Monaghan and shoved that in the coffin with Hughie's dress uniform. I suppose one ought to be grateful for that last sight of him - smiling as ever in life, no doubt sharing a joke with his dashing colleagues. Wherever they all went, they will be laughing still, and no doubt getting drunk over a hand of high stakes Poker."

Hannah placed her hand on Christina's back as she seemed to fold in upon herself and for an instant imagined she might jump into the fast flowing river below. Instead Christina rocked with pain, as tears rolled silently onto the black velvet trim of her fine woollen coat. But she contended her emotions bravely, as the true Irish Princess she was.

They had been planning to investigate a little hotel at the bend on the far side of Kinmel but Christina spun on her heel to march away with her bitter sobbing, leaving Hannah to shepherd Clarissa and Helena back into hand.

The watchful Ackroyd appeared out of nowhere to enquire if everything was okay. He seemed only too happy to park beside them on the bridge, unconscionably delaying the flow of traffic back from

Holyhead. The chauffeur looked like an off duty German sniper in puttees and trim grey uniform. He wore a flat cap bearing the Leslie family crest, with leather gloves and polished town shoes adding equivalent status of a Sergeant at Arms. The sight of a badly parked Rolls Royce might have been temptation for most lorry drivers to leer and reach for the horn, but a glimpse of Ackroyd's impassive eyes set above his square chin was sufficient to deter rude gestures.

As the sun went down they wandered into the hopeful little town of Rhyl, where hunger met with comfort. Climbing into the upholstered bosom of the fine car, sadly redolent of other adventure days spent with Hughie, Christina deployed Ackroyd in search of food. Within fifteen minutes he returned with piping hot fish and chips for all, wrapped in newspaper. The bounty gave off a zestful tang of salty steam and boiling vinegar. Really too hot to eat, the girls scoffed them nonetheless, breathing and blowing with open mouths, inside the protective shell of the darkened car.

Trundling homewards, their road climbed above fluffy evening fog bordering the Flintshire coast. Above was a starry sky, vastly cold and indifferent to their feelings of loss. Helena tried to get Clarissa to play I-spy, gazing out in wonderment at warm blue-white interiors glowing nearby and far off freighters queuing for cargoes of steel, lead and lime along the river Dee. But Clarissa was too slow, unable to think of enough possibilities for three guesses each round. Helena won their game five - one.

When the car interior had warmed and desultory conversation finally died, Christina silently handed Hannah a stack of envelopes, bound with a red ribbon which she had taken from her bag. Hannah guessed these were Hughie's letters from France. The envelopes were watermarked, personal stationery, addressed to Christina in a familiar, sweeping hand. Hannah estimated that there were nine or ten. Another buff coloured envelope appeared at a glance to have had been typed and seemingly despatched with an official War Office stamp. Without a word Christina flicked on the reading light for Hannah, then turned away to look solemnly out of the window. Hannah shifted back in her seat next to the girls, feeling alert, yet extremely uncomfortable.

Without examining the content of the letters, Hannah slipped them into her grip to read later, studying her friend with dread. Beautiful yet vulnerable, Christina gazed into middle distance across endless pastures of miserable sheep, crouching in dank air, as the Rolls Royce breezed past south eastward to circle the broad estuary. Unable to bear conversation, or meet concerned eyes, Christina was desperate nonetheless to share her grief. Hannah gently took her hand. In reflection from the glass she saw tears rolling down Christina's weather burned cheeks. Hannah reached up briskly to switch off the light. Most communication is unspoken she told herself, not for the first time. Helena and Clarissa turned to glance at Hannah, registering their own deep need for involvement in the discourse.

Hannah understood her position without the need to examine it. Christina had loving in-laws, as well as close family but they were without exception fiercely independent and competitive, self-engaged and garrulous to a fault. From what she imparted, clearly they'd driven her away, with candid engagement in speculative discussions of inheritance, and unnecessary reassurances about residency in any number of estates scattered around the globe - should Monaghan not suit her.

"Will you hold your tongue!" Christina had yelled at Philomena, Hughie's widowed mother on her last night in Monaghan, "I would give it all in exchange for one last night with my man. At least have the good grace to allow me time to grieve!"

As Hannah considered Christina's request to read Hughie's letters from France – to share what was in her heart, concerning some final vision of his sacrifice - Christina mused at the same moment on the psychology of her own motives.

The original recommendation from Lady Graham had come indirectly from Hannah's sister Elizabeth, previously described as, 'Occam's Razor, by which sobriquet I attribute to her the quality of being deterministic in the most unflustered manner, not the implication that she's holding a blade to my throat as I write.'

Christina's feeling now was synonymous with the original appraisal of Hannah Harper five years earlier, following that recommendation from Lady Graham. Writing to express appreciation she had said of Hannah, 'Mary, I thank you wholeheartedly, for she is a gem. Perhaps the most tolerant individual I have ever known, yet warm and vivacious. Her perspicacity comes not only from bright intelligence and forbearance but the self-discipline to see beyond the moment.'

In addition to her Children's governess, Christina was close to two or three members of her wide social set living near West Allerton, in whom she would confide. Other good friends, spread across the choicest rural locations of Cheshire and Lancashire, were all within a short motor car ride. Predominantly though not exclusively, they were wives of Hughie's former business partners and their wealthy professional or landed associates. Christina considered her close circle to number certain intensely disarming individuals. She was bound to them in the sense that over the years they had reciprocated interest, in social and at times deeply personal needs. These women were subtly aware of how tenuous good fortune and wealth can be – not least because they were pre-occupied with sustaining it above everything else. Unfortunately, ambition tended to make them pitiless.

But if this war goes on much longer, some of them may need to form a mutual support group.

Hannah desperately needed to sleep, yet she could feel the loneliness of Christina's tortured wakefulness going on elsewhere in the rambling house. It had been ten thirty in the evening by the time the girls were bathed and tucked into bed, with a suitably brief but compulsory bedtime story. Now that Hannah had the chance to lie down too, her instinct as always, was to reach up to turn off the lamp above the bed, to just close her eyes for a few moments.

Chapter Twenty *Vigil*

A mesmeric world of slumber surrounded Hannah in an instant, quick as a wizard's spell. Her overwhelmed mind closed unexpectedly in watchful sorrow, to suckle guiltlessly on the comforting draught of forgetfulness. But even in her deepest dreams Hannah felt the weight of Christina's need.

Alertness, with a precise sense of rigid necessity arrived before full wakefulness. It was a little after four am when she rolled out of bed, still fully clothed, to reach for the dispatches in her bag. Noting the precise manner in which Christina had bound the letters from Hughie, she realised there would be a corresponding pile written by Christina, retained as not relevant to the discussion required.

Poor Christina – I am honoured to share in her loss.

Hannah looked to see if the date stamps on the envelopes were sequential. They were. At all costs she wished to avoid mixing them up, losing or damaging them in any way.

I will be careful not to leave them lying around for the maid or housekeeper to find.

The first letter from Hughie was dated just over three months earlier. Hannah read it twice, startled by the clear resonance of his voice sounding in her head. She could not help but be amused by his alacrity, yet at the same time was stunned by his revelation of the brutal dynamics of the situation in France.

'HQ CO,
8th Rly Co. RETC
BEF/PO

St Omer,
France.

NB. Please note my new official address for all correspondence until further notice, regardless of my precise location (sic):

The Pressing Room / Wine Cellar,
Talbot Hotel,
Poperinghe,
Belgium.

9.30 pm,
Sunday,
 October 11th, 1914.

Dear Christina,
So sorry I missed my first leave entitlement, also for not finding time to write but we've had our hands full re-stocking everything the Germans ransacked for their own use as they retreated.

Thanks for regular updates from home. Your letters come within a few days of posting, similarly parcels and newspapers for which I thank you. It's nice to think there is a reality underlying this one, not geared to destruction. Sorry, but the girl at Regent's Park made judicious use of her marker pen on the precise details of Aunt Veronica complaining about her bunions. I agree that's enough to push anyone towards leaving home. I tried holding a torch behind it to read the sick-making details obscured but couldn't make it out. No actually . . . that's an invention. I wish they had used the marker.

On the subject of Miss Harper: do your best to persuade the girl but it sounds to me she has outgrown us, or at least has a notion to follow her heart.

Helena and Clarissa will survive residence at Alexandra College, despite initial strangeness; they have one other and thankfully are close, as well as mutually dependant. They will make new friends there and I'm certain will thrive. If they apply themselves half as well as you did as a child, it will eventually give them access to liberal education up to degree level. Alexandra College, being nominally

Church of Ireland now should ultimately allow them to at least think they have the 'foot in each camp' we agreed to engender. If there is an age-related issue concerning access, make a suitably large donation. Make the donation regardless. Dublin provides the best women's education anywhere in the world, so encourage them to look ahead long term, even if they don't plan to live there permanently. Tell them now Daddy advises set their sights on the male preserve of Trinity, irrespective of resistance they may encounter. Remind them of what their beloved Hannah would advocate. When the time comes, get her to arrange a demonstration outside the Provost's Office.

If the Catholic Bishop threatens to excommunicate you for planning to send our children to a Protestant University, send him an unmarked envelope with a couple of hundred in used bills. Hopefully, in the meantime, the tradition of Quaker discipline at their new school will put them off religion forever. Catholic schools would never allow such a thing – they would want our little baby's hearts and souls for the sacred heart of Jesus - not to mention their bodies. You said the school actively encourages charitable involvement in the community? Far better I think for them to become familiar with practicing a living faith, than the almost unavoidable odium theologicum of the Irish sectarian divide.

In the last century the Irish were the backbone of the professional Army incidentally. We encouraged Catholics to join and had the most eager, well organised soldiers in the world - with the possible exception of the Swedes. Diverse enemies of the Empire would justifiably shit themselves and run at the sound of bagpipes - but faced with the Irish they rarely even knew what hit them. Now Edgar's regiment can't get enough recruits because of Mr Larkin's socialist unions and the Republican movement.

I'm sorry to hear that Oscar is pining for the girls as for me, though I'm sure in my case that has more to do with macaroons I always have stuffed in my pockets. You should get out in the fields with the dog every day my dear; nothing is better for the soul. If a 42 centimetre shell lands on my staff car, I shall return to proffer an ephemeral arm each morning, ushering you through fragrant misty woodlands. I will place my steadying hand on that thoroughbred rump to prevent your slipping from a greasy stile. Sorry to joke sardonically but I am now accustomed to the absolute precept of my own mortality. Dare I speak it plainly Christina: such an admission is my only hope of exorcising the most dreadful, ubiquitous fear?

Hearing and seeing the effect of just one desultory blast from a German siege mortar - even from a confidently safe distance, provides sufficient gravitas to prepare the soul abruptly for a good confession - equivalent I would say to kneeling in candlelight for at least fifteen minutes. The first time I heard one of those rounds approach, I actually looked to see if the sky had been torn open. From initiates there is the usual exhortation to, 'keep a tight sphincter chaps!' in these all too frequent moments of outreach by the Grim Reaper. New arrivals can't resist self-consciously checking behind themselves when the dust settles and black smoke drifts away. Old hands already have the massive brown stain. There is much soldierly bravura from chaps here about dangers of getting trapped in the cellar during a bombardment with nothing to eat - what alternatives there might be for sustenance? I told them 'we could live for a week on the bread and cheese crumbs, dropped olives and sausage rinds which fall to the floor every time there is a near miss and we all dive for cover.'

I have just opted out of a card game that has been running here to the best of my knowledge for the past three weeks - with rotated personnel including officers from Smith-Dorrien's reserve companies, Supply Depot personnel and a few locals. There is a doctor, Wallahan, who sits in for an hour each night when the barrage ceases. He is smoulderingly restrained, yet unquestionably brilliant, more French seemingly than Belgian. Playing poker with some of our MOs, I imagine, is his way of adjusting to the unwelcome reality of our presence in his town. Our thoughtful pastime underscores his tacit acceptance of a vastly extended, ad hoc patient list providing opportunity for rapid advancement as a surgeon. Playing cards serves to calm the lad's mind, steadying his hands after a day of operations.

Like Pontius Pilate's soldiers, they will gamble for absolutely anything. When money runs out, the MO's have no hesitation in using bandages or medical stores, as currency. Wollahan has a local contact running a black market in imported sphagnum moss, ideal for poultices - so his credit is good.

And I must not forget Monseigneur Belfort, the one permanent fixture here apart from the landlord and his staff. He is a Canadian Chaplain who seems to have the implicit trust of the hotelier. This padre is a declared Trotskyite and dedicated alcoholic, yet will only drink what has been paid for. He looks after Talbot's delivery door key, affording card school regulars access to the cellar at all hours of the day and night, graciously avoiding disturbance to Mme Talbot and upper echelon military guests. There is a scurrilous, deeply irreligious tenor to the pattern of inferences repeated by each new arrival to the marathon poker game, regarding indulgences the padre must have bargained with The Almighty, on behalf of Msr Talbot. There is a presumption of the nature and extent of the Hotelier's sins necessitating such trust in the padre. Deplorable explanations overheard usually begin with rude speculation about his involvement with one of the parlour maids, then range through a variety of despicable allegations involving creatures in the paddock behind the hotel.

Individuals participating in the endless analogy to 'the game of life,' playing safe, or risking all like so many dug in not far from here, seem every man jack of them to have filthy bodies, filthy backsides and filthy minds. I do not include myself in that censure, as I'm here only to arbitrate adherence to the rules. Thankfully Talbot and the padre are indulgent, forgiving fellows or we'd all be sorry - squatting in some alleyway behind the marketplace in freezing rain with a thousand coarse Australians. I'm far too embarrassed to go into detail but I know you'd roar out loud at the card player's disingenuous expressions when voicing such base ribaldry. Soldiers really do make a habit of being cruel, even to a revered man of the cloth.

There are thousands of wine bottles laid down here all to be tallied and accounted for by the OIC when broken into. Nominally this is done by the padre, as the one closest to salvation and thus above reproach if a bottle or two are consumed on impulse. There is also a full wine press of this autumn's produce which cannot be shipped under prevailing circumstances, with half a million infantrymen of various nationalities trying to kill one another in the immediate vicinity. Any vehicle moving along the road during daylight hours becomes a likely target for German artillery. We have been given firm instructions by Talbot to draw off as much as we like to consume at a discounted rate. Market economics you see – Msr T is cutting out the middle man plus all distribution costs, whilst increasing his usual margins.

In order to 'create a feeling of normality, sustaining morale,' Msgr Belfort is running a book on the precise volume the wine vat contains, to be confirmed subsequently by the Mayor of Popperinghe, as President of the local wine shipper's cooperative. Talbot has his firm agreement to allow scrutiny of past records of barrels filled from his press. Whoever gets closest to the average wins the pot, which currently stand at just over £20. The vat is roughly eight foot tall and six feet across the middle at the widest point. I could work it out on the back of a matchbox for them in half a minute but in truth I'm far too drunk to even suggest that. Belfort thinks I should introduce another element of fun by outlining my method.

Incidentally this Chaplain of His Holiness is in my estimation a tutelary saint, a true emissary of Our Mother of Perpetual Help, mediating in the words of Pope Benedict, 'the suicide of civilized Europe.' He has been close to the action since the beginning (the war I mean, not the card game). Msgr Belfort has warmly afforded me the benefit of experience as a survivor amid the ruins, taking personal responsibility for my continued good health as well as spiritual wellbeing. Actually everyone who knows this fine chap, says the same thing about his concern for each of them. The Monseigneur insists we are all on the path to enlightenment, including Kaiser Wilhelm and his General Staff. Belfort prevailed upon me to wear an engineer's overall on top of my uniform and leave my cap in my bedroom, 'until you have to visit your good friend Viscount French.' He insists I must avoid any semblance of routine at all costs. I have to walk everywhere rather than venture out on horseback, which is actually the favoured means of avoiding constant traffic jams and the muddy scrum of marching columns. There is a remount depot not far from here but the horses are unhappy about exposure to continuous noise. They can be unpredictable for an occasional horseman such as myself.

'What about my staff car?' I asked him, 'F . . . that Hugh. No, never! Worst possible thing you can do!' says he, in precisely enunciated, Francophile English.

'So, what do I say when French sends his driver for me?'

'Take my advice Hugh, get yourself a civilian motor cycle. At least then when they catch you at the crossroads they already zeroed into the day before, you can leap unceremoniously into the ditch. Keep it here in the wine cellar,' he says, 'And whatever you do – never follow close behind a staff car.'

Good Lord Christina, look what I've come to! Imagine the sight of me in a navy blue boiler suit, negotiating water filled pot holes on some country lane on my way to report to the Top Brass - without even a cap in hand. Dear man – like all priests he is simply trying to save us all from our own folly. I told him he was 'misjudging the proximity of the German snipers to our key Assembly area.'

'Don't be a freakin' idiot Hugh,' he says, 'I'm not talking about snipers. It's forward artillery spotters you need to be wary of!'

Anyway, here I am at rest in the inner sanctum – if I go to my room someone will always find me! The destructive nature of warfare creates a metier of crisis management. Such is my calling – but there are times when I have to rest. I have my writing paper; a full bottle of ink, the Conway Stewart pen you gave me on our fifth anniversary. Dear girl thanks again! I also have a bottle of the finest Burgundy I could find without getting covered in cobwebs, stumbling in the dark and bashing my brains against 'un Grand Pierre a bas.' That would be a new take on 'Missing In Action' - my skeletal remains discovered when this despicable war is long over!

Yours ever,
Hughie

XX XX XX X – Two kisses each for my girls and one for Oscar.

PS. Make Clarissa wash her face whenever he licks her mouth.'

Hannah walked around her bedroom to release tension in her back. As expected, Hugh's missives to Christina brought issues surrounding his death more poignantly to bear.

Why are men of affairs so uncompromisingly arrogant? Can't they see that such brutality is utterly pointless? Thank God for Pope Benedict's influence in keeping the Italians out of it. This is why Maria Visconti came, they fear their former allies.

Hannah needed to stretch and perform breathing exercises before looking for the sequential date on the next envelope. Intrigued, she opened it to read with renewed affection for Hugh,

'The Wine Cellar,
Talbot Hotel,
Popperinghe,
Belgium.
Sunday 18ᵗʰ October, 1914.   11.57pm

My Dear Lady Christina,

Thank you for letters from all three of you. I especially liked the paw print from Oscar and Helena's drawing of workers around the thresher. Tell Hannah she is doing the right thing, investing for the future. Order the Italian statuette she likes for a house warming gift. Advise Alice - marry her Co-op manager! If they sack him they will lose all my accounts. I shall offer him a job as my supply agent on an equivalent salary. Talk to her Christina – the woman needs security for her child, regardless of where she travels with you.

Before I departed for Moore Park you told me, 'I want to know everything you are involved in - no scrabble, no varnish, no lying like a trooper.' You know me Christina, never less than candid – at least where you are concerned, my true love. Let me think . . . I'm not trying to throw dust in your eyes. I honestly find it so hard to just think for myself any more.

Bloody Germans! Imagine the cheek of them trying to take Paris through Belgium. They knew it would draw in forces from the entire British Empire, including the fighting Irish. Intelligence reports say their forward units got within ten miles of the outskirts, a little place to the north east of the city - Claye, beyond the town of Meaux. Ha! Moltke overstretched himself, failing to take account of the Belgian population resisting so bravely.

Now there are stories abounding of German troops having taken reprisals against - murdering, I mean - citizenry of local townships. These accounts are from places either liberated by us recently, or from the few survivors who managed to flee through German lines just north of here. In one place the devils locked people in a church and set fire to it. I imagine you've read something in the paper by now. Heartless pigs! There is a seed of something fanatical - at once fearfully ruthless yet also deeply oppressive, in the mentality of this German invader. Despite our common humanity this makes them seem different from us. When we win we must impose a reckoning on German army officers responsible for these atrocities – I know that all orders came from the top down. There are no exceptions to such rules, at least not on our side. Blame on the other hand always starts at the bottom with the man ordered to do the dirty deed.

At first my involvement in the campaign was low key. After finishing re-training at Moore Park I spent one week in Chatham, followed by two days at Richborough, where they are planning a sea port for troop trains. Then I spent several days in Paris where they didn't really listen to my advice, although they were extremely polite as the French invariably are.

The key meeting was not with the military but with Baron Rothschild and the Board of Hottinger, Lafitte and Blount, regarding our development of Chemin de Fer du Nord. Essentially the German's destroyed a lot of their infrastructure, so they've given us carte blanche to assist in rebuilding it to suit our needs. Joffre is gung-ho, yet I was not reassured by my counterpart from his liaison team. The man kept nodding but was very tight lipped. I suspect a major build up further south will lead to a slogging match for hotly disputed coal fields - the genuine cassus bellum. Perhaps he had that in mind when I tried to engage with him about troop movements to defend Channel Ports. Maybe my French isn't up to scratch – I found myself wishing you were here to interpret for me. My host, Colonel Dauzat, made no attempt to speak English, unsurprisingly for a Southerner. I ran up against the broad assumption that we all encounter the same difficulties of moving men and munitions. Therefore, 'BEF can sort its own problems.' In a way that's a back-handed compliment – clearly they trust us to blockade and resist the common enemy, even if they do seize Antwerp and the French ports. Despite the old rivalry, the French treat us with genuine warmth and respect. 'Entente Cordial' evidently suits their traditional mentality – roughly corresponding to the Catholic notion of Holy Matrimony, 'If you smile at her, you marry her.' Anyway, regardless of reassurances it is unfortunate that our ally seems reluctant to act spontaneously when it comes to rapid deployment. It is far too late to do anything effective now, although the allies talked one another into this joint offensive.

My latest job is to get yet another division into place for support - just in case the Germans don't co-operate with our attempts to force them out of Belgium. Despite joyous temptation, with smirks on their moustachioed faces, no one at the joint staff meeting dared respond to my jibe about the memory of the first Emperor Napoleon. I invited them with a completely straight face to speculate as to, 'what might he have done?' given the present situation. There is regret amongst the French that the father of their modern nation was a boorish thug, hated at home, who ultimately took his military campaigns too far, losing more than he won for France. At the time they cheered him like a bantam cock, loving him perfidiously like a wanton parlour maid but they unquestionably conspired with the British to get rid of him at the end. No-one here wants to admit that. The memory and guilt of waging war across Europe are still with them, despite martial boulevards, triumphal arches and their blustering contempt for Germans. I believe the French as a nation have begun to grow up, to secretly despise warfare.

Beneath all the posturing is genuine love of the land, brooding consternation at the sacrilege committed in shortening a man's life, or spoiling his days under the smiling sun. More astute officers recall ambitious trickery of the old schemer Bismarck and the posturing élan of their military a generation ago - how they were casually drawn in and swiftly routed. Nowadays they espouse caution. Others, wisely looking across the Atlantic, speak thoughtfully of a vaguely remembered civil war abruptly redefining men in subjugation to machines - the railway locomotive and the Maxim gun. Warning voices recall mass-produced machines facilitating carnage on an unprecedented, industrial scale, even as their soldiers begin to dig-in around Verdun.

I have to admit my love that I recognise the same numbing uncertainty in myself - so they can't hide it behind swaggering bravura. But there is a subtle mechanism at work here. This subdued consternation of the French military may be a promise of this world's ultimate hope for civilization. Their common soldiery has a natural instinct to share and collaborate, rather than 'force the issue.' When this nationalistic madness is over, I intend to buy a manse with a little farmland near Paris where we can settle until the girls complete their education. Maybe then some of our family enterprises can run themselves for a time.

As I write the Germans are making devious use of the occupied rail network to move forward units towards Amiens, east of the river Somme, a little to the south-west of Popperinghe. From there they threaten Paris and insinuate the more daring possibility of linking up all the Belgian and French Channel ports, possibly cutting off and encircling us here. Ultimate success would require a German naval victory of course, which we know they crave.

Thanks to Churchill's Grand Fleet chasing their battle cruisers all around the South Atlantic, that overall plan can never work. Nonetheless this deployment behind the Somme is a clever, divisive tactic. I'm no strategist, I just know how to move goods and people. But one thing is clear: despite the loss of Lille any objective for us must start from a close look at the rail network. We might advance along railway lines to take back key junctions, instead of spilling blood for open farmland and sleepy little market towns. That at least has been my advice to them. Thank God such decisions are not my responsibility, for they jeopardize the lives of millions.

At least we are over the border into Belgium - just north of Lille, near the town of Ypres. We need to push them back from the Belgian Channel ports, liberate Brussels and strike south. Ideally force them out of Belgium altogether. Then our commitment will have been honoured, as Lord Grey put it – 'our side can declare with a first innings lead before bad light stops play.' The word is that Antwerp has been relieved. The Belgian army are attacking from the north east, so it should be over soon.

All for now, as I'm too tired to finish,

Love ever, Hugh x'

'Tuesday 20th October   3.35 am
Room 203, Talbot Hotel,
Popperinghe

In case you are wondering why I write at this ungodly hour – well it's consensual with the Germans that this is rest time. In reality the only hour that is actually not ungodly. Our enemy is trying to 'up the stakes' by bombarding our salient at Ypres during the hours of darkness, when they know we move up men and equipment.

Naturally they tend to want to remind us in the rearward area at 'Pops' that they are thinking of us too. At last they too have fallen asleep it seems.

Where did I travel next? Oh yes, St Omer to fill in French's staff on the slowly crystallizing requirements of siege mentality. They at least are attentive. I was quizzed by Haig, commander of 1 Corps, Kitchener's bright star, about rapid deployment using rail. He certainly understands the complexities now – the need to plan everything in detail weeks, or even months in advance, as did our former opponent Moltke. I read in the Times that the Kaiser blames Moltke for getting bogged down in the Marne, not seizing Paris within the first five weeks. Such blithe arrogance is typical of Oberst Heeresleitung- the German Supreme Command. Naïve optimism masks bumbling uncertainty at the top - quite ludicrous really.

Now thank God, Chancellor Bethmann-Hollweg is murmuring of peace. The Austro-Hungarians wish he'd never given them their 'blank cheque.' Their new Commander here in the West, Falkenhayn wants peace with the Russians, so he does not have to take divisions away from Ypres. I pray they will all relent so we can go home for Christmas but fear there is now a military-industrial dictatorship within the nobility, much stronger than either Chancellor Theo, or Kaiser Willi. Too many personal fortunes, too many careers and reputations are at stake. Germany as a nation state lacks both circumspection and effective leadership. I Pray for them Christina. You must do so too.

At last I seem to be catching up with you in my letters - In the intervening few weeks I have raced all over the hinterland, advising on reconstruction of track, tunnels and supply depots. That at least is my excuse for not putting pen to paper. Thank you for the tin of scones – they were magnificent – I mean that. I was impressed that you made them with the girls – despite being spoilt with a staff of servants, you have not lost the touch. In answer to your questions: no you did not put in too many raisins and yes they are equally delicious with grated cheese.

I offered them round with some tea to a small bunch of Yorkshire Light Infantry heroes returning from their rotation at the front. They wandered into our marshalling yard looking exhausted, in the small hours of the morning. Three or four lads dipped gently into your OXO tin, gratefully accepting a scrape of butter I managed to procure. They ate them like they had never seen food before. One chap mumbled through his crumbs with a delightful Barnsley drawl, 'Eee that were gradely Sarnt! – a true Yorkshire-ism if ever I heard one. He naturally assumed that I outranked him because I had food to give out, but was misled by my greasy overall. I couldn't possibly have been a regimental CO because I was covered in shit.

Anyway here I am near the front, as anticipated months ago, where Field Marshall French not only welcomes my presence but seems determined to not let me leave, even though I am purportedly here to assess the situation and report back to Chatham.

I must sleep now or I will be no good tomorrow. I will post two bulletins I have written and promise to resume writing to you again at 'the ungodly hour' this time tomorrow.

Aye,

Hugh xx xx xx –
Pat on the head only for Oscar this time. Helena is right – it's disgusting to let a dog lick your face!'

Hannah was entranced. Her eyes hurt so badly that she had to rub them and she felt a slow creeping tension spreading from her crown down over the right side of her forehead. Muscles were tightening across the middle of her back and she felt a stabbing pain between her shoulders. But knowing a little of what others like Hugh were enduring at that precise moment, Hannah felt it important to finish the journey with him. In a sleepless daze she murmured, "This is my vigil for you, Hughie-my dear friend."

Stacking the letter with others she had read, Hannah swivelled out of bed again to pace around the room. Lying on the floor to stretch muscles in her back, she groaned softly in discomfort. At last she motivated herself to light a fire with the intention of ploughing on. To prepare for the imminent hiatus that awaited, Hannah searched out a half bottle of Brandy Alice had given her with the peremptory command, 'hide this for midnight feasts, in amongst your underwear.' Washing out a glass used for rinsing teeth she poured a very large measure of the fragrant Cognac. Taking a large sip Hannah found that it burned her oesophagus, making her head reel but at least it dulled an advancing migraine. She took another sip, before opening the next of Hugh's letters to Christina.

'Popperinghe / Talbot Hotel
Wednesday 21ˢᵗ October 1914

My Dearest,

Et seq:

No-one has ever encountered the sheer scale of movements here, at least not under such peculiar circumstances, myself included. French seems to think I can pick up the blower and instantly demand another fifty locomotives with a dozen Pullman cars apiece from the Board. He can then pour more bodies into the gap between us and the French, or us and the Belgians. The need is always 'critical.' I explained patiently that 'this is analogous to setting up the schedule for the FA Cup Final somewhere out in rural Devonshire, a hundred and fifty miles from the usual venue at Crystal Palace. And there is the minor irritant that Sunderland keep drawing with Villa after extra time. Currently I am planning and co-ordinating train movements for the fourth replay,' I tell him. 'In fact that would be easy by comparison,' I add with bluff indignation.

'Don't you know Hugh, Parliament commissioned the raising of another New Army?' he pleads irately, the iron jaw jutting

451

accusingly under that wonderful moustache. French's tone seems to imply that Herbert Asquith has written to me personally asking for support and I have refused.

'Oh yes, how many is that we are up to Sir?' I ask, all innocence. 'Is it two, or three now? Honestly . . . I've lost count since I've been away from my desk and a daily newspaper. I've been preoccupied by what's going on over here.'

'Well, Major General Robertson will have been authorised by now to secure new contracts with the railway companies. Why not write to your Board and get them to speak to him directly. Ask for what you need here on the ground. Bloody good business if you ask me Hugh, all assured profits old man, eh?'

I avoid disputing this half-truth, resisting at the same time temptation to mention the need for more heavy cranes for removal of mangled debris. I remind myself distractedly that I have effectively become my own authority in this arena of madness and can appeal only to God, or if I am really desperate, Head Quarters at Chatham.

We have much in common as King's Irishmen but as a professional soldier French seems resentful lately of strategic interference from Whitehall. I dread to think he might see me as complicit in that and dragging my feet in some way. I can't help imagining that had they backed him fully in the first place we would all be in Brussels now, having the sheets changed on a daily basis. Dare I say it – the man seems daunted by the risk of moving too quickly, like a heavyweight boxer pushed to the ropes in the tenth round. Meanwhile I have reluctantly slipped into the role of glorified freight-yard controller!

Chatham decided to hand me the brevet rank of Brigadier, so unit commanders are less inclined to make demands when they find out who I am - petitioning me privately about delivery of their back orders. Maybe it's because I have the unofficial status of a private contractor, with the unique privilege of nominating and commissioning my own projects. Clearly the higher up you are in the echelons of Top Brass, the less people expect of you. I actually do feel like a professional soldier now. The word 'rookie' has taken on a profound new meaning for regulars here – 'an individual who volunteered for a reason and actually knows what the hell he is doing - unlike that chump, so and so!'

Regiments and companies press me round the clock to speed up delivery of their deadly consignments. With breathtaking complacency they have begun to take the inexhaustible supply of fresh troops as a given. Once the Garrison received its siege guns and trench mortars they dug in and started blasting away. Unsurprisingly they are reluctant to go anywhere now that the Cavalry doesn't lead them. They would have to give their heavy weapons back to us and they might get broken or lost. Let's be honest – is it not every boy's dream to play with his own howitzer? So I am stuck here in the middle of the BEF's narrowly defined war.

Oh and I must not be too specific about locations in case some busy little woman at GPO, Regent's Park double checks my letter and Sgt Fawthrop lands in trouble - I'd have to put him on a charge. I gave him a bottle of the same delicious Burgundy that I'm quaffing right now and the good fellow gave me one of the censor's stamps, which I keep tucked away in my pocket. Tim would never dream of vetting my letters to you – again, I believe because of the overall recommended by Monseigneur Belfort. A German spy would never be covered in axle grease.

But here's something concerning Muintir na hEireann, that I want to share with you. The Royal Irish Regiment went through Abbeville when I was there yesterday, heading towards our southern flank! I did not see Ed but will look him up when I get the chance. I spoke instead to an officer of the 2nd Royal Irish, who told me they were heading for their usual right flank position at a village named LePilly (burn this letter in case the housemaid is a spy). I suspect that by now the Germans know they are there.

I did a little deal with a clerk at the NAAFI dump at St Omer to send up four cases of Jameson's to Edgar's Regiment in the armoured engine towing their heavy gear. I included a note telling them to, 'distribute grog to your machine gunners - courtesy of Lady

C Leslie.' A German forward unit must have spotted it through their field glasses and assumed it was carrying explosives because they took a pot shot. The engine came back for repair with large calibre bullet holes straight through the armour plating. An unusually hot reception for a unit just moving into position. Thankfully the driver and fireman were uninjured.

Word is, the precious cargo got through intact, although I don't suppose it stayed that way for long. I don't usually have to pay for things here but honour required me to write a cheque in favour of my current employer to the tune of £4.18sh and 6 pence. That incidentally was the (black market) bulk price, straight from the Quartermaster's secret bond at St Omer.

Thanks for all your delightful letters. Please tell the girls I said so! It is inspiring to hear all your news and know that life goes on as normal elsewhere. Every one of us here is fighting for just that normality. A big hug to each of my lovely dotes! Be sure and tell them what a hero their Daddy is! And now for well-earned rest!

Love ever,

Hugh x'

As Hannah sat by the fire warming ice-cold feet, darkness and exhaustion seemed not to touch her. She placed the letter back in its envelope, amused at the alacrity and openness of Hugh's perspective on events in newspapers, which she had talked so much about as an outsider.

No ordinary soldier, even an officer with the temporary rank of Brigadier would dare write home with such a degree of frankness. But Hugh Leslie was no career soldier. Had he been such he would have risen far above the token rank awarded any self-seeking aristocrat in uniform.

Knowing the final outcome for Sir Hugh, Hannah felt strong foreboding about the manner in which he spoke of his specialised knowledge required so near to the battlefront.

This place in Flanders is a tumour, rapidly growing with its own blood supply. A massive cancer in the soft tissue of Western Europe.

Hannah padded quietly to the hand basin in her en-suite dressing room to throw freezing water onto her face, rubbing it into corners of her eyes and itchy tear ducts. Filling an empty glass from a pitcher she drank a little water. Hesitating for a second before using the lavatory she considered the desperate plight of men in Belgium, wondering what was happening right now in the freezing mud. The house was silent but the sound of flushing water falling from a header tank would rouse Helena and Clarissa from sorrowful sleep. Never having used the WC without flushing, Hannah decided to set her alarm to rise and sluice it before the maid checked her room in the morning. Throwing off her clothes she donned a nightgown and braced gently with goose bumps rising on her arms and legs as she relieved herself. Her taut, blanched skin perfectly matched the bucolic scene hand-painted on delicately compressed china clay bathroom tiles.

How sophisticated we imagine ourselves with all our niceties – yet how banal we truly are in our excesses.

Hannah mused upon the protocol of living and dying graciously – of how all is revealed in a balletic symphony of impenetrable time and fate. A tear for poor dead Hugh crept into her eye, as the floodgate of sorrow began to open at last. Hannah heard her own voice crying aloud once, then quickly constrained herself. She found it difficult to dismiss the thought of how desirable it would be to die quietly in a warm bed.

Drying herself before wiping away tears on her night gown, Hannah shivered in the coldest hour before the dawn. Climbing gratefully back into bed she carefully opened another of Hugh's envelopes to read the letter it contained. Counting five more left to read, not including the official notification of Hughie's death, Hannah anticipated the last one that would be the most difficult.

'Talbot Hotel,
Popperinghe,
Belgium

11.30 pm
Friday, 24th October 1914

My Dear,

Sorry that I've so little time to communicate. I would write every day were it only possible but it's increasingly difficult to relax. Everyone here is under tremendous pressure. Ironically there is little movement but less stability in the front line. Behind the scenes I find myself spinning like a dervish, as this unimaginable conflict intensifies. Now at last I will take time – and trouble my thoughts a little to examine the unthinkable (whilst trying to avoid what is unspeakable). But to hell with censorship! As ever you are my confidante Christina, more so for distance and longing. Besides, in the unimaginable chaos of this past week I discover Fawthrop's stamp still in my pocket. I must remember to get him a spare next time there's a consignment of stationery for Divisional HQ.

Now the rearward infrastructure is rebuilt and functioning across recaptured territory, I have inherited responsibility for efficient functioning of this desperate little battlefront. Forces holding the territory around Ypres represent the rump of our shattered BEF but it is absolutely crucial we hang on. There are anything up to a hundred train movements to co-ordinate daily, between Armentieres and the Channel ports. Many hundreds of thousands of men are being moved into and around the arena, as the battleground stabilises.

I have at my disposal a company of multi-skilled Sappers: tunnelers; track layers; drivers; shunters; crane operators; firemen;

456

welders; engineers; builders; labourers; clerks; store men; buglers; cooks, officers and guards. Nothing moves through here unless they have first built a siding and storage dump, or warehousing for it, then authorised and scheduled arrival and distribution of each consignment. The officers seem to read my best intentions, often completing tasks before I express my wishes. Every day wide-eyed, scrawny reinforcements arrive to boost our regimental numbers. Yet amazingly there is always plenty for them to do. They work like dogs to prove their worth, eating up new skills like apprentices from the poor house sitting down to Christmas dinner. As a result of their finely honed collaborative sense, these men have become as highly prized by the Brass as the toughest of the Scottish regiments - but I am quite clear that is mainly due to their footballing ability, not prowess as fighting men. I jest – it's quite the opposite. These sappers are fearless. They will do absolutely anything they are asked, however dangerous, without objection.

On the subject of football: it brings me curious delight to observe secundum artem translated into 'the passing game.' Whenever there is a lull between train movements my lads get out the football and challenge the nearest bunch of field engineers. Their cries and exhortations to, 'run with it man!' or 'shoot lad, shoot!' are interwoven with booms and crackling of distant gunfire. Without hesitation any of these boys would pick up his jacket to crawl silently into a German listening post with wires and an explosive charge. Perhaps you think it ironic I wanted to avoid the frustration of flying a desk in Paris? God forgive me, instead I have become Hell's Quartermaster – the antipode, if not the antithesis of St Peter, with feet up on the desk manning the Pearly Gates. Here I have the power of a minor deity, or perhaps a wicked archon, although in truth I feel more like a beleaguered surgeon applying a tourniquet. It seems I never provide my colleagues with enough of what they need.

Christina, I have to swallow hard when an ambulance train waits to leave because the next troop transport is pulling in. It has become impossible to discriminate between the living and the dying, where killing is the only priority. One thing I can't allow myself to think about is morale, because *we* are lucky. *We* are the only people working as such, constructing *anything* amid this meandering river of destruction. Just now RCE is intensively laying light-track railway alongside heavy gauge lines, to help distribution up to the front. This makes recovery quicker after the bastards shell it, which they do every day.

We needed four hundred tons of substrate to create hard standing and decent access roads behind a screening stand of mature trees - so the boys could collect their toys under cover, without wagons and horses getting stuck in the mud. We placed an order at a local quarry and were told we had to wait a week. That night the Germans obliged us by shelling the town centre close to the station. I cancelled the order and set my men to clearing up and disposing of the rubble – they transported it a few hundred metres to the new loading dock. Sorry, I have to shower and change while the water is back on.

Love ever,

Hugh. X'

'Et seq:
Thursday 29th October.

Increasing numbers of residents are moving away from the area as the battle intensifies, not relishing the prospect of invaders rolling through a third time. Incredibly many locals still continue to live in and around Ypres itself, despite the fearsome mass of German troops and heavy guns queuing up to re-take the old town.

Here in 'Pops' we have created an immense marshalling yard, cleared back into surrounding fields with anything explosive dispersed over nearly half a mile of track. If they chance to score a direct hit on ammunition ready for transhipment it minimises damage to rolling stock, troops and buildings. Their guesswork reminds me of the game 'Battleships' I played with Ed when he was a young sprout. I oblige reserve troops to disembark in tunnels, or cargo sidings, and at night whenever possible. They march to tent villages in the salient, across fields miles from the town. Many are transported up to 'Railway Wood', East of Ypres along a branch line we constructed. Men coming back from the front line slip away quietly after an eight day stint, sooner if they have been hard pressed. Christina, their eyes betray what I cannot tell. Often reserve companies are barely rested and reinforced, when thrown back into line to retake what was lost the day before.

Infantrymen I encounter mutter insubordinately about our tactics. Thankfully however, it seems the enemy are more prepared than our side to launch themselves suicidal into the cauldron - judging from their reverse at Bixschoote (just to the north of here), about which you will have read in the paper. I understand the Germans reported to the neutral press that the action took place at the village of Langemarck, thinking it sounded Germanic. I suppose we all need a reason to sacrifice our lives.

The report spoke sentimentally of university students singing as they strode into battle through morning mist. Our troops do that too - so machine gunners on the flanks will know who they are and don't get trigger happy. The Germans learn our songs to trick men on action stations into *not* raising the alarm as they advance through the mist. They yell 'retire, retire!' in uniquely rounded, gymnasium English when advancing, to trick our chaps into emerging from their trenches to be cut down like cowards. Regardless of that, it was pitiful to see wide-eyed fear on their hairless faces as they marched the remnant through from Bixschoote. Children or not, they have done a lot of damage to our troops. The Germans couldn't take the town, so they obliterated it with artillery.

Many colleagues voice the opinion that the ferocity of their attacks there and at La Bassee to the south shows increasing desperation. As a token of national fortitude even the Kaiser's Imperial Guard have now been thrown into the mill. Although they broke through woodland near Ypres, their sacrifice made little real impression on our front line. Highland Guards soaked up their attack. As with the boy soldiers seeing startled, sour faces of the

459

remnant marching through at gun point - bloodied and humbled in their smart uniforms - inspires us to hope this despicable bloodletting will soon be over. It was widely reported last summer that the Kaiser favoured a limited war. He tried to dissuade Moltke on 2nd August when he heard we would declare war if they invaded Belgium. Maybe this massacre will prompt him to seek compromise from those seeking to prolong the debacle. Unfortunately I fear tension is more likely to push the chump into another breakdown.

Look us up on the map – Popperinghe, the 'assembly point' behind Ypres, 'the prize,' an insignificant little brewery town about ten miles from here. You've probably never heard of it before? In a couple of years it will be forgotten, by everyone except beer tourists from English universities. In the meantime don't tell anyone where I am, or leave letters lying around for casual scrutiny by domestic staff – my location and activities are a military secret. We are after all hoping to catch the enemy off guard.

Their artillery spotters are dug in on the top of a tiny mound excavated for a railway cutting south of Ypres, formally known as hill 60. From there those devils direct the unravelling all my personal handiwork, as well as wreaking havoc with General French's plans to push their army out of Belgium. Once that hill has been taken and their fusillade from hidden canons suppressed, the flank will turn and we will be going home. Or at least the Germans will be. I suspect they won't be so keen to fight tooth and nail when the battle is raging around Dusseldorf, or Cologne. But what do I really know? I'm an engineer not a psychologist. French wants to talk to me about using some of my tunnelers, with a contingent of newly arrived Welsh Engineers – coal miners in uniform. Can't be too specific or Fawthrop will require more than a bottle of Jameson!

More later

H x'

In the dead of night Hannah rose to bank the fire and partially close the flue to direct heat into the chilly room. The old house had effective central heating but it would be hours before it came on. Looking out, she could see freezing mist gripping dead woodland bordering the lane. It struck her as remarkable that any living thing could survive such deep winter. Hannah put on a cardigan before climbing back into bed to read on.

'GHQ, St Omer
12.15 pm

Saturday 1ˢᵗ November, 1914.

Dear Christina,

Thanks for the parcel. It was well received I can tell you. There has been a cold snap, so extra socks and pullover are more than welcome. I left my spare uniform with cleaners here over three weeks ago but have not had time to collect it. The Top Brass had a big pow-wow this morning which cleared the air a little, not to say that it was hostile. I intend to stick around for a few hours to have something to eat without dust in it and I can take a walk without worrying if a shell is about to land on my head. If there is a line free I will phone – which by the time you get this letter you will be aware of, ha ha!

The enemy turned up the pressure on Ypres, taking Becelare and Zandvoorde (just to the north of the town). They threw massed ranks against key positions at Gheluvelt and Messines. All regiments defending there suffered badly. The Guards lost their Irish CO, Brigadier General Charles Fitzclarence.

Did you see Top injun Fabeck quoted in the press saying this battle would, 'settle for ever the centuries long struggle, end the war and strike a decisive blow against our most detested enemy?' Didn't we come here as honest brokers to assist Belgians and French who had been invaded? I never knew the Germans felt that way about us, did you? I am deeply hurt! Moltke staked his career on six weeks, Fabeck gave himself one. They didn't bargain for the pluck of

461

ordinary British soldiers – Worcesters; Lincolns; Northumberlands, blunting their heaviest attack around Gheluvelt. Fabeck's arrogance is sublime. I wonder which colonial outpost they will send him to when he's done his worst. But enough of this sad chronicle for now! I must go get my uniform before they shut,

H: XXX , intimate pat on your sensational behind.'

'St Omer
Sunday 2nd November

10.30 am

Dearest,

You will be pleased to hear I went to mass and took Holy Communion at the magnificent Notre Dame Cathedral. The pipe organ there is formidable. I said one for all of you. In answer to your question – yes, I eat fairly well. Officers generally do – Talbot does extremely well considering, with respect to seasonal vegetables etc. Part of my role is to facilitate the inward movement of produce so our troops can be fed. On the whole they are strictly rationed but there is a healthy black market around estaminets, cafes selling beer and tobacco – from vendors taking advantage of demand from thousands of hungry men.

On a different note there are worrying rumours from HQ. I don't want to cause anxiety for everyone at home but it went badly for Edgar's regiment. They had just moved into position on our southern flank at Le Pilly, near the town of La Bassee when the Germans attacked. Sad to say they were surrounded and overrun. Communications are poor and intelligence scant but hundreds must have been taken prisoner. I will find out whatever I can and let you know immediately. Please keep this to yourself for now. Apologies for not telling you this directly but every phone line was engaged.

Besides I didn't want to worry anyone unduly, until I check on the situation myself. Don't breathe a word to my mother, or any of the wider family. Keep smiling Christina, or they will know.

I am generally fine, in good spirits despite the beastliness and folly surrounding me. I eat and sleep well between bouts of drunken singing from (not with), men on rotation. That incidentally is certainly the saddest sound I have ever heard in my life, although right now I cannot even begin to tell you why.

Unfortunately the water main in Pops was broken and I'd not bathed, or had laundry service, for over a week - the reason I stayed here overnight. I badly needed to clean up and shave! Don't say I didn't warn you Christina, my hygiene habits are slipping!

Gavrillo Princip has a hell of a lot to answer for. I honestly think even Monsignor Belfort would join me in thumping the living daylights out of him, given half a chance. I'm joking of course - but then again hypothetically . . . if one could reverse the arrow of time; change the course of History following a brief encounter with the man? Whatever would Hannah say if she could hear me? Do you think she would she accuse me of losing my humanity? God forbid I might fall in her estimation. Had she been my daughter I would have sent her to university to study Law and Politics, then found her a practice to run. More to the point, that entire episode of Serbian Nationalism was a side issue. Princip was brought to book, incarcerated and is pending execution. This accursed war has more to do with the Establishment's fear of Socialist Deputies elected to the Reichstag than the Black Hand movement. Anyhow as Voltaire once put it, 'History is but a pack of tricks we play on the dead.'

Incidentally you are right to remind me of how our army treated the Boers and how the Belgians behaved in Congo. As Belfort says, none of us has the grace to save ourselves without divine intervention. I think I am becoming a Marianist.

Hopefully I can give myself a full ten days leave at the beginning of December. If I get away on the morning of Friday the 4th I should be in Monaghan by Sunday eve. 'Advent,' I hear you say. But no, I bloody don't want to go to mass at the monastery! I want to walk in my woodlands with you and the girls then sit by the fire all evening with a bottle of Brandy, listening to you playing Chopin on the piano. I might play chess with Helena, if she agrees to let me win. I want to hear all the gossip from the village and news from the aunties and uncles – however peevish. I will read Conan Doyle's Lost World to you in bed, if you promise not to finish it on your own. All this after half an hour alone with you, not just the usual seven minutes, in any one of the master bedrooms – you choose but light a fire two days in advance to take the chill off. I wish for the girl's sake I could stay in Monaghan for Christmas . . . but with luck this will be all over then, or realistically shortly after. On that positive note, I send you my love on wings of prayer. Try not to dwell too long on the Irish Guards and dear brother Edgar. Get Daly to say mass but tell no-one at home the real reason.

     Love to Clarissa and Helena,
     as to one and all.

     Yours Aye,

     Hugh.'

'Post script

11.30 pm,

3rd November, 1914.

Dear friend,

I woke dreamily in my quarters imagining I was in bed, draped around your warmth – only to find I am deluded. Waking and sleeping long since merged into hallucination. There is no way for me to step around this, so I will say it out right – I fear poor Edgar is lost to us. I recall with dread what has preoccupied my waking thoughts for days now – deepest foreboding, with confused reports from the few survivors I could locate in field hospitals here in St Omer. Cutting through it all is an eyewitness account from Lance Corporal O'Leary, who told me this afternoon that he witnessed poor Edgar fall. By this man's word, he knew him well and says he died a hero - taking charge of a machine gun when his crew were successively hit, finally using a revolver to defend their position when he ran out of ammunition. He said poor Ed was certainly hit two or three times and not taken prisoner. O'Leary was one of only twenty officers and men of the 2nd Royal Irish who escaped being killed or taken prisoner. It galls me to accept it but they were surrounded and overrun.

Smith-Dorrien puts it down to poor intelligence, yet I swear it was decent weather and RFC squadrons were up the day before. I spoke to Harper and McDonagh in our intelligence unit, demanding to know what their basic advice had been regarding movement on our southern flank east of La Bassee. The EO Harper, said 'Colonel McDonagh is fed up of telling French and Haig precise enemy positions and apparent strength, for his word to be ignored.' Harper informed me that radio communication intercepts are numerous and accurate. I will be in real trouble myself if the girls at Regent's Park open this particular letter but I'm angry enough not to care for their censorship. The Field Marshall might take away my stamp and send me back to Richborough! It's one thing giving away military secrets but if the message gets back to Falkenhayn that *we ignore our own intelligence,* what would he make of that? Harper warned his Colonel to say nothing concerning a massive build-up to the north, which looked like the beginnings of a pincer movement.

Evidently the Brass wanted an attack at all costs - more reputations at stake you see, not to mention soldier's lives. Harper says McDonagh ignored his advice to say nothing. The good fellow was ridiculed by French, 'for warning him against any presumption of success of the planned attack by the Irish Guards.' The Royal Irish had just moved into Le Pilly, above the town of Neuve Chappelle when the enemy began an intensive bombardment with heavy siege howitzers. The rest of II Corps withdrew, leaving Edgar's regiment isolated. I got as close as possible to Neuve Chappelle, now in no-man's land. It's difficult to write about the stark scene I witnessed through field glasses, Christina - viewing the ridge where my brother fell. But if no-one speaks the truth, who at home will see the reality, until it's too late to stop this kind of murderous fiasco? How will we ever learn?

Amid paraphernalia of a broken fusilier regiment – muddied rifles lying beside lifeless, torn uniforms, the most visible feature from a safe distance were boots - protruding from the pulverised ridgeline at odd angles. Here and there lay the carcase of a swollen dray horse. There was a wrecked ammunition tumbrel, with only one wheel – the other strangely nowhere in sight on the exposed hillside. Most poignant of all was the remnant of a pathetic little dug-out hastily constructed by field engineers under fire. In front of it . . . grip fast! . . . a pile of neatly laid out, covered corpses. For all I know one of them was nineteen year old Captain Edgar Leslie. The Officer's Post had evidently doubled as a first aid station. Now it is a mausoleum, visited only by crows.

The Germans withdrew to await the next attempt to take the rise, judiciously wary of the arrival of more Irishmen. There is nothing left of the village of Neuve Chappelle. It has been erased from the world of the living, like one of the Duke of Sutherland's clearance villages.

I have to tell you that I found myself shaking uncontrollably, vomiting and bubbling helplessly like a child. There are so many battles and counter attacks that no commander even asks permission to recover corpses, or bury the dead. As Pope Benedict said, we are witnessing the suicide of European civilization.

With all my love,

Hugh x'

As she read Hannah's mouth hung open in distress. Silent tears dropped onto Christina's penultimate letter from Hugh, reviving dried ink which ran to mingle with forced handwriting, pooling across his tortured words like spilt blood. Hannah went to her writing desk to find blotting paper, cursing under her breath at ineptitude in handling something amounting to a family reliquary for two dead brothers. Yawning uncontrollably despite passion for the bereft, she carried on with the ordeal of witnessing what only the condemned had seen first-hand.

'Popperinghe,

11.20 am,
Thursday,
November 20th 1914.

Dear Christina,

Thank the Lord God Almighty for heavy snow and frost! I'd forgotten how they made my heart lift as a boy - but this morning, grown men wept with joy at the sight. I write from a smoky corner of the wine cellar beneath the Talbot - home from home - hiding from fierce recriminations abounding at St Omer. Some of that furore was intimated in my previous letter.

Even now as I relax for the first time in months, raised voices echo in my head, 'Why did Smith-Dorien counter-attack, sending precious sappers, cooks and orderlies to their doom, rather than withdraw to the designated holding position as per instruction?' and 'What does Leslie think of that? Do you support that use of your engineers?'

'Ubique Quo Fas et Gloria Ducunt,' I murmured and one or two of them shrugged. When there is nothing to be said worth saying, the regimental motto is a great conversation filler. Ideal for the tiresome business of funerals and memorials, so why not the occasional grim and blasphemous post-mortem? Leslie may think they were indeed mettlesome heroes who actually went everywhere that Right and

Glory led, even if it amounted to a disaster that no-one wants to take responsibility for. But I daren't voice that opinion, for fear it be used to vilify my Irish friend, the surly Field Marshall, who is essentially asking for my support.

Equivocation moves in a circle back towards the starting point of the argument, 'Whose bright idea was it that we open the barriers of the Yser to flood farmland West of Dixmude?' demands the commander of shattered 11 Corps.

'What, the lowlands in front of the Channel ports?' queries a fellow just returned from the close run thing at Octagon Wood, claiming he had not known what has happened.

'It was the Frogs!' bellows the Big Chief, 'and incidentally it guarantees us respite, giving them time to move up to attack Nieuport.'

'It also guaranteed the Hun would transfer units south to attack us at Ypres!' shouts back the unrepentant *Smith-Doreen*, 'You should all thank God for my Corps standing to fight and the commitment of my Cavalry, or your elite Guards would have been wiped out,' he argues defiantly. The Whisky magnate says nothing, though the Big Chief gives him a look saying, 'take note of this, Haig, for when I send you to report to Kitchener in London.'

'Bull' Allenby is praised and immediately promoted for employing essentially the same tactics as Horace. Both men advocate co-ordinated use of artillery and aircraft, with their fast moving cavalry. Unfortunately like Conan Doyle's warning of the use of submarines, the Germans will probably accommodate these new lightning war tactics more readily than the deeply fractured BEF.

They are dung hill cocks, displaying hackles and combs amid detestable slaughter, evaluating retreat not in terms of who was saved but by how many guns were lost to the enemy. In contrast they justify gross slaughter for personal ambition. Blessed be He who has given the Cock intelligence. None of them envisioned the enormity of a continental land war and truthfully none of them are in a position to give advice upon its most prudent conduct, especially Haig, who planned for these contingencies without standardising infantry equipment, or artillery. No wonder he was silent - even now there is no consensus.

Geddes (from North Eastern rail) and I both favour some of the tactics suggested by Smith-Dorrien and Allenby – anything to end the stalemate. However we are simply casual observers. There is a limit to the extent we can organise the movement of goods with a web of supply and end usage larger than the Co-operative Society - solely for the purpose of annihilation. There is a need for coherent purpose amid all this destruction.

But instead of listening to one another to identify any such principle, they turn instead to the impedimenta of modern warfare, 'Why are there no replacement buffer-springs for our field guns?' asks an RFA Major, who has come over to St Omer to plead his case. The boss looks at him sympathetically, deciding that his question doesn't merit an answer because there simply isn't one.

'Could you let us have something from one of your workshops Leslie? Woodhead's have let us down with their damned spares. Some arse gusset forgot to put in the order!'

'Let me have a broken one and I'll set someone on it,' I reply tentatively, nodding at Whitaker to take a note, 'Make a mould and put two or three men on it round the clock – get the Major's location. Deliver however many springs he wants and send the rest to the RFA Quartermaster. Garrison can wait for the order from England. But don't leave them on it too long, or they will never stop.'

'Leave who?' asks Whitaker.

'The lads at our foundry Lieutenant,' I tell him, 'Write it down lad!'

Then some sage points out, 'The Royal Artillery doesn't require a rapid rate of fire anyway old chap, because actually we have no fucking shells.'

'We used up what we had because we were defending a position that was about to be overrun!' snarls Gough.

I laugh out loud and they all look at me. After an embarrassing moment the inevitable question comes, 'Can you make shells Leslie?'

The entire Top Brass are immediately diverted away from the most invidious calumnies against one another towards mutual condemnation of those individually and severally responsible for the supply of ordnance, 'Why are there no shells Leslie? . . . No fucking shells!'

I cannot help myself . . . I laugh again but feel like shouting, 'You bunch of wafflers! Ask Haig!' But instead I say with the inherited diplomacy of centuries, 'None of this was planned gentlemen but at home we have the most efficient rail network in the world. So whatever you need we *will* deliver!'

'Bravo that man!' says my good friend from the First Colony. He is a fool but I love him.

The RFA Major seizes the opportunity to remind us all of orders from GHQ, 'The Huns continually rain fire and brimstone upon our heads, stopping only when they send in waves of infantry to winkle our lads out of their hiding places - yet we are rationed to fifty shells per gun. We have been told very firmly *not to fire those* as the enemy will probably overrun our front line soon and we will need them for the counter attack!' As usual I sit in silence, my arms folded, trying hard not to take umbrage as this is certainly not my problem.

Some poor Scottish Guards Captain, with the end of his thumb shot off and soaking crimson through a wad of bandages, croaks with the tremulous voice of a man rescued from hell - to the shame of all present, 'Gentlemen if I may venture, whilst on the subject of supplies – where on earth is the gun oil? Why was some not sent up to the siege at Gheluvelt? We were cutting their advance to pieces until our .303s began to clog! We sent a courier but he couldn't find any in the dump. I mean, do we want to win this effing war or not?'

The entire Top Brass stare sympathetically at this ardent young Laird as he delivers his final pass, 'They sent Mark 7 ammunition for infantry equipped with latest short rifles. It doesn't fit. Obviously there is a stock somewhere, which should not be given away to the Indian Police, or whoever wants the older Lee Enfield ammunition.' There is silence as this last snippet of information begins to sink in.

"What's your point lad?" asks the Earl, as if this is a personal slight, "Well, we haven't been re-equipped. Not yet sir. We have the older, long barrelled .303s.'

There is dumb silence, with teeth clenched and military jaws jutting all around the room, 'We used the last of the bullets that fit our rifles in a mad minute of rapid fire, and then charged them with bayonets. We collected up their Mausers and as much ammunition as we could carry, then moved out to wait in the woods at the edge of town. The Mauser is a damned good rifle Sir but too high velocity. The bullet goes right through. When it's tooth and nail like this you need to know your opponent won't get up.' They all look at the boy in amazement, moist pride welling in their wild rooster eyes.

'Begging your pardon sir. I spoke out of turn,' he intones self-consciously.

'That's okay my boy,' says the Big Chief, slightly concerned perhaps, with what the Viscount his father will say when he hears of this debacle, 'We need to know all the details so the same mistakes are not repeated. I want a full, written report, Captain Stewart.' The boy modestly raises his shattered hand, now urgently in need of re-dressing with a questioning look, intended to obviate the need for his formal request for a typist. They gaze at him appreciatively, one or two almost tearfully - wrongly assuming this to be an honorific gesture in remembrance of his cancelled out regiment, its fine officers and many of his bosom friends. On this solemn note they break out the Brandy and cigars.

The sun is nowhere near the yardarm but most of them have not slept in a week. I decide to make my exit, before the post mortem resumes. I return to being elusive Prospero to their floundering dreams. Stewart, the unwitting hero, now on a fast track for promotion, looks at me with a lump in his throat. The brave lad is more intimidated by this convocation of ebullient tycoons than Fabeck's 27th Corps. They ignore his gesture, mistaking it perhaps for a request to join GHQ staff, duly noted, 'Dictation lad, ask the Adjutant for a typist!" I suggest, 'You've to submit your report forthwith on the Field Marshall's order, remember.' I place my hand

471

firmly on Stewart's shoulder before making my escape. I imagine he will have his own Executive Officer and typist before long.

Now at last the Germans have given up their attempt to break us, or seize the Channel ports. Word from McDonagh is the new German Commander Falkenhayn withdrew two Army Corps opposing us, to Lodz in Poland, several days ago. There is clear evidence of them digging in for a siege. For me, the most comforting task is to move up construction material for thirty five miles of rudimentary shelters for these poor souls. There is also the most profound communal sense of disbelief which I am not at liberty to discuss in its precise ramifications. Suffice it to say this was a very close run thing, Christina. Our 'Contemptible little army' as the Kaiser labelled us, suffered appallingly, although there is respite now and opportunity to consolidate defences. We will, I'm certain, survive the outworking of the 'centuries long struggle' - always assuming there follows a tremendous expansion of the industrial economy at home.

Conan Doyle pointed out in the press recently the ultimate battle will not take place on land, nor will it be fought by soldiers. Who would change places with merchantmen at the mercy of U-boats on the open ocean? Despite our Empire Christina, we are by far the weakest of the four Armies contesting this territory. Without timely intervention by the French in a couple of places; stiff backed resolution of fearless Sikhs; in one place orderlies, cooks and cyclists armed and ready to be thrown into the fray, not forgetting our precious sappers – right now we'd all be walking to Cologne with our hands on our heads.

As Fabeck revealed, this drubbing of the British has been for decades, if perhaps not 'centuries' the secret aim of the German military. So the 1839 Belgian scrap of paper was a technicality, serving the purpose of drawing us in. I dread to speak of evil lest it becomes manifest but until they are compromised on home soil, the Germany military will never give up this murderous rivalry.

It is borne of a presumptive belief in their own superiority, accompanied by the worst paranoia that they might be overrun by their neighbours. They want an empire too - within the continent of Europe.

As winter sun sinks on a day barely begun, so does my heart. I long for peace, as I long for your touch. Also for the sound of Edgar's voice one more time. To ride with him on a summer's day round Glaslough Lake, stopping to chat with every friendly face, would be the sweetest pleasure. Why do simple things taken for granted in life gall us so deeply in the moment of despair?

On a more human note, I will answer the question from your most recent letter – When filled the vat contains 2,000 litres of wine. All present, dans les caves de Talbot, officers and gentlemen to a man drink to your good health! To you Christina! Incidentally, I have written circumspectly to my mother, so don't worry - you need not fill them in on any of the tragic details. I will telephone from Headquarters in a day or two.

Love to all, to my little ones especially.

Yours ever,

Hugh xx'

Hannah held her breath as she opened the official letter from the records office. Having searched for meaning in all Sir Hugh had said – for some touchstone for living - her eyes clouded over. Annoyingly, more tears fell – this time onto the typed page. Brushing the moisture away contemptuously, she knew sentiment was useless. As previously, Hannah read the letter twice, imagining she might have missed something essential but there was nothing of substance to be gleaned, just the standard print-run officialese with spaces for particulars filled in by a woman clerk, 'for sympathy' and with a military archivist's official stamp at the bottom for certitude.

'25th November, 1914

Madam,

It is my painful duty to inform you that a report has this day been received from the War Office notifying

the death of : *(No.) 25535 (Rank) Brigadier (Brevet)*

(Name) *Baronet Sir Hugh Leslie (Regiment) GHQ Senior Liaison Officer, Railway Companies, Corps of Royal Engineers.*

Which occurred at: *a place in Belgium*

On: *the 22nd day of November 1914 and I am to express to you the sympathy and regret of the Army Council at your loss.* The cause of death was: *Wounds received in Action.*

If any articles of private property left by the deceased are found, they will be forwarded to this Office, but some time will probably elapse before their receipt, and when received they cannot be disposed of until authority is received from the War Office. Application regarding the disposal of any such personal effects, or of any amount that may eventually be found to be due to the late officer's estate, should be addressed to "The Secretary, War Office, London, SW.," and marked outside: "Effects".

I am, Madam,
Your obedient Servant,

Mrs. Catherine O'Donnell
Brompton Barracks,

Dock Road,

Chatham.

C Halstead 2nd Lieutenant
I/C NO. 1 SECTION
Officer-in-Charge of Records
Royal Corps of Engineers'

Hannah switched off the light to sit in silence, ignoring cold encroaching at her fingers, curling toes and tightening muscles of her aching shoulders. She closed her eyes and slowly filled her lungs.

Well-developed cryptaesthetic sense took her to Belgium, to bear witness to routines of casual slaughter. She saw rats and crows feasting hastily in freezing mud, wherever terrible red eyed men scuttled away breathless from the wheeling carnival of butchery. Into her night watch came cries of alarm and pain, fearful soldiers struggling and stumbling and the surprising debasement of a million horrific woundings. Sudden breathless expiry exuded the only certitude amid endless fear and blood. Hannah reached into tortured silence of so many last desperate thoughts to see slow, pleading death bleed out from uncountable venial youth, their eyes turning in final expiation to the wisdom of Sophia, Lady of Life. Her mind darkened, exploring what Christina's eyes had pleaded but could not ask.

How could Hughie have been taken so abruptly when in his letters he seemed so alive?

Hannah knew this unanswerable question lay at the very heart of the matter – in essence this was the true nature of war. Monstrous injustice, creating nothing but incoherent grief.

So many straight backed postmen carrying messages as streamlined as any bullet. So many hearts bursting with sorrow on the front step. So many brows pressed against a font in the hallway, weeping for the Holy Mother's mercy. The same story repeated many thousands of times each day, across Europe and the whole of a world in turmoil. Behind the blossoming of the black flowers of evil, a thousand cultured voices speaking with the same vain reasoning.

What consolation lay in her vision? What could she possibly say to Christina and the girls? Hannah sat hunched in bed hugging her knees, sickened by The Beast, awaiting peace that would not come.

To be continued.

If you have enjoyed reading FEVER THERAPY and HANNAH DUFF go to www.jimburnside.com for sample extract and details of how to purchase GOING HOME book three, GOLDEN DAWN.

Lightning Source UK Ltd.
Milton Keynes UK
UKOW05f1013101014

239873UK00008B/78/P